P9-DOB-196

RECEIVED
NOV 07 2012
By_____

No Longer the Property of
Hayner Public Library District

HAYNER PUBLIC LIBRARY DISTRICT
ALTON, ILLINOIS

OVERDUES 10 PER DAY, MAXIMUM FINE
COST OF ITEM
ADDITIONAL $5.00 SERVICE CHARGE
APPLIED TO
LOST OR DAMAGED ITEMS

HAYNER PLD/ALTON SQUARE

The Silvered

*The finest in Fantasy and Science Fiction
by TANYA HUFF from DAW Books:*

THE SILVERED
* * *

THE ENCHANTMENT EMPORIUM
THE WILD WAYS
* * *

The Confederation Novels:
A CONFEDERATION OF VALOR
Valor's Choice/The Better Part of Valor
THE HEART OF VALOR (#3)
VALOR'S TRIAL (#4)
THE TRUTH OF VALOR (#5)
* * *

SMOKE AND SHADOWS (#1)
SMOKE AND MIRRORS (#2)
SMOKE AND ASHES (#3)
* * *

BLOOD PRICE (#1)
BLOOD TRAIL (#2)
BLOOD LINES (#3)
BLOOD PACT (#4)
BLOOD DEBT (#5)
BLOOD BANK (#6)
* * *

THE COMPLETE KEEPER CHRONICLES
Summon the Keeper/The Second Summoning/Long Hot Summoning
* * *

THE QUARTERS NOVELS, Volume 1:
Sing the Four Quarters/Fifth Quarter
THE QUARTERS NOVELS, Volume 2:
No Quarter/The Quartered Sea
* * *

WIZARD OF THE GROVE
Child of the Grove/The Last Wizard
* * *

OF DARKNESS, LIGHT, AND FIRE
Gate of Darkness, Circle of Light/The Fire's Stone

TANYA HUFF

The Silvered

DAW BOOKS, INC.

DONALD A. WOLLHEIM, FOUNDER

375 Hudson Street, New York, NY 10014

ELIZABETH R. WOLLHEIM
SHEILA E. GILBERT
PUBLISHERS

http://www.dawbooks.com

Copyright © 2012 by Tanya Huff.
All Rights Reserved.

Cover art by Cliff Nielsen.

DAW Book Collectors No. 1604.

DAW Books are distributed by Penguin Group (USA) Inc.

Book designed by Elizabeth Glover.

All characters in this book are fictitious.
Any resemblance to persons living or dead is strictly coincidental.

The scanning, uploading and distribution of this book via the Internet or via any other means without the permission of the publisher is illegal, and punishable by law. Please purchase only authorized electronic editions, and do not participate in or encourage the electronic piracy of copyrighted materials. Your support of the author's rights is appreciated.

Nearly all the designs and trade names in this book are registered trademarks. All that are still in commercial use are protected by United States and international trademark law.

First Printing, November 2012
1 2 3 4 5 6 7 8 9

DAW TRADEMARK REGISTERED
U.S. PAT. AND TM. OFF. AND FOREIGN COUNTRIES
—MARCA REGISTRADA
HECHO EN U.S.A.

PRINTED IN THE U.S.A.

HuF

b20114357

Saw five rabbits on the way to the beach, there were two deer on the road when we walked the dogs, and I took three hornworms off the tomatoes last night. But now I have no one to tell . . .

Albert Copp
1918–2012

Chapter One

S ENSES NEARLY OVERPOWERED by the scent of sweat and gunpowder and onions, Tomas followed his nose through the 1st Aydori Volunteers, searching for his greatcoat. When his uncle, Lord Stovin, had ordered the Hunt Pack out before dawn, Tomas had left his coat folded on Lieutenant Harry Kyncade's saddle, up out of the dew. His cousins might think it funny to hide his uniform, mask the scent, force him to hunt it out, to go naked or stay in fur, but not Harry. Since their first days at school, they'd been as inseparable as duties and responsibilities allowed, and Tomas trusted Harry to keep safe the only clothing he had with him.

Unfortunately, the 1st—along with the remains of the armies from the overrun Duchies of Pyrahn and Traiton—had moved into battle formation while he was gone and Tomas had only a vague idea where Harry was.

He felt the soldiers' attention on him as he passed. They might not know for certain who he was, but, given that he currently looked like a black wolf, they knew *what*. For many of them, this had to be the first time they'd seen a member of the Pack so close. Because they couldn't know how acute his hearing was, he chose to ignore comments on his size, his color, and the unfortunate fact he had burrs in his tail.

"Finally decided to join us, Lord Hagen?" Harry's voice cut through the ambient noise.

Tomas raised his head. Harry stood by his pony, a little apart from his men, holding the missing greatcoat.

Two quick steps and a leap over the head of a sitting soldier, too startled to do anything but swear, put him at Harry's side. He changed and turned at Harry's gesture, allowing the other man to slide the sleeves up over his arms, grimacing as the fabric came in contact with filthy skin. He needed a long bath and the vigorous application of a scrub brush.

"If you mean did I decide to spend the remainder of the day sitting around with you doing nothing," he replied, tightening the belt and turning, "then, yes."

"Then I'm thrilled to give the pleasure of my company." Reins looped over the crook of his elbow, Harry straightened Tomas' collar. "Where were you? Off chasing rabbits?"

"I wish." Not that he'd have objected to a rabbit; the duckling he'd grabbed on the riverbank hadn't been much of a meal. "Scouts got sent out just before dawn."

Harry's eyebrows rose until they almost disappeared under the edge of his plumed shako. "And?"

"And nothing," Tomas admitted. He nodded across the river at the Imperial army lined up and waiting, helmets gleaming in the afternoon sun. "They had sharpshooters with those new rifled muskets stationed along both flanks. Shitheads were shooting anything that moved. No one could get close."

"They shot at you?" Eyes, flecked with Fire-mage red, gleamed as Harry ruffled Tomas' hair. "But you're so adorable."

"Shut up." At eighteen, he remained slight enough he could pass in low light as a very large black dog, but he drew the line at adorable. Leaning against the shoulder of Harry's pony, he scratched at the mud drying on his left foot. The Imperial army would have expected scouts from upstream, so he'd crossed downstream where the banks were marshy and found himself expected anyway. "They're waiting for something."

"Really?" Harry snorted, and gestured expansively at the surrounding Volunteers, who pointedly ignored both young men. "I wouldn't have guessed, given that we've been waiting for them. This is no way to run a war."

Straightening, Tomas rolled his eyes. "Next time I talk to my uncle, I'll tell him you think you could do things better."

"Ass."

"Idiot."

They turned together to stare at the command post. Harry's men had taken up a position close enough to Command that Tomas could see Lord Stovin, one bare foot up on a stump, talking with General Krystopher, military commander of the Duchy of Pyrahn. General Lamin, leader of the Traitonian army, was conspicuously absent.

General Lamin had a problem with the Pack and had been heard to refer to them as *no more than vicious animals*.

Lord Stovin had been forced to show teeth to prevent the younger members of the Hunt Pack from provoking an incident. As it was, Tomas knew for a fact that after the *no more than vicious animals* comment made the rounds, his cousin Jared had honored the Traitonian Lancers with a visit, panicking their horses. The sturdy mountain ponies used in Aydori were exposed to the Pack from birth, but nothing panicked enemy—or allied—cavalry like a large predator suddenly up close and personal.

Before the Duchy of Traiton had been overrun by the Imperial army, General Lamin's prejudices hadn't mattered much. But the Imperial army had pushed the retreating Traitonian army over the border into Pyrahn and kept pushing until the elderly Duke of Pyrahn had brought his grandchildren into Aydori for safety and asked for help. Where only a few short months before there'd been two independent Duchies as a buffer between Aydori and the Kresentian Empire, now there was a river. And not a very deep river at this point, Tomas noted.

There was a bridge about a quarter mile southeast, but the Imperial commanders had concentrated the bulk of their forces at the shallows rather than be caught in the shooting gallery the bridge and the road, deep in a rock cut, would become. In answer, the 1st Aydori and the Hunt Pack had set up on the ridge across from them. The ground angling down to the river was rocky and steep, but the Hunt

Pack didn't care and the 1st held the high ground—they could wait for the Imperials to come to them.

Tomas frowned across the river. Adding insult to injury, they were facing barely half a division of the Imperial army. Of the three divisions, the regiments that made up the Shields never left the heart of the Empire, the Spears were quelling rebellion in the northeast, so the emperor had only the Swords to aim at Aydori. Or those Swords not bringing the Imperial boot down on the recently conquered Duchies, at any rate.

"I wonder if that's why they're hanging back so far." Squinting didn't bring their colors into any better focus, but there had to be cavalry. There was always cavalry. "So their horses don't spook if the wind comes back up." There'd been heavy gusts of wind in the early morning, but, by the time the sun reached its highest point, the air was barely moving.

"Possible. But it looks like mostly infantry and artillery over there. You don't end up ruling most of this continent by being stupid enough to send horses against you lot." Harry bumped Tomas' shoulder. When Tomas growled softly, Harry laughed. "Yeah, you're tough. Besides, even if they were loitering about close enough for our nine pounders to reach their lines, that'd still be too far for an Air-mage to send scary wolf scent."

"If they were close enough for our artillery to hit them, their artillery could hit us."

"And that," Harry snorted, "is pretty much the whole point of war."

"Danika could do it."

"To my knowledge, your sister-in-law has no experience with artillery."

"What?" Tomas twisted and stared. "Is your hat too tight again? I meant that Danika could send our scent across to them!"

Harry grinned.

Tomas felt his cheeks heat. Harry had never let differences in social standing stop him from pulling Tomas' tail. "Oh, bite me!"

"Not likely. You bite back. Besides, moot point," Harry reminded him. "Your brother would never allow Lady Hagen anywhere near a battle in her condition, no matter how powerful an Air-mage she was."

"True." Tomas sighed and returned to trying to force an explanation for the delay by power of will. He hated waiting.

"Maybe the Imperials took one look at us and were so scared they shit themselves and we're waiting for the laundry to return their trousers."

"They didn't smell scared."

"Joke, you ass." Harry drove his elbow into Tomas' ribs. "If we don't move soon, the sun'll be against us. Go tell Lord Stovin I'm willing to lead a sortie against their lines. Draw them out. Prove to him I'm the right man for Geneviene."

"You haven't enough mage-craft for the artillery," Tomas told him, elbowing back. Most of the Fire-mages in the army were artillery, but poor Harry hadn't been able to pass muster. "What makes you think you have enough mage-craft for Geneviene?"

"Love makes my fire burn hotter."

"Oh, puke. She's probably going to marry Gregor."

"What's he got that I don't?"

"Fur."

"I hope he gets mange," Harry muttered sulkily. "I hope he . . ."

Raising a hand to cut Harry off, Tomas stepped forward. "Something's happening."

A pale blue bulge rose above the heads of the closest Imperial ranks.

"What the . . . ?"

"I don't know."

It continued rising until it looked like an upside-down teardrop.

"What's that underneath it?"

"I don't know." Squinting, Tomas leaned forward. "A basket? Is it mage-craft?"

"If it is, it's not like any I've ever heard of."

Another time, Tomas might have needled Harry about testing too low to get into the university, but something about that *thing* in the air made him uneasy. "If they've put one of their long nines in that . . ."

"Too heavy," Harry interrupted and, although he sounded as sure of himself as he always did, Tomas could smell the beginning of fear.

Tomas glanced over at his uncle. Lord Stovin had his eyes locked on the Imperials, one hand on Colonel Ryzhard Bersharn's shoulder.

Ryzhard, married to Stovin's oldest daughter, was one of the most powerful Air-mages in Aydori. Not as powerful as Danika, but he was *here*.

After a long moment, Ryzhard shook his head.

What did that mean?

An Aydori lieutenant galloped in from the south, his pony sitting back nearly on its haunches as he hauled on the bit. Tomas thought he recognized the officer attached to General Lamin. Ears pricked forward, he tried and failed to separate words from the noise. The lieutenant was still talking when General Krystopher pulled out a telescope and turned back toward the Imperials.

Telescope.

"Harry." Tomas reached out blindly, and closed his hand around Harry's wrist. "If they've got a man with a telescope in that thing, they could see right into our lines. Locate our commanders."

"Yeah?" Harry sounded calm, but then Harry always sounded calm. "And how would they get the location back to the ground?"

"Air-mage. Either up in the basket sending their voice down on a breeze or on the ground listening to the breezes and non-mage observer's voice. Or both, just to be sure; it's really up there."

"The Imperials think they're too good to use mages."

"Then they write the coordinates on a piece of paper and drop it in a weighted pouch."

"Fine. Doesn't matter. We've already established we're too far away for the artillery to . . ." Harry pulled free of Tomas' grip and took a step forward, his pony following. "Now what?"

As the first few ranks of Imperial infantry peeled back, Tomas' hands fell to his belt, working the buckle free. Whatever was about to happen, he needed to be back with Lord Stovin and he'd get there faster in fur. He saw sparks, heard a whistle . . .

"Incoming!"

Several voices.

"We're too far for artillery!"

Harry.

The blast wave slammed Tomas face-first into the ground. Something heavy landed on his right leg, pinning him. He felt it jerk from multiple impacts as he fought to get free. He could smell smoke and blood and shit and gunpowder. Over the ringing in his ears, he could hear screaming.

Finally, scraping skin off against the ground, he dragged his leg free and rolled over to see that he'd been trapped by the bulk of Harry's pony. Its head and one shoulder missing, its body had absorbed a number of small balls of shot from a secondary explosion.

Silver.

His lip curled off his teeth as he fought his way out of his sodden greatcoat and changed.

The scents separated into their component parts and his nose took him to Harry, lying in a crumpled heap against his pony's head, both legs gone at mid thigh. He changed again—this needed hands—and grabbed up the reins to tie off the stumps.

Harry's fingers touched his wrist. "Don't bother."

"You're in no shape to cauterize them."

"Idiot. Can't cauterize myself."

"Then shut up."

"Tomi . . ."

"Shut up."

Even in skin, he smelled Harry's bowels let go. Felt Harry's last breath against his shoulder. Let the reins drop from shaking fingers.

Changed.

Spun on one hind foot, nails gouging the dirt, and raced for the command post. Lord Stovin would have orders. Lord Stovin would . . .

He heard another whistle.

Saw General Kystopher point. Saw Lord Stovin change.

The blast flung him head over tail.

"Mirian, concentrate! I can barely see you."

Mirian frowned at her sister's image in the small, brass-bound mirror propped up on her dressing table. "I *am* concentrating."

On the other end of the mirror-link, Lorela's face grew larger as she moved closer in. "So you are. Sorry." An extreme close-up of an embroidered handkerchief momentarily filled the glass, then Lorela's face reappeared, much more sharply defined. "One of the boys spilled his milk this morning. I didn't realize how far it had spread, and it's impossible to keep this place clean when . . ."

Mirian let the monologue drift into background noise as she searched her portmanteau for her jewelry case. Her mother wanted her to wear her pearl earrings tonight and had refused to listen when told they'd already been packed. Hardly surprising since her mother refused to pack.

"There's nothing to worry about, Miri, not with Lord Hagen here. The Pack Leader will keep us safe."

"Miri! Are you listening to me? You have got to convince Mother and Father to leave Bercarit tonight!"

All right, *that* she should have been paying attention to. Apparently her sister's stories about husband and children had segued into a topic of actual note. Pushing her hair back out of her eyes, Mirian turned to face the mirror again. "Leave the city?" She pitched her voice higher, imitating their mother. "The Pack Leader says there's no need. Aydori will not fall to the empire."

"Cedryc says the Imperial army will be over the border before dawn and marching on Bercarit before breakfast."

Mirian rolled her eyes. "Has Cedryc turned Soothsayer now?" When Lorela didn't answer immediately, she frowned and leaned closer to the mirror. "Lore? Has he?"

"Of course not!"

Mirian waited.

Finally, Lorela shrugged, her face expressionless. "He has dreams sometimes. When he's asleep. That's all."

Soothsayers eventually went insane, their minds in the future, their bodies in the present; Lorela wouldn't have admitted it even if Cedyrc had been having waking dreams. All things considered, Mirian didn't blame her. "So if he's not a Soothsayer," she said lightly, and noted the way her sister's shoulders relaxed, "who do you think Mother and Father will believe? Lord Ryder Hagen or your charming but otherwise unremarkable husband?"

You have to make them believe."

"The Pack Leader is never wrong," Mirian muttered wearily.

"You're ready to leave."

She glanced down at her portmanteau, a little impressed the mirror-link had depth of focus enough to show it. The blue Air-mage flecks in Lorela's eyes hadn't changed and her sister had never been more than fourth level, merely maintaining the link was already at the edge of her abilities.

"Miri . . ."

"Traiton fell." Mirian drew a line through the spilled powder on the dressing table. "Pyrahn fell. My mage-craft may be too diffuse to be viable . . ." The opinion of her kinder professors; the less kind accused her of being lazy, stubborn, and superficial. Occasionally all at once. ". . . but no one ever said I was stupid. We're only seventeen miles from the border and refugees have been arriving for weeks." Bercarit's hotels were full of people from both Duchies with money enough to pack up and escape the advancing Imperial army, and the streets were filling with people who'd left without anything more than a desire to survive. "Mother says the refugees are proof positive the border will hold." Mirian thought they proved only that Pyrahn had fallen. "But it's not just the refugees," she continued through gritted teeth. "The Hunt Pack is on the border and the Pack leadership has come to Bercarit in case defending the border requires their personal touch. Mother and Father couldn't possibly miss this chance to present me at the opera like a dressed side of beef!"

With four and a half years and a dead brother between them, Lorela had carried the weight of their parents' expectations until her marriage to a young man she'd met at school had taken her out of the social advancement game. It would never occur to her to say *Mother and Father just want what's best for you.* Their father wanted the Pack's business at his bank. Their mother wanted to be invited to all the best parties. The only way that would happen was if their remaining daughter married into the Pack.

"They think because my mage-craft was strong enough to get me into the university, it's strong enough to attract a member of the Pack."

"Have you told them you won't be going back?"

Mirian frowned, and bent to grope among the folds of a sprigged muslin day dress.

"Miri?"

What she thought might be the pearl earrings turned out to be the two polished bone buttons that closed the top of the bodice.

"Miri!"

"No!" She straightened so abruptly that Lorela's image flickered. Drawing in a deep breath, Mirian forced herself to concentrate. Forced herself to calm enough to anchor her end of the link. "No," she repeated quietly, "I haven't told them. It seemed a little pointless what with Emperor Leopald suddenly deciding this year would be all about conquest. Besides, you know how Mother thinks. I was tested, I was accepted, I was schooled. I can, therefore, attract a member of the Pack."

"Well, you won't," Lorela said bluntly. "Not with only first levels. So, it's the opera and parental disappointment tonight. What about tomorrow?"

Mirian kicked the portmanteau shut. Tomorrow she'd try again to get her parents to leave the city, to head to Trouge, higher up in the mountains where the land itself would give the Imperial army pause. Of course, as long as the Pack leadership remained in Bercarit, the odds were high her parents wouldn't be moved and she'd be expected to smile and dance and pretend that disaster wasn't on the doorstep. "Tomorrow," she sighed, "never comes."

"Tomorrow, I'll take Jaspyr and Sirlin down to the border and have a sniff around." Shifting the brass candlestick that held a curling corner in place, Ryder Hagen stared down at the map spread out over the sitting room table.

Danika sighed, set down the book she'd been trying to read, and stood, shaking out her skirt. Ryder had spent the afternoon studying the map, pacing, studying the map, arguing with his cousins, studying the map, changing, and pacing some more. Although her husband weighed the same in both fur and skin, an agitated wolf took up considerably more space and the room, even emptied of half of its owner's overly fussy furniture, was not large.

"The Hunt Pack will have closed with the Imperials this afternoon," he continued. "There should be news by morning. Tomorrow . . ."

"Tonight," Danika interrupted, wrapping both hands around Ryder's arm and tugging him around to face her, "we are invited out to dinner before the opera and a reception after. You'll be expected to be in clothing."

"My greatcoat . . ."

"That's a field uniform and you know it." She allowed him to pull her close, her hands sliding up and around his neck. "Tonight requires trousers . . ." She kissed him before he could protest, then continued kissing him after each piece of required clothing. ". . . and shoes and a shirt and a jacket and a cravat."

Dark brows drew in. "If I have to change . . ."

"There should be no reason for you to change at either dinner or the opera, but if there is, I know for a fact you can get out of your clothing in . . . Ryder!"

"As I'm already out of my clothing, it seems a pity to waste this opportunity." His grin, twisted by the scar he'd gained in the fight that made him Pack Leader, was distinctly wolfish as he carried her over to the settee.

Danika thought about protesting the time or the place but, as Ryder's callused fingers began unbuttoning her bodice, she chose not to. She needed to begin dressing for their evening's engagements and the unlocked sitting room door meant any of the Pack members in Bercarit with them could walk in, but in a very few months she'd be in no condition for semi-public lovemaking on an extremely uncomfortable piece of furniture, so she might as well enjoy it while she could.

As though he were reading her mind about the furniture, Ryder flipped them so she straddled his lap.

"Better?" he asked nuzzling her throat.

She buried her fingers in the thick, dark mass of his hair and tugged. "Much. Now get on with . . . Oh!"

After, lying on the wool carpet, not entirely certain how they got there, Danika turned her face into Ryder's shoulder and murmured, "Why now?"

She felt as much as heard him laugh, a rumble deep in his chest. "I'm afraid you'll have to be more specific, love."

"The empire. There's been peace for four years, why did the emperor suddenly toss out the Treaty of Frace and decide to attack Traiton?"

"Why does that shit Leopald decide to do anything? Ego. He hates there's still free people not kissing his ass."

"It's just . . ." She laid her hand on his where it cupped her belly, warm against her cooling skin.

"I know."

They'd been married for almost seven years. Danika had begun to fear that she would never be able to bear a child of the Pack when Jesine—the Pack's strongest Healer-mage and married to Ryder's cousin Sirlin—had told her she'd finally caught. And now, with their first child on the way, the Imperial army was as close as it had ever come.

"Tell me they'll be stopped in Pyrahn, that they won't cross into Aydori."

"They'll be stopped in Pyrahn." She felt his mouth against her hair, his lips warm, his breath warmer. "Would you be this close to the border if I thought differently?"

No. She wouldn't be. As Pack Leader, Ryder's duty was to Aydori; he could send the Hunt Pack into battle, but he couldn't cross the border himself. Bercarit was his compromise. It would, after all, be the first city attacked should the unthinkable happen. He'd asked her to accompany him as much for politics as a dislike of being apart. Clearly, in spite of the Pack Leader's presence, there could be no *real* danger or the Pack Leader's wife and unborn child would be safe behind stone walls, high in the mountains in Trouge, the ancient Aydori capital. And she'd much, much rather be here, even considering the drift of dark hair she could see under the settee. If Ryder had shed that much since the housemaid had last swept the room, he wasn't as sure as he sounded.

They'd left the bulk of the Imperial army before it had entered Pyrahn, had traveled quickly across country, and slipped across the border into Aydori about forty miles north of Bercarit. Their first day in enemy territory had been spent angling carefully toward the east road out of Bercarit to Trouge; toward the road a forced evacuation from Bercarit would have to take. The dense woods had made the men skittish, all of them familiar with the tales of the giant beastmen who kept Aydori safe. As the day went on, and the largest animal seen had been a small, white-tailed deer bounding away in terror, the men had begun to calm and, finally, to laugh at their fear.

"Cap'n?"

Pulled from his thoughts, Captain Sean Reiter shifted his focus to the man who'd fallen into step beside him. "Sergeant Black."

"Scouts say there's a river up ahead." The sergeant shoved a branch out of the way with his musket and waited until the captain passed before he released it. "Not a deep river, like, but running fast. No way to avoid being seen while we cross if there's anyone about."

Reiter glanced up. The thick canopy prevented him from seeing the sky, and the shadows by the ground were either too constant or too broken to be of any use determining the time. He took a reading, mentally marked his path, tucked his compass carefully into a pocket, and pulled out his watch. Just past six. They'd lose the light soon.

"Can we cross after dark?" He snapped the case closed.

"Like I said, Cap'n, she's running fast." Black spat, cleared his throat, and spat again. "Wouldn't want to risk it in the dark myself."

"We'll cross it by squad, then. No more than three men visible at once. You cross with the first squad. I'll cross with the last."

"Four men visible, then."

"Thank you, Sergeant. I'd never have managed that math on my own."

Black grinned. "I live to serve, sir. And Lieutenant Geurin?"

Reiter snorted and lengthened his stride to clear a fallen sapling. "Lieutenant Geurin believes he walks on water, so put him in the middle of the river directing traffic."

They walked in silence for a few moments.

Lieutenant Lord Geurin, Viscount Tribuline, had been a pain in Reiter's ass from the moment he'd been assigned to this mission. He resented that Reiter, his superior officer, had been promoted out of the ranks. He expected blind obedience from men with significantly more time in, men who'd been handpicked for this assignment by General Loreau because of their skills rather than their bloodline. Reiter'd be willing to bet serious money that Geurin had been the sort of boy who'd spent his school days bullying the weaker boys and snitching on the stronger.

Dumping him in the middle of the river sounded like a great idea. However . . .

"He goes across with Four Squad. I'll have him check that the tangles crossed safely when he gets to the other side. That'll keep him busy until I get there."

"Tangles affected by water are they, sir?"

"Could be." Reiter knew Black could handle the young lieutenant, but that would lead to the men taking the sergeant's side—more than they were naturally inclined to anyway and, eventually, that would lead to trouble. Inspecting the tangles, the ancient artifacts given to them to neutralize the mages, would suit the lieutenant's sense of self-importance.

"Figure they'll still work? Them being so old and all."

"They'd better. Or it's going to complicate things."

"Complicate." Black punctuated the word with another mouthful of saliva. "Murphy says there's Soothsayers behind our orders."

"Does he?" Murphy had a habit of stating the obvious. Shields were never deployed outside the empire and seldom outside the capital unless the emperor went on progression. The regiment acted as the palace guard, they supported the city guard, and they spent one fuck of a lot of time looking martial to impress the empire's citizenry. But every man on this insertion team had been pulled from the Shields. Some of them, like Reiter himself, had only just been rotated in. All of them had been happy for a chance to be more than ceremonial soldiers, but the point remained—Shields were never deployed outside the empire. Only Soothsayers could convince the emperor to interfere to that extent with the natural order of the Imperial army.

"I'm thinking the lieutenant knows more than he's letting on," Black added. "Being part of the Court and a cousin of the emperor and all."

Distant cousin by marriage, as Reiter understood it, but the little shit did have the smug air of a kid keeping secrets. He moved a dangling caterpillar out of the way with the barrel of his musket and realized he could hear the river. They must be close. "We have our orders, Sergeant."

"Yes, sir."

"When we capture these mages and return them to the empire, we control the beastmen. We control the beastmen, we spend fewer men taking Aydori. It's as simple as that."

Black's snort spoke volumes about how they'd both been in the army long enough to know it was never as simple as that. But all he said was, "If you say so, sir."

"Is that thunder?"

Mirian closed her mouth, reply cut off by her mother's raised hand. With her head cocked to hear beyond the evening sounds of city outside the carriage, thin face bracketed by the emerald feathers trailing from her hairpiece, Mirian thought her mother looked a bit like a startled peahen.

She caught her father's eye, realized he was thinking the same thing, and had to bite her lip to keep from laughing.

"Lirraka . . ." He leaned forward and placed a hand gently on his wife's knee. ". . . the sky is clear. It's only the wheels rumbling over the cobbles."

"No." A dismissive shake of her head set the feathers swaying. "I have mage-craft enough to know thunder when I hear it in the distance."

"Ah, in the distance."

"Yes, Kollin, in the distance." She blinked, slowly, deliberately, drawing attention to her eyes and their few flecks of green. Given how very few they were, Mirian thought drawing attention to them wasn't the best of ideas, but her mother clearly disagreed, having gone so far as to dust her eyelids with green powder. "But distant thunder may not remain distant. What will we do if it's storming when we leave the opera?"

"There's umbrellas in the door pockets, Mother, we can . . ."

"Oh, yes, *umbrellas*." Lip curled, she made it sound as though she were expected to stand under a canopy of dirty rags. "We cannot carry umbrellas into the Opera House, Mirian, what would people think?"

"That we wanted to stay dry?"

"We would be perfectly capable of staying dry if you'd studied harder. It's a simple, low level Air—stay dry in the rain—and yet you can't seem to manage it."

"I can blow out a candle from across the room."

A disdainful sniff. "First level."

"I can light the candle again," Mirian pointed out, knowing she couldn't win but was unable to stop herself.

"And again, first level." Her mother's thin fingers pushed a curl back over Mirian's ear, then pulled it forward again. "You squandered your year at university. First levels in everything but Metals and no second levels at all? Honestly, Mirian, next year I expect you to pick a discipline and apply yourself. The Pack expects their mages to shine."

This was not the time to explain why next year wouldn't be an issue. Not in the carriage on the way to the opera. Not when her parents' reaction would become fodder for the city's gossips.

"Did you see how the Maylins were looking at their younger girl? I wonder what Mirian's done to disappoint them now."

"Oh, didn't you hear? The university released her."

"Poor Lirraka."

"Poor Lirraka? Poor Kollin, he might as well close the bank."

Definitely not the time.

"Mirian, stop slouching."

She straightened and endured her mother twitching at her bodice—forcing the neckline lower, higher, then lower again. "The Imperial army is in Pyrahn," she began.

"And the Pack Leader is in Bercarit," her father pointed out. "I think we're safe."

"Pack Leader or not . . ." And honestly, it wasn't like he could perform miracles. He was, when it came to it, flesh and blood, the same as everyone else. ". . . we're only seventeen miles from the border. We should . . ."

"We need to use this opportunity the Lord and Lady have granted us. We have never had so many members of the Pack in Bercarit." Her mother's tone declared this was the final word on the matter. "Unless you know something no one else does?" The words hung between them, taking up all the extra room in the carriage, then her mother wrapped her hand around Mirian's wrist and added, tone now speculative, "You don't, do you? Your marrying into the Pack would be preferable, but if your father and I were able to provide them with a good Soothsayer, I'm sure they'd be grateful. In fact, as there's no telling what member of the Pack you'd attract, that might . . ."

"I'm not a Soothsayer, Mother." Her father, at least, looked relieved she didn't face insanity. "And I'm not going to attract a member of the Pack."

"Not with that attitude, you're not. I'm not sure about this hairstyle on you." She poked a finger into the mass of tousled curls. "It looks disheveled."

"Isn't it supposed to look disheveled?" Mirian sighed. Her mother's maid had spent half an hour torturing her with a hot iron and pins, the chambermaid who usually assisted her having been declared too inexperienced for such an occasion.

"*Artfully* disheveled," her mother sighed. "You look as though you just climbed out of bed. With Lady Hagen setting the fashion for golden hair and your hair so entirely unremarkably brown, we'll have to use what we have. All things considered, a little suggestiveness can't hurt. Once you're part of the Mage-pack, you can cut it all off, and I'm sure that will make you happy." As the carriage came to a stop, she leaned in, a fingertip on Mirian's right cheek, pulling her eye open wider. "Still gray. Paler if anything," she sighed. "We'll have to hold to the knowledge that your entrance tests were strong and I've made sure everyone knows that. Brush against them when you get the chance," she added as the door opened. "The Pack is very tactile."

Even if Mirian had been able to respond, her protest would have been lost as her mother emerged from the carriage, one hand in her husband's as he assisted her down the step and the other trailing shawl, and reticule, and attitude. As Mirian stepped out a moment later, she was surprised to see her father waiting, and put her hand on his with a smile.

"Your mother has spotted one of her particular friends," he said, with a nod toward the wide plaza outside the Opera House and familiar green feathers bobbing above a cluster of women.

"Father, if I can't attract . . ."

"You can do anything you put your mind to, Miri, and my bank can very much use the Pack's attention. Smile, be pleasant. You may not be this season's fashion, but you're a pretty girl; it'll work out." He tucked her hand in his elbow as the carriage pulled away, its place taken immediately by another. "So, why no first in Metals?" he asked as they started up the broad steps.

"Pardon?"

"Your mother said you had a first level in everything but Metals. Why no Metals?"

"The Metals-master . . ." Had been scathing about her inability to stay with one craft and had refused to examine her. ". . . felt I wasn't suited."

"Well, I'm sure he knows best." He patted her hand then released her as her mother reclaimed him.

"Stop dawdling, Kollin, I want to be seated before the Pack enters so we can see who's attending."

Mirian dropped back behind her parents, smiled at a truncated greeting from a friend hurrying past, and paused between the wings of the huge glass-and-wrought-iron doors. The sky over the city was clear, but, as much as she hated to admit it, her mother had been right.

She could hear the bass rumble of thunder in the distance.

The tragic love story of *Onnesmina* was the gem of the Bercarit Opera Company and they hauled it out for polishing every other season. Mirian had seen it half a dozen times and not even Emilohi Okafor, the visiting soprano—lauded in the program for her beauty of tone and dramatic acuity—could capture her complete attention.

Lord and Lady Hagen were in Lord Berin's great box, across the theater and a tier lower from the much smaller box that came with her parents' subscription. Lord and Lady Berin, who had grandsons with the Hunt Pack, were the height of Bercarit society, and Mirian's mother had fought to get the box with the best line of sight. It looked as though the Pack Leader and his wife had been accompanied by every member of the Pack currently in Bercarit.

"If there were only a way of telling which of the men were unattached," her mother muttered, peering at the box through her opera glasses. "Do you feel an attraction to any of them, Mirian?"

"I don't . . ."

"Well, you won't if you keep staring at the stage!"

Catching a sigh behind her teeth, Mirian directed her own glasses away from the stage to Lord Berin's box. With the glasses, the blur her own eyes would have offered at that distance resolved itself into individual faces all staring enthralled at Okafor whose performance was definitely giving those who'd never seen *Onnesmina* before an amazing introduction to the opera.

"Well?"

"No, Mother."

"Try harder."

A second glance showed they weren't *all* staring enthralled. Lord Berin appeared to be dozing and Lord Hagen seemed distracted. All things considered, Mirian found that unsettling and watched the Pack Leader with an intensity that made even her mother happy.

At the first intermission Lord Hagen was up and out of his seat almost before the curtain had closed. The male members of the Pack charged out of the box after him, leaving the women to follow more sedately.

Mirian found herself nearly lifted out of her seat and dragged onto the upper concourse, her mother's hand like a steel band around her wrist.

"The Pack will, of course, have gone to the café in the lower lobby," she said, moving purposefully toward the stairs.

Wishing for the courage to dig her heels in, Mirian lifted her skirt in her other hand, trying not to step on her small train and end up taking the stairs headfirst. "Your subscription doesn't allow you into the café," she pointed out a little breathlessly as they reached the lower level.

"We don't need to go in. We'll just walk by so they can get your scent."

"Mother!" Feeling the blood rush to her face, Mirian began to wish she *had* taken the stairs headfirst. A fall would have been significantly less embarrassing. It didn't help that the makeup of the crowd swirling about the wrought-iron barrier between the café and the lobby suggested the idea was not her mother's alone.

"You mark my words, Annalyse. In your lifetime there will be a Pack member on the stage."

Danika kept half her attention on the discussion going on across the small table between Lady Berin and her granddaughter-in-law—the Pack loved opera and many of them had amazing voices, but not even the youngest and most rebellious would do anything so vulgar as take to the stage—and half her attention on her husband standing over by the far wall. He was deep in conversation with Neils Yervick—his wife had sent her excuses and Danika had to admit she was just as glad not to have her attention split by Kirstin's sharp tongue. While their verbal fencing often made her more boring social obligations bearable, tonight the Imperial army was at the border and Danika neither wanted nor needed the distraction.

Among the uniformed men surrounding Ryder and Neils, she could see General Narvine of the 2nd, Colonels Greer and Aryat of the 2/2 and 2/4, and a number of younger officers she didn't recognize. To a man, their expressions whether talking or listening were so completely neutral, she shivered. She could almost hear Ryder instructing them to hide their reactions from the surrounding civilians.

Tucked behind her own mask of polite interest, she noted that while facial expressions might be under control, some Pack members were visibly agitated, shifting their weight and pulling at their clothing. Jaspyr, usually among the most levelheaded of Ryder's cousins, worried the three pewter buttons on his jacket in and out of their holes, his fingers in constant motion. What news had they heard that . . . ?

"Lady Hagen?"

Danika turned toward the soft touch on her arm to find Annalyse had shifted her attention from Lady Berin—now arguing the lack of vigor in recent hunts with the equally elderly Lady Evanjylan. When Annalyse inclined her head toward the front of the café, Danika followed the younger woman's line of sight and suddenly understood Jaspyr's problem.

The mass of people passing back and forth in the lobby outside the café was almost entirely made up of mothers and mages of a marriageable age. A quick glance around the café confirmed the unmated Pack members were most affected by the scents rising from the crowd.

A word to one of the officers of the Opera House and Danika could have the crowd dispersed, but that hardly seemed fair as she, herself, had caught Ryder's attention as part of a similar promenade. Here and now, however, the Pack needed to remain focused on the security of Aydori. Reaching out with power, she combed through the air currents and redirected them so that they flowed from the café to the lobby.

After a moment, she glanced back at the men surrounding her

husband in time to see Jaspyr move his hand away from the front of his jacket, the buttons now securely fastened. When she shifted her gaze to Ryder, he caught and held it long enough to nod his thanks before returning to his conversation with General Narvine. The general nodded in agreement when Ryder stopped speaking and, although Danika couldn't see the general's face, must have said something in turn as the lieutenant beside him snapped to attention, pivoted on one heel, and all but ran from the café.

That didn't look good.

Behind her, Annalyse drew in a sharp breath, and Danika remembered the younger woman's husband was with the Hunt Pack and the Hunt Pack had met the Imperial army some hours before.

The Pack healed so quickly they were very hard to kill. Silver poisoned them, but they'd been careful to keep that knowledge from their enemies.

Still, only three months married and hours without news . . .

Reassurance would be meaningless as Danika knew no more than Annalyse did, so it would have to be distraction. Tugging on the cuff of her lace mitten as she turned, she waggled the fingers of her right hand and said softly, "Forced by circumstance to a public display of mage-craft, how very vulgar."

Annalyse's green-flecked eyes widened, then she smiled. A polite smile, a society smile, but it lifted a little of her distress. "As the Alpha Female, Lady Hagen, you set the fashion. At least, that's what Geoffrey told me when I joined the Pack."

"So I cannot, therefore, be vulgar?" Danika lifted her cup and grinned over the rim. "That could come in handy."

This smile reached Annalyse's eyes, crinkling them at the corners. "My much more vulgar solution would have involved washing the scent from the air."

Sixth level Water at least, Danika realized, setting her cup down, and she clearly had a more delicate touch than most Water-mages managed. "You could actually make it rain inside the building?"

"If there's moisture enough. With so many people and the ceilings so high . . ." She waved off her ability to perform an impressive bit of mage-craft, her gaze sliding past Danika's shoulder, back to the men around the Pack Leader. "Do you think something has happened? Something bad?"

"Of course something bad has happened," Lady Berin growled. "To the Imperials. The Hunt Pack will have sent them howling home with their tails between their legs." She reached across the table and gripped her granddaughter-in-law's wrist, the back of her hand grown hairy with age. "Our Geoffrey will be back in no time. Isn't that right, Lady Hagen?"

If she'd been born Pack, Danika would have bared teeth at Lady Berin's tone even as she was aware she was demanding reassurance, not challenging. Instead, she smiled carefully and said, "The Hunt Pack is the best Aydori has to offer."

Lady Berin nodded in satisfaction, but Danika could see that Annalyse knew her words meant nothing at all.

Mirian spotted an acquaintance from school and maneuvered her mother alongside. Given that Bertryn wouldn't be competing for the same attention from the Pack, her mother settled in beside his mother, leaving the two of them to follow obediently behind.

"Better odds for me than you," Bertryn murmured, as the four of them reinserted themselves into the slow moving promenade.

"True enough." Behind the wrought-iron barrier, the café's small, round tables were surrounded by women, born Pack and Mage-pack. The male Pack members stood together by the rear wall, talking with men in uniform. Probably officers of the 2nd. Mirian wished she could see their expressions, but distance made that impossible. Judging by their posture, they weren't happy. And why would they be? Seventeen miles from the border . . .

Air currents shifted.

"Did you feel that?"

"Feel what?" Bertryn glanced down at her, irises dominated by rich brown flecks. He'd had five levels at the end of first year, and the Earth-master had practically refused to allow him out of her sight. Rumor had it that she'd cried when he left at the end of the session. All things considered, asking if he'd felt Air move had been a stupid question.

"Never mind." Mirian waited until they'd turned and started back again before saying, "What are you even doing here? I thought after graduation you were going to return to the university to teach?"

He shrugged. "I'm the eldest of eight and the only one with any power; teaching won't help situate them, but getting into the Pack will. With so many of the Pack in Bercarit, this is an opportunity. Given your . . ."

Mirian frowned into the pause.

". . . difficulties," he continued diplomatically, "I'm a little surprised to see you."

"My mother wants invitations to better parties." His brows rose at her tone, and she sighed. "Sorry. Being a part of this is just . . ."

"Frustrating because it's futile?"

"Entirely." More than he knew. The air currents now blew the mage scent away from the Pack. Glancing into the café past a couple of giggling girls who couldn't have been more than sixteen, their eyelids stained Healer gold, Mirian found herself looking into a pair of very blue eyes. It only lasted for a moment and the movement of the promenade broke the connection before Mirian realized that the eyes were Lady Hagen's.

Lady Hagen was said to be the most powerful Air-mage in Aydori. If she hadn't shifted the scent, she'd approved it being done.

Why would . . . ?

Because she hadn't wanted the Pack distracted.

That couldn't be good.

"Mother." Pulling her hand from Bertryn's elbow, she touched her mother's shoulder. "We should . . ."

The gong for the end of intermission rang out on the upper level, amplified by a low level Air-mage in the employ of the Opera House.

"We should take our seats, yes, Mirian."

"No, Mother, Lady Hagen . . ."

But the rest was lost in the chaos created by just under a thousand people returning to their seats. Back in the box, Mirian tried again.

"You're being ridiculous," her mother hissed under the sound of the orchestra, nodding toward Lord Berin's box. "Would Lord Hagen be at the opera if there were any danger?"

"If he didn't want people to panic."

"There is nothing for anyone to panic about. Now be quiet!"

Teeth clenched, Mirian watched the curtain rise for the second act and wondered if she were the only person in the Opera House putting two and two together and actually arriving at four.

When *Onnesmina* finally ended, with the lovers reunited and a final aria sung, Mirian found herself with her hand firmly tucked into the angle of her father's elbow and her mother close up on her other side as they made their way down the stairs to the reception in the lower lobby. Their clear concern that she might make a run for it was almost funny, and Mirian amused herself during the descent by imagining the dash through dark streets, her hair spilling down, her satin slippers worn through, one glove lost and abandoned in the gutter. She'd reach the house, push past Barrow, who'd be so astonished to see her an emotion might spill past his perfect butler facade, then she'd lock herself in her room and . . .

And what?

Might as well stay here.

Her stomach growled.

At least there'd be food.

During the last act, the wrought-iron barriers that had previously separated the café from the lobby had been moved to create a corridor those not attending the reception could use to exit the building. At the entrance for the favored, an employee of the Opera House checked their invitations, then stepped back and bowed.

Mirian thought her mother might have enjoyed the bow just a little too much.

In a room filled to capacity, with everyone wearing the same loose, easy to remove clothing dictated by Pack fashion, it still wasn't hard to identify the visiting members of the Pack. Like those of the Pack who lived in Bercarit, the visitors were so much more present. Those not in the Pack outnumbered the Pack about ten to one, but the latter dominated the room with a vitality and an assurance no one else could match.

Although the four women and three men who were Mage-pack came close. Mirian suspected she could actually see the power surrounding them if she squinted a little.

They had the power—mage and otherwise—to actually accomplish things, to not waste their lives on clothes and card parties and social positioning. She objected to the way her parents felt they could use her to solve all *their* problems and she objected to time wasted on futility—as she was clearly not suitable—but she had no actual objection to being a part of the Mage-pack. Who would?

"Miri. Stop squinting!" The accompanying pinch was more to ensure her attention than to cause pain, but it hurt nevertheless. "And keep your head down, so they can't see the lack of color in your eyes. Kollin, isn't that Regin Fortryn, from the Council? He knows Lord Berin, and he's certainly borrowed money enough from the bank. We shall have him introduce us."

Fortryn seemed pleased to see her father—not always a given when someone had "certainly borrowed enough from the bank"— and the two were soon happily deconstructing the city's finances.

Her mother waited, more or less patiently, until it became obvious no introduction to the Pack would be immediately forthcoming, then she tugged Mirian aside and murmured, "You must be hungry."

Most of both Pack and Mage-pack had gathered around Emilohi Okafor—as beautiful and charismatic offstage as on—but there were four young men—three members of the Pack and a lieutenant from the 2nd—standing at one end of the buffet table. As it was nearly midnight and she *was* hungry, Mirian didn't bother pointing out that, given how close they were standing to each other, it was unlikely two of the young men would be interested in her.

And besides, there was always the chance she'd meet the lieutenant's gaze and they'd fall desperately in love. The thought of her mother's reaction to a match with a junior officer who was neither Pack nor mage kept her amused all the way across the room and she was still smiling when she accepted a white china plate and a linen napkin from the server stationed at one end of the tables.

Given the number of Pack at the reception, the dishes were heavily skewed toward small pieces of meat on sticks, nearly all of it cooked. There were also tiny meat pies, a plate of cold tongue, several varieties of cracker, and three platters of tiny cakes made to look like sleeping lambs, chicks, and piglets. Mirian picked up three sticks of chicken and two of beef, added a puddle of sauce to dip them in and moved out of the way, her back against one of the lobby's marble pillars.

Ignoring the young men her mother had sent her to attract as well the trio of giggling girls suddenly surrounding them, Mirian searched the crowd for Lord Hagen. He couldn't have gone to the border; there were still far too many officers of the 2nd around, but where . . . ?

"Lord Hagen, is it true? Is it true that the Imperials are at the border?"

Mirian stiffened. The young woman's worried voice came from the other side of the pillar. She swallowed a mouthful of chicken and began to inch sideways.

"I think that's a given." Lord Hagen's reply lifted the hair on the back of Mirian's neck. "Or we wouldn't have been able to hear their artillery."

Not thunder, then, as they'd arrived at the opera. Cannon.

"But that," the Pack leader continued firmly, "is all we *know*."

Another step brought her far enough around the pillar to see Lady Hagen link arms with a mage no older than Mirian and draw her away, speaking quietly. She thought it might be the youngest Lord Berin's new wife, but as she'd only ever seen her pass in a moving carriage, she couldn't tell for certain. Lord Hagen watched them go, eyes locked on his wife as though he were memorizing her in this place and time.

Dark eyes under a mass of thick, dark hair—in spite of the scar that twisted the corner of his mouth, he was handsome enough, Mirian allowed, but it was the sense of barely contained energy that drew her attention. He was like a thunderstorm just before it broke, the potential for danger barely harnessed.

"And who do we have here?"

Mirian spun on one heel and looked up. Pack member, definitely. Amused, fortunately. The same dark eyes as Lord Hagen, his hair the pale gray his fur would be and short enough the points of both ears rose through it.

One pale gray brow rose. "Your eyes have no color, but your scent . . ." He leaned toward her, nostrils flared. "What makes you smell so good?"

His proximity made her cheeks flush and her heart beat faster. He was close enough she could see the puckered edges of the scar that ran down his cheek over his jaw to disappear under his collar, and he wasn't young, thirty at least, with a fan of lines bracketing his eyes.

When it appeared he wanted an answer, she managed a shrug and lifted her plate up into his line of sight. "I have no idea, my lord. Perhaps it's the beef."

He blinked, looked down at the food, then laughed and straightened, putting a little more distance between them. "Perhaps it is. I am Jaspyr Hagen."

The Pack Leader's bloodline. Her mother would be thrilled. And insufferable. Mirian sent up a quick prayer to the Lord and Lady that her mother wasn't watching.

"And you are?"

"Mirian Maylin, my lord."

His nostrils flared again. "Would you share your food with me, Mirian Maylin?"

There were undertones to that question that raised goose bumps on Mirian's arms and a look in his dark eyes that made it hard to breathe. Mouth suddenly dry, she wet her lips, realized he was watching the movement of her tongue, and thrust the plate toward him. "I would be honored to share my food, Lord Hagen."

"Jaspyr." He picked up one of the beef sticks. "Or people will think you're talking to my cousin."

His teeth were very white.

Well, of course they were.

"Jaspyr, what are . . . ? Hello!" One of the young men who'd been at the end of the buffet charged around the pillar, and only Pack reflexes kept him from knocking her over. His eyes widened and his nostrils flared. "Wow, you smell amazing."

"It's the beef," Mirian sighed.

Jaspyr laughed again and Mirian felt her mouth twitching in response. When the younger man leaned closer, Jaspyr grabbed his shoulder, turned him away from the pillar, and gave him a little shove. "Go away, Bayor."

Bayor kept turning until he faced them again, looking startled. "It's like that?"

"It could be."

"She has no mage marks."

"She's standing right here," Mirian snapped.

Both men turned to look at her, Jaspyr smiling, Bayor frowning slightly.

"Jaspyr, Ryder wants you to . . ." The young man racing around the pillar slid to a stop, one hand clutching Bayor's jacket for balance. His eyes widened and his nose twitched. "Is that *her* scent?"

Mirian rolled her eyes. This was getting ridiculous.

"Yes," Jaspyr told him. "It's her. Now take Bayor and go."

At first Mirian thought it was Bayor growling, and then she realized the sound came from the far side of the lobby, by the doors.

A woman screamed.

The crowds parted, and a black wolf raced through Bercarit's finest, straight for Lord Hagen. Claws skittering on the marble, he managed to stop at the last moment and become a young man, covered in mud and bruises, his chest heaving as he gasped for breath.

"Tomas!" Lord Hagen closed the distance between them, gripping the young man's shoulders.

"The Imperials, they're across the border." Voice rough, Tomas sounded on the edge of tears. "Everyone is dead. The 1st, the Hunt Pack. Ryder, they're using silver!"

Chapter Two

DAWN TINTED THE MOUNTAINS pink and gold, and chaos reigned on the cobblestone street outside Mirian's parents' house. Those servants who hadn't run off to be with family of their own loaded and unloaded carriages and wagons, trying to find room for one more trunk or one more family heirloom that couldn't be left behind. Children cried, adults shouted, and through more than one open door came the sound of breaking glass.

Mirian, unable to spend another moment listening to her mother scream at her maid, stood on the walk in her traveling clothes tasting *I told you so!* on the back of her tongue. She wondered if she had time to go to the Lady's Grove at the end of the street, took two steps in that direction, then decided that with the Imperial army already over the border, it was too late for prayer. Cook had taken the little round Lady of the Hearth with her, but as far as Mirian knew, the Lord's Regard remained half hidden in the small back garden.

"Do you see him?"

She half turned as her mother came out onto the porch, confused for a moment about which *him*.

"Your father, Mirian! Do you see your father?"

"No, not yet."

The circles under her eyes nearly the same green as the tint still on the lids, Mirian's mother clutched a pair of silver candlesticks closer to her chest. "How could it be taking him so long?"

Mirian had no answer. Not that it mattered.

"We could be murdered in our beds, you unnatural child! How can you be so calm?"

Calm? That would do, she supposed. Although it felt anticipatory, more like the calm before the storm. "We aren't *in* our beds, Mother."

"Why would that matter?"

She looked so distraught, Mirian moved closer to the house. "We're in no immediate danger. The Imperial army won't advance further until dawn."

"You can't know that!"

"I can; it's obvious. There was no moon last night, and starlight alone isn't enough to move men and equipment over unfamiliar ground."

"Obvious?" The snort had the force of imminent hysteria behind it. "So you've decided to be a general now you've failed as a mage? Perhaps Lord Hagen should have sent *you* to the border!"

Mirian took a deep breath and abandoned logic for reassurance her mother would actually believe. "Lord Hagen said the carriages would leave at dawn—all the carriages, his family's as well—so he must believe the Imperial army won't reach the city until much later."

A double blink and a deep breath. Then: "Well, if Lord Hagen believes . . ." Hysteria averted, grip on the candlesticks visibly eased, her mother ran back inside.

Although the city was by no means calm, Lord Hagen had managed to prevent more than just her mother's panic. After his brother's dramatic entrance at the opera house and his declaration of defeat, Mirian knew he'd had mere moments to take control of the situation before it descended into chaos. He'd handed his brother into the care of the red-haired Healer-mage suddenly at his side, looked to his wife, and said levelly, "Can you be ready to leave for Trouge by dawn?"

Lady Hagen had nodded. "I can."

She'd made certain their voices had risen above the shocked silence and filled all the available space, leaving no room for panic to grow into.

The Pack Leader had swept a calm gaze over the watching crowd, his tone and body language declaring, *I am in control of this. There is no reason for you to fear.* Common sense said at that point he was in control of nothing save his own reaction, but, even knowing that, Mirian had felt as though a weight had been lifted from her shoulders.

"Carriages heading for the capital will leave at dawn. The Trouge Road will be closed to all but foot traffic until then. Go. Make ready."

Had he not made it clear his family would remain in the city, the wealthy would have rioted. Although no one had asked for her opinion, Mirian thought his reasoning was sound. Panicked drivers in fast carriages on a narrow, winding road at night could only be a recipe for disaster. One accident would block the way and destroy any hope of an orderly evacuation.

Now, it was dawn and then some. Mirian wondered if Lady Hagen had left yet.

She could see nearly to the boulevard by the time she spotted her father hurrying home. The other families on the street were gone.

"The cabbies are using their cabs to take their families from the city," he said, when he was close enough. "As long as they weren't taking the Trouge Road, they've been permitted to leave. There's none about. I had to walk from the bank."

He sounded so indignant about not having a cab at hand when required, that Mirian nearly laughed.

"Oh, Kollin!" Arms clasped around the ornate porcelain vase that usually sat on the mantel in the morning room, Mirian's mother burst out of the house followed by Nyia, her maid, and Burrows who closed the door and locked it behind him. "Kollin! Please, tell me we're leaving. I can't take much more of this!"

"We're leaving. Get in the carriage, Lirraka." He plucked the vase from her hands as she hurried past and handed it to Mirian. "Leave the ugly thing for the empire," he muttered as he turned and followed his wife, coat flapping around his calves.

Mirian set the vase on the path, straightened, and frowned. She could hear singing from the boulevard, rising up over the sound of marching feet—the remainder of the 2nd heading out to the border. She hadn't known so many soldiers were still in the city.

The younger Lord Hagen had said the Hunt Pack and everyone in the 1st was dead. While that couldn't possibly be accurate, there had to have been death enough for him to believe it.

So why were these men singing?

At first she thought the creature running toward her was a small pony, escaped from the soldiers. It was the size of a small pony, yes, but the shape was wrong—too narrow, too pointed, too . . . much a Pack member racing down the center of the street, moving so quickly it seemed his paws never quite touched the cobblestones. The early morning light made him look more silver than gray.

He was almost close enough to touch when he changed. "When this is over . . ." The growl smoothed out of his voice with every word. ". . . and we have a moment to ourselves, you and I will have to talk."

She kept her eyes on his face. Mostly. There were lines and shadows there hadn't been last night at the Opera House. Lines at the edges of his mouth. Shadows in and under his eyes. He looked older. He looked like he hadn't slept. His intensity was still . . . disconcerting. "We have a moment now," she said.

"No. Promises made before battles bring bad luck. But after . . ." He grinned, showing teeth. "After the battle, Mirian Maylin who smells amazing, I will find you and we *will* talk."

Mirian took a deep breath. He smelled like sweat, just on the edge of becoming rank and she wished she had his nose, his certainty. But he made her feel as though she trembled on the edge of an abyss and that uncertainty would have to be certainty enough. Discarding half a dozen responses, she reached out, laid two fingertips against the damp skin over his heart, and said, "Yes."

That seemed to be answer enough. A heartbeat later, the wolf stood where the man had been and a heartbeat after that, he turned and raced back toward the boulevard.

She watched him for a moment, then pivoted on one heel, walked to the carriage, accepted Jon the coachman's hand with a smile, and settled into the seat beside her father.

"Mirian!" Her mother's eyes were so wide the whites showed all the way around. "That was Jaspyr Hagen. Cousin to the Pack Leader!"

Mirian discarded another half a dozen responses, wiped damp palms on her skirt, and settled for, "I know."

"You will stop them at the border."

"Is that an order, my love?"

"It is. And here's another . . ." Danika wrapped her hands behind Ryder's neck and locked her eyes with his. ". . . return safely and soon."

He bent his head and kissed her, then buried his face in her hair, inhaling her scent. It was something he'd done a hundred, a thousand times over the years of their marriage, and Danika refused to read anything more into it now.

She let him go when he stepped away, even though holding on seemed a perfectly reasonable thing to do. When he changed, she stroked the soft fur on his muzzle and murmured, "Do try to stay out of the burrs, beloved. You know how much you hate having your tail brushed."

He licked her hand, pushed his face up against her belly, then pivoted on one rear foot and raced along the wide boulevard that led out of the city, toward the border. Tomas and Jaspyr fell in behind, with them the other four males who'd stayed in Bercarit to help maintain order.

"Lady Hagen, we need to leave."

Lady Berin. Lord Berin had gone to the border. Although Ryder wouldn't have sent him, he hadn't stopped the old wolf.

Danika raised a hand to acknowledge she'd heard. The Pack's carriages were among the last remaining in the city, the five of the Mage-pack tasked to guard the rear of the column. She whispered, "I love you." Sent it on a breeze to Ryder. Turned, much as he had given the differences between two legs and four, and took her place in the carriage.

"I can't see how this'll hold anything, Cap."

Before Lieutenant Lord Geurin could find words to go with his scowl, Reiter carefully gathered the gold net dangling between two of Chard's fingers, and piled it into the soldier's palm. "You just have to throw it, Private. None of us has to understand how it works."

"The tangles are ancient artifacts," the lieutenant snapped. "They'll do their jobs if we do ours."

"But . . ."

Reiter raised a hand to cut off Chard's protest. "Up the tree, throw the tangle among the carriages, down the tree, take the neutralized mages to the empire. Simple. Now, get your ass up the tree."

As he settled into the underbrush by the side of Trouge Road, Reiter had to admit the Soothsayers had chosen the perfect place for an ambush. The road back to Bercarit was visible for some distance—allowing them to identify the last carriages—then climbed steeply, forcing the carriages to slow, the sharp turn at the top of the hill cutting them off from the rest of the evacuation. While there'd been signs of lumbering back away from the road, massive oaks still pressed in close on either side, providing stable platforms for the men with the tangles.

Reiter had to admit, he saw Chard's point about the artifacts. The delicate gold nets didn't look like they could hold an infant let alone an adult, high-level mage.

He'd known mages when he was a boy—an elderly woman with brown-flecked eyes whose garden fed half the village, a legless veteran with a few blue flecks who could make himself heard over distance—but he hadn't seen one for years. There were probably a few selling their services in the capital because everything was for sale in Karis, but as far as he knew, none served under the Imperial banner. Science had replaced magic in the army. When soldiers carried fire-starters in their pockets, they had no need to waste time seeking out a Fire-mage. Even Colonel Korshan's blasted rockets blew up over enemy lines more often than not.

Science could do anything mage-craft could and, more importantly, anyone could use it.

Given that he had six men in trees holding ancient magical artifacts, Reiter saw the irony in believing this fight had anything to do with the rise of intelligence and training over random talents caused by a lucky dice roll at birth.

He'd just checked with Sergeant Black that everyone was in place when the first of the evacuees from Bercarit appeared, the cursing that came with them in Pyrahn working-class accents. Twice refugees, the poor bastards on the run again before the might of the Imperial army. Able to be first on the road because they could carry everything they owned on their backs. The funny thing was—although probably not funny for them, Reiter admitted—for the most part, they ran from rumor. While opposing armies were destroyed with brutal and practiced efficiency, the emperor preferred his conquered work force alive and working.

Reiter settled more comfortably behind his screen of brush, aware that around him his men were doing the same. Their orders concerned the last few carriages only; the rest could pass.

Tomas had wanted to return to the border immediately, but Ryder had ordered him to eat and sleep. His protests had been ignored; the Pack Leader's word was law. So, hungry and exhausted, he'd done as he was told. He woke just before dawn, remembered Harry was dead, and he couldn't believe he had to wait longer still. In fur, he watched Jaspyr head off on personal business—as though anyone with a nose didn't know it was about a woman. He watched Ryder deal with half a hundred stupid, unimportant, petty details. Lip curled, he watched him *finally* say good-bye to his wife, and change to fur.

Ryder snapped at him as he passed, but Tomas didn't yield, merely fell in on his left flank as Jaspyr took the right, four distant cousins following behind. Once he was moving, the need that had been chewing at him, the need to return and make the bastards who'd killed Harry pay, began to ease. By the time they left the city, he'd given himself over to the run.

Noses to the west, Ryder led them across country, cutting off the two large loops that eased the Border Road for carriages. Tomas had no clear memory of the route he'd run the night before, but they crossed his scent so instinct must have led him straight and true.

He heard the artillery before he smelled the gunpowder. The wind was against them. Didn't matter. The Imperial army stank, but their noses were useless.

He tried not to think of what they were running toward. Tried not to think of bodies blown to pieces. Of silver slamming bloody holes through fur. Of Harry. He thought of running, and of revenge, and how Ryder would fix this.

Then they came out of the woods, and the blood scent hit him like a physical blow. Blood. And shit. And fear. And memory. He stumbled, but Ryder ran on, so Tomas pushed the terror back and followed. He could see the Aydori line, shattered in places, the living sheltering behind bulwarks of the dead. He could see the Imperial army advancing, another score of infantry in reserve to replace every man shot down. He could hear gunshots and cursing and an Air-mage screaming on the breeze.

There were bodies in fur where the dead lay thickest and death too thick in the air to know if any Pack still lived.

He saw Imperial cavalry charge the exposed Aydori flank. They'd held the horses back then, until they thought the Pack was dead. Hackles up, Ryder raced to intercept, Jaspyr and the cousins following. But Tomas had caught another scent. Knowledge warred with instinct. Knowledge won, sending him away from his Pack Leader toward enemy lines.

Toward the weapon that had killed Harry.

A line of pain burned across his shoulder, but the ball was only lead and the wound healed as he ran.

He pushed off a fallen Imperial, breastplate keeping the body from compacting under his weight, and threw himself up over the heads of the corpse's company. Heard the Aydori infantry rally behind him and knew that, with them returned to the fight, he needn't fear a bayonet in the back. Dodged through chaos, still at full speed.

The impossible range of the new weapon kept it back from the front lines. Far enough back there'd be no reason for a heavy guard.

Speed and agility and the terror the Pack evoked in the unfamiliar kept him alive as he moved deeper and deeper into the Imperial ranks. The part of him trained to war recognized the Imperials' fast advance had opened up their lines and that worked to his favor.

The weapon, up on a small rise, didn't look like much. A fat tube on a cradle. The men around it smelled of curiosity and excitement, distant from the death they were dealing. Men who fought with heads instead of hearts. They smelled of gunpowder, familiar but a more concentrated scent than he was used to.

They smelled of silver.

He had to circle around behind the weapon to approach it.

Heard a man with a telescope shout, "There, a black beast! Huge bugger! And a gray one! I see four, no, six abominations with them!" And then coordinates. Tomas thought they meant him at first, then realized the big black beast had to be Ryder.

But Ryder and Jaspyr and the others were safe in among the Imperial cavalry,

They wouldn't shoot their own horses, their own men to bring their enemy down.

He thought that right up until they lit the fuse.

His teeth crushed the gunner's wrist a moment too late.

The carriage slowed and slowed again as the ponies struggled up the long, steep hill through Whelan Forest. Not that they'd been moving all that fast since leaving the city. As far as Mirian could see, the biggest difference between those on foot and those on wheels wasn't speed, but possessions. Lord and Lady forbid the wealthy not take the good dishes and silver and linens when fleeing for their lives.

Although, in all fairness, the less than wealthy had made a valiant attempt to carry their possessions with them. A wide variety of objects had been discarded by the side of the road even before the road left the city. Pots and pans, bundles of clothing, a bed—Mirian was impressed they'd gotten it as far as they had—a single shoe, a striped stocking, a broken confectioner's jar still half filled with red-and-white candies. Fortunately, the people no longer moved packed tightly together in a solid line of desperation as they must have through the night. The stragglers didn't even look up as the carriage passed. Too many carriages had already gone by, and they were still walking. When they passed two women with three small children, the youngest screaming his displeasure to the world, Mirian's mother had reached past her and pulled the blind down over the carriage window, her action saying as loudly as words that the concerns of the common were no concerns of hers.

Her concerns were unmistakable and had entirely replaced any panic.

"When did you meet Jaspyr Hagen?"

"At the reception."

"And it never occurred to you to tell me?"

Mirian shrugged. "It seemed unimportant."

"Don't shrug, Mirian; you look like a shopkeeper. Tell me, how could meeting Jaspyr Hagen be considered unimportant?"

"The Imperial army . . ."

Her mother cut her off. "Is not as important as attaching Jaspyr Hagen. Do you have an understanding?"

They had a something. Jaspyr didn't seem to care she had nothing more than first levels in five disciplines, certainly not enough Magecraft to bear children to the Pack, but they had nothing as definite as an understanding. An attraction? An acknowledgment? A hope? A dream? A chance? Mirian couldn't define it, even to herself, so the thought of explaining it to her mother made it simpler to say, "No."

Not that her mother listened.

"He is older than you by at least a decade, but you act like an old woman most of the time . . ."

Apparently, only old women could be practical.

By the time the carriage slowed for the hill, Mirian's mother had planned the wedding—who she'd invite, who she'd snub, who'd make her dress. She'd wanted Jon to pull over to the side of the road so that Lady Hagen's carriage could catch up. Her father had refused to give the order, but Mirian wouldn't have been surprised to discover he'd planned the delay at the bank in order to claim this position. It certainly wouldn't hurt business if they were close enough to offer any necessary assistance to the Pack.

When the first shot rang out, and her mother shrieked for Jon to put the whip to the ponies, Mirian wasn't surprised by that either.

The coachmen were armed. One managed to get a shot off and died a moment later, the other two just died. Tangles released, the men in the trees dropped onto the wolf's-crest carriages, as Reiter led the rest of his men out onto the road.

A quick glance to ensure the carriage up ahead continued moving around the curve at the top of the hill, then he yanked open the door of the last of the carriages they'd stopped. As he leaned in, an elderly woman ripped the buttons open down the front of her dress, clawed the fabric down off furry shoulders, and became a huge gray wolf. Had it not tripped over its discarded skirt, he'd have died. Claws scrabbled at his clothes, teeth closed on his shoulder not his neck, and they slammed together down onto the hard-packed dirt of the road.

Reiter froze, hands gripping the thick fur of the beast's throat, as three shots slammed into its side. He squeezed his eyes and mouth closed as a fourth shot went in behind its jaw and sprayed hot blood over his face. He'd got his eyes closed in time. His lashes had already started to stick together, so he forced them open and heaved the body off to one side. Rolling up onto his knees he spat, dragged his sleeve over his mouth as he stood, and refused to think of some of the more lurid stories.

"You okay, Cap?"

Easy enough to hear what the sergeant meant, even over the screaming.

Did it break the skin?

He shoved a hand under his clothes. "Didn't get through the jacket," he said, bending to retrieve his bicorn.

"Good." Sergeant Black finished reloading his musket with silver shot, and yelled, "Behind you!"

The creature dove off the top of the carriage, blood on its muzzle, fur gleaming gold in the filtered light.

They fired together, muskets snapped up to their shoulders, and it crashed to the ground, eyes wild even in death.

Reloading, Reiter swept his gaze over the road, saw another three dead beasts, a small cluster of sobbing servants, one holding an infant, and five women on the ground at the lieutenant's feet, hands clutched to their heads, breath coming in pained gasps.

Reiter hadn't expected the mages would all be women. Young women. Young, terrified women. Although their sex did provide a simple explanation of how they controlled the beastmen. . . .

"This one's had pups," Sergeant Black grunted, heaving the golden body over with the toe of his boot. The extended teats protruded through the thick fur.

"Leave her alone!" One of the servants broke from the group and threw herself down beside the beast, cradling its head on her lap and bending to sob against the bloody fur. The woman holding the infant wept against the child's hair.

Uncomfortable, and unsure why—he was a soldier, death was his job—Reiter looked away, dragged his gaze across to the old beast who'd attacked him, and realized it wore a pair of gold hoops in its ears.

Young women. Old women. The rulers of Aydori had always been named beastmen. They were to take their women back to the empire to control them. This wasn't . . .

"Where's the sixth?" The lieutenant held a tangle in his hand. "We need all six!"

"I forbid it!"

Mirian rolled her eyes and slipped out of the carriage and into the brush at the side of the road. With her father trying to calm her mother's hysteria, she'd managed to shout an order to stop that Jon had chosen to obey.

"Mirian! Do you hear me? Get back in the carriage this instant!"

"Mirian!" Her father leaned out the open door. "Your mother . . ."

"Wants me to join the Pack." She turned and threw the words at him. "You want me to join the Pack. This is what the Pack does."

The words meant nothing in and of themselves; the Pack had no monopoly on doing the right thing, but they were the words her mother needed to hear to stop shrieking and the words her father needed to hear to nod and sit back.

"I will accompany you, Miss Mirian." Barrow climbed down from his seat beside the coachman and twitched invisible wrinkles out of his immaculate black coat. "You should not go alone."

Barrow had been with them as long as Mirian could remember. Some years older than her father, he'd recently stopped tying back his thinning gray hair and had cropped it short in an old man's style. Fitting, she acknowledged, given that he was an old man. But Jon had to hold the ponies and her father was clearly not going to leave the safety of the carriage and Barrow was all there was if she was not to go alone.

There had been shooting. And screaming.

In all honesty, Mirian didn't want to go alone. She nodded once and the two of them made their way quickly back to the top of the hill. Slipping off the road and into the trees, she motioned for Barrow to follow as she cut across the arc of the curve until she could see back the way they'd come. Dropping to her knees, she crept forward as far as she could. To her surprise, Barrow dropped to his knees in turn and threw himself down beside her.

The wolf's-crest carriages had been stopped and were surrounded by men wearing deep purple jackets over black trousers and boots. They wore black bicorns on their heads and held muskets. Imperial army uniforms. Imperial army weapons. The one gesturing, gold glittering as he waved both hands, was so pompous, even at this distance she knew he had to be an officer. She could see two wolves on the ground, one of the coachmen under guard and all five women of the Mage-pack kneeling in the circle of men, bodies bent and twisted, hands clasped to their heads. They looked to be in pain, but she couldn't be sure as she couldn't see their expressions. As she watched, Lady Hagen dropped her hands to the fabric of her skirt and straightened, the effort obvious even to Mirian's less than perfect eyesight.

A breeze lifted Mirian's hair, and she heard Lady Hagen's voice as clearly as if she were kneeling with her.

"You have us bound, so kill us and be gone."

Bound. Magically bound, or the Mage-pack would not be kneeling there waiting for death.

The officer waved his hands again. It looked almost as though he was sprinkling gold dust from his fingers. He had to be responding, but Mirian couldn't hear him. Did he speak Aydori? Lady Hagen was speaking Aydori, but that didn't necessarily mean she expected the enemy officer to understand her.

"We are only five." She sounded angry. Imperious. Not stooping to insult him personally even while her tone insulted his entire nation.

Mirian strained to hear what the Imperials replied, hoping hearing at distance meant she was finally showing some of the mage-craft everyone seemed to think she had. The breezes refused her command. It must be Lady Hagen then, not bound so tightly as they thought and doing what she could.

The officer raised a hand as though to strike her. The man beside him, covered in enough blood for it to be visible even at a distance, grabbed his wrist.

"The emperor? What does Leopald want with us?"

What did the emperor want? Mirian hoped Lady Hagen was stalling for time because it should be obvious to anyone what the emperor wanted. Control the Pack Leader's mate. Control the Pack Leader. She had no idea how the emperor's men had managed to neutralize the Mage-pack—although the gold she could still see glinting in the officer's hands was so out of place it had to have something to do with it—nor did it matter.

She leaned in close to Barrow's ear. "The Pack Leader must be told his mate's been taken. He *has* to stop them before they cross the border!"

Barrow, who was, after all, sensible above all else, nodded and then proved he was after all not as sensible as all that when he said, "Go back to the carriage, Miss Mirian. I will find the Pack Leader and give him this information."

"You won't be able to get near him. I will."

He stared at her for a long moment, then he nodded. "Jaspyr Hagen." Seated on the outside of the coach, Barrow'd had a better view of her conversation with the Pack Leader's cousin than her mother had.

"Yes." *And a run to the border would probably kill you.* She couldn't say that, but neither could she have it on her conscience. "Tell my parents where I've gone and then get them to safety."

"They will not . . ."

"Tell them I've gone to join Jaspyr Hagen." She struggled to keep the edge from her voice, but didn't entirely succeed. "That should calm them."

After another moment's scrutiny, he nodded again. "As you wish, Miss Mirian." His tone had changed and, for the first time, he didn't seem to be addressing the child she'd been. Rising to his knees, he ignored the leaf litter on his coat and touched her lightly on the shoulder. "Lord and Lady keep you safe."

"Our orders were to return with six mages. There must be six!"

Reiter resisted the urge to visibly count their captives again no matter how much he'd enjoy irritating Lieutenant Lord Geurin. Lingering this far behind enemy lines would get them killed. "Five will have to do. Sergeant."

"Sir."

"Divide the captives among the squads and get ready to move out."

"No!"

Reiter stiffened and turned to face the younger officer. He'd had to accept a certain amount of aristocratic attitude since they'd left the bulk of the army, but this was over the line. "No?"

The soldiers surrounding them froze, and even the lieutenant had brains enough to flinch although he tried to hide it. He wet his lips, glanced down at the women, and stepped forward. "A word alone, Captain Reiter."

Secret orders, as suspected. War was bad enough without Soothsayers getting involved. "Sergeant."

"Sir."

"As ordered."

"Sir."

As Reiter followed Geurin behind the carriages, he could hear Black barking orders and the baby screaming. It sounded hungry.

"This one's had pups."

No. He wasn't going there.

Safely out of sight of both their men and the captives, Geurin turned the sixth tangle over in his fingers and said, "Our actions follow the visions of the Imperial Soothsayers."

"No shit. We're ass-deep in enemy territory with ancient weapons, capturing mages," Reiter continued as Geurin's eyes narrowed. "Soothsayers are a given. Now, tell me something I don't know."

"There's a prophecy about the fall of the empire."

That was something he didn't know. "Concerning these women?"

Geurin straightened and stood as though he were reciting. "When wild and mage together come, one in six or six in one. Empires rise or empires fall, the unborn child begins it all."

"Seriously?" Reiter let his musket hang off the strap, lifted his bicorn, and ran his free hand back through his hair, the front sticky with blood. "That's the reason we're here? My eight-year-old niece writes better verse."

"Is your eight-year-old niece an Imperial Soothsayer?" Geurin's lip curled. His tone remained respectful enough that Reiter ignored his expression. "Or the Soothsayer's Voice? Or a Court Analyst? Or

His Imperial Majesty Emperor Leopald himself who gave the order to release the tangles from the vaults? One of these six women . . ."

"Five." Reiter pulled a handkerchief from his pocket and smeared the blood around a bit. He'd need water to get it off.

Geurin's nostrils flared dramatically. "One of the *six* women we have been ordered to capture is pregnant with the child who could bring down the empire!"

Could. Prophecy hinged just a little too much on *could* in Reiter's opinion. However, as the lieutenant had pointed out, he wasn't a Soothsayer, or a Voice, or a Court Analyst; he was just a soldier, and he had a soldier's response. He wasn't proud of it, but he owned it. "If they haven't had the child yet, why not kill them here? Why drag them back to the capital?"

"Empires rise or empires fall," the lieutenant repeated. "If His Imperial Majesty controls the child, he determines what the child sets in motion."

That sounded reasonable, as far as anything connected with Soothsayers could be called reasonable. Soothsayers were a remnant of the old ways, still around for the advantage they could give. Where *could* was, once again, the operative word, referring to men and women who were undeniably crazy, their words translated by political expediency. Still, he had his orders and now they even made a certain amount of sense. Controlling the beastmen through their women implied the Imperial army would fail to take Aydori by more direct means, and the Imperial army had not yet met a defense that could stand against them.

"You and Sergeant Black escort the women back to the army with squads one to five. I'll take squad six and find our missing mage." Reiter held out his hand for the unused tangle. "This is my command. That makes it my responsibility she's found."

And I don't trust you to find your ass with both hands and a map, he added silently as Geurin hesitated, no doubt weighing the cost of showing up a mage short against the benefit of being the first to report. *I definitely don't trust you to find your way back to the border on your own.*

"Sergeant Black . . ."

"Will go with you." Thus ensuring they'd actually make it out of Aydori.

Geurin nodded, although at what, precisely, Reiter wasn't sure. "We were sent to this place on the road because all six mages were Seen here. She can't be far."

The tangles were surprisingly heavy given how little substance they had, and the last tangle seemed to weigh as much as all six had combined. As Reiter slid it into his pocket, he wondered if that was because it carried the weight of the Soothsayers' prophecy or the weight that would come down on his ass if he returned without the sixth mage.

The pain had faded, no longer knives driven in through her temples but a dull, unpleasant, albeit bearable, throbbing. Fresh knives stabbed in if she attempted to use her power. A lesser but constant pain if she remained quiescent. Danika gritted her teeth and squared her shoulders. Her power was not all she was. If these creatures who had slaughtered Lady Berin and Marinka thought she would crumble and beg, they could think again. She was the Alpha Female of the Aydori Pack and would not show her throat to the enemy.

Moving only her eyes, she checked on the captured Mage-pack.

Annalyse still had her head down, shoulders shaking as she wept— probably for Lady Berin, possibly for them all. Jesine, Sirlin's wife, was sitting up, weight back on her heels, eyes closed, chest rising and falling as she breathed deeply. The highest level Healer-mage in the Mage-pack, it was possible she could control the pain caused by the net. Beside her, Stina Menkyczk, wife to one of the senior officers of the Hunt Pack—widow now if Tomas was right and the entire Hunt Pack had been destroyed—dug her hands into the dirt of the road and whimpered. Danika didn't know if her pain came from fighting the net or because her niece lay dead and her niece's baby daughter continued to wail, not understanding that her mama could not rise and change and go to her. Kirstin Yervick stared wide-eyed around her, met Danika's gaze and bit her lip hard enough to draw blood. She'd left twin ten-year-old sons with their grandparents in Trouge to travel with her husband to Bercarit. Danika was actually impressed that Kirstin was holding her tongue. It wasn't something the other Air-mage was known for. Sarcasm, yes. Silence, no.

Danika couldn't turn far enough to check the servants, but now that they'd stopped fighting to get past the soldiers, they seemed safe enough. She could hear Natali, Lady Berin's maid, murmuring a string of complex curses and could only hope none of the enemy spoke more than the very basic Aydori the lieutenant had attempted.

The golden net wrapped around Danika's head stopped her from raising the winds and throwing these men back across the border like ragdolls, but voices were only air given form and texture and the breeze blew past the two officers talking quietly behind the carriage.

"When wild and mage together come, one in six or six in one. Empires rise or empires fall, the unborn child begins it all."

Her hand moved unbidden to her belly. Soothsayers who lived far enough in the future to give voice to "prophecy" were so insane every word could have a dozen different meanings. Danika had heard rumors that Emperor Leopald kept Soothsayers at the Imperial Court, but she'd had no idea he was actually mad enough to use them to determine policy.

As the lieutenant explained why they weren't to be murdered, the sound of retching pulled Danika's attention back to the road in time to see one of the soldiers send Jesine sprawling as she tried to move toward Annalyse, now bent double, spewing her half-digested breakfast onto the dirt.

Time to stop pretending she didn't speak Imperial.

"Sergeant Black!" He started and turned, drawn by the command in her voice. "That woman is a Healer." Danika nodded toward Jesine, who drew herself up onto her knees, gold-flecked eyes narrowed, teeth bared. "And that woman . . ." A nod to Annalyse, a line of saliva stretching between her mouth and the stain on the road. ". . . requires her services."

"She can't do a healing with the tangle on," the sergeant pointed out, one hand raised to hold the surrounding men silent and in place, his eyes locked on Danika's face.

"Healing isn't only about mage-craft, Sergeant."

After a long moment he nodded, hand moving so his thumb could stroke the thick scar along his jaw. "No, it ain't. All right, then. Tell her she can do her healin', but if her hands touch the tangle, Hare'll shoot her." As Sergeant Black spoke his name, a soldier slightly older than the others, his dark hair streaked with gray, lifted his weapon to his shoulder. "And just so you know, m'Lady, Hare's got one of the new rifled muskets and he never misses."

"Thank you for the warning, Sergeant. You can go to her, Jes," she continued in Aydori. "Don't touch the gold net."

"Or what?" Jesine muttered, crawling to where Annalyse was now dry heaving. "They'll shoot me?"

"Yes."

"Wonderful."

"Not really."

"This doesn't mean you lot can start talkin'." Sergeant Black cut Stina off before she managed more than an indeterminate sound. Understanding the tone, if not the words, Stina shut her mouth with a snap and glared up at him. If looks alone could kill, the sergeant wouldn't have survived the encounter.

"You speak Imperial very well."

Although her heart slammed against her ribs, Danika kept herself from visibly reacting to the sudden presence behind her. The younger Pack members were always playing stalk and pounce; those who reacted, soon became a favorite target. "Thank you, Captain Reiter." His voice was deeper than the younger officer's.

"And how well do the *others* speak Imperial?"

"Everyone speaks a little Imperial, Captain." Stina spoke a *very* little, but Danika had no idea how much she understood. Jesine could manage if everyone involved spoke slowly. Kirstin was as fluent as Danika was—there was no way she'd allow her rival the advantage. Danika wasn't certain about Annalyse as she'd known the younger woman for barely a week. "The language, like the empire, is . . . pervasive."

"True. Stand up."

"You don't give me orders, Captain."

"And I don't have time for this."

His hand around her upper arm was more competent than cruel, but intent mattered very little given the sudden flare of pain when he hauled her to her feet. When he released her, she staggered forward, stumbled, and flung out her arms to stop herself from falling. The sudden movement added yet more pain, and it raged through her body like a storm before dissipating through the soles of her feet.

She sagged with the relief of its going, then straightened her back, slowly lifted her head, and turned to face the captain.

Reiter was younger than Danika expected; tall but lean with pale eyes, a beak of a nose, hair that indeterminate color between blond and brown, and reddish-brown stubble over a pointed chin. He might have been attractive if not for Lady Berin's blood still smeared over his face. The competence in his touch extended to his expression. He had the look of a professional soldier, a man who would get the job done no matter how distasteful he personally found it.

"Good, they can walk." He spoke Imperial with the careful diction of a man promoted from the ranks and thrown in among the sons of aristocracy. "Tie their hands behind them."

"They can't remove the tangles, Captain." The lieutenant, whose name Danika hadn't yet heard, was clearly one of those privileged sons. His uniform had not merely been tailored, but made-to-measure, and his accent had the supercilious sound of the Court about it. "Removal requires another artifact."

"Does it? Tie their hands anyway," the captain continued, "as I doubt they'll take your word for it and I don't want them damaged beyond their ability to walk."

"So kind," Danika murmured, carefully inclining her head toward him.

His cheeks under the patina of blood flushed slightly, but that was the only sign he'd heard. "One man in each squad keeps them upright and moving. You go back the way we came in."

Was he not going with them? Danika wondered. The lieutenant's youth might make him easier to manipulate, but he looked like the type who felt he had to keep proving his power.

Before the lieutenant could acknowledge the captain's order, Natali's cursing grew louder as, finished with the soldiers themselves, she began to wish nightmares and diseases on their descendants. Danika heard Kirstin giggle and then bite the sound off before it slid into hysteria.

The next sequence of sound began with a musket butt slamming against bone, the impact of a body with the ground, a slight scuffle, and a sudden uneasy silence broken by the baby's hiccup.

Captain Reiter turned just far enough Danika could see past him to where Natali lay crumpled on the ground. The others stood glaring but still, and Marinka's maid—Danika hated that she couldn't remember the girl's name—cuddled little Talia, her cheek pressed against the baby's golden hair. When the captain turned back, his gesture took in all five of the captured mages. "Is one of you the mother?"

She did not look at Marinka's golden-furred body, not wanting to bring the contempt these men had for the Pack down on her child. Hands curled into fists, she could feel her fingernails cutting into her palms. "No." She didn't trust her voice with more than the single word.

"Good." The captain also did not look, a muscle jumping in his jaw as he stopped himself from turning his head. "Tie the servants. Make sure the girl can tend the baby." When no one obeyed immediately, his lips drew back off his teeth. "Move!"

Ryder couldn't have done it better.

The thought brought a different kind of pain. Danika whispered her husband's name, allowing the breeze to take it. It *would* find him.

She missed the captain's instructions to the lieutenant, but heard the younger man ask, "Where will you search?"

Search? And then she remembered. The prophecy had sent these Imperial soldiers into Aydori to capture six mages, not five. Six. *One in six or six in one.*

"She can't be far." He glanced back along the long curve of the road toward the city. "I see no carriages heading up from Bercarit, so I'll take the boys up the road; take a look at what's around that corner. Move as fast as you can. Don't wait if you get to the wagons before we catch up."

Danika got the impression that the last bit of the captain's order was more for Sergeant Black than the lieutenant. It seemed that the captain believed the lieutenant less than capable in the woods. That could work in their favor, slowing them enough to allow Ryder to find them before they reached the border.

As for the sixth mage, Danika had no idea who the Soothsayers could have meant. Only eight of the Mage-pack had been in Bercarit and the three men had gone to stop the advance of the Imperial army. While it was more likely that the Soothsayers' crazed babbling had been misinterpreted, it was possible that one of the others had been alerted by the refugees arriving in Trouge and was even now heading back toward Bercarit to help.

Barely parting her lips, she breathed out a warning. Unrestrained, any one of the Mage-pack could send these Imperials across the border, tails between their legs.

They retrieved their packs before moving into the woods, both to cut off the corner and maintain the element of surprise. Reiter could hear raised voices even before they regained the road.

At his left shoulder, Chard snickered. "Someone's gettin' an earful, Cap."

"Captain."

"Sergeant Black calls you . . ."

"You're not Sergeant Black. You haven't earned the right." Without Black, Chard would push. But Reiter had been a sergeant once himself; he could handle young men with delusions of experience.

The carriage, pulled as close to the far side of the road as it could go without putting the far wheels in the ditch, was a little smaller than the three they'd stopped. Reiter knew squat about carriages, but it seemed of similar quality—shiny reddish-brown paint, tarted up with unnecessary brass. No wolf's-head crest, so it was unlikely it belonged to the mage they sought. Still, the Soothsayers had said *six*, six at this place in the road and it was the only carriage in sight.

The upper-class woman leaning out the open door, one hand clutching the overcoat of the equally upper-class man standing on the road, was clearly demanding he get back in. Some situations needed no translation.

The man was neither one of the beastmen nor a soldier.

The old servant at the pony's head—gray hair, neat black clothes—was equally no threat. The coachman had a musket, but, in spite of their situation, hadn't pulled it from the scabbard. If he was smart, that lack of foresight could save his life. Civilians died in wars, but Reiter avoided adding to their numbers when he could. He assumed there'd be a maid of some kind inside the carriage. Unless Aydori maids were combat trained, he doubted she'd give them much trouble.

He sent Best to the front of the carriage, Armin to the rear, and kept Chard with him.

The coachman, as expected, saw them first. He froze and remained frozen, hands lifted well away from his musket when he realized Chard could drop him where he sat. By the time the woman's eyes widened and she fell silent, Best and Armin were in place. She jerked the sleeve she held until the man wearing it turned.

Reiter ignored them both and pulled the tangle from his pocket. The coach was already stopped; he could have flung the artifact from the trees had he thought of it. Not that it mattered. It hung limp from the end of his finger.

"Maybe it's broke," Chard muttered.

Possible. Unfortunately, Reiter had no way of checking without a mage. *One not already wearing a tangle*, he corrected silently.

Gesturing with his musket, he moved the man away from the door and glanced past the woman. The plump, middle-aged redhead pressed against the far door, glaring daggers at him, was clearly the maid.

"She not here!"

The maid looked as astonished as Reiter felt. He stepped back and they both stared at the woman who continued in fractured, accented, but understandable Imperial.

"She gone to Jaspyr Hagen!" Reiter took another step back as a slender finger jabbed toward him. "He come rip you throat!"

The beastmen had names.

"Lirraka!"

This close, he could see the few flecks of green in her eyes. Mage eyes. But the tangle hadn't taken her. The tangle needed a younger woman. A stronger mage. A woman with the strength to run for the beast she controlled.

Up on the carriage step, Reiter ignored the fluent Imperial directed at him by the man—who was either bragging about the money he had or offering a bribe—and the continuing death threats by the woman. Glaring the coachman's ass back down onto the seat, Reiter grabbed his weapon and jumped back down to the road. "Let's go."

"We're just leaving them, Captain?" Chard asked, falling in beside him.

"They're harmless. We have a line on the sixth mage," he added when all four of them were back across the ditch and under the trees. "She's headed for the fighting, to warn the beastmen."

Not even Chard needed him to point out they had to stop her. If the beastmen got their scent from the road, and if even half the stories were true, none of them would reach the border.

"Why doesn't she just use mage-craft to tell them?" Best asked as they began to move back down the hill.

"Could be she's a Fire-mage," Chard pointed out. "He's not going to be sitting around a campfire scratching his fleas and waiting for her to pop out of the flames, now, is he? Not with our bloody army attacking."

From the road behind them, they could hear the argument their presence had stopped start up again.

"Sounds like my mum having a go at my dad," Armin muttered. "I thought they'd be more different, laying down with beasts and all."

In all honesty, so had Reiter.

Chapter Three

"BEWARE THE NET FROM ABOVE."

The underbrush grabbed at Mirian's skirt. She caught her foot in a tangle of fallen branches and stumbled through a spiderweb. Resolutely not thinking of spiders in her hair or down her collar or climbing into her ears, she flailed at the strands hanging off her face as she ran.

Did Lady Hagen's warning of a net refer to the gold glitter Mirian had seen hanging off the officer's fingertips? It was hard to think of what else that glitter could be. Her father had spoken approvingly of the empire's advances in technology—was this one of them? Had someone created a technology to neutralize mage-craft?

One foot dropped into a hole masked by ground cover and she fell, biting back a startled cry. The impact drove her hands wrist-deep into the leaf litter. As she pushed up, something cracked then compacted under her right palm. Soft and moist and horribly warm, it left a dark smear on her skin. Back up on her feet, she swiped her hand against her skirt and kept running.

The Mage-pack had been holding their heads in pain, unable to fight back.

The net from above, probably the gold glitter, neutralized mage-craft by wrapping around the head. Logically, the net had to do something more than merely wrap, but how it did what it did wasn't as important right now as what it did.

Mirian ducked under a branch and wondered if the net would've worked on the Mage-pack had they been wearing hats. Last season, the style in Aydori had been for little knots of flowers and lace perched precariously on shell combs that dropped off during the change to fur. Would the Imperial army have taken fashion into account?

She jerked to one side as the pocket on her skirt caught then tore, bounced off a tree trunk, and through another web.

"Beware the net from above."

The soldiers wouldn't want her regardless of what the net was or where it came from. She wasn't Mage-pack. Her professors had made it clear they considered her barely a mage. Still, Jaspyr Hagen had said she smelled amazing and Lady Hagen had sent a warning. . . .

An evergreen branch slapped her cheek. She gasped, inhaled a bug, and had to stop to cough. As soon as she could breathe, she ripped tender new tips off the branch and tangled them in her hair until she wore a sticky green circlet. She'd probably have to shave her head to get it free. In Aydori, only the women of the Mage-pack cut their hair short to match the Pack who didn't have hair but caps of fur.

Her mother would have fits.

Her mother might be the only person in Aydori currently worrying about hairstyles.

It seemed brighter off to her right, so Mirian clambered over a fallen trunk and headed toward the light, hoping it meant the underbrush had thinned and she could move faster. She had to get to Lord Hagen. She had to let him know.

Pushing through a thicket of shoulder-high, red stems, the sharp ends of oval leaves scored the bare skin above her collar and clusters of buds smeared sticky fluid on her clothes. Suddenly stepping out over nothing, she clutched at branches, but they bent with her, folding down into the ditch and springing back into place when impact opened her fingers and she released them. Scrambling up the opposite slope on her hands and knees, Mirian stared at the hard-packed clay of the road. Had she gotten turned around? Had she been running in circles?

Lifting her head, she saw the road to the left curved around a stand of silver birch and disappeared, cutting off the sight of carriages and the captured Mage-pack. Cutting her off from the sight of the Imperial soldiers.

To the right, a family—a group of people anyway—plodded toward Trouge. Two women older than her but younger than her mother pulled a low cart piled high with goods and topped with three small children. An elderly woman plucked the limp body of a chicken as she walked.

Mirian stared at the old woman and wondered if the children perched so precariously on the cart were her grandchildren. Lady Berin had no grandchildren, although her son's winter marriage no doubt meant there'd be some soon. Except her son was in the Hunt Pack and the younger Lord Hagen, Tomas, said the Hunt Pack had been killed. And her daughter-in-law was in the Mage-pack and they'd been taken by Imperial soldiers. And Lady Berin . . .

Lady Berin . . .

Mirian remembered a gray-furred body lying limp on the road, a shadow spreading beneath her.

Lady Berin was dead.

Dead. Killed.

And one other of the Pack. And at least one of the coachmen.

But Lady Berin . . . Mirian had just seen her at the opera. Had just seen her laughing and talking and alive. And now she was dead.

Shoving her fist into her mouth, Mirian muffled a noise she couldn't stop herself from making. Scream, sob, pain, protest—she didn't know what it was, but she couldn't breathe around it and it hurt! After what seemed like hours, but was more likely moments given how much farther the family had progressed up the road toward her, she wiped her hands off on her skirt, took a deep breath, and stood.

Her legs felt shaky, disconnected from her body. Stepping forward, she wobbled. Took another step and had to spread her arms for balance.

She didn't have time for this.

Lady Berin was dead. The Mage-pack had been taken. And Lord

Hagen needed to know. Lord Hagen would fix this. She swallowed a giggle before it could emerge and turn to hysteria. Her mother would be so pleased. It was the first time they'd agreed in months.

A deep breath. Another. She started to run.

As Mirian passed the family, someone yelled, "You forget your dancing shoes, lady?" and all of them laughed. The children laughed because the adults did, the adults laughed because the Imperial army was marching on Bercarit.

They didn't try to stop her.

She brushed a chicken feather off her sleeve and ran faster.

At least the road ran downhill to the city.

Around another curve, she staggered to a stop beside an abandoned trunk, hand pressed hard against the pain under her ribs, and realized walks along the promenade and weekly dances at the Assembly Hall were not enough to prepare for this kind of a run. It occurred to her as she tried to work up spit enough to swallow, that she should have warned the family what they were walking into. Warned them about the soldiers. About the bodies.

"Too late . . ."

A raven investigating a pile of cloth on the other side of the road looked up as if to ensure she wasn't speaking to him. There was a raven on the Imperial flag. A raven in flight over a shield, a spear, and a sword, each representing a division of the Imperial army. Each division an army on its own as smaller countries understood the definition of *army*. They studied the Kresentian Empire in Aydori schools; it was too powerful to ignore and forewarned was supposed to be forearmed. Except it didn't seem to be.

A line of sweat ran down her side and she unbuttoned her jacket. The jacket, a military-styled gray wool with black braid and the new tucked sleeves hadn't been too hot for a spring dawn, but she was starting to understand those evacuees who'd abandoned bundles of clothes.

Jacket open, she began to run again, fists tucked up under her breasts to keep them from bouncing painfully.

Her heel came down on a rock, her foot rolled, but she caught herself before she fell and ran on in spite of the throb in her ankle.

Ran until she had to walk to catch her breath.

Ran again.

Eyes on the road, concentrating on breathing, on moving her legs, she was at the outskirts of Bercarit before she realized.

It was quiet. The sky was clear, no smudge of smoke from cooking fires hung over the city. If there were people still around, and there had to be, then they were lying low.

She could see a smudge of smoke over the border. Except that the border was seventeen miles away and she only had first level Air so whatever it was she saw, it couldn't be smoke from the battle.

Could it?

Did it matter?

She couldn't run another seventeen miles. Every breath tasted like copper and it felt like steel spikes had been driven in under her ribs. Her feet hurt all the way up to her knees and she was drenched in sweat.

But Lord Hagen still had to know.

If she could find a pony . . .

Stupid. No one would have left a pony, and anyone who'd stayed wouldn't *have* a pony.

They said that in the old days the strongest Air-mages could ride the wind. Lady Hagen was the strongest Air-mage in Aydori and, as far as Mirian knew, her ladyship had never gone flying. Not that it mattered what *they said*.

Limping, she started down the wide avenue the Trouge Road became when it entered the city. Bercarit, unlike Trouge, was built for commerce. It had no city wall; trees and shrubs gave way to the homes of the very wealthy, each individually walled. Private gardens in front of large sprawling houses on property that ran down to the bank of the Navine. This was where the Pack lived. Where Lady Berin . . .

Scrubbing at her cheeks with her palm, Mirian caught a glint of silver. She turned toward it, and realized she'd glimpsed the river between two of the houses.

The Navine looped around east of Bercarit, slowing as it deepened. This early in the season it would still be running fast, fed by the snowmelt and by runoff from a hundred mountain streams. Okay, maybe not a hundred. Mirian had no idea how many mountain streams fed the Navine and didn't care. The river not only ran to the border, it curved to *become* the border for a part of its length. Somewhere there *had* to be a boat small enough for her to use.

She knew where the docks were. They topped her mother's list of where good girls didn't go. Good girls didn't cross Beech Street.

Beech Street was nearly all the way across town.

Mirian weighed distance against the garden wall rising up beside her and turned to the wall, hurrying back to the last set of iron gates. Too large to squeeze through the vertical bars, she put her right foot on the lower crosspiece and jammed the toe of her left boot between the gate and the stone post, just above the hinge. Metal digging into her palms, she dragged herself up until her weight was on the hinge, braced her right foot on a bit of scrollwork, and pushed. Releasing the gate, she threw her upper body at the top of the post, moving her right foot to brace against a higher bit of ironwork, digging for imperfections in the mortar with the toe of her left boot.

Then her right foot slipped.

She lurched forward, trying to hook her fingers under the capstone. Began to slide back.

A delicate touch against the back of her hand.

Just a leaf . . .

The shriek didn't count if no one heard it.

Where there was a leaf . . . Her fingers touched wood. Shoulder screaming, Mirian stretched an impossible amount farther and curled her hand around a thick piece of vine. With no choice, she trusted it with her weight. Squirming and kicking against the side bars of the gate, she managed to get up onto the top of the wall.

The vine made getting down a lot easier.

Boots sinking into the soft earth between clumps of daffodils, she sagged against the vine for a moment, and watched the bud closest to her hand swell and unfurl into a pale pink blossom. A few more, then a few more, until a spray of blossom bobbed up over the wall scenting the air with the promise of summer. First level Earth. Pretty, but useless and worse than that, unintentional. Given the way exhaustion ate away at her control, it was a good thing she hadn't managed to learn anything more dangerous. As it was, it was still too cold at night for so delicate a flower, so all she'd done was expose the vine to an early death.

More death.

Eyes locked on the ribbon of silver, Mirian staggered toward the water. Just a little farther and she could sit down. Just a little farther and there'd be a boat and it would take her to the border and she could find Lord Hagen. Jaspyr, too, if the Lord and Lady felt she was due some personal return for a horrible day.

Just a little farther.

The dock at the bottom of the garden was empty.

"Shit! Shit! Shit! Shit! SHIT!" Mirian had learned to swear at university from a woodcutter's daughter who'd tested absurdly high for her station—although no one had pointed that out more than once. Only Mirian had tested higher and that had thrown them together for a few months until Adine had progressed as expected and Mirian hadn't.

Uncertain of what she should do now, or rather how she should do what she needed to do, Mirian turned in place, the dock creaking ominously beneath her.

There was a dinghy tied at the dock at the bottom of the garden next door and the wall between the two properties only came down as far as the shore.

The water was ridiculously cold. The shock almost made her swear again.

Her waterlogged skirts were heavy, and the dinghy tilted dangerously when she stepped in. It nearly threw her out when she tried to cast off, but she managed to push away from the dock with one of the oars and force the boat out into the current.

It was faster even than she'd expected. The water dragged the oar from her hand and she almost went overboard reaching for it.

"A single oar can be used as a rudder," she told herself, watching the second oar move farther away, her knuckles white around the edge of the seat. At least theoretically. All Mirian knew about boating she'd learned on the still pond at her brother-in-law's farm and that had mostly consisted of not allowing her older nephew to fall in.

As the small boat sped past increasingly less affluent properties at a dizzying speed, not falling in seemed like an excellent idea.

If the Soothsayers were right, the carriages they'd stopped had been the last out of the city. If the Soothsayers were right, the only people they'd meet on the road back toward Bercarit would be tired and not likely to challenge four Imperial soldiers even if they were armed.

But *not likely* was not a sure thing, particularly not when Soothsayers were involved, and Reiter wasn't going to lose a man by assuming the citizens of Aydori wouldn't fight back. They needed to move fast in order to catch the sixth mage so they'd stay on the road, but they'd keep their weapons ready.

"Shoot if they look at us wrong, Cap?"

"Shoot if they aim a weapon at us," he snapped. "Musket, pistol, cannon if it comes to it. Otherwise, leave them alone."

"Crossbow?"

He turned to frown at Armin, who shrugged without breaking stride.

"Da's got a crossbow in the shop, from *his* days in the army. He'd take it if he had to haul ass out of town."

Reiter had once seen an old-timer put a crossbow quarrel through a plank. It might take forever to cock it, but a loaded crossbow was as deadly a weapon as a loaded musket. "Fine. If they're pointing a crossbow, shoot."

"What about a rock, Cap? You could get killed with a rock," Chard protested over Armin's laughter.

"Not if it hit your head," Best jeered.

"More running, less talking," Reiter growled.

"But, Cap . . ."

"A lot less talking from you, Chard."

None of them seemed to have any trouble with the idea of hunting down another young woman and dragging her back to the empire. She was a mage, she was an enemy, and they were at war. The mages of Aydori lay with beasts and that made them . . . less. His men had their orders; their only concern was following them.

He gave the orders.

The beast had gold hoops in its ears. Her ears.

You have your orders, too, he reminded himself. And they were at war.

They heard a child complaining, high-pitched and peevish, as they rounded a corner and that was the only warning they got before coming face-to-face with a small family trudging up the road toward Trouge. Trudging up the road away from the inevitable advance of the Imperial army.

As the closer of the two younger women ran for the cart and the children, Reiter wished he was still a part of that faceless mass. Killing soldiers was one thing, they knew why they were there, but he had no stomach for killing civilians.

Suddenly in the sights of four muskets, she froze, both hands in the air. Her eyes were brown. No mage marks.

"I can ask her if she saw the mage, Cap," Chard murmured.

"You speak Aydori?"

"I can say *girl* and *how much*."

Of course he could. Probably in the same sentence. "Stick with girl."

The old woman snarled and spat at Chard's single word. The woman with her hands in the air lowered them, wrapped them around her body, and shook her head. The other one stumbled back, stopped by the crosspiece of the cart.

"They think," Armin began, but Chard cut him off.

"I know." He shook his head in turn, and ran in place.

The youngest of the children shrieked with laughter. The two elder all but sat on him to shut him up.

The old woman spat again, but the one by the crosspiece glanced up at the children and pointed down the road.

"Captain, if they have a weapon . . ."

"You run slow enough you're still in range by the time they find it and load it, I'll shoot you myself." Reiter lowered his musket. Aydori eyes tracked the movement. "Let's go."

"I'd do the one on the left," Chard observed, falling in behind Reiter.

"You'd do a diseased Pyrahnian whore," Best grunted.

"If the price was right," Chard admitted cheerfully.

Imperial infantry didn't run into battle; the empire expanded and war waited for them. Oh, they'd all done some running—toward the front, away from the front, for their lives as one of Colonel Korshan's rockets went off in a random direction—but Reiter couldn't remember the last time he'd pounded down a road like a child escaping chores. Breathe in for two strides, out for two. Under his pack, his uniform stuck to his skin.

"We running all the way to Bercarit, Cap?"

"If we have to."

They had to.

They took a breather on the last rise overlooking the city. It seemed calm, peaceful even. It reminded Reiter of Karis, the empire's capital, in miniature. Gridded streets with frequent squares of green surrounding the city core—modern, built to design.

Armin snorted and said what they were all thinking. "Not burning yet."

"Swords must be taking their own sweet fucking time at the bor . . . Cap!"

A flick of gray skirts against paler gray stone.

"I see her." Reiter pulled the tangle from his pocket, thought he felt it tug against the end of his finger before it fell to hang and sway. They were still too far from the mage for it to take her. "Come on."

By the time they reached level ground where the road to Trouge turned into a wide avenue that split the city in half, she was gone.

If she was heading to warn her beast, she was heading toward the fighting. That meant they'd have to cross the city after her.

"Stay close to the walls. Someone heads toward us, you shoot." The people who remained were likely thieves, taking advantage of the evacuation to fill their pockets and more than willing to take on four Imperial soldiers far from the might of the army.

"What about children, Cap?"

"No one's left their children behind."

"But what about puppies? What if they left the little beasts behind to guard . . ."

"We don't shoot children!"

Gold earrings . . .

"Just as glad to hear that, actually. I like puppies. You know, the kind that aren't likely to turn into a . . ."

Reiter stopped so suddenly, he felt Best's musket hit his back before he could stop. When he turned, Best took a step back, Armin took a step away from Chard, and Chard looked confused. "Private Chard." His voice was a threat he didn't bother to find words for.

"Captain?"

"Shut up."

Chard's default squint widened, and he swallowed. "Yes, sir."

A quick glance at Best and Armin showed the other two soldiers staring into the city like there was actually something to see.

Drawing in a deep breath, Reiter let it out slowly and . . .

Honeysuckle.

It was barely spring at this altitude. The honeysuckle on his mother's cottage bloomed in high summer.

Mage-craft.

It didn't take long to find the spray of flowers dipping over the wall and less time for the four of them to climb it and drop down the other side. Last time Reiter had gone over a wall, enemy soldiers had been shooting at him. This time, they found a woman's bootprint heading toward the water. It could have belonged to anyone—there'd probably been women in the house that morning—but the honeysuckle suggested otherwise.

They reached the dock in time to see a small boat bob out of sight around one of the larger river wharfs. The person in it appeared to be attempting to steer with a single oar.

"Why's she not using mage-craft, then?" Armin wondered.

Best snorted. "She's Earth-mage, idiot. Made the vine blossom, didn't she? Nothing she can do about water. A boat that small in water running that fast, that's like a leaf in a fucking gale."

"What do we do, Cap?"

Reiter touched the tangle, shoved back into his jacket pocket. "We follow the river."

The oar twisted and bucked in her hands, dragged left then right by the river. Mirian fought to keep the tiny boat from running into the end of wharfs, from being smashed to pieces by a log nearly as big around as the boat—escaped from the lumberyards above the town, the deeper part of her mind observed while the surface bits jumped frantically from dealing with one near disaster to the next.

Finally, curving past the center of Bercarit, the river slowed and the oar stilled. Arms and shoulders aching, Mirian relaxed her grip enough to get blood flow back to her fingertips. On the shore to the left, the Lady's Park slipped past and she realized, given the distance she'd covered, she couldn't have been traveling as insanely fast as it had felt. As she watched, the rough land beside the park that gave the Lord his due became warehouses, each with their own pier and some with broad double doors that came all the way down to the water and likely hid interior lagoons . . . ponds . . . catchment basins? She had no idea what such a thing would be called and, right at the moment, didn't care.

She jerked as a voice yelled out from the shore, and flattened against the seat as far as her grip on the oar allowed, then straightened, calling herself an idiot. An Imperial soldier wouldn't call out to her, he'd shoot. Stupid of her to think the city had completely emptied, that all the thousands of people had left. Scanning the line of buildings, she couldn't see anyone and, whoever it was, they didn't yell again. If she could have spotted the warehouse worker or even an owner foolishly staying to try and protect his property against Imperial might, she would have landed and told them what she'd seen, and she wouldn't have been alone any longer with the knowledge that the Mage-pack had been taken.

Except she had no idea how to get the boat to shore.

Tightening her grip on the oar, she swept it back and forth as hard as she could and managed to turn the bow slightly. Relieved by this small indication of control, Mirian sagged on the seat, breathing heavily. It would take some work, but she could . . .

Three huge, wooden squares rose out of the river in front of her.

The forms for the new bridge.

The newspaper she'd read—had it only been yesterday morning?—said that, with the rough work finished on the piers, the stonemasons would begin laying the dressed stone as soon as the spring runoff ended.

Her boat was at the forms between one breath and the next. Mirian pushed the oar hard to the right. The boat twisted, kept twisting, and slammed into one enormous upright, the impact knocking her from the seat. Struggling against already wet skirts made even heavier by the water sloshing around the bottom of the boat, Mirian heaved herself up onto her knees, grabbing for the wildly swinging oar.

It clipped her on the bottom of the chin. Her teeth slammed together, and she dropped back to the bottom of the boat.

The boat spun again, wood scraping against wood, then bobbed free.

The oar swung past Mirian's vision one last time.

She thought she heard the splash as it hit the water. Might have been the sound of the water rushing past the cradles.

It seemed hard to care.

Mirian made a face as she swallowed a mouthful of blood, then blinked up at the sky, knowing she needed to sit up but not entirely certain why.

The thing she was lying on dipped suddenly sideways and she got an unexpected face full of icy water.

Boat!

She was in a boat, on the river, on her way to the border and the battle to tell Lord Hagen about the Mage-pack. And she'd lost the only way she had of controlling the boat's progress. And her head hurt. Gingerly moving her jaw, she swallowed another mouthful of blood, unable to overcome society's stricture against women spitting regardless of how unobserved she might currently be. The wave that had brought her back to herself had soaked the last dry bits of her clothes. Scrambling back up onto the low seat, Mirian noted how heavy even the finest wool got when wet and how unpleasant it felt against the skin.

With nothing to do but hope, she stayed afloat as the eastern half of Bercarit slid past and tried to make sense of what she'd seen that morning.

She'd heard the empire—so omnipresent almost no one bothered with the full name—had begun accepting women in the ranks because of its need for a constant supply of soldiers. Caught between expulsion from the university and her mother's social expectations, she'd somewhat wistfully thought that joining the army would solve all her problems. But women of Aydori didn't go to war. The female half of both Pack and Mage-pack were the last line of defense. In a worst case scenario, she'd been taught that the function of the Aydori military was to delay the Imperial army long enough for the women to get to Trouge. Carved out of the mountain by ancient Earth-mages, history said the walls of the capital couldn't be breached. Not only would the unpredictable mountain weather keep sieges short, but there were rumored to be secret ways out of the capital and a besieging army would be whittled away, night by night.

For all the years Mirian had been in school, that worst case scenario had involved the Kresentian Empire and the Imperial army.

If a dozen or so members of the Imperial army captured the women of the Mage-pack before they got to Trouge—and killed as

many Pack as possible, she admitted even as memory skittered past
the bodies lying on the road—then the defense of Trouge would be
weakened should Lord Hagen have died at the border.

Emperor Leopald wanted it all, Mirian reflected, holding her wet
jacket open and away from her shirtwaist in the hope that one or
both might begin to dry. Everyone knew the emperor wouldn't stop
until he had nothing left to conquer.

If Lord Hagen survived the battle at the border, then Lady Hagen
in the hands of the emperor was a way to control him.

Unless it had nothing to do with Lord Hagen at all—regardless
of her mother's belief that the world revolved around the Pack
Leader—and the emperor had a use for high-level mages. Who he
couldn't allow to use their abilities.

Maybe his scientists had built a machine that could suck the
mage-craft out and then feed it into creatures belonging to the emperor, creating super-mages he controlled completely and could use
as weapons.

Mirian swallowed another mouthful of bloody saliva and sighed.
Maybe her mother was right about novels rotting her brain.

"Tell her to stop."

"To stop?" Danika asked. She hadn't overheard the lieutenant's
name; he hadn't asked theirs. People had names. Those who inter-
sected with prophecy apparently did not.

The lieutenant gestured at Annalyse. With her hands tied behind
her, she leaned on a sapling, trying to stay upright as she retched. All
three of the soldiers assigned to her looked disgusted, but the one
charged with keeping her moving maintained his hold on her arm.
"She has nothing left in her stomach," the lieutenant sneered. "This
is a delaying tactic that will not be tolerated."

Given the prophecy he followed, he had to know Annalyse was
pregnant, had to assume the rest of them were as well. Danika found
it hard to believe that five of them traveling together were in a similar condition, but that was exactly the sort of cascading coincidence
that Soothsayers relied on. Or caused, according to some philoso-
phies. Given the conversation she'd overheard between the lieutenant and the captain, the men had not been informed about the

prophecy they followed. She wondered if they'd be more sympathetic or less if they knew. They could be kinder to their captives or use the information against them. Could she risk the latter for the chance of the former?

Hare, the man who never missed his shot, frowned thoughtfully as Annalyse straightened, breathing heavily. Old enough to have a wife and children, it looked as though he suspected the reason behind her illness.

Fingers digging into her arm, the lieutenant dragged Danika around to face him. "Stop pretending you don't understand me . . ."

Because, of course, it was all about him.

". . . and tell her that if it happens again, we won't be stopping. I'll have her dragged all the way to the border if I have to."

He'd moved close enough that Danika could smell his breath and the stale sweat of a man who'd been in the same clothing for days. Over that, the bitter scent of the bile Annalyse had managed to spew, and, under it all, something pungent in the underbrush that had nothing to do with any of them. The mix of smells combined with the throbbing pain wrapped around her head by the Imperial artifact, caused her stomach to roil in spite of nearly two weeks free of sickness in the morning.

And it *was* a good delaying tactic, she acknowledged as she threw up on the lieutenant's boots.

Tomas remembered the gunner's wrist in his mouth, tasting salt and blood and gunpowder. Remembered seeing the lit taper fly out of his hand, hearing screams, smelling sulfur . . .

He could still smell sulfur and gunpowder and charred wood and flesh and blood and horse and shit and urine and ash. But mostly blood. And meat.

He blinked. It was darker than he'd expected.

Although he couldn't remember what he'd been expecting.

He blinked again, and stared into the face of the Imperial gunner. The man's blue eyes were open, he had freckles on both cheeks, and he looked surprised. Dead, but surprised.

Lips pulled back off his teeth, Tomas tried to move away. His front feet were trapped under the gunner, but his back feet were free.

He drew them up tight against his body and pushed, nails scrabbling against wood. They caught the edge of a board. He pushed harder. Felt something give. Jerked his shoulders far enough into the space he'd made to free his front legs.

The gunner rolled, upper body slamming into Tomas' shoulder with a squelch of trailing intestines.

The next thing he knew he stood panting in the sunshine, squinting at the pile of lumber and bodies that had once been a wagon and a gun crew. He scrubbed at his nose with both front paws then, low to the ground, tail close to his body, he circled the pile. Stopped and stared again. The blast radius was . . .

Large.

Beyond the crater, the land bore the marks of the shells that hadn't merely exploded but had taken off and cut a swath through the lines of infantry, leaving bodies and smoking holes scattered about where the Imperial army had been.

A voice called out over the moans of the wounded and the buzz of flies. Tomas ignored it.

Where the Imperial army had been.

He spun around toward the river. The fighting had moved up into the trees. He could hear the distant sound of weapons.

A glance at the sky told him it was midmorning, maybe later. How long since he'd left Ryder to take out the weapon and . . .

Ryder!

A wound high on his shoulder sent waves of pain through his body every time his right front foot hit the ground. Didn't matter. He ran for where he'd seen his brother last.

He scrambled up the rocky slope that was to have given the combined Aydori, Traitonian, Pyrahnian armies the advantage. Scrambled over bodies in Imperial and Aydori uniforms. Found the place he'd last seen Ryder.

Found Ryder . . .

Part of Ryder.

Parts of the Pack. Cousins.

Whining deep in his throat, he dug at a half-buried leg, the silver fur matted with blood.

He needed hands.

With hands he could . . .

The flash of pain in his shoulder as he tried to change slammed him to the dirt.

The Imperial army had been using silver. The explosion he'd survived must have driven the silver deep. Twisting around, he licked at his shoulder but couldn't get to the wound.

He could hear fighting in the distance. He could smell the bits of meat that used to be his brother all around him. He could hear a constant high-pitched litany of loss and despair. Wondered who'd bring a cub to a battle. Realized . . . Forced himself to be quiet.

He didn't know what to do.

It wasn't thunder in the distance. It so obviously wasn't thunder, Mirian wondered how they could have ever convinced themselves it was. Each distant boom she could hear in the east shouted out death.

Clutching the left side of the boat, she stared at the shore and wondered if the reinforcements had been in time. Wondered if the Imperial army had been pushed back across the border or if they were even now pressing into Aydori. Wondered if fighting uphill in the woods put an army that marched in straight lines at enough of a disadvantage. Wondered if Imperial numbers would tell as they always had. Wondered if the fighting would come down to the river. Wondered what she'd do if it did.

Wondered how she'd find Lord Hagen in a battle.

In an extended lull in the shooting, she relaxed into the quiet and realized, after a moment, that it wasn't as quiet as it had been. This new sound reminded her of a winter wind roaring through the trees in the park. But it wasn't winter and the new leaves on the poplars along the shore were nearly still.

Shifting on the seat, Mirian stared past the front of the boat at the river. The banks rose, narrowed, and the river itself . . . She squinted, trying to force the distance closer.

The river itself disappeared.

The roaring grew louder, like a storm through the chimney pots.

Rivers didn't just disappear. That was impossible. Therefore, there had to be a logical explanation. Lower lip caught between her teeth, Mirian glanced over at the shore, back at the river . . .

If the Imperial army had to fight its way uphill into Aydori, then in order to get to the border the river would have to flow downhill. And water didn't so much flow downhill as fall.

She had a vague memory of her mother mentioning a recent social column and a report of Lord and Lady Berin picnicking at Border Falls with their household. The writer had gone on at length about how fast and dangerous the falls were in the spring.

The paper hadn't mentioned exactly where Border Falls was.

Geography suggested Mirian had found it.

Without the oars, she had no way to steer the boat. The only thing she had any command over was herself. Moving quickly, before she could change her mind, Mirian stood, stepped up onto the seat, and launched herself into the river.

She surfaced closer to the shore than the boat, although that could have been because the boat was moving faster now without her in it. Wet wool wrapped around her legs as her skirt soaked up water. *Stupid! You should have taken it off before you jumped!* The water was so cold it drove the air from her lungs, and she had to clench her teeth to keep them from chattering. Her hands felt as though they were covered in a thin layer of grease. Not swimming as much as steering diagonally through the current, she kept her eyes locked on a muddy bit of riverbank and struggled to keep her head above water.

Just don't panic and you'll be fine.

She didn't realize there were rocks close to the surface until her legs slammed into one. The impact spun her around, coughing and choking. A wave closed over her head. If not for her skirts, the water would have tumbled her end over end, but the weight kept her upright enough that when her legs hit another rock, she managed to push off and surface. A glimpse of quiet water between her and the shore, then she was under again.

The next rock she hit, she hit with the entire right side of her body. Before the river swept her away, she managed to get her arm around it, leg bent high, foot jammed into a crack. Pushing off with everything she had left, she rose up out of the water far enough to twist down over the rock into the quiet pool.

Cold and hurting, she thrashed her way to the shore and flopped out onto the mud.

Every movement disturbed the flies that covered the dead. Clouds of them rose from where they were feasting and laying eggs to swarm around his muzzle, trying to land in his mouth and on his eyes. Tomas shook his head to dislodge them and wished he could shake a thought back into it. Should he join the battle still going on, deep in the Aydori woods? Or should he join what was left of the Pack in Trouge and bring them—bring Danika—the news that Ryder was dead. She'd need to know. They'd all need to know. The Pack was leaderless now.

Tail clamped tight, he limped back and forth across the scar in the earth that still smelled of his brother, wishing someone would just appear and tell him what to do.

Because Ryder was dead and . . .

Ears up, he turned toward the river. He could hear voices; two men speaking Pyrahn. Pyrahn soldiers, having run from the duchy with the Imperials on their heels, had fought and died beside the Pack and the Aydori 1st. Maybe these men were wounded. Maybe he could help them. Maybe they'd know what he should do.

It wasn't easy covering uneven terrain with one front leg unable to bear his full weight, but for the sake of doing something, of doing anything, he managed it. Moving toward the voices, he picked his way diagonally down the slope toward the river, going around obstacles he'd have jumped without thinking another time. At the water's edge, he turned upstream. The men were no longer talking, but he thought he knew where they were. Or had been. He moved a little faster.

Rounding one of the many stumps created by artillery fire, he saw a pair of old men bent over a body, stripping it of its uniform. An Aydori uniform. The same green and brown Harry'd worn yesterday morning when he'd died standing between Pyrahn refugees and the Imperial army.

Not soldiers. Scavengers.

Tomas launched himself forward, forgetting the pain. He couldn't stop the howl from ripping free. He was close enough the warning didn't matter. The scavengers jerked away from the half-naked body, but before they could run, he crushed the scream in the throat of the man nearest the water, taking him down, tearing out mouthfuls of flesh. When he turned, blood dripping from his muzzle, the other man was running up toward the larger trees.

Stupid man. He had hands. He could climb after him.

No. The silver in the wound kept him from changing. He had to end the chase before his quarry reached a tree large enough to climb.

Leaping the body, Tomas stumbled and nearly fell as the impact of his paw with the ground shot lines of pain out from the impacted piece of silver. He switched back to three legs and kept going. Uphill was easier than down and rage lent him strength.

They reached the ridge together. Tomas lunged forward and closed his teeth on a mouthful of filthy fabric. This close, even over the blood still coating his muzzle, he could smell young man, not old and under that, something sharp, bitter . . . if hunger had scent . . .

A bare heel slammed into his bad shoulder.

Tumbling back down the slope, Tomas landed on his left side, pawed the cloth from his teeth, and, snarling, fought his way back onto his feet in time to see the surviving scavenger dive through a break in the trees and run deeper into Aydori. He had to be trying to get to the river above the rapids. It was the only way back to Pyrahn that didn't go past Tomas.

Pushing himself past the pain, Tomas followed, holding tightly to a single coherent thought: *Stop him.*

A scrap of fabric caught on a branch.

Fresh blood in a footprint.

The only living scent in the woods, impossible to lose.

Snapping and growling as he shoved through the underbrush, Tomas emerged onto bare ground, looking down over the river. He could hear the roar/hiss of water dropping over a jumble of rock. Saw the scavenger fling himself from ledge to ledge then suddenly end his wild descent, realizing there was no safety here. If he tried to cross, the river would take him. White showed all around his eyes as he twisted and looked up.

Tomas had no intention of allowing the river to take his prey.

He could smell the fear.

Growling low in his throat, he gathered himself to . . .

Froze.

Another scent.

An almost familiar scent.

He straightened, lifting his head into the breeze.

Almost Pack.

Alive.

The scavenger no longer of any importance, Tomas turned and ran upstream. The scent came from above the rapids. He plunged back into the trees, the river on his left, following the slope of the ground as it dropped back toward the river. He staggered, bounced off a tree, kept going.

Up ahead, the underbrush grew thick again, marking the edge of another clearing. He slowed and dropped to his belly to crawl past the older wood, below the long thorns. The silver flashes of water he could glimpse to the left moved around until he could see them out in front as well. A creek? Spring runoff?

Gray where it shouldn't be caught his attention and he crawled toward it.

She wasn't dead. She didn't smell dead. As he watched, she tried to move a little farther out of the water without much success.

About to rise and risk the thorns, a new scent froze him in place. Men. He lifted his head as high as he dared, nostrils flaring, forcing himself to smell something other than the warm, amazing scent of *her*. Three . . . no, four men, Imperial soldiers, moving fast.

Gold glittered in the air between the soldiers and the woman, too small and moving too fast for Tomas to identify it, but it smelled bitter and cold like old mage-craft. She flinched as it touched her and disappeared into the wet, tangled mess of her hair.

Three pairs of boots stopped just at the edge of his vision, bodies masked by half grown leaves. The fourth pair moved close enough he could see they belonged to an officer, a captain. From what Tomas could see of his face, he looked like a professional soldier. A man who'd do what he was ordered to do whether he liked it or not. As Tomas watched, he reached down, grabbed the woman's arm, and hauled her up onto her feet.

Instinct fought with reason and reason won although, deep down, Tomas knew that had he not been wounded and exhausted, reason wouldn't have stood a chance. He'd have charged out and gotten himself shot by the three men who, given their position, had to be holding muskets on their captive.

Whoever she was, they thought she was dangerous.

Well, they weren't stupid because given the way she smelled, she was a high-level mage of some kind. He recognized the almost Pack scent now—Mage-pack. Potential Mage-pack anyway. She didn't smell mated.

He watched as the captain efficiently bound her arms behind her. Watched as he half carried her over to where his men waited.

Whoever she was, she was the only thing that had smelled like Pack since Tomas had come back to consciousness facing the dead Imperial gunner.

At least he knew what he had to do now.

"So what now, Cap?"

Reiter stared down at the girl—woman, *very* young woman—and frowned. He could see the tangle glinting in the wet mess of her hair, more obvious than it had been on the others for all she had a lot more hair, but she hadn't tried to escape with mage-craft, so he had to assume it was working. She looked annoyed, exhausted, and frightened in that order. He appreciated the lack of weeping and wailing. Actually, there'd been a distinct lack of weeping and wailing from all six women the Soothsayers had sent them after. Was it bravery or did they not understand what was happening to them?

"Cap?"

"We take her to Karis, as ordered."

"Do we go back and join up with the lieutenant?" Armin wondered, and all three of them turned to look back, as though they could see the distance they'd covered.

Best snorted, bicorn in his hand, fingers scratching through damp hair. "He won't be there, you dumb shit. We're coming on late afternoon and he started moving when we left."

"No one told you to lower your guard," Reiter growled, pulling out his map.

"But, Cap, the tangle . . ."

"You want to bet your life on an artifact that's been gathering dust in the treasury for a couple hundred years? Or on the Tower .625 caliber musket you're holding?"

Chard swung his weapon back around to point at their captive. "Well, if you put it that way . . ."

"Armin. Best."

"Yes, sir!" They snapped it out together, although Best's musket rose noticeably faster. Seemed Armin didn't much like holding a weapon on a helpless woman. Well, neither did Reiter, but what he did or didn't like had no bearing on what he would or wouldn't do. He had his orders. They all did.

"We'll follow the river around to the ford, and cross into the Duchy of Pyrahn . . ." What *had been* the Duchy of Pyrahn and was now a part of the empire; or would be as soon as politics caught up to war. ". . . then we follow the border until we meet up with Lieutenant Geurin and the wagons."

"Begging your pardon, Captain, but there's no ford marked on that map and even if they didn't blow the bridge, it's still a good five miles out of our way."

Reiter turned just far enough to meet Armin's eyes. The soldier tried not to look like he'd been reading the map over his captain's shoulder, gaze sliding sideways to lock attentively on their captive. "If the army's crossed into Aydori . . ." Reiter paused so they could all hear the sound of distant gunfire. ". . . then there's a ford."

"Probably more than one," Chard snorted. "Trust me, I've spent a stupid amount of time on dig the crap back *out* of the river duty 'cause that's way too much actual work for *engineers*." When Reiter turned to glare at him, he grinned. "And no one cares. Right. Shutting up now, sir."

Not for the first time, Reiter wondered how Chard had managed to survive his few years in the army without losing the skin off his back. Insubordination was still a six-stroke offense, but even Geurin, the very definition of an officious prick, had put up with Chard's mouth. Still, sometimes, his mouth was useful.

Their captive had been watching Chard through her lashes as he spoke; listening, not merely hearing.

"Everyone speaks a little Imperial, Captain. The language, like the empire, is . . . pervasive."

Something to remember, although, here and now, he had nothing to say to the mage nor did he need to hear anything she had to say to him.

"Armin, you and Chard keep her on her feet and moving. Best, you're on our six." Of the three, Best had the most traditional view of the beastmen of Aydori and Best's beliefs wouldn't let him get complacent. The job wasn't done until their captive was in Karis.

"You think if the lieutenant gets there first, he'll leave us a wagon, Cap?" Before Reiter could speak, Chard sighed and answered his own question. "Yeah. Me, either."

If her hands hadn't been tied, Danika would have struggled until the two soldiers keeping her upright in the current lost their footing on the slick rock, sending the three of them into the river. She was a strong swimmer and her clothes were designed to be easily removed. The soldiers, on the other hand, weighted down by boots and weapons and packs would be at the mercy of the icy water, swept away, and drowned. Two less enemies of Aydori.

Were it not for the golden net suppressing her abilities, it wouldn't matter that her hands were tied. She could take air into the water with her. Of course, if it were not for the golden net, they'd still be on the road to Trouge arguing that they should have kept one of the enemy alive to question. Jesine was a strong Healer, but not quite strong enough to question the dead.

But her hands *were* tied and she had access to only the most basic mage-craft, so to drown the enemy, she'd also drown herself and her unborn child. While that would still result in two less enemies of Aydori, she was a long way from the point where death seemed the only escape. Where there was life, there was hope. Where there was life, Ryder would find her.

From what she'd overheard, the artifacts restraining them were ancient and everyone knew time weakened even the strongest mage-craft. Danika tested the net's control constantly, barely allowing the pain to fade before she tried again. From what she'd seen of their expressions, Stina and Jesine were doing the same. Annalyse looked so miserable her expression could have been hiding anything, and Kirstin had remained strangely quiet. But then, Kirstin hadn't been herself for some days, although preparations for the war had kept Danika from inquiring. She'd thought to have plenty of time to speak to her on the road to Trouge.

In her defense, this was not something she could have anticipated. Soothsayers had a way of complicating the most basic of expectations.

Her own face as expressionless as she could make it, Danika remained passive in the grip of the enemy, walking between them because being dragged would accomplish nothing but leave her less able to fight when the time came.

"Sarge! These wet skirts weigh a fucking ton! Can we strip them down?" The shout came from behind, from one of the soldiers charged with keeping Jesine on her feet.

"You can stop bellyaching and put some effort in!" Sergeant Black called from the shore.

"Effort, he says," muttered the soldier on her right as he half guided, half dragged Danika forward another step. "Didn't see him crossing at the same pace as the prisoners. My balls have climbed so far up into my body they're sitting on my shoulder."

"Shut up, Murphy, you fool!" snapped the soldier on her left. "She can understand you."

"What's she going to do, Tagget? Tell the sergeant on me?" Murphy's grip tightened and he shoved her down until the water that had been up to her chest slapped against her face. "You're not going to say anything, are you, sweetheart?" he murmured as he pulled her upright again.

Coughing, Danika fought to get her feet back under her, helped by Tagget's arm around her waist. When she could speak again, she turned her head to the left and nodded as graciously as her position allowed. "Thank you." Murphy, she ignored.

Then there were hands reaching down from the bank, and she was hauled up and left to lie on dry ground while the others were pulled from the water. For the last few weeks, as her body adjusted to pregnancy, she'd been too hot, but now, in cold, wet clothing, her teeth started to chatter. A warm body rolled up against her back, and Jesine whispered, "I can still control my temperature. Maybe it'll help."

It didn't make her less wet or less cold, but it did help.

"If there's a breeze," Danika told her, lips barely moving, "it carries sound both to and from, but I have no control."

"Seems we're first level again. Stina should force the rockweed into bloom."

"What . . ."

"Allergies." Jesine's tone made it clear her teeth were showing. "Might as well make them as uncomfortable as possible until the Pack arrives."

"Shut up!"

The wet wool of her skirts absorbed most of Murphy's kick and, as it was Tagget who hauled her to her feet, Danika allowed herself to be hauled, teeth gritted against the growing pain in her shoulders.

"Come on, get up, you great bloody cow!"

The soldiers lifting Stina were handling her a lot less neutrally, grunting and cursing at her weight and grabbing both breasts and buttocks as they maneuvered her upright. When she jerked away, calling them names, it was probably just as well for her safety they didn't understand. One of them reached inside her open jacket to pinch a nipple, visible through wet shirtwaist and chemise.

"You lay with beasts, don'cha? You should be grateful for a bit of human touching."

"Enough." The lieutenant sounded bored. "We haven't time for that nonsense. Get them moving." He peered westward, eyes slitted against the late afternoon sun. "This is taking too long. We're following our own tracks out. We know exactly where we're going. We should have been able to make it over the border and meet up with the wagons before dark."

"We won't be able to manage that, sir."

"I know that, Sergeant! That's why I said *should*." He sighed, as though he carried the weight of the world on his shoulders. "Fine. Then we need to reach the camp before dark."

"The camp, sir?"

"The place where we camped on the way in, Sergeant. I want to leave as little indication of our passage as possible."

"Sir, the beastmen track by scent. It doesn't matter where we make camp for the night."

"Then we make it where we ..." The lieutenant frowned. ". . . where we made it."

"Yes, sir."

Danika bit her lip at the sergeant's tone, fighting the rise of hysterical giggles.

Lieutenant Geurin turned his frown on her, as if he sensed her reaction. "The beastmen close enough to track us," he said, his words meant for the sergeant but spoken to her, "are being dealt with by the Imperial army. If there are others, either beast or mage, they're both too far away. Get them moving, Sergeant Black."

"Yes, sir. You heard the lieutenant." His voice was a nearly familiar growl. Danika bit her lip harder. "Keep them on their feet, keep them moving. And Kyne?"

"Sergeant?" The soldier who'd assaulted Stina now had one hand tucked up into her armpit, waiting for the man on the other side to take his place.

"Keep your hands to yourself."

"Ah, she doesn't mind, Sarge. Do you?" As he leaned in, Stina reared back and slammed her forehead down onto his nose.

The next thing Danika knew, Stina was on the ground and Kyne had both hands clamped to his face, blood seeping out past his palms, his profanity varied and extensive. Murphy shoved her toward Tagget and charged forward, raising his musket to strike Stina with the butt. Danika stretched out a foot and tripped him. As he hit the ground, she saw Kyne put his boot to Stina's hip, saw the marksman Hare prevent him from taking a second kick, saw muskets coming up . . .

"Enough!" Sergeant Black grabbed Kyne's arm and threw him away from Hare, now standing over Stina. "You deserved that hit for letting her past your guard."

"She took me by surprise!"

"And I'm sure that's an excuse the Record Keeper is tired of hearing from the newly dead. Corporal Carlsan, take Kyne's place. Kyne, you're behind the redhead."

"But . . ."

Danika couldn't see the sergeant's expression, but it shut Kyne up.

"Ma'am . . ."

The lieutenant's frown deepened at the honorific, but Danika gave the sergeant the attention an Alpha deserved.

". . . tell the women not to try anything like that again. We *will* knock you out and drag you if it comes to it."

She met his gaze levelly for a moment, then nodded. "Nicely done, Stina," she said in Aydori. "But the sergeant says that if anyone tries something similar, they'll be knocked out and dragged. As I doubt it will slow them any more than if we're stumbling along conscious, and as we can't do enough damage to free ourselves, and as I'd rather none of us were irreparably damaged, passive resistance only for now."

"You'll tell us when we can be a little more active, Alpha?" Stina showed teeth. The Mage-pack inevitably picked up their spouses' expressions.

Danika returned her smile. "I will."

Head pounding, shoulders burning, Mirian collapsed to the ground the moment the two soldiers released her. The one named Chard looked a little surprised and bent to touch her cheek.

"You hurt?"

"Why are you shouting?" the other one, Armin, asked him.

Chard glanced up and shrugged. "She went down like a one-bit whore, I thought she was hurt."

"But why," Armin sighed, "were you shouting?"

"In case she doesn't speak Imperial."

"She speaks Imperial."

Chard moved away as the officer, Captain Reiter, came to stand over her. Mirian didn't look up. She wasn't entirely certain she could; her head felt like it weighed a hundred pounds.

"How do you know, Cap? She hasn't said nothing."

"She's been listening too intently for someone who doesn't understand what's being said."

Mirian heard Chard and Armin move away and the captain move closer. She couldn't stop herself from crying out as he cupped her jaw and lifted her head.

"I'm not hurting you, I . . ."

Blinking away tears, she gritted her teeth as he tilted her head to better see the bruising under her chin.

"Chard."

"It wasn't while we had her, Cap. Must've happened in the river."

"If I find out . . ."

"It happened in the river." Chard hadn't exactly been kind, and he'd had his hand on her bottom as often as the terrain made the excuse plausible, but he hadn't needed to wait for an excuse and he hadn't been cruel and he hadn't looked at her like Best had. Like she was something he'd found on his shoe in the gutter. When the captain frowned, she added, "The current pulled the oar from my hand and it hit me."

"You speak Imperial very well."

"My father is a banker." She paused to wet dry lips. "He says money doesn't stop at borders."

He was studying her face, so she studied his. Late twenties, maybe early thirties—he had the look of a life lived hard. Pock marks on one cheek and the thin white line of an old scar through an eyebrow and across his temple—old enough he must've been a boy when he got it. His eyes were a sort of mix of blue and gray and his hair a sort of mix of blond and brown. Not mixed the way Pack hair was mixed but lighter where it had been longer in the sun. His face was narrow with high cheekbones and a pointed chin, his stubble darker and redder than his hair. There was a newer scar just visible above the collar of his uniform. His eyelashes were absurdly long and thick and his lower lip had a sort of dimple in the middle of it.

Objectively, he wasn't unattractive.

Except that he was an enemy who'd taken her captive along with five members of the Mage-pack, killed at least one coachman and two Pack, and it was impossible for her to be objective regarding him. Given a chance, she'd push him off a cliff and laugh as he hit the ground. Well, maybe not laugh, but she'd definitely see it as justice served.

"You saw us take the others on the road," he said at last. "So you know this has nothing to do with you personally."

A part of her wanted to tell him that he'd made a mistake, that she wasn't the mage he'd been searching for. A larger part of her realized that he'd have no reason to leave her alive if he knew his mistake. A very small part looked forward to the amount of trouble the captain was going to be in if he showed up with her instead of a sixth member of the Mage-pack. Her lip dragged as she bared her teeth. "And yet, I'm taking it personally. Funny that."

Chard snickered.

"Chard, get wood for a fire. A small one. We don't want to attract attention. Are you thirsty?"

It took Mirian a moment to realize the last question had been directed at her. Pride warred with thirst and, finally, she nodded.

"Armin. Tie her hands around this tree and leave her with a canteen. You'll eat what we eat later," he added.

She whimpered as Armin pulled her arms out in front of her body, unable to move them herself. When the captain turned away, a muscle jumping in his jaw, she whimpered again. She wouldn't be her mother's daughter if she didn't know how to use guilt as a weapon.

The water was warm and tasted of the inside of the canteen. It was awkward drinking it around the sapling, but it was still the best water she'd ever tasted.

By the time the soldiers had the fire going, it was full dark. Heavy cloud covered the moon, so even had the captain wanted to keep going, they couldn't. From the way he kept glancing up at the sky, then back the way they'd come, Mirian suspected he wanted to. Smart man. The Pack Leader couldn't cross the border, but Jaspyr Hagen could, and once he got her scent he'd be able to follow her to the ends of . . .

"Captain." Best had his musket in his hand. "There's something out there."

All four of them froze and over the crackling of the fire and the beating of her own heart, Mirian could hear a crashing through the underbrush, a yelp of pain, more crashing, and a big black dog limped into the circle of light on three legs, the broken end of a rope trailing from around his neck. When it . . . no, when *he* saw the men, he dropped to his belly and crept forward, tail sweeping the ground.

The gunshot nearly stopped her heart, and she shrieked.

Branches broke. The dog yelped and ran.

Over by the fire, Chard held the end of Best's musket and glared at him. "It's a dog, you stupid prick! It had a rope around its neck. Probably some farm dog abandoned when the army rolled past. It broke free and it's frightened and it came to the fire to find people and you tried to shoot it!"

Best yanked his weapon free. "It could've been one of the beastmen!"

"We're in Pyrahn, and it had a rope around its neck!"

"I didn't see the fucking rope!"

"I did!"

"You wouldn't know the difference between a beastman and a dog if it licked your ass!"

Breath coming shallow and fast, Mirian fought with the confining weight of her skirts to put the sapling between herself and the soldiers. The captain turned toward her, noted her reaction to the gunshot, nodded, and turned away. He wouldn't ask, he'd assume she'd lie, but he thought he could read the truth in her reaction.

"Sit down. Both of you."

"Captain . . ."

"It had a rope around its neck, Best."

"Sir, the size . . ."

"This close to the Aydori border, I expect large dogs are the rule."

"You think the beastmen bred with . . ."

The captain raised a hand. "I don't want to think about it."

"No, sir. Me, either," Best agreed, smirking.

Food kept them quiet. Mirian was nodding off, stretched out by the tree, her head against her arm, when she heard Chard murmur, "Who's a good dog, then? Are you hungry? Thirsty? Come on, I won't hurt you."

The dog was a shadow against the ground, creeping forward toward Chard's outstretched hand. His eyes locked on the Imperial soldier, he stretched out his neck and took the dried meat from Chard's fingers. The next thing Mirian knew, he was on his back, three feet in the air, dark lines against the firelight, with Chard rubbing his belly.

"Who's a good boy, eh? Who's a good . . ." He paused when the dog yelped, bending forward. "He's been shot, Cap. Wound's up high on his shoulder. Feels like there might still be something there."

"Leave it."

Chard paused, his knife already in his hand. "But, Cap . . ."

"It's a black dog on a dark night; you try to clear the wound by firelight and you'll end up cutting off his leg. You can do it at dawn before you send him on his way."

"But, Cap . . ."

"You're not keeping him."

Mirian laid her head back down again and closed her eyes. She'd need her strength later. She was dreaming about the opera, Captain Reiter singing the tenor role, when a cold nose stuffed into her ear woke her. Best snickered as she jerked and squeaked.

The big black dog stared at her from no more than a handspan away. Beyond him, Best kept watch by the fire while the others slept.

"Scram."

The dog cocked his head. One of the soldiers, probably Chard, had removed the rope.

"Go away!"

Tail wagging, he sniffed her vigorously then stretched out, his back against her stomach, his head curled around on his front paws.

"I don't want you here, you stupid dog!"

"You sleep with beasts," Best sneered. "Maybe he thinks he'll get lucky. If you let him fuck you, keep it down."

Then he turned his back, as though she wasn't worth his attention.

With the warmth rising up off the younger Lord Hagen, relaxing muscles pummeled first by the river and then by the forced march into Pyrahn, Mirian wondered if, after the war was over, she might have a career as an actress.

Chapter Four

M IRIAN WOKE A SECOND TIME with the younger
Lord Hagen's face so close her eyes nearly crossed trying
to focus on him. He had one enormous paw still pressed
against her shoulder, so she assumed he'd woken her. Looking past
him, she could see Armin sitting by the dying fire, his musket on the
ground beside him, and his head down on his crossed arms. She
couldn't tell for certain if his eyes were open or closed, but had to
trust that the younger Lord Hagen wouldn't have risked waking her
if it wasn't safe.

"What?" she whispered when he leaned closer still, a silken ear
brushing her cheek. He leaned back with a whuff of warm breath and
jerked his head toward the leather thongs tying her hands around
the tree. A little surprised he hadn't already gnawed through the
bindings, she frowned and realized that, while the leather itself
would cause him no problem, Armin had tied her in such a way that
there wasn't room for the younger Lord Hagen to gain purchase
with his teeth.

When he saw he had her attention, he crept silently around until
his shoulder brushed up against her fingertips.

He had an itch?

She wiggled her fingers against his fur. He pushed back against her touch. When she pressed against a spot both sticky and damp and he flinched, she remembered Chard telling the captain that the dog had been injured and he could feel something still in the wound. She couldn't, but with her movement so restricted that wasn't surprising.

"They're using silver!" That was the news the younger Lord Hagen had brought his brother at the opera. With a bit of silver shot still in the wound, the younger Lord Hagen wouldn't be able to change and he needed hands to get her free.

Bracing her bindings against the tree, Mirian pulled herself as quietly as possible up into a sitting position. Well, half sitting, half leaning against the slender trunk. The bark was smooth and cool against her cheek as she rested and wondered how she was to get silver out of a wound in the middle of the night while tied and guarded, however laxly, by enemy soldiers? She didn't have the mobility to use a knife even if she'd had one, which she didn't, and besides, Captain Reiter's observation about using a knife around dark fur on a dark night was a valid one—however little she wanted to grant him the acknowledgment.

Had she been able to reach her fingers down far enough, she might have been able to work the shot out of the wound like a splinter. Poking the younger Lord Hagen to get his attention brought his head around and he frowned, his expression so clearly saying *get on with it* that he might as well have spoken aloud.

Fine. Get on with it how?

Lower lip between her teeth, Mirian worried out an answer. Jaspyr Hagen had said she smelled amazing, reacting to her in the way Pack reacted to Mage-pack. If Tomas Hagen also thought she smelled amazing—and the odds were high he did as the two younger Pack at the opera had—then he had to think she was more powerful than she was. He therefore expected her to be able to use magecraft to get the silver out. Fortunately for him, it would take nothing more than first and second level metals. Unfortunately, she had no idea if she had even first level metal-craft and, given that the Metals-master had refused to test her, the odds were very high she didn't.

But unless she wanted to remain a captive of the empire, she had to try.

Bracing her fingers around the wound, she took a deep breath, tried to remember the one hundred and one ridiculous ways to center herself in her power—ridiculous because they were all essentially the same way—and froze.

The net!

The golden net had prevented the Lady Hagen and the others in the Mage-pack from using their abilities. It had also caused them pain it hadn't caused her, but perhaps the amount of pain was related to the amount of mage-craft being blocked. Hardly surprising then that she didn't feel it at all.

She gave the younger Lord Hagen an emphatic poke and when he turned to look at her, lips off his teeth, she dipped her head and whispered, "You have to take the net off me first."

His eyes narrowed.

"Off my head."

When he paced away, she thought he still didn't understand, but he circled the tree and she felt warm breath on the back of her neck. Then a tug at her hair. The tugging grew stronger, moved from tugging to pulling, pulling to yanking, and she clenched her teeth to hold back a yell as what felt like a handful of hair ripped free. Blinking back tears, she nearly dislocated a shoulder twisting around in time to see him shake what looked like gold spiderwebbing from his mouth. Even in limited starlight, it gleamed. It would have been beautiful, but stuck to it was more hair than Mirian was comfortable losing and what looked like a small bird's nest made up of evergreen needles and gobs of solidified sap.

She'd forgotten about her response to Lady Hagen's warning. With the mess of her hair keeping the net from contact with her head, she might have been able to use her mage-craft the whole time. It wasn't until the younger Lord Hagen pushed at her impatiently with a paw that she realized she was shaking with barely suppressed hysterical giggles at the thought of facing down four Imperial soldiers by lighting a candle and then blowing it out again.

Awareness of the incipient hysteria only made it harder to control. In a moment she wouldn't be able to control it at all and the noise would wake Armin. Awareness of *that* didn't seem to help and the small, rational bit of her that remained could only watch ineffectually as their chance to escape seemed lost.

Then the younger Lord Hagen bared his teeth and growled low in his throat. Mirian didn't so much hear the growl as feel it reverberate through her body at every point they touched and her reaction was so primal it overwhelmed everything else. She froze again, barely breathing, unable to look away from the teeth inches from her face. The terror was instinctive . . .

And then she remembered.

The people of Aydori are part of the Pack's protectorate. If they appear to threaten, they do it only to make a point.

The Pack and You had been a popular pamphlet at the university. Late night conversations about actual *interaction* more popular still.

If Mirian allowed the younger Lord Hagen's point to stand, allowed him to believe she needed his protection like some kind of wilting heroine in a bad romance novel, it would define their relationship from this moment on. She needed his help, yes, but with that silver in his shoulder, he needed hers in return. Heart pounding, she swallowed, narrowed her eyes, and growled back at him.

He closed his mouth and leaned back to get a better look at her face. Given how little definition black fur and a dark night allowed, he was surprisingly good at looking annoyed; it was all in the line of his tail and the angle of his ears. She took a deep breath and refused to allow the hysteria to rise again. If she wasn't fine, and she suspected she really wasn't, she, at least, had herself under control.

After a moment, he moved and pointedly settled his shoulder back under her fingertips. Staring at his silhouette against the dim glow of the fire, Mirian took a deep breath and readied herself.

If he was to free her, the younger Lord Hagen had to change. In order to change, the silver had to come out. He couldn't get it out himself, so she had to remove the silver.

It was really just as simple as that.

Pressing the first two fingertips of her right hand against the wound, Mirian closed her eyes. She didn't need to identify this metal. She knew what it was; it was silver. Given its effect on the Pack, silver was, if not forbidden, a seldom used metal in Aydori. But, given its effect on the Pack, the university made very sure its students could recognize it—from raw ore to polished metal—in order to help protect those who protected them. As silver was expensive and since small amounts did damage disproportionate to size, the shot would most likely be the size of the birdshot her brother-in-law used to hunt partridge and quail.

This silver piece would therefore be tiny, round, but not necessarily perfectly smooth. It would be a soft gray with slivers of shine where friction had burnished it. It would be warm, trapped within the younger Lord Hagen's body. Poison, but only because of where it was, not intrinsically of itself.

Another deep breath and Mirian suddenly realized the difference between knowing there was a piece of silver in the wound and being *aware* of the silver in the wound. She felt as though she could reach out and touch it. Hold it. As she could neither touch nor hold it where it was, it would have to come to her.

It seemed logical to Mirian that identifying a metal could only be the first step. Knowing there was metal in the earth—or a shoulder— was pointless if that metal remained in the earth—or a shoulder. High-level metal-craft could bend and twist and refine raw ore to a thing of use or beauty or the incredible tackiness of the iron dryad firescreen in her parents' bedroom, but first it had to be in hand.

A trickle of heat in her fingertips and she opened her eyes in time to see a glistening silver stream roll over the younger Lord Hagen's fur like liquid moonlight. When it hit the ground, it solidified again to become nothing more than a tiny dark shadow on the earth.

Tomas Hagen changed to skin crouched on the other side of the tree Chard had tied her to, the damp skin of his shoulder pressed up against her fingertips. Mirian found herself unable to stop staring at the gleaming curve of his buttocks.

Sooner or later every child in Aydori, Pack or otherwise, asked where the tails went. While she'd never been entirely happy with the answer—apparently, they just *went*—Mirian hadn't thought about the question in years. Here and now, she couldn't get it out of her head.

Although in my own defense, I've had a tiring day.

The memory of her mother declaring that exhaustion was no excuse for bad manners hit strongly enough that she snapped her gaze up and focused on the triangle of black fur that grew past the bottom of Tomas Hagen's neck as far as his first vertebrae. She hadn't seen the back of Jaspyr's neck, not on two legs anyway, not without a high-standing jacket collar over the area in question, so she had no idea if this was standard among the Pack or if it was unique to the younger Lord Hagen. Did it feel the same, she wondered, as the fur he wore on four legs?

He was just over a year younger than she was. She'd sat through her mother's list of the unmarried Pack so many times she should be able to recite his entire history, but that was all she could remember.

The knots securing her had clearly been tied so that they'd released easily under the correct pressure. The younger Lord Hagen just as clearly knew the correct pressure.

Free of the bindings, her hands dropped to the ground. Mirian sucked a breath in through her teeth. Her wrists burned as blood rushed back into the deep creases pressed into her skin. Moving slowly and carefully, trying not to cry, she folded her arms close against her body, hands curled against her chest as she worked mobility into her fingers.

Up close, the girl's scent was nearly overpowering. She was dirty and her hair was weird and her gray eyes had no mage marks in them at all, but she smelled like home and like safety and a little like Danika. He needed to tell Danika what had happened to Ryder! She had to hear it from him. They had to get moving.

Grabbing both the girl's arms above the elbow, Tomas hauled her to her feet. Although her clothes were damp, her skin was warm where he buried his face against her neck. When he realized what he'd done, he jerked back, face burning.

She wasn't even looking at him.

She was looking past him at . . .

"Where'd you come from, kid?"

Tomas spun around to see the Imperial who'd been asleep by the fire standing only a few feet away. He'd been so caught by the girl's scent he hadn't realized the man was awake and moving. He was Hunt Pack! Forgetting to keep part of his attention on the sentry was a stupid cub mistake.

"I don't want to hurt you, kid, so just stay calm." The Imperial raised his left hand, palm out, musket loose in his right. How did the empire keep winning with idiots like this in the ranks? Had he forgotten he was at war? Who he was at war with?

Wool scratched against his side as the girl lunged past him to touch the Imperial's forehead with two fingers.

"Sleep." Her low voice had rough edges. She sounded like she'd been chewing twigs.

The Imperial blinked twice, opened his mouth, then slowly collapsed to the ground. He rolled up against Tomas' legs, eyes closed, mouth open, chest rising and falling.

Before he could change to rip out the man's throat, warm fingers wrapped around Tomas' wrist and held on. Her breath hot against his ear, the girl whispered, "Change. I'll hold your tail and follow you through the woods!"

"Wha . . . ?" When he turned to face her, there were still no mage marks in her eyes.

"You can see in the dark. In fur." She jerked her head toward the fire and the other three soldiers. Still asleep, Tomas noted, but that was luck alone. "I can't."

When she released him and spread her hands, her gesture said *get on with it* as clearly as if she'd spoken out loud.

She smelled amazing. But she was bossier than Danika, and his brother's wife was Alpha.

His brother's wife was a widow.

He changed and lunged for the throat of the mage-slept Imperial.

Only to come up short as two hands grabbed the scruff of his neck and yanked back. She'd taken him by surprise, or she wouldn't have been able to stop him. That, and her fingers were dug in by the healing wound in his shoulder and were hurting him! He twisted free and turned to snap at her, catching the edge of her jacket in his teeth, tearing it free.

She stumbled back, arms flailing. When she'd regained her balance, she gave him a look he almost physically felt, turned on her heel, and ran for the woods.

"Armin?"

The captain was awake!

Fine. Not a problem. First, he'd kill the man at his feet and then . . .

The shot hit the ground by the Imperial's head, spraying dirt over his face. Tomas could smell the heated silver pellets.

He turned and ran, his nose leading him along the path of the girl's footsteps. Quickly catching up, he pushed past her, changed, and grabbed her arms to keep her from slamming into him.

"Fine! Hold my tail." He tightened his grip. "But don't pull it!"

"You're hurting me!"

"I am not . . . Ow! You kicked me!"

"And I'll kick you again if you don't let me go."

Tomas resisted the urge to shove her away as he released her, but only just. He opened his mouth to remind her that, if not for him, she'd still be tied to that tree at the mercy of the enemies of Aydori when he noticed her rub her arms, right where he'd been holding her.

He was Pack. Pack protected. He was more than Pack. Ryder was dead. He wasn't the younger Lord Hagen any longer. He was Lord Hagen because Ryder was dead and Ryder's son, if it was a son, hadn't yet been born.

Lord Hagen would never hurt a girl he was trying to save.

He wanted to tell her he was sorry, but he couldn't force the words out past the grief.

When she touched his chest, he started, unaware she'd moved.

"I won't pull your tail. I promise. But we have to go now, Lor . . ."

He flinched.

". . . Tomas. I can hear them shouting in the clearing."

So could he. Better than she could, that was for sure. They were trying to wake the soldier she'd slept. They were distracted. Easy prey. Easy to kill. He needed to go back and kill them. Kill them all!

"Tomas! Tomas, listen to me, we have to run! They're using silver! If you go back to kill them, they could kill you!" Her palm pressed warm against his chest. "Tomas! I can't see in the dark. I can't get to safety without you!"

The breeze shifted, blowing her scent into his face. He took a deep breath and felt the edges that had been pulling apart move back into place. When he met her eyes, she looked worried and frightened and confused, but she held his gaze until he nodded and looked away.

He changed. When he felt her hand close around his tail, he

moved as quickly as he could away from the Imperials. He used to lead his cousins in the Mage-pack like this. He moved more quickly as she grew confident in him. Then they were running.

"Armin! Come on . . ." Reiter slapped the sleeping soldier lightly on both cheeks. ". . . wake up!"

"Sir." Best's hand, holding a canteen of water, appeared in his peripheral vision.

After a moment's hesitation, Reiter took it and dumped it over Armin's face. Armin sputtered, sneezed, and slept on. In the spill of light from a hastily lit lantern, he looked peaceful. Wet, but peaceful.

"Has he been mage hit, Cap? Did the girl do it?"

Turning to answer Chard, Reiter saw a glint of gold and, using the mouth of the canteen, scooped the tangle out of the dirt. There were two sizable hanks of hair attached to it, sticky with evergreen sap and needles. It hadn't come off easily, but it had come off. So much for Geurin's belief that the mages would be unable to remove the tangle without another artifact.

He frowned as two sections of fine chain swung free of the pattern. The ends of both pieces were blackened, the gold links of the broken segments misshapen. Not melted though, so it hadn't been heat . . .

"Wait! Where's the dog?" Chard's question snapped Reiter's attention off the net. "She better not have hurt the dog!" Chard pursed his lips to whistle but before he could make a sound, Best punched him in the arm.

"It wasn't a dog, you ass. It was one of the beastmen, and it freed her!"

Squint narrowing, Chard glowered at the older man. "Yeah, right. A beastman who let me scratch its belly."

"So you'd believe it was a dog."

"Because it was a dog!" Stepping closer to the tree where the girl had been tied, Chard scooped the leather straps up off the ground. "See these, not chewed. Untied!"

"You saw the women!" The dim light couldn't hide Best's incredulous expression.

The beast had gold hoops in its ears. Her ears.

"What women?" Chard demanded waving the ties. "There was one woman!"

"This one's had pups."

"Not here, idiot! On the road! The women looked like people before they became beasts!"

"That dog didn't look a person."

"You are too stupid to live."

"Enough!" Reiter rocked back onto his heels and stood, leaving the lantern on the ground and Armin lying beside it. Mage hit yes, but only asleep. Given what the girl had been through, she'd shown considerable mercy. Of course, there was no proof Armin would ever wake. "Dog or beastman, the animal is not our concern. The girl is. Chard, watch Armin. Best, you're with me." Best wouldn't hesitate to shoot a big black dog.

"A beastman would've killed us," Chard muttered under his breath.

He'd spoken quietly enough the others could ignore him and let the argument die. Besides, Reiter acknowledged silently, he had a point. They'd all heard the stories of attacks in the night. Of sentries who'd found everyone in camp dead, throats ripped out so silently they hadn't heard a thing. Of farmsteads emptied of people and live-stock both. Of travelers who disappeared, their torn and bloody clothing found strewn over the road.

They'd all heard the stories, but Reiter couldn't think of anyone who'd actually witnessed such a thing.

Some of the cloud cover had cleared, exposing brilliant swaths of stars and a crescent moon that shed light disproportionate to its size. Scientists at the observatory outside Karis had declared that the moon had no light of its own, that it was no more than a large orbital body—which Reiter had translated as "rock"—reflecting the light of the sun. The recently appointed Prelate had been quick to deny the teachings of the Sun-as-metaphor and claim the science as proof of His mercy, throwing light into the dark. Reiter was not a religious man, but right now he'd take what help he could get. That said, they were lucky the girl hadn't tried to cover her tracks. If she'd had time to be more careful, they'd never be able to find her.

"Captain, what if she's leading us into an ambush?" Best was close behind his left shoulder, speaking so quietly Reiter barely heard him. "It's said the beastmen run in packs."

He also had a point. But if Chard's dog *was* one of the beastmen, Reiter'd bet his life the . . . the *creature* was as lost as it had pretended to be. Soldiers' pets roaming the battlefield after their master's death quivered with the same barely contained sense of panic. Of not knowing where they belonged. If it wasn't one of the beastmen, it might have gone with the girl because she was up and moving.

"If there's a pack," he told Best, "we'll deal with it."

"But, Captain . . ."

"I said we'll deal with it. Our orders are to return with six mages. No one's going to be happy to hear we had one in the tangle and she got away." *One in six or six in one.* The Soothsayer's prophecy brought to mind, Reiter suddenly realized the girl they hunted had to be pregnant. *Empires rise or empires fall; the unborn child begins it all.* Realized all the women under the tangles had to be pregnant. *When wild and mage together come.* They'd lain with beasts, but . . .

Was Chard's creature the father? He was young, yes, but old enough for that. Remembering the girl's reaction, Reiter would've sworn she'd never seen the beast before. Had she played them? He could have admired that had she not put his balls in the fire by escaping.

A surprisingly large part of him wanted to let her go. Bad enough to make civilians a part of a war, making war against the unborn was . . .

Empires rise or empires fall.

He was a soldier sworn to the protection of the empire. He was an *officer* sworn to the protection of the empire. He had his orders.

"Captain?"

"I hear it."

She was moving faster than expected—although he should have expected it. With the tangle off, she had full access to her mage-craft again. And, she was determined. So far today, she'd survived an ambush planned by Imperial Soothsayers, a run to Bercarit, a river still dangerously swollen with spring runoff, and an ancient artifact specifically designed to stop her. Reiter remembered how annoyed she'd looked when she'd first been taken and couldn't prevent a smile. She'd studied him, much as he'd studied her, her pale eyes narrowed with disapproval as though four Imperial soldiers rated no higher than the wrong-colored gloves. The smile disappeared as he frowned. He admired her no more than any other competent enemy.

She *wasn't* moving quietly. With no breeze stirring the leaves or rubbing branches together, she was making the only noise in the wood.

Because Mirian had promised not to pull, when she needed Tomas' attention, she released her grip on his tail and waited for him to notice. Three steps and he turned.

"I can't keep going." Her grip on a branch was all that kept her upright. Her thighs trembled, her knees threatened to buckle, and the pain in her side felt as though someone had stuffed hot coals under her ribs. "You have to find us a place to hide." She paused just long enough to check that the sounds of pursuit hadn't stopped. If they'd already given up . . .

They hadn't.

"It's dark," she added, "once we're not moving, they won't be able to find us.

It was too dark to read Tomas' expression, but his body language as he stared past her was clear.

"I know you could kill them now they've separated. But they're still using silver, and I still can't get away without you." And there'd been enough killing today. The younger Lord Hagen was Hunt Pack; he wouldn't understand why she wanted four of the enemy to live. Mirian wasn't sure she understood it herself, only that four more bodies sprawled limp and bleeding wouldn't bring Lady Berin and the others back. "Please, just find us a place to hide."

He shot her a look it was too dark to decipher—the shifting silhouettes of his ears the only indication he'd turned—then he snorted and disappeared into the underbrush.

Mirian flattened the black ruffle along the lapels of her jacket and pulled the edges together over the white vee of her shirtwaist. Shaking her hair down over the pale oval of her face, she leaned back against the tree and tried to become one with the night. It was a phrase from the last novel she'd brought home from the book-shop on Upper Cryss Road. The hero became one with the night when he hunted. Of course, in the novel, the hero hadn't had to deal with a swarm of insects that tried to make a meal off any bit of exposed skin. Novels, she noted, wondering how much noise she'd make if she slapped at the back of her neck, were nothing much like real life.

Over the high-pitched whine of the insects, it sounded as though pursuit had slowed.

Give up. Give up. Give up. It was a sort of a prayer, although Mirian had neither faith nor expectation that either the Lord or Lady were listening.

Her head fell forward. She jerked it upright and bit back a cry as something large brushed past her legs. And again! Tomas was Pack! He was supposed to be protecting her! Where . . .

Oh.

Teeth in her skirt, Tomas jerked her away from the tree. Mirian stumbled and nearly fell, but managed to stay on her feet by clutching at a handful of fur. They danced like that for a moment, shuffling about together in a half circle before she found her footing and was able to let go, murmuring an apology as she slid her hand along Tomas' spine until she could close it around his tail.

He led her on what seemed to be a stupidly long, looping path; through a clearing, around to the left, over two fallen trees . . .

Was he lost?

. . . .to a low rock face, a sudden splash of pale gray rising knee-high out of the darkness. Tugging his tail free, he dropped to his belly, changed, and crept out of sight. Mirian had to move right up to the rock and collapse to her knees before she could find the narrow opening and then flip onto her side to inch her way in, arms over her head, fingers scratching for purchase. Even in her exhausted state, Mirian realized the rock extended both vertically and horizontally far beyond what was visible.

When her right hand finally flailed about in the open, callused fingers closed around her wrist and yanked, nearly dislocating her arm. A second yank with the same result. Tomas' help wasn't moving her any faster than she could manage on her own.

The moment her left hand came free, she slapped at bare skin until he released her, muttering something rude under his breath. Mirian ignored him and concentrated on freeing her head. Skulls didn't compact and it felt like she'd lost more hair and scraped a line of skin off her forehead shoving past the last bit of rock. Once her shoulders were in the cave, she exhaled, dug in the toes of her boots, braced her hands, and shoved.

Her mother had always wished she'd been more buxom, like her sister. Mirian had never been more thankful her mother's wishes could not come true. There was a limit to how far even squishable body parts could be squashed and more buxom would have jammed her in the crack like a cork in a wine bottle.

To be fair, her mother couldn't have envisioned this situation.

When her hips came free, Tomas grabbed her under both arms and, this time, Mirian let him pull.

"Stay here!" he growled when she lay panting, half propped against a curved rock wall trying to decide if it was worth trying to count her new bruises.

And then she was alone. In the dark. A musty smelling dark—animal musty, not closed-up rooms under dust covers musty. Drawing in her skirt, she cautiously patted the floor around her and felt twigs. Very dry twigs. With no bark. Maybe bones?

Did they have bears in Pyrahn?

There wasn't a bear here now. Tomas would have seen to that, but that didn't mean a bear wouldn't come back when Tomas was somewhere else.

Somewhere else killing Imperial soldiers?

"I was covering our tracks."

Her thoughts had been so loud she hadn't heard him return.

Tomas frowned. He could smell blood. "Are you hurt?"

"I don't . . ." A rustle of cloth. She was probably raising her arm. It was so dark in the old den, he couldn't even see gradations of black. "It's a scrape. From the rock. It's nothing."

He knew the Imperials hadn't hurt her. Not the way soldiers took what they wanted from the conquered. Not even Best, who'd clearly despised her. He'd have been able to smell the evidence if they'd forced her and then he'd have killed them. She wouldn't have been able to stop him no matter how much sense it made not to risk four-to-one odds and silver shot.

His shoulder ached, but the itching told him he'd healed.

"You shouldn't scratch at it."

Fingers flexed over the scar, he froze. "What?"

"I can hear you scratching at it. It'll scar."

"It's already scarred. And it's not my first."

She sighed, the gust of breath warm against his chest. This close, this enclosed, her scent was intoxicating, and he felt himself begin to respond physically. By the time he realized he was leaning forward, his face was almost tucked in the curve between her shoulder and neck.

"I don't think you should . . ."

He snapped upright, his fingers pressed against her mouth. When her teeth touched his skin, he leaned back in, mouth against the curve of her ear, not even wondering how he could find the curve of her ear so effortlessly in the dark, and said, "They're close."

"Anything?"

"No, sir. I've lost them."

Lost her, Reiter corrected silently. They still had no proof Chard's creature was with her. They could barely see broken branches and crushed greenery; it was far too dark to see actual tracks and the tangle hanging off his finger gave no indication she was near. "She's probably heading back to the border."

"The beast could be leading her," Best acknowledged thoughtfully.

"She's a mage."

"Yes, sir." Clearly, in Best's mind, a potential beast outweighed an actual mage.

"Let's head back. We'll try again at first light. She's exhausted, she can't have gone far." If she'd collapsed under a bush, or in a hollow behind a fallen branch, they'd never find her in the dark. Once she'd stopped moving, they'd had very little chance. Even given the small amount of time he'd spent with her, he should have known she'd keep her head and not flail about in panic, allowing herself to be recaptured.

He checked his compass bearing—the dot of luminescence on the magnetic needle proof Imperial army scientists weren't completely useless—and led the way back to the camp. As he slipped the compass into his tunic pocket, his fingers touched the strand of hair he'd pulled from the tangle.

"They're gone." Tomas kept his fingers pressed against her mouth for a moment longer, withdrew them hurriedly when her lips began to draw back. She wasn't Pack, but that was a Pack reaction and even blunted teeth hurt. Given her previous reactions, he had no doubt she'd bite if he pushed. He guessed he liked that about her although she'd be easier to rescue were she more compliant. "We'll rest here until dawn. Even if they keep hunting, they'll never find us. Not in the dark and probably not in the light." The lingering scent of its previous occupant had led him to the cave; no one in the Imperial army had any kind of a nose.

He could hear her breathing. She didn't sound panicked, or shocky. She sounded tired.

"I'll escort you back to Aydori in the morning," he continued when it became clear she wasn't going to speak. As soon as she was safe, he'd pick up the trail of the four Imperials and hunt them in turn. They were the enemy. They were part of the army who'd destroyed the Hunt Pack, killed his brother, and forced their way over the border into Aydori. They were only alive now because the girl needed him.

The girl who smelled so, so *good*.

He inhaled the scent along the soft curve of her neck, nuzzled into the hollow of her jaw, rutted once against her leg, unable to stop himself and . . .

. . . and . . .

"I'm moving outside air in through the bottom part of the entrance and pushing inside air out the top. Better?"

It hadn't been *bad*. His skin so hot he knew he had to be flushing a deep red, Tomas shuffled back until they were as far apart as the small cave allowed. Unfortunately, that wasn't far. If she hadn't been able to disperse the scent, he was horribly afraid he wouldn't have been able to control himself. "My apologies. I'll . . . It might be better if I . . ." He changed and curled up into a miserable ball, trying not to think about Ryder's opinion of such an appalling lapse into instinct. Willing to take the cuff he deserved if only to be able to hear Ryder call him an unthinking cub one more time.

Mirian eased herself down onto the floor of the cave until she lay curved around Tomas, her head on her folded arm, her other hand resting on thick fur near where she'd removed the piece of silver. Stretching out her thumb, she could feel the scar. The Pack healed quickly.

He wasn't asleep.

If she had to guess, given how rigidly he held himself, she'd say he was too embarrassed to sleep. She supposed she should be embarrassed as well, after all, a young man she'd never been formally introduced to had just gotten intimate with her thigh, but after a moment's consideration, she realized she didn't *feel* embarrassed. Exhausted, in varying amounts of pain, emotionally stretched to the point where kindness would bring involuntary tears, but not embarrassed. After the day she'd had, she was almost grateful to have a problem so easy to deal with. Lady Hagen had adjusted the airflow to ease the Pack response to the promenade at the opera, so Mirian had done the same. She may have been stuck at first level, but air moved when she used mage-craft to blow out a candle, so, logically, she knew how to move air. In order for Tomas to regain reason and stop thinking with his nose, she did nothing more than move a little more air than usual. And if she had to visualize a candle to do it, no one needed to know.

Mirian flushed, becoming aware she'd been stroking the soft fur on Tomas' shoulder in time with the rhythm of her thoughts. Although she stopped the motion—she didn't have the excuse of instinct for her lack of manners—she left her hand where it was, needing the contact. Society could just cope.

Tomas continued to hold himself stiffly, painfully stiffly if she had to hazard a guess. Almost as though he were afraid to relax. Afraid of what might happen if he let go. Mirian knew *that* feeling.

And, maybe, his emotional state had nothing to do with her at all. Tomas Hagen had been in the battle that had destroyed the rest of the Hunt Pack, had run from the border to report to the Pack Leader, and then had run back to fight in another battle today.

Today.

Just this morning, she'd listened to the 2nd Aydori Volunteers sing as they marched toward the border. It seemed like a lifetime ago. There'd been a battle fought today and Tomas had been in it. She had no idea of what he'd seen. No idea of what kind of day he'd had before he'd appeared by the soldiers' fire. Given the silver she'd pulled from his flesh, only an idiot would think he'd had a good day.

But she had no idea of how to ask him what had happened, or even if she should.

"I was looking for your brother." Her jaw hurt so she spoke softly, her lips barely parted. He hadn't asked either, but Tomas had to have wondered why she'd been taken by the soldiers.

Taken might not have been the best word, Mirian realized, her mouth gone dry and a sudden sweat beading out all over her body. She wasn't a child. She knew how some men chose to prove they held power.

How long before Chard's harmless interest became something darker? Or Best's disdain found a physical outlet? Armin might do as the others did or he might turn his back, but he wouldn't choose her over men he fought beside. Would Captain Reiter have allowed it? He seemed to be an honorable man, but all she knew of men were bankers and boys.

A quiet growl and she opened her fingers, releasing a tufted handful of Tomas' fur.

"Sorry." Forcing herself to stop panting, Mirian drew in a deep breath and let it out slowly. Things were bad enough; why borrow from the list of things that hadn't happened.

"Those four men," she continued, when she was certain she'd regained control of her voice, "they were part of a group of Imperial soldiers who ambushed Lady Hagen's carriage on the Trouge Road. They killed Lady Berin and someone I didn't know. She was gold; her fur was gold." Beautiful, golden, sprawled on the road, bleeding. "They used the nets to control the Mage-pack and they intend to take Lady Hagen and four others back to the emperor. My parents' carriage had stopped just up the road, so when I heard the shots, I went back and saw . . ." She paused and tried to untangle the story. "I already told you what I saw, didn't I? When I heard they were being taken to the emperor, I ran to tell the Pack Leader what had happened. Bercarit was farther away than I realized, so when I reached the city, I remembered that the river came to the border and found a boat. I didn't know about the rapids. I jumped out before I reached them and . . ." And nearly drowned, but, again, from the list of things that hadn't happened. ". . . and they captured me on the shore. They thought I was Mage-pack, but I'm not."

Even if just this morning Jaspyr Hagen had told her that promises made before a battle brought bad luck.

When silence was the only response, when that silence grew, and lengthened until it couldn't be called a pause, when it had gone on long enough it was clear Tomas wasn't going to respond, Mirian shifted into as close to a comfortable position as she could find and sighed. The younger Lord Hagen wasn't her sister, having crossed the hall to her bedroom so they could share confidences in the dark. He wasn't even a friend. They'd been thrown together by circumstance, and she had no right to resent his silence.

Then the fur shifted under her hand, flesh and bone changed—not quite instantly, she realized, this time not distracted by the visuals—and she cupped a bare shoulder, the skin cool and slightly damp.

"My brother . . ." Mirian felt his ribs rise and fall, as though he fought his own bones to breathe deeply enough for what he had to say. "My brother," he tried again, "is dead. Killed by the weapon that destroyed the Hunt Pack. It was new. More power and a greater range. When we reached the battle lines today, I found it and destroyed it. Too late. I found . . ." Another deep breath. Mirian rubbed small circles on pebbling flesh as though he were many years younger, instead of just the one. "It exploded, the weapon exploded, and I was knocked out. By the time I woke, the battle had moved on, but I found . . . Ryder was . . . he was in pieces. Dead."

"I'm so sorry." Her mother's belief denied; the Pack Leader would not be saving them. A tear dripped off the bridge of her nose and fell to join the rest dampening her sleeve. Dead. The Pack Leader was dead. What happened now?

"The battle had moved inland. But Ryder . . . I didn't know what to do and then I saw them with you on the riverbank. I knew I had to rescue you."

"Rescue me?" Mirian heard her voice rise, bouncing around the inside of the cave, and quickly lowered it in case Captain Reiter had doubled back. He was smart. It was the sort of thing he might do. She rubbed her nose against her sleeve. "I kept you from getting shot."

"I untied you and I found this cave."

"I took the piece of silver out so you could change."

"I'm going to take you back to Aydori."

"That's tomorrow."

"Tomorrow," he repeated. "Tomorrow, I'm going after Danika. She's carrying my brother's baby."

Mirian frowned as she tried to remember Lady Hagen's profile and failed to remember any indication of a pregnancy. She thought about arguing that the baby was decidedly as much Lady Hagen's as his brother's, but his brother was dead and he was grieving, so all she said was, "I didn't know that."

"Why would you?" He sounded angry, but even as emotionally flailed as she was, Mirian knew he wasn't angry at her. "All I have left of my brother is the two of them. I have to save them."

With the net off, Lady Hagen could easily deal with a few Imperial soldiers. With any luck, those soldiers would be on the edge of a cliff and she could blow them off it. All Tomas would have to do to save her, was remove the net.

Mirian rubbed at a sore spot on her head, felt dried blood under her fingertips where a clump of hair had been pulled out, and thought about her own tomorrow. Back in Aydori, whether Becarit had fallen or still stood, she'd have to get to Trouge. Her mother would want to know about Jaspyr Hagen. *She* wanted to know about Jaspyr Hagen, but was afraid to ask. As long as she didn't know, he might be alive. And even if Mirian left out the river and the soldiers and Tomas Hagen, her mother would see the loss of the Mage-pack as a social opening. Mirian didn't think she could stand that.

"Who is Pack Leader now?" she asked.

"I don't know." After a moment, "I don't care."

"Shouldn't you . . ."

"No!" His teeth snapped together. Biting at the air. Biting at denial. Mirian could hear the quaver in his breath. "I'm getting Danika and the baby back. And the others," he added after a moment. "All of them."

All right.

"I'm going with you."

"No, you're not." He shifted position. It was obvious he wanted to turn and face her. She was darkly amused that even with the breeze moving her scent from the cave, he didn't trust himself enough.

"Alone you're either a stray dog—and Best isn't the only one out there who takes shots at stray dogs—or you're a naked young man." She used her most reasonable tone. Exhaustion helped. "I can act as your *owner* and keep you from getting shot, and I can carry your clothes. You won't get far without me."

"You're a Soothsayer?" She could hear the curl in his lip.

"No, I'm sensible. If those soldiers are still hunting me, they'll never think to look for me going toward the empire. If you want to keep me safe, that's the best way to do it, and if you want to travel on four feet, it won't seem strange to see a young woman with such a big dog for protection. "

After a moment, he snorted. "You've thought of everything."

"Probably not."

"Your family . . ."

"They didn't stop me from trying to reach your brother." Granted, she hadn't given them the chance, but her mother had told her time and again not to ask questions when she already knew the answers. "They'll be thrilled I'm going after Lady Hagen." They'd be thrilled she was with a Hagen.

With a Hagen . . . If they ever found out she'd spent a night with Tomas Hagen, skin to skin—however little skin was involved—they'd be planning the wedding. Even if he'd stayed in fur the entire time, she'd never make them believe it. There'd be petitions to the Pack, speculations in the papers, arch looks over a hundred tea tables. And she did not want to go home to that.

Besides, the Mage-pack needed help, and it seemed there were only the two of them to provide it. Mirian couldn't walk away from that now any more than she'd been able to up on the road.

She'd wanted her life to have a purpose.

Now it did.

"You're warm."

"What?"

"You're warm. Your clothes were wet from the river and you should be freezing, but you're warm. And mostly dry. The damp bits . . ." The heavy facing of her jacket pressed against his bare back. ". . . the damp bits are warm, too. It's mage-craft, right? If you're going to accompany me, I need to know what you're capable of."

She could hear the junior officer in his voice, feel it in the stiff line of his shoulders, recognized a retreat to what he was sure of. "First level healing. Body equilibrium."

"You had to have been raising your body temperature all along. The net wasn't stopping you, but you said it stopped Danika and the others."

"Lady Hagen warned me. Well, not me specifically, but she sent words on a breeze, *the net comes from above*. I twisted my hair up with pine gum and twigs and then it got wet; my hair gets thatchy when it's wet and . . ." Lord and Lady, she was babbling. ". . . and I guess it didn't stop me because it couldn't reach my head."

"So a hat could stop it?"

"I wondered the same thing."

They wondered together for a moment.

"You should've brought the net with you," Tomas said at last.

"*We* should've brought the net with *us*," Mirian told him. "Your fingers weren't broken."

It sounded like he'd picked up one of the twigs—or bones—and was fiddling with it. "One of us should have picked up the net."

"Agreed."

"Putting that soldier to sleep?"

Mirian blinked. Eyes open, eyes closed, there was no change in the darkness. "I don't understand the question."

"What put the soldier to sleep?"

"Second level healing." She blinked again. Second level. *Sleep gives our bodies and minds time to restore and renew. Sometimes the greatest gift a Healer-mage can grant a patient is the gift of sleep.* Mirian had known what to do, she'd just never been able to do it. Perhaps all she'd needed was the possibility of having a Pack member shot with silver and herself recaptured by Imperial enemies—although, should she be given the chance, she didn't think she'd mention that to the Healer-master.

"Your eyes have no gold."

"Trust me, I'm aware of that."

She heard him yawn. Yawned in response. She'd slept tied to a tree; she could sleep here.

"You smell amazing." He sounded as though sleep had come on him suddenly and he hadn't yet realized he was falling.

"Tomas . . ."

"What's your name?" Another yawn. "I don't even know your name."

"Mirian Maylan."

"I mean, really amazing." He shifted, pushed back against her, and began to turn over.

Mirian closed the hand around his shoulder, hard enough she felt flesh dimple under her fingers. "Tomas. No." She kept her voice gentle because it was comfort he wanted as much as anything and a part of her wanted it, too. Wanted to lose herself in something just long enough to forget. But he wasn't a *something*, and it wouldn't be right.

He stopped moving, made a noise she couldn't identify, then pulled his shoulder from her grip and changed.

She could put her arm around him in fur, rest her cheek on his head, and if that wasn't enough comfort to forget—for either of them—it was at least enough to grant them sleep.

It wasn't the distance they'd traveled that had left them so exhausted, but the constant fight to retain balance with their hands tied behind their backs.

"*It's to keep you from using magic,*" Hare, the marksman, had reminded her as he waited yet again for Murphy and Tagget to haul her back up onto her feet.

"*I thought the net on our heads was doing that.*" She'd layered her words onto a passing breeze, leaving a trail of information for those with the ability to hear.

Hare had merely shrugged, but Tagget had sighed and said, "*It's old. Captain, don't trust it.*"

"*The captain isn't here and I notice the lieutenant, who keeps nagging about how much time this is taking, doesn't have to lift one of us back onto our feet when we fall.*"

Murphy had snorted. *"Catch an officer do something like work."*

Now the five of them sat awkwardly on the ground in a half circle, too far apart for private conversation, but close enough that even in the fading light Danika could see that Annalyse still looked too pale, Stina, who had a purple bruise on her forehead, still looked angry—Danika envied her energy—Kirstin looked as though she'd folded in on herself, and Jesine looked worried about Kirstin specifically, barely taking her eyes off her face and inching as close as she could.

Each of them had an Imperial soldier standing over them, musket ready. The other soldiers were setting up camp—reusing two of the three old fire pits. Danika wasted a moment wishing that Allyse had been with them in Bercarit. Not that she wished this captivity on yet another friend, but if the nets allowed first level mage-work, then a first level Fire-mage could light a candle. Or a sleeve. Or a pant cuff. Or a series of ammunition pouches.

On the other side of the camp, by the fast-moving stream where Kyne and Tagget were filling canteens, Sergeant Black and Lieutenant Geurin were talking.

Danika tipped her head so the breeze brushed over her right ear.

"We need to make better time tomorrow, Sergeant."

"Private Murphy has a point, sir. If we tie their hands in front of them, they won't fall as often."

"And Private Murphy is giving the orders now?"

As pleased as she was that Murphy had done as she wanted, Danika thought Lieutenant Geurin sounded like her sister's five year old, and a five year old with the power of life and death was a terrifying thought.

Smart enough not to answer what was so clearly a rhetorical question, the sergeant remained silent.

"Fine." The lieutenant started across the camp, the sergeant falling into step behind him. When he stood in the center of their half circle, he smiled and said, "Call the squads back around them."

Sergeant Black frowned, but obeyed the order.

With Murphy on her left, Tagget on her right, and Hare behind her, Danika tucked her chin in to her chest and watched Lieutenant Geurin through her lashes. He would think it made her look weak, afraid of him. She knew it masked expressions she might not be able to hide.

"Tie their hands in front of them. Do not," he added before the men began to move, "allow them at any point to get a hand free."

The dull ache in her shoulders turned into fiery pain as her arms moved in ways they hadn't been able to all day. Annalyse cried out, and one of the men who held her arms made soft clucking sounds. Through her own pain, Danika made note of that sympathy for later use.

When they had all been retied, the lieutenant stepped forward, pinched Danika's chin between thumb and forefinger and lifted her head. She gave serious thought to seeing if she could bite the end of his finger off, but, in the end, merely met his gaze.

"Translate this," he said.

"Drop dead," she said pleasantly in Aydori.

He nodded, not imagining for a moment a bound captive would argue and stepped away.

"You'll notice your hands are now bound in front of you," he said, and paused.

"The lieutenant thinks we're so stupid we have to be told our hands are in front of us now," Danika translated.

Jesine coughed.

Danika did not look over at Sergeant Black.

"I know what you're thinking. You're thinking you can now remove the tangle and use your mage-craft against us. Well, you can't."

That, she translated as spoken.

"Attempting removal without a second artifact will cause extreme pain."

And that.

"I realize you have no reason to believe me, so I'm going to prove it to you."

Prove it? Danika shifted so she was not staring up at him at quite so acute an angle. "How?"

"By attempting to remove one of the artifacts of course. Now, translate."

"Sir, I don't think . . ."

"No one asked you to think, Sergeant. Translate, or it'll be you for sure instead of a one-in-five chance."

Danika showed teeth. "Then it'll be me."

"As you wish."

She swept her gaze across the others and while none of them looked happy, she was Alpha and they'd abide by her decision.

But before the lieutenant could either step forward or order the net removed, Kirstin, who'd sat limp and unresisting while her bindings were changed, met Danika's eyes and gave a nod so tiny Danika wasn't positive she hadn't imagined it. A heartbeat later, she dug the fingers of both hands into her hair, hooked them around the barely visible net, and screamed.

And screamed.

And screamed.

Sergeant Black grabbed her bound wrists and yanked her hands free.

Kirstin collapsed as though she were a puppet in a winter pantomime and her strings had been cut.

"You!" The sergeant moved men aside so Jesine had a clear path. "Do what you can."

Jesine was already moving.

The lieutenant opened his mouth, but before he could speak, before he could make a smarmy pronouncement on what Kirstin had done, before he could claim her pain as his, Danika said softly, "They have very good hearing, our beasts."

The lieutenant's mouth snapped shut. He glanced up at the darkening sky with wide eyes, looked for a moment as if he were about to order a march through the night, then he snarled, "Get those fires lit!" Turned and strode to other side of the camp.

Danika glanced at the sergeant, who nodded.

"Jesine?"

"Pulse is fast but strong. Her nose is bleeding, but I think it'll stop soon enough. The net's left white lines on her fingertips."

"Burns?"

"More like frostbite."

"I think the lieutenant's point's been made," the sergeant said softly.

Danika nodded in turn. No one else would try to remove the net. But from the way the men glanced into the darkness between the trees, the way they jumped at every sound, her point had been made as well.

They ate the same food as the soldiers: dried meat, army biscuits, and water. The lieutenant had Carlsan heat water for coffee and the smell made Danika's stomach roil, but she managed to keep her food down.

When she knew the lieutenant was watching her, she looked at the fire and smiled an *I've got a secret* kind of smile.

"Douse the fire," the lieutenant snapped. "The beasts aren't blind!"

"But, sir . . ."

"Douse it!"

Danika remembered hearing a lecturer at the university say that the first fear was fear of the unknown and the dark was the unknown's representative. Everyone feared the dark, at least a little. Feared what the darkness hid.

The night was cloudy, no moon or stars, and the shadows under the surrounding trees were nearly thick enough to have substance. She could feel that fear rising from the men around her.

"If they smell us on you when they come . . ." Soft words to the breeze that circled the camp. Had there been a fire, some of the men might have tried to prove they weren't afraid. Had they been anywhere else, those men might have been what the darkness hid.

Here and now, in the forests of Aydori, knowing that the beast-men were somewhere in the darkness, they had other things on their minds.

It was as close to safety as Danika could arrange.

Chapter Five

TOMAS WAS DREAMING of Harry. He knew it was a dream because he knew Harry was dead, had died with his legs blown off and his life pouring out of the stumps. Dream Harry was laughing, the mage marks in his eyes glittering nearly the same shade of red as the wine in the glass he held up to the firelight.

"So let me get this straight; sex is connected to your nose?"

They'd had that conversation, Tomas remembered, but not in uniform. They'd been thirteen, the first year they'd spent together at school. "It has to smell right," he said, realizing too late he was in fur. Fur had many advantages, but words weren't one of them.

It didn't seem to matter as Harry laughed again and said, "What smells right, then?"

Tomas looked down at Mirian Maylin, lying on the floor of Harry's study in a gray wool traveling suit and black ankle boots. Her hair was a tangled mess, her hands were filthy, and a purple bruise covered the lower half of her face. He didn't remember the bruise being that bad. She was attractive enough, he supposed, average to tall, brown hair, gray eyes, maybe a little on the *sturdy* side . . .

"Tomi!" Harry was still laughing. "What smells right?"

"If it's not Pack, power."

"And if it is Pack?"

He could feel himself blushing, which was weird because he was still in fur. "None of your business."

"I have power." The mage marks gleamed.

"Yeah, but you're dead, Harry."

Harry's legs were gone, and the floor was covered in blood. Mirian Maylin lay in a puddle of it, her skirt darkening as the fabric soaked it up. He couldn't see her boots anymore. The skirt just . . . ended. Tomas was sure she'd had legs when they went to sleep. Of course, she smelled so good, he supposed legs weren't actually necessary.

He was still half asleep as he pushed himself out of the cave in skin, her scent in his nose and Harry's laughter ringing in his ears. He changed to fur as he emerged, gouges the rock had taken as payment for his panicked exit, healing. Tail clamped between his legs, he sucked in a deep breath, forcing the dream and his reaction to it away.

It took a moment for him to realize he was an idiot.

And a lucky one.

It was barely dawn. The light hadn't quite made it under the trees, but his shadow stretched across the small clearing in front of the rock. He flattened into it, slowly, and froze, nose turned into the breeze. The faint scent of the Imperials was old. Last night, not this morning.

If they weren't moving now, they would be soon. The last watch would wake them at dawn, and if they ate at all, they'd eat what cold food they had as they broke camp. They'd assume their captive would head back toward the border and, because they knew she was a mage, they'd assume . . . what?

If Miss Maylin was to be believed, they'd already survived an encounter with Danika and those of the Mage-pack traveling with her. They'd have faith that this last artifact would do its job as well as the others had.

As he'd been stupid enough to leave it behind, the net was there for them to use.

With the net, the Imperials would be overconfident, unaware of what the Mage-pack could do. They had the artifact. They had silver bullets.

But he had Mirian Maylin.

Lying alone in the dark, Mirian took inventory of aches and pains and decided first, that she'd live, and second, that she desperately wanted a drink of water. No, she desperately wanted tea, and toast with honey, and maybe a boiled egg, but she'd settle for water.

Right after she emptied her bladder. Unfortunately, caves didn't come with water closets. Still, if Tomas had left—and he had—it must be safe to go outside. Unless he'd left more than the cave. He could have left her entirely. Gone to kill the soldiers, gone back to the army, gone after Lady Hagen—it didn't matter, the point was he'd gone without . . .

The soft scrape of skin against stone and a quiet, almost inaudible grunt stopped the thought. That could be him returning, but there was no way to guarantee it. The soldiers could have killed him. Tracked him back to the cave. He'd be able to smell the difference between friend or foe, but she wasn't Pack.

Shuffling around until she was as far from the sound as possible, she removed her right boot and held it ready by the toe. The stacked wooden heel was only an inch high, but it was the closest thing to a weapon she had. In the world of *Onnesmina*, women carried a discreet dagger in their bodices; her world having gotten slightly operatic of late, that seemed like an excellent idea to Mirian.

"Good, you're awake." From the sound of his voice, Tomas' upper body had cleared the entrance. "You're right. We need to work together. You deal with the silver. I'll take out the Imperials."

"What?"

"You deal with the silver," he repeated. She could almost hear his eyes narrowing. "Leave the Imperials to me. Let's move. They'll be up and after us soon, and we left a trail a blind, one-legged priest could follow."

"How do I deal with the silver?" Leaning back against the rock, Mirian concentrated on putting her boot back on. It was more difficult than she expected. She *knew* where her foot was, she shouldn't have to see it.

"You're a mage." *Don't be so stupid*, added his tone. "Melt it out of the air or turn it to lead or whatever a Metals-mage does. I don't care."

Fingers through the side loops, she shoved her heel down. "I'm not a Metals-mage."

"What?"

Mirian sighed and crossed her legs, the childish position hidden by the darkness and her skirt. "After a year at the university, I had first levels in every discipline but metal-craft."

"But you removed the shot."

"Yes, I did. It seems I've finally completed the set. But I have no second levels."

"You said the sleep thing was second level. So you're a Healer-mage?

"No. I'm not an anything mage." In memory, silver ran warm and liquid over her finger. Not only identified, but called. Two second levels. Still, that didn't change anything. How could it? "I suspect any advance in ability arose in reaction to an extreme situation." She tried to sound surer than she felt. "There's no guarantee I could do it again."

He did nothing but breathe for a moment, then he growled, "So if you're a nothing mage, why did they want you?"

That shouldn't have hurt, but it did. "I told you, they wanted *a* mage, not me. Now, if you'll excuse me, Lord Hagen . . ." Rolling up onto her knees, she reached out, touched his shoulder, and used his position to find the slightly less dark line of the cave's exit. He flinched away from her touch, or maybe the title, but that only made it easier to get by him. When halfway out and slightly stuck, she kicked and her foot impacted with something solid but not hard enough to be rock; she half hoped she'd hit him hard enough to raise a bruise.

Eyes squinted nearly shut against the gray dawn light, she crossed the small clearing and went into the underbrush, trying not to leave a trail a blind, one-legged priest could follow. Although, given that there were no blind, one-legged priests around and there *was* an annoyingly bloodthirsty, junior member of the Hunt Pack, most of her attention went to listening for his approach.

It wasn't until she was returning to the clearing that she realized she should have been listening for the Imperial soldiers, not for To-mas Hagen.

He was leaning against the rock face, arms folded. Mirian locked her eyes on his face, and waited.

After a moment, his nostrils flared, he drew in a deep breath, and sighed it out again. "Can you light fires?" he asked quietly.

It wasn't an apology but, in fairness, he'd only stated the truth. In truth, she wasn't much of a mage. "Small ones," she told him, matching her volume to his. They wouldn't be hard to find if the soldiers could hear them talking. "Candle fires."

"A fire in an ammo pouch would throw off their accuracy. There'd be no explosion without the constriction of a barrel, but the gunpowder would ignite," he added when she frowned.

Apparently, he believed a lack of mage-craft meant a lack of functional intellect. Mirian folded her arms as well. "What about Lady Hagen?"

"After we deal with . . ."

Mirian cut him off. "They're taking her, all of them, to the emperor. You don't think they're going to walk all the way to Karis, do you? They'll have coaches waiting on the other side of the border, fast ones." She frowned, thinking of maps and of what she'd read in the newspapers. "If he wants them badly enough to send soldiers into Aydori with ancient artifacts, he'll have sent mail coaches. They'll be able to stop and change horses at every posting house and get from the border, the old border, to the capital, in four days. You can add an extra two days to cross the conquered duchies, but if the soldiers reach those coaches with Lady Hagen, we'll never catch them."

"You've thought about this." He sounded suspicious. Like she'd been privy to the emperor's plan all along.

"I may not be much of a mage," she snorted, "but I'm not stupid. And you have to decide, which is more important: revenge or rescue?"

He stiffened. "They're Imperials. It's not revenge, it's war."

"There's at least a dozen soldiers with Lady Hagen and the others. If you want to make war, make war with them." She didn't know them. Not their names, not the dumb jokes they told each other, not what they believed about the Pack.

Tomas' eyes were very dark and his skin very pale, as though he only went out into the sun in fur, giving it no chance to darken. After a long moment, he unfolded his arms and pointed. "The Imperial camp is there. The quickest way to the border is that way, due south. We were moving toward it last night before I left you to find shelter, following the trail the five of you made yesterday. Hopefully, they won't notice where we left it, and they'll think you're still heading home. It's the *sensible* thing to do."

"*Are you a Soothsayer?*"

"*No, I'm sensible.*"

"That way . . ." He turned and pointed past the rock. ". . . to the northeast, the way your Imperials were taking you, a Pyrahn logging trail goes nearly all the way to the border.

About to ask how he knew, Mirian bit the question off. He was Hunt Pack. Hunt Pack patrolled the borders. And they weren't *her* Imperials.

"The Teryn Valley juts out of Aydori into Pyrahn. It's one of the few places there's no natural demarcation. The entire valley used to be part of Aydori, but about a hundred years ago when they straightened the border in return for building up the road into Bercarit, well, Ryder says . . . said . . ." He stopped. Swallowed. Continued. "You could get a coach down the trail if you needed to. It has to be where they're taking the Mage-pack. We'll stop them there."

"Just like that?"

"Or we could argue some more until your Imperials show up and shoot us both," he said, and changed.

She could finally stop looking at his face. "They're not *my* Imperials."

"She's definitely heading back toward the border, Cap." Chard pointed down the trail the girl had left the night before; crushed undergrowth, broken branches, the occasional bootprint, all obvious in the dim gray light of dawn. "She's heading right back the way we came. How could she find that in the dark?"

Reiter glanced past Chard to Armin, yawning but finally awake. One hand holding the net, the other his musket, he didn't have a hand to spare to close around the lock of hair in his pocket. "She's a mage."

"Can she see in the dark, Cap? Because if she can . . ." Chard shrugged. "If she kept moving all night, we'll never catch her."

"She was exhausted," Reiter reminded him. "She wasn't faking that."

"And me and the captain heard her crashing through the brush," Best added. "Then we didn't. She went to ground." He stopped and waved a hand.

If she hadn't been a mage, if they'd had more than one tangle or any other guaranteed way to subdue her, he'd have already sent Best on ahead with it, full speed along the back trail to the border while the rest of them spread out and searched more slowly. But she *was* a mage, and they had only one tangle.

And it was broken. Reiter had no idea if it was functional. Or if it ever was. He did, however, have a very good idea of what would happen if they just let her walk away.

They were soldiers. The Imperial army had trained them to shoot and march and follow orders and give orders and kill and die, but it hadn't trained them to track a single woman through the empty lands buffering the border between Pyrahn and Aydori. They'd been lucky finding her yesterday and they'd only managed it because they'd known if she was heading for the border, the river limited the possibilities.

She had to be going back to the border today.

Back home.

Back to safety.

If they didn't find her asleep behind a fallen tree or hiding in a hollow, they'd catch her at the border. Her mother had told them the mage was looking for her beastman. If the black creature was a beastman, he wasn't hers or they'd all be dead—their lives the best argument he hadn't been a beastman at all. She had to still be looking for *hers*, heading back across the border and toward the battle.

Where else could she go?

Best to his left, Armin, then Chard to his right; he thought they'd covered the ground he and Best had covered last night, but nothing looked the same as it had in the darkness and the four pairs of boots—*five pairs*, he amended silently—had made enough of a mess he couldn't tell for certain if the girl had gone back over it in the other direction.

"Cap, if we see the dog . . ."

"Best, if you see the dog, shoot it."

"Yes, sir." Best didn't sound happy as much as justified.

"But, Cap . . ."

"Shut up, Chard."

The emperor expected six mages. Reiter had his orders.

He wished he'd asked her for her name.

"The emperor knew you'd be returning with women." Six women. Six pregnant women given the Soothsayer's rhyme, but Danika had no intention of letting Lieutenant Geurin know she'd overheard that. "The emperor is married, I'm sure he knows that women take longer to perform certain tasks than men. Especially if their hands are tied. And they have an audience."

The lieutenant leaned toward her and smiled. "I don't care if you piss yourselves. My orders are to get you to Karis alive; they say nothing about how you're to smell." He pulled out a pocket watch and made a show of snapping open the ornate case. "You have three minutes. I suggest you stop wasting time."

Danika had never wanted to throw up on someone so badly in her entire life, but, this morning, her stomach had settled.

Tomas could move faster without her. Why hadn't he said that? Without her, the odds of him reaching the border before they piled Danika and the others onto coaches were considerably higher. He could avoid people—not that there'd ever been many people in the borderlands—and even if he were seen, any Pyrahnian who lived this close to Aydori knew better than to take potshots at something that could be Pack. Or their neighbor's dog. He'd never been able to decide if the big dogs they preferred in this part of the duchy were intended as flattery or protection, nor had he ever much cared.

Harry, who'd actually taken the time to read *Mind and Matter*, a book by a popular Traiton doctor making the rounds of Aydori drawing rooms and lending libraries, said it was a subconscious way of dealing with the Pack. *See, we leash things that look like you here.* Tomas had almost believed Harry'd taken that bullshit seriously, then he'd burst into laughter and . . .

Died. Harry had died.

He wanted to run full out. Away from the place where Harry and Ryder and so many others had been killed. Run to a place where he could make a difference. The odds of anyone shooting him while he ran were slim to unlikely and it was less unlikely the Imperials searching for Mirian Maylin . . . Mirian. *"A little respect, Tomas."* His mother's voice in memory. *"You do not refer to an unmarried woman you are not related to by her first name without her permission."* It was unlikely the Imperials searching for Miss Maylin were following. Anyone with half a functioning brain would assume she'd head back to the border instead of heading off to help rescue five people she didn't know with only first level mage-craft to call on. Of course they didn't know she had only first level mage-craft. They thought she was one of the mages they'd been sent to capture, thought she was Mage-pack, which was a stupid case of mistaken identity since they couldn't catch her scent in a bucket.

Maybe the *artifact* had chosen her.

Behind him, she made a frustrated noise, almost a Pack noise, and he turned to see her trudging around the root fan of a downed cedar he'd jumped without thinking. He looped back beside her, then almost immediately pulled out in front again. She wasn't talking, he'd give her that, saving her breath for the scramble through low scrub and around the occasional weed tree.

Crap cover for someone on two legs. There was, after all, no guarantee the Imperials had half a functioning brain between them.

Why hadn't he told her he could move faster without her?

Tomas had no idea.

The breeze shifted, and he fought the urge to turn and twine between her legs.

When they reached a small, fast moving creek, he bent his head to drink, stomach growling. The bits of dried meat he'd been fed at the Imperials' camp had been all he'd eaten since before they left Bercarit and it hadn't been nearly enough. He was always hungry these days, even when he was home and eating regularly. When the Hunt Pack was out with the 1st, he'd haunted the field kitchen.

Harry laughed about it.

Used to laugh about it.

His stomach growled again.

No, not *his* stomach.

He turned to see Miss Maylin kneeling by the creek, scooping water in her cupped hands but breathing too heavily to drink. Stepping away from the shore, he changed. "We can't stop for food."

She glanced up at him with those strange, pale eyes, face shiny with sweat. "I didn't ask to."

He'd never spent much time with non-mages. It was weird to look at her and see a total lack of mage marks. She'd said her father was a banker. That meant money, didn't it? Had she ever sweated before? Had she ever been hungry? "I just . . . I heard . . ." Three long strides moved him upwind and he breathed easier, not having to constantly try and suppress his physical reaction. "When we get there, to where Danika and the others are, I'll still be facing Imperials armed with silver."

Hair falling in a tangled mess over her face, she managed to suck up two handfuls of water before answering. "I know."

"It's just that's why you didn't want to kill the four who'd taken you, because of the silver and how you couldn't get away without me . . ." He couldn't seem to stop talking. ". . . but now, I'll be facing even more Imperials armed with silver, and you still won't be able to get away without me."

She shrugged. "Now, the risk is worth it."

Two could play that game. He shrugged as well, then realized she couldn't see him. "Long odds," he growled, annoyed at her disinterest.

Sitting up on her heels, she wiped her hands on her skirt and dropped her head, looking over at him from under the tangle of her hair. "Not if we work together. You draw the attention of the soldiers while I get the net off even one of the Mage-pack. Even odds."

"They're Mage-pack." Tomas showed teeth. He could see she knew it wasn't a smile. She knew that much at least. "Better than even odds." Because she didn't tell him how to draw the attention of the soldiers, he didn't ask how she intended to get the net off one of the Mage-pack. He'd pulled hers off easily enough and the Mage-pack had a lot less hair. "Can you run?"

Pushing herself up onto her feet, she squared her shoulders. "For a while, I think. Are you sure you know where you're going?"

"Yes." If he kept the pull of the border on his right and headed northeast, they had to cross the logging trail.

He thought she might demand an explanation, but she only nodded and said, "All right, lead."

He waited until she got across the creek before he began to run. Run slowly. Jog really. Still, it was faster than they'd been moving.

He'd be able to move a lot faster without her, but she was right. The two of them together raised the odds. Her scent had nothing to do with it.

Her feet hurt. Her legs hurt. The cold water had eased her throat but made her stomach hurt. She ran, she walked, she ran again, swallowing the taste of iron.

Tired and hungry and just as pigheaded as her mother had called her, Mirian was not going to quit.

Together, they had a chance.

On his own, Tomas Hagen would be one more body sprawled on the road.

"I heard that mages can talk to animals. And make trees walk." Although he spoke quietly, Chard sounded excited by the thought of talking animals and walking trees.

"Why?" Armin sounded confused.

"Why what?"

"Why would they make trees walk?"

"I don't know about every mage, but our mage, if she could make them walk, she could make them walk out of her way. Make the path easier for her. Or she could move them to hide her tracks as she left the path and headed to a secret mage hideout!"

That, Reiter admitted silently, would be a useful skill. Chard's secret mage hideout was a figment of the soldier's overactive imagination, but they hadn't found their mage beside the trail and they hadn't caught up on the way back to the border. He stood by the river, by the discarded wagons the Imperial army had emptied of gravel to stabilize the ford, and stared into Aydori.

"Where to now, Captain? Do we rejoin the lieutenant?"

"No." He spoke without thinking and then had to find words

beyond his belief that the lieutenant was an officious little shit. "You heard her mother . . .

"She gone to Jaspyr Hagen! He come rip you throat!"

". . . she's looking for her beastman. He'll be in the battle."

"With luck, he's dead." Best spat to one side. "One less abomination."

"Do they only have one?" Chard wondered, reaching between the buttons on his tunic to scratch. "Because my Nan has three little yappy things and I heard Lieutenant Geurin say he had a pack of hunting dogs, so maybe the women in Aydori have whole packs of beasts to service them."

"It doesn't work like that," Reiter growled, his tone reminding them that he was a captain and they weren't, so they'd better not ask him how he knew because all he could tell them was she hadn't seemed like the kind of girl who had a pack of beasts to service her. And he couldn't tell them that.

"If I had a pack of girl beasts . . ."

"Chard."

Proving he wasn't entirely stupid, Chard shut up.

There'd be a command post at the bridge. Staff officers. Swords, not Shields. Who'd ask what he was doing there if he was under orders and if he believed the girl those orders told him to capture had headed for the battle. The leadership of the Imperial army was, among other things, predictable.

He pulled his boots from the mud churned up by hundreds of similar boots, felt them slipping off his heels as the mud pulled back, and stepped into the river. "Come on."

"What if we got in front of her, Captain? Passed her without seeing her?" Unlike Chard's casual idiocy or Best's religious fundamentalism, Armin asked questions weighted only by the facts as he knew them. "What if she's just not here yet?"

"Yeah, but if we're in front of her," Chard snorted, "why isn't she using her magic to pick us off, one by one?"

"Because she's a lady?"

"She lies down with beasts!" Best snarled.

"Well, yeah, but . . ."

Reiter reached the other bank and turned in time to see Armin's frown. *Well, yeah, but* indeed. They could only act on the information they had, and the mages of Aydori lay with beasts. They didn't even deny it. "What if she changed into a bird and flew away?" he muttered.

Chard smiled up at him. "It'd have to be an owl, Cap. It was dark. Or a nightingale. Oh, or she could have waited until morning and slipped into that flock of starlings."

"Can they do that?" Armin wondered, stepping up out of the river onto a rock and avoiding the mud.

"No." Best seemed positive.

"But they're mages," Chard protested.

"Mages can't change shape."

"The beastmen change shape."

"Mages aren't beastmen."

"But they lie down with beasts? Right? Maybe they catch the changing thing from them."

Reiter ignored the rest of the argument. If she was heading for the battle, they'd head for the battle. If they found her searching for her beastman among the bodies, good. If the tangle still worked, it would take her down again. If she'd broken it, he had no way to capture a mage and there'd be ranking officers on the battlefield who understood a soldier couldn't put his faith in ancient artifacts. He'd happily dump the whole mess in their laps and walk away from the problem entirely.

Danika couldn't feel the border like Ryder could, like their baby would be able to if it was Pack, but she knew exactly where she was when she saw the wound cut into the forest, the stumps radiating out from the logging trail. Straightening the border between the Duchy of Pyrahn and Aydori had given the duke access to the timber of the Teryn Valley. The empire had a need for timber, and the duke had been happy to supply it at a price. She bit back a laugh that threatened to tumble over into hysteria. It seemed like the empire would be getting its own timber from here on.

Kirstin made a noise at the sight of the three mail coaches, a choked-off cry that brought a laugh from one of the men beside her.

"Well, that's it for your beastmen, then," Murphy smirked. "Thank fuck they can't cross the border. Everyone knows that," he added when Danika turned toward him. "It is true, right? They can't cross the border?"

"Why would she tell you?" Tagget muttered as the lieutenant strutted forward to meet the drivers and Sergeant Black corralled them in a lose semicircle of soldiers.

The horses were larger than the mountain ponies used in Aydori, but still sturdier looking than Danika had expected given that the speed of the mail coaches crossing the ever-expanding Kresentian Empire held the conquered pieces together as much as the army did. The newspapers Ryder had brought into Aydori in monthly bundles praised the growing network of roads and posting houses that delivered news and laws and letters from sons and daughters who'd been drafted into supporting the empire's massive infrastructure. Of course, that same network had taken those sons and daughters away in the first place, but even allowing for Imperial propaganda, the citizenry seemed to approve of being connected.

"*Leopald may be a dangerous egomaniac,*" Ryder had declared, "*but he's not stupid. He has a lot of disparate peoples to govern and conformity will wipe out rebellion faster than force.*" Dropping the folded paper onto a lopsided pile, he'd snorted and added, "*Not that he isn't willing to apply force.*"

Ryder should have caught up to them by now. Gripping a fold of her filthy skirt between her bound hands, Danika told herself he was needed at the battle, needed to drive the Imperial army away from Aydori, needed to organize counterattacks and needed to be there where Aydori soldiers could see him and know that with their Pack Leader in the battle, they couldn't lose. However much he might have wanted to race after her, he couldn't do it without delegating at least some of his responsibilities. But he'd be here soon.

He couldn't cross the border, but he wouldn't have come alone.

Danika could see the same thought on the faces of the women around her. Their husbands could leave Aydori even if Ryder couldn't.

They were standing upwind of the horses, but after a day and a half, the scent of the Pack had apparently faded past the point where it could panic prey. Pity. Standing as he was between the first and second coach, Lieutenant Geurin would have been crushed beneath the wheels had the horses bolted. The horses continued to stand frustratingly still.

"Sergeant Black!" The lieutenant smiled as he turned. It looked as though both men and officers had relaxed upon crossing the border, no doubt believing as Murphy did that none of the *beastmen* could cross. Danika's hands began to cramp, and she forced herself to loosen her grip. Lieutenant Geurin's smile was triumphant, as though moving his captives a quarter mile out of Aydori meant he'd won.

"They hold four passengers inside," he told the sergeant, waving toward the track as if the sergeant had never seen a mail coach before. "I want two women, two soldiers in each. Let the fat one ride on her own so her enormous ass . . ." He smirked at Stina and cupped the air with both hands. ". . . doesn't slow the coach."

"Your father was a syphilitic weasel," Stina growled, recognizing the gesture if not the words. She grunted as Carlsan poked her in the ribs with the muzzle of his musket, but it didn't sound like pain. Danika suspected Carlsan had reacted for form's sake only, responding to an obvious insult rather than draw the lieutenant's ire toward him. Danika hadn't yet been able to make use of the soldier's dislike of the lieutenant, but she promised herself she would.

"One man sitting up with the driver," Lieutenant Geurin continued. "One man on top facing back the way we came, on guard."

Danika did the math and frowned. If there were two soldiers riding inside with Stina, that accounted for only fourteen of the seventeen Imperials.

"Hodges."

The youngest looking of the soldiers stiffened to attention, surprised at being directly addressed, high cheekbones flushing red beneath tan and dirt.

"They say you're fast. Is it true?"

Hodges swallowed, angles shifting in a skinny throat—Danika lowered his age to his mid-teens—and said, "I run fast, sir."

Lieutenant Geurin waved off the reply. "I have less than no interest in what else you may do at speed. Once the coaches are loaded," he continued, ignoring the sniggering from two or three of the men, "run for the battle. Leave a message with the ranking officers reminding Captain Reiter . . ." The lieutenant's lip curled, not bothering to hide how much he resented the other man's rank. ". . . that his orders are to return *immediately* to Karis with the sixth mage."

Even Danika could see that Hodges had questions. The lieutenant ignored them.

"Cooper and Mylls, you two will stay here. Shoot anything that comes across the border after us. Hare, you're riding guard on the last coach. Anything that gets past these two, you put down."

Hare nodded. If he believed he could hit moving Pack from the top of a moving coach, he was indeed a crack shot. Or, Danika hoped, delusional about his skill level.

"Well?" Looking more petulant than commanding, Lieutenant Geurin spread both hands. "Let's go, Sergeant!"

Danika watched a muscle jump in the sergeant's jaw as he ordered the men to move her and Kirstin into the first coach, Jesine and Annalyse into the second, and Stina into the third.

Hungry and tired, her head throbbing, Danika didn't have a lot of fight left in her, but they had to delay. The farther they were moved from the border . . . She sank to the ground and heard the others follow her lead.

Eyes narrowed, the lieutenant closed the distance between them. "Get into the coach!"

Danika bared her teeth.

She'd expected the blow, but it still rocked her back and she let it carry her to the ground as she fought to catch her breath, the pain chasing it from her chest. His knuckles had caught her cheekbone and she could feel it already beginning to swell.

"One way or another . . ." He stepped forward to stand over her. ". . . you will get in the coach!"

Blinking away tears, Danika stared up at him and said, "Another." Heard Jesine and Annalyse echo it. Didn't hear Kirstin at all. Grinned as Stina muttered, "Have fun, skinny boys, carrying my fat ass up those tiny steps."

In the end, they were dragged and groped and bruised for very little delay, but every little delay had to count for something. Swearing under his breath, Tagget dumped her onto the narrow seat and dropped into place beside her. Opposite, a Corporal Berger sat beside Kirstin who slumped against the seat back, eyes closed. The center well barely had room for all four sets of legs and the women's skirts filled the remaining space.

The inside of the coach was utilitarian, as well as less than spacious; the walls, floors, thin cushion on the seat, all black. Like a hearse, Danika realized and was a little surprised to find herself pleased that while most of the exterior was also black, the doors were Imperial purple stenciled with the gold Imperial crest. A large horn of polished brass curved up beside the driver's seat, the mechanism that sounded it in a polished purple box. *Not* like a hearse. They weren't dead yet.

She glanced over at Kirstin who'd whispered, "*Someone had to.*" in a voice torn from screaming and then not spoken again. This wasn't the Kirstin she knew. This wasn't the Kirstin she'd argued with and competed with since university. The Kirstin she knew would have found a way to blame Danika for getting them captured and then declared she supposed she'd have to see about freeing them. The Kirstin Danika knew was irritating, but familiar. This Kirstin worried her. Perhaps believing they were safe from the Pack would make the soldiers less rigorous about conversation.

She looked out the window in time to see Sergeant Black speaking to Hodges. The younger soldier held a map and a compass and nodded so enthusiastically Danika couldn't help thinking of pigeons. It seemed they weren't turning him loose to find the battlefield on his own. As she watched, Hodges took off running and the sergeant moved to speak to Cooper and Mylls, probably giving the orders on how long to wait and what to do afterward that the lieutenant hadn't bothered with. When Cooper and Mylls moved off, she could just barely hear him yelling at Kyne, moving the soldier out of the coach with Stina and up onto the seat by the driver. She had no doubt that locked away from the more honorable men, Kyne would have gotten his own back at Stina for the black eyes, but Danika trusted the sergeant to keep his hands—and the hands of whoever else was in the coach—to himself.

A sudden flurry of shouting made it apparent that the lieutenant had forgotten to assign himself a seat. Boots on the lacquered wood overhead tracked Murphy's movement from his seat by the driver, over the stowed packs, to join whichever of the men sat at the rear. The coach rocked with the force of the lieutenant taking his seat.

Tagget snorted and Corporal Berger shot him a look of complete agreement.

"Is it . . ." Danika began.

"No talking." The corporal shifted slightly and his boot pressed Danika's leg back against the seat.

"The lieutenant didn't . . ."

"Shut the fuck up, lady. Do not make this shithole smaller than it is." When Berger shifted again, the movement looked more like nerves than anger.

"You don't like it in here, ride outside," Tagget told him.

"Yeah, I'll just tell the sarge you miss Murphy and need him snuggled up with you."

"Ass."

"That's Corporal Ass, you dick."

"Like ass outranks dick," Tagget muttered settling back into the corner. He looked as though he were sulking, but he also looked fully capable of stopping either her or Kirstin or both of them from trying to escape.

It wasn't the musket. A musket would be almost impossible to aim in such cramped quarters. It was the man himself. Both of the men. Neither she nor Kirstin were particularly large—Kirstin had often been referred to as delicate by those who didn't know her—and they had the babies to consider—which ruled out throwing themselves from a moving coach in the first town they reached, assuming the newly conquered locals would hate the empire enough to hide them. Of course, pregnancy should have also ruled out trying to rip the net off. Danika desperately wanted to talk to Kirstin about what she'd done and why, but it didn't seem like she'd get a chance anytime soon.

As the coach pulled away from the border, she sagged back against the seat and closed her eyes. She'd gather her strength, consider her options, and she *would* come up with a way to escape and return her small Pack back to Aydori.

Where Ryder would be waiting.

Had to be waiting.

There had to be a hundred reasons why he hadn't made it to the border in time.

The logging road wasn't so much a road as two tracks cut ankle-deep into the forest floor, packed hard with the weight of wagons carrying away—well, if the stumps were any indication, carrying away everything of any size. Had it been a wet spring, they'd have been filled with so much muddy runoff they'd be impassable. Then again, the little Mirian knew about waging war suggested the dry spring had been part of the Imperial timetable. Feet screaming in pain, chest burning, she collapsed onto one of the larger stumps and rubbed the sweat off her face with a fold of her skirt as Tomas raced forward.

Either the coaches were still on the way and the Mage-pack hadn't yet been dragged across the border, or they'd been and gone and the Mage-pack was on its way to Karis.

Tomas lifted his head and snarled, hair lifting along his spine, and Mirian bet on the latter. He certainly didn't seem hap . . .

The sudden crack of a musket jerked her back off the stump, the sound a physical blow. She could see Tomas pivoting left, then right, then left again as another shot rang out. Closely followed by a third, and fourth. Two shooters. He couldn't attack one without the other taking him down.

Heart pounding, Mirian dragged herself up onto the stump, on her knees first, then up onto her feet. So far, the shooters had ignored her. *She* was supposed to take care of the silver. With the underbrush not fully leafed, she could see a purple sleeve. Traced it back to a shoulder. Down to a belt. Along the belt to a pouch. How was she supposed to know if it was an *ammo* pouch?

She could light a candle. Create fire where no fire had been. Logically, then, she didn't need the candle; she only needed to create the fire. Easier to do if the world wasn't swaying . . .

No, wait, *she* was swaying.

Fortunately, swaying didn't affect the fire.

Gunpowder burned. She hadn't needed Tomas to tell her that.

The screaming from the soldier she'd found brought the second out of cover. Before she could find her focus again, Tomas was on him.

She had to blow the candle out now, but the screaming made it hard to concentrate.

Blow it out . . .

Blow!

Trailing smoke, but no longer wrapped in flame, the soldier flew back about twenty feet, slammed into one of the few standing trees, and slid silently down it to the ground. When he didn't move, she turned her attention to Tomas. It took her a moment to find him. She hadn't expected him to be on the track, running away from the border, toward the empire, as though he hadn't been running all morning. His head was up, but she supposed he didn't really need a scent to follow given coaches had to stay on the track.

When she stepped off the stump, her knees gave out, her legs folded, and she continued descending all the way to the ground. That was okay, the ground was soft. And from the ground, she couldn't see the soldier she'd set on fire.

"So," she said, brushing an insect away from her face, "what now?"

She could follow the trail the soldiers and the Mage-pack had left back to the border, back into Aydori, back all the way to the Trouge Road and Lady Berin's body.

It took her a while to push her left boot off her swollen foot, but her right came off immediately, pulling most of the bleeding blister on her heel off with it. When the blood stopped spreading, she peeled off her stockings, tossed them aside, frowned, and nearly toppled over retrieving them. They were unwearable now, but she might need them later. Besides, she could tie them around her shoes and hang them over her shoulder. That would leave her hands free.

Because the soldiers probably had canteens. And maybe food. And they'd killed Lady Berin and captured the Mage-pack and they were the enemy and it was entirely possible that the man she'd burned wasn't dead.

She couldn't hear him moving. She couldn't hear anything but a few birds and the pounding of her heart.

But she could smell burned wool. And cooked meat.

After a long moment, she stood. Picking her way carefully over brown grass and tiny yellow wildflowers, the pain of bare feet different at least than the pain while wearing her boots, she kept her eyes locked on the tree. When she bumped up against something yielding and cloth covered, she stopped walking and counted to ten, breathing shallowly through her teeth. Then she unlocked her gaze from the broken branch and looked down . . .

. . . backed up two hurried steps, turned, fell to her knees and doubled over with dry heaves as her empty stomach tried to turn inside out. His right side had been a mass of char, uniform merged with flesh. It looked like the fire had just reached his face when she'd blown it out. His hair had been singed and there were blisters climbing past a swollen eye to where half his eyebrow had been burned off. The thick piece of the broken branch protruded from just under his right ear, the thin end was just barely visible inside the left curve of his tunic's collar, his skin stained red, the fabric not so much a darker purple as black. He might have been alive when he hit the tree, but he was dead when he hit the ground.

Burned so badly, dead was better than alive. And not just for the soldier, Mirian was honest enough to admit. If he'd still been breathing, she'd have had to . . .

"I'd have had to sit beside you and wait for you to die. Maybe read to you, to take your mind off the pain. I couldn't kill someone." She could feel hysterical giggles rising and forced them back. "Except I killed you, didn't I? But you're a soldier and we're at war, so you must've expected to die, right?"

It was said, although not in polite company, that high-level Healer-mages could talk to the dead. Didn't seem so hard to Mirian. Hysteria rose again, and again she forced it back. It wouldn't help. It wouldn't even make her feel better, so what was the point. Reaching out, her hand dirty but steady, she touched the charred fabric of his trousers. "I'm sorry. I didn't mean to."

Standing, even slowly and carefully, she had to steady herself against the tree. She'd be okay as soon as she got to where she could breathe deeply again. At school she'd learned that they burned their dead in the empire. In Aydori, they exposed the bodies and, in time, gathered the bones and returned them to the earth.

"Six of one, half a dozen of the other," she said softly, not looking down.

Back where he'd been hiding, facing toward the border, guarding against whatever came after the Mage-pack, the grass around his pack hadn't even been scorched.

"Sensible," Mirian reminded herself, easing back down to her knees.

She pulled a pouch about a third full of dried meat and hard biscuit from his pack, slipped a cheap compass into one jacket pocket, a worn coin purse into the other. He had a folding knife, a fire-starter, and a telescope worth more than everything else in the pack combined. The shaft was rosewood bound in brass—ornamented brass—and there were extra lenses under the heavy cap. It looked nearly new. Mirian stroked the polished wood and thought about leaving it with him. It had the kind of worth that felt like stealing rather than the slightly less reprehensible scavenging.

After a moment, she laid it carefully on the small pile with the rest.

Not taking it seemed like disrespecting the man she'd killed. Which wasn't exactly sensible, but it had been a long day.

He didn't have a watch.

The pack itself was too obviously Imperial army for her to carry, but the blanket was gray wool, indistinguishable from a hundred others. Mirian dropped her finds and boots into it, rolled it up and tied off the ends with her stockings, leaving out only the half-full canteen and one biscuit. Her stomach protested at the thought of anything more and, besides, she had no idea of how long the food would have to last.

The other man would have more food and coin and maybe something else she could use.

She could see the line of his back. Tomas had killed him. Ripped out his throat . . .

Making her way to the track, she sighed at the feel of the smooth, cool dirt under her feet, gave thanks that the open blisters were up on the backs of her heels, and began walking toward Karis.

Danika's scent had been strong on the ground, and the coach they'd locked her into wouldn't be able to move quickly on the rough track. He could catch them. Hamstring the horses. Kill the guards. Save Danika. Save Danika and Ryder's unborn child. And the others . . . He'd save the others, too.

He followed the scent off the track, onto what passed for a country road. The horses' stride had lengthened, so they were moving faster. Let them. He could catch them. There was a town, no more than five or six miles from the end of the track. He had to catch them before they reached the town and potential reinforcements.

He heard them before he saw them. The pound of hooves against packed earth. The long whips cracking above the horses' backs. He rounded a curve and saw the back of the last coach. There wasn't enough dust raised to give him cover, but he didn't care. They'd die. They'd all die. Every last one of . . .

The first shot slapped dirt up into his face.

He didn't even break stride. They couldn't hit him.

His front legs stretched out, rear legs bunched up under his belly driving him forward. He was close enough to see the differences in the barrel bands that said this man had one of the new rifled muskets. Close enough to see his face as he finally finished reloading. The Imperial army required four shots a minute, skilled infantry could fire five, but no one could hit a moving target from a moving coach. No one.

Pain exploded out from his shoulder as silver shot plowed through flesh and shattered bone. Flung up and back, Tomas hit the ground, rolled . . .

". . . and we followed her back to the battlefield but were unable to find her." Report finished, Reiter stared over General Lord Denieu's right shoulder at the billowing wall of the command tent. The army was in control of Aydori from the border to the outskirts of Bercarit while remnants of the Aydori army used the city as cover. And occasionally as a weapon.

The general refused to march his soldiers down streets that had become shooting galleries. *"He's waiting for more artillery and more ammunition for the guns we have," Major Gagnon said cheerfully, leading Reiter to the tent. "He'll bomb it flat, then we'll march over the rubble."*

Reiter waited as the general's valet poured a glass of wine and the general took a long swallow. "There's beastmen in the south continent, too," he said, thoughtfully, turning the glass so the wine gleamed ruby red in the light. "I hear they're different than our lot, slighter, but, still, I always thought they were purely a northern problem. Turns out there's vermin all over the flaming place. Now then, Captain . . ." He picked up a pen and poked at the tangle, lying like a glimmer of gold across his desk. ". . . I think I can answer one of your questions at least. Gagnon!"

"Sir!" The major stuck his head back into the tent.

"Is that captured mage still alive?"

"He was last time I looked, sir."

"Get him in here."

"Yes, sir."

"You know, it's funny . . ." Denieu took another swallow of wine. ". . . we spent so much time figuring out how to kill the beastmen, raising taxes, gathering silver, we forgot about the mages. They blew up the rocket station. The one by the bridge. Reports say there was a fireball." Another swallow and then he had to raise his voice slightly over the sound of approaching soldiers. "They can throw them now. Well, not throw them exactly, it's that they blow them our way, but the effect is the same. So much for the *common* . . ." He threw a bitter emphasis onto the word. ". . . belief that mage-craft has dwindled to parlor tricks and creature comforts; killing the beastmen seems to have motivated them. And I always thought it was the female mages that . . ."

The open flap cut off the general's thought as Major Gagnon led two soldiers—one of them a woman, Reiter noticed, evidence of the new draft—dragging a bound and half-naked, middle-aged man, his torso marked with bruises, into the tent. They dropped him and stepped back by the canvas.

"He's still breathing, sir."

"Good." Denieu gestured with his glass. "Captain Reiter, test the artifact."

"Yes, sir." The women in the carriages had been farther from the tangle than this captured mage. If the tangle were still working, it would have done its job by now. Reiter hooked a finger through a strand of the net, carried it to the captive mage and draped it over his head. It slipped down over one swollen ear and remained entirely visible on top of the blood-streaked hair.

"Is that it?"

"No, sir." The tangle had worked on the girl through more hair and more debris, pulling from his hand and fitting itself against her skull. "Looks like the damage she did when she removed it is enough to keep it from working."

Denieu grunted. "Or it never worked."

Or this mage is too close to dead. Reiter kept the thought to himself. He didn't want the tangle to work. He didn't want to continue hunting the girl.

"Get him out of here, Major. I'd love to know," the general continued as Reiter retrieved the artifact and the major beckoned the two soldiers forward, "what courtier with his head up his ass convinced the emperor to put his faith in the leftovers of ancient magic."

As the lengthening pause seemed to indicate there was a response required, Reiter said, "Most likely the Soothsayers, sir."

"Of course. You said they were involved. Inmates running the asylum. You want to put your faith in anything that isn't a Morrisville smooth bore musket at three volleys a minute, you put your faith in science, Captain. That's the future of the empire; science. Even Korshan's rockets have a place if he could just get the flaming things to move in a straight line. They certainly performed as advertised against the beastmen." Denieu drained his glass and held it out to be refilled. "The question now before me, Captain Reiter, is what do I do with you? I've got holes you're more than qualified to fill, so . . ."

"General Denieu?" Major Gagnon stuck his head into the tent. "There's a messenger out here from General Ormond. She says it concerns Captain Reiter."

Ormond was staff, his position back at the bridge the one Reiter had decided to skip.

"You know what this is about, Captain."

"No, sir."

"Then send her in, Major. Her," he added under his breath, "still not used to that."

As far as Reiter could see, the messenger, red-faced and breathing heavily from her ride, looked like half the boys he'd had under his command. Eager and far too young.

She came to attention in front of the desk.

"Let's have it, Corporal."

"Sir. General Ormond's regards. He says that if Captain Reiter makes himself known to you, he's to be reminded his orders are from the emperor and he's to return immediately to Karis with the mage."

"And the general knows this how?"

"Runner from Lieutenant Geurin, sir."

Hodges, Reiter figured. The boy was fast.

"Does the general want a response?"

"No, sir."

"All right. Check with the major before you head back. I'm sure he's got something you can take as long as you're going."

"Yes, sir!" The messenger snapped off a perfect salute, spun on one heel, and left the tent.

"She must be good on a horse," the general said as the flap closed. "Even a scent of a beastman drives the big dumb brutes wild, and we can't be sure we got all of them. I suspect there's a few slinking around between Bercarit and the border."

Was the girl's beast one of them? He wasn't sure how he felt about her finding him.

"I know Geurin's father." From the general's tone, his opinion of the father was close to Reiter's of the son. "It's his uncle you have to watch, though. Smarmy bastard got himself a place at court. Looks like you're returning immediately to Karis, Captain."

"I don't have the mage, sir." The tangle hung limp from his fingertip.

"I'd lend you one of mine, but they're all men."

"It has to be a woman, sir."

General Denieu took a long swallow of wine. "Then I guess you'll have some explaining to do when you get to the capital."

Mirian had no idea how long she'd been walking. Staggering. Stumbling. The best she could say about her pace was that she continued to move forward and time was passing.

Walking in the city, she'd never had to worry about the time. The clock on the Pack Hall and the clocks on the larger of the guild buildings rang every quarter hour. At home, there was the standing clock in the hall, the carriage clock in the parlor, the old mantel clock in the kitchen, and, if he was in the house, her father's pocket watch. She'd asked for a watch of her own for the Lady's Gift at Summer Solstice although it seemed unlikely she'd receive one; her mother considered women who carried watches overly masculine.

"But why do you need to know what time it is, Mirian?"

She hadn't really had an answer for that. She still didn't. Knowing how long she'd been walking wouldn't get her to Karis any faster.

It took her a moment to realize that the track had ended, that she'd stepped out onto a rough road, traveled enough that only a narrow ridge of grass remained down the center line. She stopped and frowned and tried to remember what direction she'd been traveling and what direction she needed to travel in now. Her head ached almost as much as her feet and legs, and trying to pull up a coherent thought was a little like trying to pull matching ribbons from a sale bin.

Eventually, she worked out that turning left would take her back to the Aydori Road, the somewhat obvious name the Duke of Pyrahn had given the road that led to the bridge over the river. She didn't want to go back to Aydori. Not yet. Didn't think she could, even if she wanted to.

"Sometimes, you can only go on," she announced to a pair of sparrows as she turned right. Yesterday morning, she'd been a different person. Today, she was walking to Karis.

It seemed to be taking a very long time.

Squinting up at the sky, she wondered what time it was. Afternoon, certainly, but how much past noon? The pocket watch she wanted had a beautifully enameled case—leaves piled one on the other, a hundred shades of green lying in a circle smaller than her palm. The pocket watch she'd likely get, if her father could overrule her mother, would be less beautiful and more practical. She was practical. She admitted it. *Sensible*, as she'd told Tomas Hagen.

Something on the ground stuck to her foot. Pulling her skirt in against her legs and looking down, she saw the something was black. When she lifted her foot, her sole was red. Although her broken blister had started bleeding again, it wasn't her blood.

She found Tomas just off the road, a pile of damp, black fur, barely breathing.

His left shoulder looked like raw meat. On the one hand, he'd been lucky; the bone had stopped the silver from reaching any internal organs. On the other hand, she could see shards lying like ivory inlay about to be decoratively set into the exposed muscle.

Laying her bundle on the ground, Mirian sat, and gently lifted Tomas' head into her lap. The Pack were very hard to kill; everyone knew that. Silver killed them because silver kept them from healing. There were professors at the university, Healer- and Metal-mages, working together studying why this was so, but as they couldn't ask the Pack to injure themselves for science, the common belief was they weren't making much progress. Tomas wasn't healing so, once again, he must have silver in the wound.

Calling the metal to her was second level metals. Second. Until last night, she hadn't even had first. But she'd cleared the metal out last night; therefore, she could do it again. She *had* to do it again, or Tomas Hagen would die. If duress was required, that would have to be duress enough.

Spreading her hand a hairsbreadth above the wound, she tried to think of silver but was so exhausted her mind kept wandering.

A tremor ran the length of Tomas' body.

"Oh, Lord and Lady, Mirian, at least you're not tied to a tree!" She bit her lip. Hard. The pain cleared her head enough for her to grab the litany of silver and hold it tight. Deadly and beautiful. Beautiful and deadly. Deadly and . . . "Enough! I want that shot out!" The silver slapped up into her palm, warm and no longer entirely solid. She tossed it aside and stared down at the wound. Was less bone visible than there'd been only a moment ago, or did she imagine what she wanted to see so badly?

First level healing maintained body temperature. Healer-mages neither sweated nor shivered. As society frowned on ladies sweating, Mirian's mother had been thrilled when she'd passed the level. Mirian had never been able to master second level, a healing sleep, until she'd used it to stop Armin and, in all honesty, she hadn't been thinking of healing when she'd touched the Imperial soldier. At third level, the professors began teaching the healing of light wounds, the students learning on pinpricks and small cuts sliced into the back of their hands. They spent weeks healing themselves before finally moving on to healing equally small wounds on each other.

Tomas' wound was not small, and Mirian had never healed as much as a hangnail on herself.

She spread her hand just above the wound again and thought of flesh and bone and skin all growing back together. Thought of Tomas up and running. Thought and thought and never managed to find the place where she *knew*.

When she moved her hand, nothing had changed.

Tomas had certainly healed quickly from his more minor wound. Although, he'd changed almost immediately . . .

Did the change, and its reworking of flesh and bone see the wound as a flaw and correct it?

If he healed as he was, taking the time that kind of a wound required, he'd never use the leg again.

But if the injury was corrected . . .

"Tomas! You have to change." She didn't know if he could even hear her. "Tomas!"

Another tremor, more powerful than the first. Was he trying to change?

"Look, you think I smell amazing, so pay attention to me! You have to change!" Bending forward, she exhaled over his muzzle, unsure of how much more of her scent she could get to him given that his head was in her lap. "Tomas!" Another exhale. "Change!"

The tremor became a shudder, arms and legs lengthened, grew pale, he turned his face into her skirt and screamed. His shoulder looked better, not healed completely but, as far as Mirian could tell, the bone was whole and the flesh beginning to knit.

"Hurts." She could feel the word against her skin.

"I know." His skin glistened with sweat. "I have water."

"I . . . have to . . . to change . . . again . . ."

"Drink first."

"No. Won't have . . . the courage if I . . . wait."

The second change resulted in an oval scar, shiny and smooth. No fur grew on it or in the swollen flesh around it. Tomas lay with his mouth slightly open, panting rapidly, eyes wide.

Mirian settled them both into a more comfortable position, stroked her thumb over the soft black fur between his eyes and said softly, "Sleep."

Karis wasn't going anywhere.

Chapter Six

ANIKA HAD HEARD TWO SHOTS not long after they'd turned onto what passed for a road in this part of Pyrahn, but as the bouncing had to be worse on top of the coach than it was inside, she very much doubted Corporal Hare had hit anything, regardless of how good a shot he thought he was. Given that that they were still moving, that the horses hadn't been hamstrung, that the soldiers hadn't fallen screaming, that they *continued* to bounce about, she knew Hare couldn't have missed a shot at any of the Pack.

And he couldn't have hit what he shot at.

Couldn't have.

A sudden lurch threw her sideways and Tagget grunted as he shoved her away. Between the sound of the wheels on the road, the creaking of the coach, and the pounding of hooves both before and behind, she had no idea if his grunt was a complaint or merely an observation.

The Hagen family coach she'd been taken from had been designed to absorb much of the road's roughness, cushioning the necessity of travel from the unpleasantness. Imperial mail coaches were designed to get across the empire as quickly as possible. Sufficient padding had clearly been considered an unnecessary extra so when she bounced off the seat, her landing was, for all intents and purposes, uncushioned and the only reason the four of them weren't tossed about like leaves on the wind was that the interior of Imperial mail coaches provided so little room they supported each other whether they wanted to or not.

Private Tagget was as insufficiently padded as the seat, his elbow and shoulder both annoyingly bony.

Danika was aware it might be considered foolish to resent a lack of comfort in her current situation—captured by enemies of Aydori, hands bound, her mage-craft contained, her unborn child threatened—but it helped to keep the hysteria at bay. The farther they moved from the border, the more she wanted to weep and scream and throw herself at the soldiers guarding them, ripping their throats out with her own entirely inferior teeth.

She remembered reading an article about the Imperial army drafting women and thinking it wasn't a terribly practical idea. If an army of men should be wiped out, the women remaining could manage with only the men who'd been unsuitable for war, but it took strong and healthy women to have strong and healthy babies. Of course, the Imperial army had no intention of being wiped out so, perhaps, extended as the army was, they were, in their own mind, being entirely practical. Here and now, she merely wished she'd had the same opportunity as those unknown women to learn how to fight.

Tagget had jammed himself into the corner of the coach, both hands wrapped loosely around the barrel of the musket he held between his legs. His eyes were closed under the flat brim of his bicorn and he seemed to be as relaxed as possible under the circumstances. Corporal Berger held a position similar to Tagget's, but his slouch was a lie; every muscle tense, his eyes locked on the blur outside the small window in the top half of the door. He gripped his musket so tightly that the knuckles of his right hand were white, the fingers of his left tapping patterns across them.

Unbound, she could pull the air from their lungs and hold it from them until they collapsed, gasping for breath. She'd never used her mage-craft to hurt anyone, but she thought . . . no, she knew she could hurt these two men who were taking her away from her home.

As though it sensed her desire, the net increased its constant pressure against her head. Or within her head; Danika wasn't sure which. She breathed shallowly, almost panting, until the pain passed.

What could she do with the limited mage-craft it allowed her?

Berger bounced into Kirstin, swore, and jerked away. He was panting, much as she'd been. Was he in pain?

"Do not make this shithole smaller than it is."

Oh.

She studied the movement of the air inside the coach. Found the paths it took, guided by breath and movement and body heat. Then she exhaled words toward the corporal's ear.

Too small.

He twitched.

Another breath.

Too close.

He shuffled his feet and kicked at the fabric of her skirt. His knees knocked up against hers, and he swore as he shoved her aside. Her knees pushed up against Tagget's and Kirstin's and when Tagget shoved back, Berger's feet got tangled in her skirt.

"The flaming fuck!"

Trying to avoid being kicked as the corporal struggled to get free, Danika drew her legs up, toppled sideways, and elbowed Tagget in the stomach. He snarled and shoved her away. She worried for a moment he might start to yell, but something—Berger's rank perhaps—kept him silent. A fight might have released the rising tension. She didn't want the tension released.

Danika watched Berger's chest rise and fall as he finally freed himself. Before the rhythm could slow, she breathed, *Trapped.*

And then began again.

Too small.

Too close.

Trapped.

Too small.

Too close.

Trapped.

Trapped.

Trapped.

"Trapped!" He surged up out of his seat and had the bolts thrown, his hand on the door latch before she realized what he was about to do. A heartbeat later, he pushed the door open.

"Berger! What the fuck?" Tagget tried to get past her, but there wasn't room, so he grabbed her shoulder and threw her nearly onto Kirstin's lap. Danika clutched at Kirstin's arm, trying to prevent herself from sliding to the floor as the coach rocked.

"Berger!" Tagget stumbled. He stopped his fall, one hand clutching the side of the opening, the other palm against Berger's shoulder. His fingers were just beginning to close as Danika stretched out her leg, the movement hidden in the folds of her skirt, and pushed.

Berger seemed to hang in the air for a moment, then he disappeared.

The coach lurched.

She heard the wet crunch even though the creaking and pounding were as loud as they'd been. Even though the breezes were moving the wrong way to bring her the sound. Then there was shouting from outside and the horses began to slow and there was more shouting and the coach rocked one last time before it was still and she wished whoever was screaming would stop. The coach was too small for that amount of noise to be anything but painful.

She felt gentle hands against her face, looked up to see Kirstin looking down at her, gaze more focused than it had been since trying to remove the net. If it wasn't Kirstin screaming, it had to be her. And she *had* to stop so as not to waste this chance of escape while they remained so close to the border. Tagget still blocked the open door, but there was a door in both sides of the coach and they certainly knew now how fast the bolts could be thrown and . . .

"Out! Move it."

Hands grabbed her skirt and pulled and Danika found herself outside the coach blinking in the sudden sunlight, unable to stop herself from looking back along the road at the bloody, misshapen lump that had been a man. Alive, then dead. So easy.

"Corral them," Sergeant Black pushed her toward the others. "Keep them from talking."

"He went nuts, Sarge. I mean we all fucked around with him about hating small spaces, but he just . . ."

"Shut it, Tagget."

Danika ignored them, stumbling forward under the concerned

gazes of her Mage-pack until she could rest her head on Jesine's shoulder. They thought she was reacting to seeing a man die. They didn't know she'd killed him. She didn't know yet if she'd tell them. She didn't think she could stand it if they were pleased about it. So easy to say *I'll kill them.* So different to actually do it.

When rough hands pulled her away, she didn't fight them. Took a deep breath, squared her shoulders, raised her head, and looked past Murphy at Lieutenant Geurin.

"I think," the lieutenant said, smiling, "that it will take us over three days to reach the capital and those three days will be frequently punctuated by stops in order to change the horses, this might be the time to inform you of what will happen should one of you actually succeed at an escape attempt. Should that happen, I will punish those left behind, making the escapee directly responsible for their pain. My orders are to deliver you alive to the emperor, but that still leaves me a great deal of leeway. It would be foolish, therefore, to believe you can take advantage of the distractions offered to my men by either the common business of the road or such unexpected happenstances as the corporal's misfortune."

"And doesn't he love the sound of his own voice," Stina muttered as Danika stepped forward.

She wiped her nose on her sleeve. "The corporal's misfortune?" She spoke loudly enough to be heard over the drivers calming their horses. "A man under your command has been killed and you call it a *misfortune?*"

His lip curled. "Shut up." He wasn't as stupid as he looked.

Danika ignored him and raised her voice. "Sergeant Black, if our Healer-mage can . . ."

"I said shut up!" His knuckles hit the same place he'd hit her before. As her swollen cheek dimpled under the blow, she cried out and crumpled to the ground. They were still captive, but the lieutenant's men saw him disdainful of the death of one of their own, and she had the pain to help ease her guilt.

They rolled Berger's body up in his blanket and tied it to the roof of the last coach.

"We'll give him to the new garrison at Abyek for the rites," the sergeant said as they passed the body up and Kyne secured it. No one seemed to care that the blanket had already darkened in places and that they'd be traveling for miles with a corpse. No, they cared, Danika amended, they didn't mind. To be a soldier was to grow used to death.

Although perhaps not this manner of death . . .

"Are you all right?" she asked as Tagget latched the door.

"Why wouldn't I be?" he growled. "He threw himself out. It's not I like pushed him."

"Of course not." No one knew that better than she did.

"Who'd have thought Berger would go like that?" Murphy muttered, having been ordered to the second place inside. "Coach, horses, coach, horses, coach. Fuck."

"Shut up."

"I'm just saying . . ."

"And I'm just saying shut the fuck up!" Tagget slammed the butt of his musket down into the floor with enough force Danika felt the impact through the soles of her boots.

Murphy stared at him for a long moment then said, "Lyone says both his ladies puked riding backward. You didn't notice the stink?"

Danika hadn't, although both Jesine and Annalyse's skirts had to be stained. She had to stop thinking about Berger, about how she'd killed him, and concentrate on getting her Mage-pack free.

Tagget stood, shoved Kirstin into the place he'd vacated, and dropped onto the seat beside Murphy. "Happy?"

"I only want one thing more." Murphy made a rude gesture, but when Danika ignored him and Kirstin continued to stare into the middle distance, he snorted and slumped back into the corner. "Fine, I'm happy."

Tagget wasn't. Danika could see the memories playing behind his eyes, over and over and over. He saw his hand on Berger's shoulder. Then he saw Berger disappear out the door. She wished it had been one of the others, one of the men who saw them as things not people. Kyne, or even Murphy rather than Tagget, but she'd work with what she had.

The coach lurched forward. Murphy's musket cracked against her knee, and he stroked her leg as he retrieved it, grinning broadly when she refused to react. When both men finally closed their eyes, Kirstin reached over and took Danika's hand.

With the other woman's fingers warm around hers, Danika breathed in. Breathed out.

It was all your fault.

Tagget shuddered.

As she inhaled, Murphy opened his eyes, glanced down at the joining of their hands, and leered. Danika exhaled without words.

By the time they stopped to change the horses, she'd been able to prod Tagget only twice more, unable to trust Murphy to keep his eyes closed for any length of time. Her lips barely moved, but if he saw her, if they realized she'd killed Berger . . .

Truth be told, her greatest reaction to Murphy's casual lechery was relief. Manipulating Berger had been an experiment. Knowing the result, manipulating Tagget made her feel unclean.

The Duchy of Pyrahn hadn't been a conquered territory of the Kresentian Empire long enough for the network of posting houses to have been extended out from the old borders. But, as they thundered up to the village of Herdon, their driver sounded the mechanical horn as though expecting grooms to be ready and waiting with new horses. Herdon had grown up around the lumber mill at the point of the valley, and Danika assumed it had a public house, perhaps even two, but it couldn't possibly be prepared for the sudden arrival of three coaches demanding twelve fresh horses.

Except it was.

The coach rocked to a stop abrupt enough to throw both women forward out of their seats then back again. At the sergeant's command, the men inside the carriage switched with those riding outside—Danika doubted that included Hare, the sharpshooter, and hoped it didn't include Sergeant Black—and during the exchange, as Tagget and Murphy were replaced by Corporal Selven and the lieutenant, Danika saw a team of sleek bays being led past the open door. With narrow heads and long legs under muscular withers and haunches, these were horses intended for speed, not for hauling loaded coaches over rutted forest tracks. These were the horses Danika had envisioned when she thought of post horses.

She'd just never thought of them this far into Pyrahn.

Lieutenant Geurin had no intention of riding backward, so Danika faced him while Kirstin sat across from the corporal. She stared out the window and Corporal Selven stared at his musket, leaving her and the lieutenant to focus on each other. As they left the village and picked up speed, the horses proving their pedigree, the ride went from uncomfortable to unpleasant.

Danika watched the lieutenant's face and waited. He was, as Stina had noted, too fond of his own voice to stay silent for long.

"In the empire," he snarled, shouting above the noise, "we know how to build roads."

We? Danika would have wagered a year's pin money that the lieutenant had never built anything in his life.

"You should thank us for pulling your pitiful little country out of the darkness and into the illumination of science and development."

Did he think they lived in mud huts crouched around an open fire? There were gaslights about to be installed on the main streets of Bercarit and a complete restructuring of the sewer system intended for Trouge. As tempted as she was to defend Ryder's planned civic works, Danika kept her comments to their more immediate concerns.

"And should we thank you for tearing us away from our homes, our husbands, our children?" The corporal's gaze flicked to her face, surprised. It had apparently never occurred to him that they had lives beyond being captives of the Imperial army. Soldiers seldom got to know those they faced in war—which made sense, if they thought of the enemy as other people, how could they kill? Had she been arranging this . . . journey, the reason behind changing the soldiers with the horses would be to keep them from getting to know their captives in the forced proximity and relative privacy of the coach. It seemed the Shield commanders thought the same way. Although it left her unable to continue escalating Tagget's guilt, Danika decided to see the change as a chance to unsettle a greater number of the men.

Linking her fingers in her lap, she fixed Lieutenant Geurin with her best drawing room stare, reminding him they shared a social class. "Are you aware that you've left five children crying for their mothers?" Kirstin made a pained sound. Two of the children were her ten-year-old twins, the other three were Stina's. "Five children whose grief you are directly responsible for."

"I have deprived a great many children of their fathers," the lieutenant drawled as they passed over a relatively smooth bit of road. "I hardly think the grief of five tiny abominations will bother me." She thought she'd controlled her reaction, but when he continued, voice dripping false concern, she realized she had not. "Oh, hadn't you heard? His Most Imperial Majesty, the Emperor Leopald, has had the church declare your beastmen and your children by beastmen abominations—that which has not passed through the Holy Fire and is unclean. I heard the old Prelate became so concerned about the issue, it killed him. But he was an old man, and these things happen."

Danika wondered if Geurin understood he'd as much as told her the emperor had the old Prelate killed. Or if he was stupid enough to be bragging about it.

"Abominations have no protection under the law," he continued. "I, personally, am not a religious man, but some dictates of the church it pleases me to follow. You, personally, are unclean by association. You lie down with dogs . . ." He grinned, suddenly pleased with himself. ". . . you get up with fleas. Not a metaphor in this case, is it?"

"It's a metaphor you'd do well to remember," Danika snarled, hands curled into fists. Beside her, Corporal Selven stared across the coach at the tears running down Kirstin's cheeks. It was probably the first time in the corporal's career that he'd been forced to spend time with the consequences of his actions. And it couldn't hurt that those consequences were presented by a young and beautiful woman of good birth.

She raised her hands to touch the bruising on her cheek and, shielded by the motion, sighed, *It breaks your heart.*

A muscle twitched in Selven's jaw, and he shifted in his seat. She could only see his profile, but he didn't look happy. Good.

Leaving the corporal to think about what exactly he was involved with, Danika listened to the lieutenant speak of his uncle, high in the emperor's council. He was, he informed her, Lieutenant *Lord* Geurin and she wondered how he'd react if informed in turn that she was *Lady* Hagen. Given that he hadn't bothered to find out the names of any of his captives, she doubted he'd care.

"When I deliver you to the emperor, His Imperial Majesty will grant me a colonelcy and a regiment."

"Above those who have worked for it? Above men who have the experience you lack?"

"I don't need experience!"

She felt the corporal's leg jerk where it pressed against hers. "Weren't you supposed to bring six mages back?"

"The sixth mage is Captain Reiter's problem."

Danika widened her eyes and looked concerned. "I hope His Imperial Majesty sees it that way."

"He will!" But he sounded more like a petulant six-year-old than a confident man in his twenties, and the sulky way he settled back into his corner only emphasized the resemblance. He did no more talking, but Danika figured both he and Corporal Selven had enough to consider.

She stared out the window and watched time pass in the small patch of sky.

It had been nearly noon when they'd reached the forest track and not long after that, even considering the delay of Berger's death, when they'd made the first change from work to post horses. It was almost dark when the horses were changed the second time. As the horses were changed for the third time, the lieutenant ordered the Mage-pack out of the coaches.

They were in an inn yard, an actual inn yard; the inn to the left, the stables to the right, a gate in both of the connecting walls to allow a coach the luxury of driving through without turning. There were one or two dim lights in windows in the black slab of buildings beyond, but Danika expected no help from that quarter. There was just barely room to change all three teams at once. A dozen steaming, sweating horses and their handlers gave the Mage-pack an excuse to huddle together and their guards insufficient geography to separate them.

All the men in sight were Imperial soldiers—even those changing the horses—but moving closer to the spill of light and glancing through the open door into the kitchens, Danika could see a number of local women. It looked like they had fared much worse than her small pack. Although, given the swelling that had forced her left eye nearly shut, the way Kirstin remained closed within herself, a bleeding cut on Jesine's lip, a certain dishevelment of Annalyse's clothing, and the care Stina took walking, they didn't look much better.

The inn yard gave no clue to where they were although, given the size, they had to be on the outskirts of a city. Given the speed they'd been traveling, they had to be out of Pyrahn and over the border into Traiton. Fraris, then, the Duke's Seat and the only city of any size in the duchy.

"They have fifteen minutes, Sergeant." The lieutenant flicked open his watch. "For the privy *and* for food."

Danika suspected they were intended to use the privy in the same pairs they traveled in—keep them from sharing information, keep them from knowing how their friends were faring—but Jesine slipped in front of Kirstin; Carlsan, clearly annoyed at being forced to guard the privy while the others were already eating, either didn't notice or didn't care.

"Has she said anything?" the Healer-mage asked when the door closed.

"No." Danika raised a brow at the rough wood, but needs must. "She hears what's being said, though. And she's reacting."

"I'd like the time to examine her properly. Annalyse is pregnant."

It sounded like a non sequitur, but Danika had known Jesine long enough to know differently. "Yes."

"And so are you. And I think, although it hasn't been long enough to be certain, I think I am as well." Jesine shot her a glance heavy with implication.

"We all are. They're following a prophecy." She frowned trying to recall the exact words she'd overheard. "*When wild and mage together come, one in six or six in one. Empires rise or empires fall, the unborn child begins it all.*"

"Six in one?" Jesine stood and let her skirts fall. For all she wore the calm and practical manner taught to Healer-mages, Danika heard hysteria barely held at bay in her laugh. "I certainly hope not. Do the soldiers know?"

"No. Even the captain was only told when they came up a mage short."

"Should we tell them?"

"The soldiers? I don't know." How would soldiers feel about their orders coming from Soothsayers? Would they care about risking their lives on the word of the insane? Or would they see the order as coming from the emperor himself? "I do know that separated as we are, there's no way we can all escape together, so we'll have to wait."

"They're taking us to Karis, Dani."

"I know."

"If they keep moving all night at post speeds, we'll be in the empire before morning and at Karis no more than two days after that. You think we can escape from the emperor himself and make our way home across half the empire and two recently conquered duchies still crawling with Imperial soldiers?"

"I think . . ." Danika stood and settled her skirts in turn. ". . . we will do whatever we have to and we'll do it together. All of us."

After a long moment, Jesine nodded and showed teeth. "I think you're right. Danika . . ." She paused, hand on the privy door. "Berger was an enemy."

Danika didn't want to know how much Jesine suspected. "I know," she said, and pushed past her into the inn yard where a young woman, girl really, handed her a bowl of stew and a spoon, wincing as she moved. With her hands bound, Danika had to hold the bowl at her mouth. She hadn't realized how hungry she was until the first bite; she finished the rest so quickly she barely tasted it. She thought the lieutenant might have lingered, that the time limit would apply to everyone save him, but after fifteen minutes, they were loaded back into the coaches and, a moment after that, the horses were given their heads, horn sounding to clear the road.

It appeared they were to travel at post speed through the night.

It was nearly dark by the time Tomas began to stir. Mirian had slept a little herself, stretched aching muscles, drank a bit of water, ate another biscuit, and wished she had her mirror so she could talk to her sister. Lorela would be horrified by the situation and tell her to return to Aydori at once. Mirian would tell her why she couldn't, and that would make the whole impossible situation real in a way saying the same words to herself couldn't.

Tomas was going after Lady Hagen.

All the evidence so far indicated he couldn't do it without her help.

But mostly, sitting in last year's grass by the side of the road, Tomas' head on her lap, she just wanted to talk to her sister. She wanted Lorela to make it right, like she always had when they were growing up. Lorela would sit on her bed, wrapped in a shawl, and explain that the world as they wanted it to be and the world as it was weren't always the same place. Their mother's drive for social advancement, their father always putting the bank first, that was how it was. A smart girl would figure out a way to work around it.

Mirian ran gentle fingers over Tomas' shoulder, trying to decide if the skin around the scar felt hotter than the rest. The road to Karis went through two recently conquered duchies—logically, therefore, full of Imperial soldiers—as well as through half the empire. The coaches carrying the captured Mage-pack already had a full day on them and unless the people of Pyrahn or Traiton decided to spontaneously block the road and stop them, she and Tomas wouldn't catch up. Emperor Leopald would have the Mage-pack for days, maybe weeks before they could be rescued. This is how the world was.

She stared down the road toward Karis—eventually Karis—and then back toward Aydori. In the gathering dusk it would be impossible to see something even the size of a small gray pony racing down the road to the rescue. That didn't stop her from looking, from hoping to see Jaspyr Hagen suddenly appear, leading the Hunt Pack, coming to her rescue.

Jaspyr Hagen.

She wanted to talk to Lorela about that, too. About Jasper and Tomas and things that seemed like they should be unimportant next to war and capture and burning a man to death, but weren't. Unfortunately, her mirror was probably in Trouge by now, wrapped in a silk scarf her mother had given her after having accidentally dipped the end in a glass of sherry. Mirian had no idea of how to enchant another, it needed at least fourth level air and second level metals, and mirrors, backed with silver, were both rare and expensive in Aydori.

Of course, she wasn't *in* Aydori.

Tomas' ear flicked, then his back legs began to kick at the air. Mirian moved her hands away, just in case, as he pushed against her thigh with a front paw. Then his eyes snapped open and an instant later he was on his feet, growling, hackles raised, ears tight to his head.

"They're not here. They shot you and kept going. It's just me." Moving slowly, carefully, she reached into the soldier's pouch and pulled out a piece of dried meat. "There's food and water. I'm assuming, given how much healing you required, that you won't be strong enough to hunt right away. I could be wrong but . . ."

His teeth grazed her fingers.

"You'll have to change to drink," she said as he swallowed. She pulled out another piece of meat and tossed it to him. He snapped it out of the air. "Or you'll have to lap from my hands. The only water we have is in this can . . ." Sitting on the ground, it was harder to look at his face now he was on two legs, so she stared at his knees instead as she passed him the canteen. His knees were dirty.

He tried to make it look like he chose to sit, legs folding as he collapsed to the ground. It looked more like a barely controlled fall to Mirian.

"There's hard biscuits, too."

"More meat?"

"Yes." This must have been why she'd only eaten the biscuits. She'd known he'd need the meat. Known he'd get shot running after the coaches like an idiot, right down the center of the road where any decent marksman could take him out. Known she'd have to pull the silver out of him again. Known he'd nearly die and leave her alone to save . . .

"Are you okay?"

"I'm fine." She wiped the biscuit crumbs off on her skirt and put half of it back in the pouch like she'd meant to break it.

Still chewing, he turned his head to peer down at his shoulder, working the arm and wincing. Against his pale skin, the scar was an angry pink—not a shade Mirian had previously been familiar with, even considering Lorela had ribbons in every other imaginable shade of pink.

"Does it hurt?"

"I'm fine."

They sat in silence for a moment. Bats dipped and soared overhead, irregular shadows against the deepening dusk. In amidst the ash and birch behind them, an owl made its first cry of the night.

The moment after that, Tomas said, "So what do we do now?"

"We free the Mage-pack."

"We'll never catch them."

"We know where they're going."

"No."

"No?"

"I've been thinking about it . . ."

"While you were unconscious?"

". . . and I should have stopped you." His tone suggested he knew what was best for her. He was a year younger, and he'd needed her to save him not once but twice, but he was Pack. As Mirian stiffened, he added, "I should never have allowed you to come this far."

"Allowed?" Mirian forced the word through clenched teeth.

"I need to take you home."

"How?"

They were sitting close enough she could see him blink. "I beg your pardon?"

"You can't convince me to return home and you can't physically force me, so how did you plan to *take* me home?"

"Miss Maylin . . ."

"Mirian. If I'm not to call you Lord Hagen, you may use my given name as well."

"Fine. Mirian." His tone slid from barely excusable concern to patronizing. "You have no idea of what dangers you could face on the road."

"Apparently," she snapped, "neither do you." Yanking her stocking tight around the end of the bedroll, she slung it over her shoulder and stood. "I've come too far to quit now, so *I* am going to free the Mage-pack. As you're no longer bleeding to death by the side of the road, and therefore no longer need my assistance, you may accompany me or not as you see fit." The pivot on one heel would have worked better had she been wearing her boots and not winced at the movement, but she stepped out onto the road with her head up.

One step.

Of all the arrogant . . .

Two steps.

You're welcome. Next time, you can remove the silver yourself.

Three steps.

It's not like I didn't kill someone to keep him from shooting you.

Four steps and Tomas stood in front of her, growling softly.

Mirian kept walking. "You're not going to attack me and I'm certainly not frightened of you, so I don't know what you think you're trying to prove."

As she brushed by him, he grabbed her skirt in his teeth and yanked.

"Really?" she said, as she stumbled. "Really?" She grabbed for the bedroll with one hand as it slid off her shoulder and reached out with the other, pressing the first two fingers down into the fur between his eyes. "Sleep."

Tomas woke lying in the middle of the road, one front leg tucked under his head, the other stretched out, shoulder throbbing. It took a moment to figure out where and why—he'd been shot, again, there'd been pain and darkness and then a voice . . . Mirian! He scrambled onto to his feet and shook, trying to throw off the lingering effect of the mage-craft.

How dare she!

And, more importantly, how long had he been asleep?

The night smelled young; the hunters and hunted who roamed at dusk and dawn still out and about. In the west, the evening star lingered on the horizon. He'd been asleep for minutes then, not hours. Turning to face east, the direction the coaches had been traveling, he saw, no more than half a mile down the road, a single figure walking away. Downwind, so he couldn't catch a scent, but there could be little question of who it was.

Mirian Maylin, walking to Karis to free the Mage-pack.

She had no idea of what she was walking into.

She had no mage marks in her eyes.

She couldn't fight.

She'd barely been able to cover the distance between the cave where they'd spent the night and the track where the Mage-pack and their captors had emerged from Aydori. He'd have been there on time if not for her.

He'd have been dead if not for her.

She smelled like power. And home. And . . .

Of course, she smelled so good, he supposed legs weren't actually necessary.

. . . and something more he was not going to think about right now. Or like that, at least.

Clearly, she wouldn't turn back no matter what he said or did, and she'd proven that, while he couldn't stop her, she could stop him.

He was either going to help her free the Mage-pack, or he wasn't.

He sat and scratched for a moment, putting off the inevitable, then he sighed and stood. Even in a small pack, pack members needed to know their place; it kept the world from degenerating into chaos and confusion.

She didn't look down when he caught up. He limped along beside her for a few steps, but every time his left forefoot hit the ground it sent a shock of pain up into his shoulder, so he changed and, cradling his left arm against his chest, matched her pace on two.

When it became obvious she wasn't going to speak first, Tomas cleared his throat. "Thank you for saving my life. It was rude of me to not mention that before."

He heard her snort although he suspected he wasn't intended to. "You're welcome. I would have done it for anyone."

Polite, but still angry. "I apologize for not respecting your decision to carry on. I have no right to dictate your actions and . . ." Frowning he tried to work out just what it was she wanted to hear. ". . . and you have certainly proven yourself capable. I mean, you got captured by Imperials, but that wasn't your fault."

"Thank you."

Her tone dropped the temperature, already almost too cold to be out in skin, another few degrees. He didn't know what he'd said wrong and had no idea of what to say to fix things between them. A memory of her fingers stroking his shoulder suggested a better way than words. He changed and butted his head against her hip.

When she ignored him, he did it again, putting enough weight behind it that she staggered. When she turned to glare at him, he hit her with what Harry'd called the puppy eyes of doom.

"You can take down a doe on your own, snap her neck between those monster jaws, and cover yourself in blood and guts, but you give me that look and all I want to do is bury my hands in your fur and tell you what a good boy you are. So stop giving me that look, you walking carpet, it creeps me out."

Mirian laughed, as though she hadn't intended to, and finally said, "All right. You're forgiven. We're in this together." She reached out to stroke his head, then snatched her hand back, embarrassed. "I'm so sorry. I know better, it's just . . ."

Tomas shoved his head up under her hand. It was the two of them against the empire. They could both use the comfort of touch. It didn't have to mean anything more, not if she didn't want it to. No matter how good she smelled.

A few moments later, he reluctantly pulled away from her hand and changed. "It's almost fifteen miles to Herdon. If I stay in fur, I'll be on three legs when I get there."

"Before Herdon . . ."

"A few small farms, but Herdon's the first town. It's where the sawmill is. Where they take the logs," he amended. She'd said her father was a banker. Two days ago, her life had been shopping and card parties and dances; why would she know what a sawmill was. "The logs they cut in the forest," he added, just in case.

"I know where logs come from." But he heard her smile, so that meant she wasn't angry. "Why wouldn't they build the sawmill closer to the trees?"

"They did. A hundred years ago."

"But these trees . . ." She waved a hand at the woods surrounding them.

"Softwoods. They cut them, too, but they're what grew up when the hardwoods were gone, so every year, if they want the good stuff, they have to cut farther away from the mill."

"How do you know all this?"

"Herdon's the biggest town in the borderlands. You can't protect the border unless you know why people are there. And, the duke's been after Ryder to send some Aydori timber to Herdon. Says it would open up new sections of our woods for cutting if we could send floats down the Vern directly to Herdon and the mill pond rather than having to feed everything into the Nairn and down to our mill at Bercarit. Trouble is, the Vern's not exactly deep in places, but the duke even offered to deepen the pool under the falls on our side of the border because Herdon lives or dies with the mill, and he doesn't intend for it to die. Ryder said that's an admirable thought, but if we gave the old weasel access, he'd strip the mountain bare in a decade. I had to go to the meetings as his aide. The most boring four days of my life." Suddenly realizing he'd just repeated the highlights of the most boring four days of his life, he flushed, thankful it was too dark for Mirian to see his face. "But more importantly," he added hurriedly, "is that fifteen miles is a long walk. I need to stay off my front leg for a while, but the night's getting colder. Too cold for skin. Trouble is we need to reach Herdon before dawn if we're going to find out what happened when the coaches went through. I'm trained to get in and out of town with no one knowing, but it works better in the dark. I'm a little obvious in the daylight."

"All right. How long will it take us to reach Herdon?"

Tomas had no idea what *all right* referred to, but she wasn't laughing at his stupid timber babbling, so he supposed it didn't matter. "At this speed, three or maybe four hours."

She was silent for so long Tomas was unsure if she was thinking or despairing.

"I have a blanket and a knife. If we cut a hole in it for your head, and you wore it, would that keep you warm enough?"

Thinking, then. Muscles he hadn't realized were tense relaxed. He'd made the right choice. As for her suggestion . . . "It should." The Hunt Pack had done winter training up in the mountains, just fur, no greatcoats, and one shitload of snow. Three or four hours in skin on a spring night would be no problem as long as they kept moving. He stopped walking as Mirian dropped to one knee and let the bedroll slide off her shoulder. It took her a minute to get her . . . Tomas frowned . . . her stocking untied, then she unrolled it and set the contents aside. Her boots, a folding knife, a fire-starter, a telescope, the pouch that smelled of meat and biscuits . . .

"Where did you get all that?"

"I took it from the soldier I killed."

"You killed?"

"While you were running at the other one, I set a fire in his ammo pouch like you suggested. He went up like . . ." She waved a hand, unable to find a comparison or unwilling to voice those she'd found. Her fingers were trembling. "He was dead so, logically, he wouldn't need any of this anymore. There's a purse with a bit of money, too."

"The other soldier . . ."

"One," she snapped, "was enough. He was dead and I killed him, but the other one wasn't my . . . I mean, I didn't . . . I couldn't . . ." She wiped her nose on her sleeve then tried to open the knife.

"Here," Tomas knelt beside her. "Let me."

She shoved it into his hand and when he glanced over at her face, her eyes were shut and he could smell the salt tang of tears.

"We're at war," he said quietly, hooking his thumbnail in the grooved steel edge and forcing the blade out. "He was a soldier. Soldiers die in wars." He cut a slit in the center of the blanket, hearing Harry reminding him to be careful. Hearing Danika telling Ryder to return safely and soon. "Soldiers kill in wars."

"I'm not a soldier." Her eyes were open now, pale and free of mage marks. "I'm not an anything."

He pulled the blanket over his head, the scent of the man who'd slept in it lingering long after the man himself. There might have been a slight scent of char; it might have been his imagination. When he could see again, Mirian had unbuckled her belt and was in the process of hanging her boots and the pouch from it. She'd lost the bedroll, but her hands would be still be free. Smart. "Then why are you here? If you're not an anything," he added when she looked confused.

"Because someone has to be." She hung the telescope around her neck and tucked it inside her jacket, stared at the fire-starter then slipped it into a boot. The knife followed when Tomas handed it back. "And I'm all there is."

"*We're* all there is."

She looked at him for a long moment. He could see her clearly, but he had no idea of how much of his expression she could make out even given how close they were. Enough, apparently. She took a deep breath and smiled—mostly smiled, partially bared her teeth. "We're all there is."

As she reached for one stocking, he reached for the other. "May I?" She nodded and he wrapped it around his waist, cinching the back of the blanket tight around his body, leaving the front loose enough to tuck his arms inside if he needed. Then he stood and held out a hand.

She needed more of his help to stand than she'd be comfortable admitting. Or maybe not, he reminded himself; she was sensible. Her skirt came to just above her ankles, her feet more obvious bare than they had been in boots. He could smell blood, but she hadn't mentioned an injury, so he wouldn't bring it up. Her jacket fit loosely—ease of removal dominated Aydori fashions. Anything under her skirt and jacket, he had little experience with, but it seemed a reasonable outfit for tromping around the countryside. It smelled of mud, and ash, and crushed plants, and sweat, and girl.

"What? You're looking at me like it's the first time you've seen me."

It was, in a way. They hadn't been Pack before. He shrugged, not wanting to admit to more than she could work out on her own.

She shook her head, then forced her fingers through her hair and used the other stocking to tie it back. When she caught him staring, she almost smiled a true smile with no aggression in it. "I know what you're thinking; it was in a boot for two days and even I can smell it. But it's better than having hair fall in my face all night."

"That wasn't what I was thinking."

"Then what?"

He shrugged again, knowing that if he said *sensible*, she'd misunderstand. Knowing he couldn't explain and that at some point, according to both Harry and Ryder, girls wanted to hear more than, *"You smell amazing."*

After a moment, when she finally realized that was all the answer she was going to get, she rolled her eyes, took a deep breath, and started walking. "Three to four hours to Herdon? All right, let's do it in three."

What wind there was came from the northwest, so he fell into step upwind behind her left shoulder. The blanket rubbed a bit, not in a good way, and that helped. He wondered if she was going to talk now they were only walking not charging along the border. His limited experience with young ladies of quality, at least those he wasn't closely related to, had involved rather a lot of staring over teacups and inane conversations about the weather.

Mirian Maylin walked—limped—as quickly as she could and said nothing at all.

So Tomas said nothing as well for about an hour until he picked up a scent he couldn't ignore. "Wait. Someone died here."

"Here?"

"Right there." Wrapping a hand around her elbow, he tugged her back two paces, and dropped to one knee. The dirt was still damp, the pattern complicated under the bootprints. Tomas could smell blood and guts and horses and steel. "I think he was run over by a coach wheel. More than once." Rising, he moved forward slowly, following his nose. "They stopped the coaches here. Everyone got out. Stina Menkyzck here." He ran forward. "Jesine and Annalyse Berin here." Further. "Danika and Kirstin Yervick here." He moved off the road to a rough circle where the grass had been crushed under boots. "They gathered together here." Their scents would be easier to separate from the Imperials if he changed, but none of the women were strangers. "Geoffrey Berin was Hunt Pack. Colonel Menkyzck was a senior officer. The Hunt Pack . . ."

"I know. I was at the reception when you arrived."

"Ryder sent Sirlin and Neils Yervick to the front with the 2nd." Sirlin was a Hagen. Another cousin. He was years older than Jesine, but they were stupidly in love. Jesine had laughed at the age difference and said Healer-mages were always more mature. She was beautiful and Tomas had been a bit in love with her himself.

Mirian had stayed where he'd put her. She was watching him, but he had no idea how well she could see in the dark. "Are they all right?" she asked softly. "No, stupid question; widowed and kidnapped, of course they're not all right. Are they hurt?"

"They're all walking. They're not dripping blood." He wanted to howl. "Other than that . . ."

"They're all walking." She held out her hand and he went to it, her scent stronger than the lingering evidence his brother's wife and baby lived. "Let's go get them."

Mirian had no idea how long it had been when Tomas stretched an arm out in front of her; it felt like she'd been walking for her entire life. She hoped he had a good reason to stop her because she wasn't entirely certain she could start moving again.

"We're at the edge of the mill property," he said quietly, bending close to her ear. "It smells like the mill's still running in spite of the war. Not surprising, since the duke sold a lot of his high-end lumber to the empire. Ryder says that's why he wanted our oak and . . ."

Tomas stopped talking when Mirian turned to face him, their mouths suddenly so close together she could feel his breath on her lips. "I appreciate the depth of your knowledge . . ." She did. It was a lot more interesting than fashions or her mother's nerves or who had recently gotten married to whom, but would, unfortunately, have been as out of place in a drawing room as it was in the middle of the night outside a small town in the recently conquered Duchy of Pyrahn. ". . . but why have we stopped?"

"What?"

His lower lip was slightly chapped. She hadn't noticed that before. "You stopped me."

"Yes."

"Why? Has someone else died?"

"No."

His jaw was as smooth as hers. Did the Pack not need to shave? "Then why have we stopped?"

Instead of responding, he shook himself then shoved her behind him, taking half a dozen steps down the road, dragging the blanket off over his head as he moved, changing on the last step, hackles up, looking even bigger than she knew he was. He'd pulled the blanket out from under her stocking, not stopping to untie it, and it hung around his . . . waist? . . . the middle of his body, a dirty white stripe around the black, like some kind of weird medieval favor.

What was he protecting her from?

Now that all her attention was no longer locked on putting one foot in front of the other—or, she reluctantly admitted, on gazing at Tomas' face like a simpering ninny—she could see an irregular landscape made up of piles of wood and, beyond that, a cluster of buildings topped by the distinctive shape of the mill wheel. Past the mill, the road turned to the northeast and followed the glint of the river for a while until it disappeared into a cluster of shadows showing only one or two scattered lights. Herdon. Only a little farther now.

Movement caught her attention and, looking back toward the mill, she could see a pair of shadows cutting diagonally across toward the road. She couldn't see what they were, but she knew what they had to be. Captain Reiter had said they kept big dogs in this part of the duchy.

The profanity she'd learned from Adine suddenly seemed remarkably limited.

Not until the shadows reached the edge of the road did they finally resolve into dogs. They had a look of Pack about them, although they were smaller and their heads proportionally narrower.

Tomas growled, a low rumble Mirian felt roll across her, and took a stiff-legged step forward.

The dogs snarled and mirrored Tomas' position.

Tomas took another step and stopped.

The three of them held their positions long enough Mirian had to bite her lip to keep from swaying in place, then the dogs lowered their heads, sniffed the dirt around their front feet—it looked very much like they were trying to convince Tomas they'd just run out to check that particular bit of ground—turned, and trotted back toward the mill, disappearing into the night.

Tomas stayed where he was for a moment before he turned and changed. "Guard dogs," he said, retrieving the blanket, as though she hadn't figured that out on her own. "Anyone coming down this road at night probably intends to help themselves from the mill yard."

He sounded like he'd been reenergized by the encounter, moving as though his skin could barely contain him. All Mirian felt was tired. "Why didn't they raise an alarm?"

"We're upwind."

"That's how they knew we were here." She started walking again before sitting down in the middle of the road and remaining there until someone provided a hot bath and a change of clothes became her only option. "But why didn't they raise the alarm?"

"Dogs recognize the dominance of the Pack." Tomas fell into step beside her, still holding the blanket. "They don't challenge us. But guard dogs are both bred and trained to challenge, so they need more convincing. Geese," he added after a moment, "are a bigger problem. They're mean."

Mirian had never met a goose that hadn't been plucked, roasted, and served with chestnut stuffing. The thought of Tomas, hackles up in the dining room, facing down a holiday dinner made her giggle. Once the giggles started bubbling up, she couldn't stop them. They kept coming even with her eyes closed and her hands clamped over her mouth.

"Mirian?"

Her ribs ached with the effort of keeping things in, and she felt as though she was going to shake apart. Her knees started to buckle, but something pushed against her legs when she threw out a hand to keep from falling, her fingers sinking into fur. She opened her eyes to see the top of Tomas' head and to feel his warm weight against her, supporting her. He wasn't watching her. He wasn't judging. He was just a quiet presence lending her his strength until she could get herself back under control. Letting her know they were in this together.

She took a deep breath. If it still sounded a little shaky on the exhale, at least the terrible noises she'd been making had stopped. A second breath. A third. She forced herself to relax. Mage-craft came from calm. That lesson, at least, she'd always excelled at.

The outer layer of fur slipped cool past her fingers, the inner softer, warmer. Stroking his ears reminded her of the gray velvet evening cloak her parents had given her at Winter Solstice and the list of events that had accompanied it, including the parties for her to be paraded at before she returned to the university at the holiday's end.

Tomas glanced up at her when she laughed.

"It's okay," she told him, stepping back to give him room to change. "I'm okay. Just putting things in perspective. As horrible as the last two days have been, I'd rather be doing this than nothing at all."

"When we get through Herdon, we can look for a place to hide and rest."

That was the best suggestion she'd heard for hours. "Good."

The road entered Herdon between a large house by the river and lines of small cottages disappearing into the darkness on the other side. Mill owner, mill workers, Mirian assumed, tugging the blanket from Tomas' hand and kneeling to retie the bedroll. She assumed that should they run into anyone awake, a young woman out at this hour with a big black dog would be less notable than a young woman out at this hour with a nearly naked young man. They *had* to find Tomas some clothes.

"Will there be soldiers?" she asked, untangling her bootlaces.

"Why would there be soldiers?"

"Maybe because the duchy was recently *conquered*."

"The emperor wants the mill to keep producing. The people of Herdon want the mill to keep producing. There'll be someone new in the mill house taking orders from the empire. Probably new workers brought in to replace those killed in the war." He shrugged when she looked up at him. "Ryder says most people don't care who's in charge as long as someone is."

Mirian thought of the empire absorbing Aydori. Of the emperor thinking he could just send soldiers in to take what he wanted. To take *people* he wanted. "I care."

"Yeah, well, we've established that you're not most people." Tomas grinned. "You're sensible."

They reached the town square without being seen. When Tomas took two steps toward the inn then turned and looked back over his shoulder, Mirian raised the canteen and pointed at the well. He nodded and disappeared into the shadows.

There was moonlight and starlight enough she could maneuver past the three trees that made up a kind of cut-rate Lady's Grove. The grass around them felt colder than the pounded dirt of the road, and she hissed in disgust as a slightly warmer lump squished under the ball of her foot and up between her toes.

Something hissed back.

She froze.

The windows surrounding the square were dark, no lights showing through any of the tiny squares of thick glass.

After a moment, or two, or ten, she took a tentative step forward. Then another. Alone in a silent night when she reached the well, she let out a breath she hadn't remembered holding and stepped onto the worn path around the stone curb, frantically scrubbing the bottom of her foot in the dirt, gagging a little at the smell.

She'd never actually worked a pump before, but how hard could it be? Cook had one in the kitchen. Sticking her foot under the metal nose, she slowly raised the handle, wincing as steel hissed against steel . . .

And something hissed back.

Something very close.

Heart pounding, Mirian leaned around the pump and came face to face with a scrawny orange cat. Relief was short-lived as she realized the cat was sitting on the legs of a man so ragged his edges feathered off into the night. The smell wasn't coming from the mess on her foot, but from him. She had to hold her own breath before she could hear him breathing, but that was infinitely better than touching him. He wasn't dead. She could wash her foot and fill her canteen and . . .

His eyes snapped open.

Given the way her last two days had gone, Mirian had to admit she wasn't surprised.

"They know!" The words bounced off the surrounding buildings. "They know!" he repeated, arms flailing. The cat gave a disgusted noise and jumped up by the pump. Mirian shrank down into the minimal shadow thrown by the curb, but no windows opened, no one appeared to find out what was going on. When he looked directly at her without seeing her, Mirian understood why.

The townspeople had to be used to the Soothsayer's random yelling. He'd be one of the familiar noises in the night. A noise that would excuse any noise she might make.

She turned back to the pump and nearly screamed as a clammy hand wrapped around her ankle.

"White light!"

Pulling free, she turned. They said touch compounded a Soothsayer's madness. If he was speaking to, or about her . . .

He was mumbling into the fur of the cat who'd returned to knead against his belly.

If she wanted more details, wanted a clarifying vision, he'd have to touch her again. Or she'd have to touch him.

She reached out a hand. Puffed up twice its size, the cat spun around toward her then raced away into the darkness leaving the Soothsayer clutching his belly and moaning.

"He'll wake the town," Tomas muttered.

"They're used to him." He wasn't in vision anymore. He was just a crazy old man. "What did you find?"

"They changed horses here. Switched local horses for twelve post horses bred for speed, and they'll be changing every twelve to sixteen miles all the way to the capital."

"You could smell all that?"

"No, there were a couple of boys up in the mow over the stable talking about the horses."

"What were they doing awake?" When he snickered, she raised a hand and went back to the pump. "Never mind. So they're moving the Mage-pack faster than we thought." She'd half hoped the soldiers had decided to lock the Mage-pack in Herdon for the night. Close to the border. Easy to rescue.

"You stepped in . . ."

"I know."

With the aid of Tomas' night sight, they cleaned her foot off with one slow push of the pump handle—the back of her heel had scabbed over, but she still had to bite back a shriek as the cold water rushed over the broken blisters—and filled the canteen with the second. As they crossed to the north side of the square, they heard a cackle and a soft, "Nice doggie."

"And the emperor uses men like that to plan his campaigns," Tomas snorted and changed.

Mirian glanced back toward the silhouette of the Soothsayer by the well. "It seems to be working for him so far.

Chapter Seven

DANIKA STARED OUT the tiny window at the sun rising over the Kresentian Empire and remembered how Ryder used to come back into the house after his morning run, how she'd hear his toenails against the oak floor in the hall and then the pad of his bare feet as he crossed the bedroom. It always woke her although she often pretended it didn't just so she could shriek in indignation as he dove into the bed and wrapped his body around hers, his skin damp and cool. Every morning since she'd told him about the baby, he'd paused by the bed to stand and stare and she'd stopped pretending sleep so she could open her eyes and see his expression. See how much he loved her and his child to be.

If he was alive, he'd be going crazy, unable to leave Aydori and come after them.

If he was dead . . .

She pressed her bound wrists against the slight curve of her belly. If he was dead, she'd mourn him once she got their child safely home.

Once in the empire, the smoothness of the roads had finally allowed the sleep insisted on by exhaustion, both friend and foe closing their eyes and surrendering. Danika had forced herself to stay awake until she could whisper the suggestion that they were better men than this into Tagget and Carlsan's dreams. She sent what comfort she could to Kirstin although the other woman gave no indication she'd heard, even though she was nearly as strong in air as Danika herself, the bright blue mage flecks brilliantly obvious against her dark brown eyes.

They changed the horses just after dawn at an actual posting inn designed for moving Imperial mail coaches in and out again as quickly as possible. Danika had the sudden image of an anthill stirred with a stick as the horn sounded. There were no soldiers standing around the yard, watching and guarding, just terribly efficient grooms hustling the spent horses away and slipping fresh horses between the shafts. Yawning kitchen staff handed out bowls of porridge as though they started every morning serving Imperial prisoners. For all Danika knew, they did.

Their soldiers relaxed again now they were not only out of Aydori but out of the duchies. Everyone from Lieutenant Geurin down to Private Kretien—young enough his five days of beard made a barely visible shadow edging plump cheeks—was less tense on this side of the Imperial border.

The old Imperial border, Danika corrected herself. The border was now at the edge of Aydori and trying to extend further.

Only Sergeant Black continued to split his attention a dozen different ways, but, as Danika understood it, that was part of being a sergeant. Even he had relaxed, however, no longer keeping his prisoners from talking in the line for the privy.

"The emperor's spending a fortune on this," Stina muttered, scraping the bottom of her porridge bowl. "Three sets of posting horses at each stage, arming his soldiers with silver shot . . . Do you think his Soothsayers came from conquered nations and they're trying to bankrupt the empire?"

Annalyse giggled and, although there were dried tear tracks on her cheeks, the sound contained more amusement than hysteria, Danika noted gratefully. She caught Jesine's eye over Kirstin's shoulder as the two of them came out of the privy. The Healer shook her head and, as Stina pulled Kirstin into the circle of her warmth and began gently chivying her to eat, Danika moved to join Jesine at the water barrel.

"As long as I have this net on, I'm limited to a visual diagnosis," Jesine growled. "I can't tell if attempting to remove the net injured her, or if she's suffering emotionally more than the rest of us."

"She has to be thinking of her twins."

"Granted. But Stina has three in Trouge, and thinking of them hasn't shut her off from the rest of the Pack."

"Have you met Stina's children?"

Jesine grinned. Stina's eldest had once disemboweled a rabbit under her dining room table, ruining an expensive rug. "Good point." Then she sobered. "It could also be the new pregnancy, but I couldn't get her to talk to me about how she's feeling."

"Maybe she doesn't know she's carrying. You told me that you only suspected you were and you're a Healer."

"That's possible." Jesine took a long drink and sighed. "I'm so tired of my head aching and afraid I'm getting used to the feeling. They won't remove the nets when we get to Karis, will they?"

Danika showed teeth. "Not if they're smart."

In novels, the heroine would wake, not know where she was, and enjoy a moment of blissful ignorance before facing the day. Mirian knew where she was the moment she opened her eyes; burrowed into a pile of old straw in the corner of a three-sided shed. Having nearly drowned then been captured by Imperial soldiers, she was on her way to Karis to rescue the Mage-pack and faced another day of sore feet, aching legs, needing a bath, and not having enough to eat.

Up by the rough boards of the roof, a fly struggled to free itself from a tattered spiderweb.

Mirian snorted. The Lady could be less than subtle, but she didn't actually need Her reminder. Sore feet, aching legs, hunger, unpleasant odors . . . they all beat attending card parties with her mother, listening to monologues about unmarried and available members of the Pack, and ignoring the Imperial advance.

"Good. You're awake."

Tomas no longer radiated warmth beside her. Mirian blinked and pushed herself up on her elbows, peering around until she found him sitting in a patch of sunlight spilling through the open side of the goat shed. All she knew about goats came from a childhood misunderstanding about her late grandfather's gout attack, so she'd taken Tomas' word for the identity of the shed's intended occupants.

He had clothes on. Tomas, not her grandfather. Her grandfather had always been impeccably dressed, wearing the stiff brocades of his youth until the day he died. Tomas, on the other hand, wore brown wool trousers, a shirt of unbleached linen, and a frayed tweed jacket that looked like he'd grown out of it and hadn't been able to afford to replace it. His feet were bare and dirty, but then so were hers.

"Where did you . . . ? Never mind." She emerged from the straw, using both hands to brush bits off the front of her clothes. "I suspect I'll be happier not knowing. You're going to stay on two legs?"

"It'll be less frustrating than running circles around you on four." He reached into the jacket's pocket. "But I also got this."

This was a thick collar with a brass buckle. Mirian took it from his outstretched hand and squinted down at the brass nameplate attached to the leather. "Duke?"

Tomas shrugged. "Not everyone likes their landlord."

"Or they really liked dogs and considered it a compliment." The collar looked huge dangling from her finger, but it wouldn't have been overly large on the guard dogs they'd seen last night. "Does it fit?"

"I don't know. I didn't want to put it on and change in case it was too tight."

"Should we . . ." Mirian suddenly found herself at a loss for words. The Pack didn't wear collars; they weren't dogs. When she thought of buckling the heavy leather around Tomas' throat, her cheeks grew almost painfully hot. "Not now," she said, answering the question she hadn't quite asked and silently handed it back.

"It's a better disguise than a frayed rope." Tomas shoved it back into his jacket pocket like it meant nothing at all and held out a small, round loaf of bread. "I got this, too," he said, and offered her half.

It was chewier than she was used to, and her stomach growled as she struggled to swallow the last mouthful.

"You're still hungry. I had a couple of mourning doves, but . . ."

Mirian waved off the thought of raw mourning dove for breakfast and turned to deal with the blanket. Folded around the hole she'd cut for Tomas' head, it was still the best way to carry everything. By the time she finished packing up, Tomas had gone outside, so she followed him, squinting up at the sun. "It's late. You let me sleep."

He shrugged, pulling at a loose thread on his cuff. "I had to get clothes. And some food." As the thread came free, he looked up at her from under the fall of dark fur that nearly reached his eyes. He had the longest fur in skin she could remember seeing on any of the Pack. It completely covered the points of his ears. "Getting to Karis isn't going to be easy."

He was watching for her reaction, Mirian realized, not even trying to hide that he was waiting to see if she'd changed her mind. She shrugged and enjoyed the absence of her mother's objection to the gesture. "We'll have to tell the emperor we object to his scheduling. If it were fall, we could forage for apples and nuts and . . ."

"Snow."

"You forage for snow?"

The points of his teeth just barely showed as he grinned and said, "Snow falls in the fall. And there's apple trees in that fence bottom."

"But no apples." Mirian frowned at the tangled branches, only just leafed out. "How can you identify an apple tree with no apples?"

"You said you had first level earth."

"Which has surprisingly little to do with botany."

"Apple wood has a distinctive scent. Here, I'll prove it."

"You don't . . ." But he was already gone. She had no idea why Tomas Hagen needed her to know he knew apple wood, but, since he seemed to, she followed.

As she reached the fence bottom, he bent a branch down toward her. "See that bud with the pink? That's an apple blossom. My grandfather is an Earth-mage. I used to spend time with him in the orchards outside Trouge."

Mirian stared at the bud and remembered the honeysuckle in Bercarit. She'd always thought forcing flowers to bloom was a silly parlor trick that allowed equally silly girls to be tested for earth-craft without getting their hands dirty, but that was before half of a small loaf of bread had become her entire breakfast. Reaching past Tomas, she wrapped her hand around the branch beside his.

Felt the life inside the tree.

Nudged it.

Delicate pink-and-white blossoms released their scent into the morning air.

Logically, if she could speed the blossoming then she should be able to speed the entire process. It was, after all, only a difference of degree.

One more nudge.

"Mirian?"

Her stomach growled, and she *shoved*.

Petals fluttered to the ground, covering her nearer foot. The base of each blossom swelled and kept swelling until the branch sagged under the weight of a dozen dark red apples the size of Mirian's fist. Sagged until it cracked and broke. Tomas caught it before it hit the ground.

He looked at the apples, rubbed the back of his neck with his free hand, then looked at Mirian. "My grandfather says you can't force a to tree bear fruit, that the best orchards have mixed varieties because each blossom has to be pollinated from another tree."

"I didn't know that," Mirian admitted, picking an apple and taking a bite. The flesh was white with a few pink streaks. It was crisp and sweet and juicy and the most delicious apple she'd ever eaten. "It doesn't seem to matter."

"It should."

Mirian rolled her eyes and waved the apple at him. "But it doesn't."

Tomas ate one of the apples because Mirian looked at him like he was an idiot when he didn't want to. He didn't enjoy it. It smelled more like Mirian than like an apple and while that wasn't exactly a hardship, it *was* strange. His grandfather helped keep Trouge fed, went out into the fields and orchards with the other Earth-mages in the Mage-pack and got his hands dirty because that's what Earth-mages did.

His gray eyes were nearly brown with mage marks.

"Maybe because he's not at first level, it never occurred to him to try."

He turned as Mirian closed the pouch over the last of the apples. "Him?"

"Maybe it never occurred to your grandfather to try," she explained, then added, "you were obviously still thinking about it."

"It's weird."

She made a face but didn't object when he took the blanket roll from her and hung it from his good shoulder. He followed as she crossed to the pond where she wrapped the bulk of her skirt up onto the front of her legs before she crouched and filled the canteen.

"That's mostly frog shi . . . waste," he amended at the last minute. Long-legged shadows dove for the depths around clumps of greenish-black translucent eggs.

"First level water purifies." She took a drink then offered it to him.

"Why?" The water in the canteen definitely smelled better than the water in the pond.

Her brows drew in deep enough to make a little vee over her nose. "Why?"

"I'm no mage, but it seems a strange place to start."

"Strange like the apples?"

"Strange like complicated."

"Oh. They say it's because convincing water to be nothing but water is easy."

That didn't sound easy, but as the water tasted like it had come from a spring and not the next thing to a cesspit in a goat pasture, he was impressed.

"The next level involves parting water," she continued, almost absently as he handed back the canteen. "The university built an artificial stream in back of the Water Hall. To move into second level, you had to cross it without getting your feet wet. It seemed a bit precious to me because *parting* water means *moving* water, so if you could get across the stream with dry feet, you should be able to move any water anywhere." Canteen refilled, she straightened and swirled one foot then the other in the pond. At first Tomas thought she was making a point, her mouth pressed into a thin line of disapproval at the university. Then he realized she was washing off the dirt and blood, the cold water painful against blisters on her heels. He hoped first level healing—or whatever level she was at—would be up to the contents of the pond. Hunt Pack learned not to wash a wound with dirty water. It seemed Mage-pack didn't care.

When her feet were as clean as they were likely to get, she took a long careful step back onto new grass instead of mud and said, "My mother could keep her feet dry, as she informed me every time we passed a puddle even though *she* hadn't tested high enough to attend the university."

Until she mentioned her mother and started to smell angry, he'd thought she was talking to distract him from the apples.

"When you get right down to it," she added, heading toward the road, "it's a fairly useless skill. If there's a puddle in your way, go around. If there's a river, build a bridge. By third level, you can convince rain not to fall on you. Or you could carry an umbrella."

Tomas frowned at the pond, decided he wasn't hungry enough for frog, then hurried to catch up. "Are you sure that's how it works?"

"The university may have been confused by my breadth of mediocrity, but they did let me in."

The Mage-pack had no first level mages. Harry was no more than second, but Harry was a soldier and his friend, not a mage, and while he'd been upset about not qualifying for the artillery, he'd only really cared when it came to his stupid crush on Geneviene. He did, however, always make sure the soldiers under his command had hot food and coffee. Had been. Made sure. When he finally remembered to always refer to Harry in the past tense, would it be real? "Maybe they start with purifying because it's useful."

She shot him a glance that made him think his voice hadn't been entirely steady. When the brittle edges were absent from her reply, he was sure of it. "Maybe, but it's still a matter of degree. If you're only powerful enough for first level, there's a limit to how much water you can purify. First level Water-mages usually find work in high-end restaurants. First level Fire-mages are thrilled about the new gaslights because they have to be lit every evening and first level Earth-mages work with florists—which is almost respectable. First level Air-mages can blow out a chandelier, one candle at a time, without getting a ladder, so there's always domestic service for employers with low expectations. A couple of girls had suggestions I'm not going to repeat about uses for maintaining your own body temperature."

Wait . . . "*Girls* had suggestions?"

Her laugh felt like fingers rubbing behind his ears. He smiled freely for the first time in days as they reached the road and he took his position upwind of her right shoulder.

"You'd be surprised at what women talk about when there's no men around. The point is," Mirian sighed, the exhalation exaggerated, "with five first levels and *only* five first levels, my classmates made any number of useful suggestions. Oh, wait, I can do first level metal now, so there's always a future of finding coins in sofa cushions."

"It's just . . ." He hadn't forgotten the two second levels, but they seemed incidental. The apples had been more worrying. ". . . you don't smell like a first level mage."

"So I've heard."

Now she sounded sad. Lord and Lady, was it him or was she always that confusing?

Mirian had a feeling that every time she let an opportunity to mention Jaspyr Hagen pass, the memory of what they'd shared, already ephemeral, was shredded a little more. But she refused have her mage-craft defined by the interest of a man. That would make her no better than the silly girls who wafted their scent toward the Pack, as though that and that alone would validate their existence.

"We could move faster if we'd stolen a horse in Herdon."

She counted ten strides before Tomas caught up to the change of subject.

"Horses and the Pack don't exactly get along. Not unless they're raised together. My cousin Jared unseated half the Traitonian cavalry."

"Weren't they on our side?"

"You'd think. Their general was a bigot, and Jared was . . ."

Dead. She could feel his dead pile up in the pause, so she reached out and squeezed his hand. Words like *I'm sorry* were so inadequate they'd be insulting. After a moment, he squeezed back and, when she released him, cleared his throat and said, "Can you ride?"

"No."

"Then why did you think we should have stolen a horse?"

"Because you could run on four legs, too, and it would be faster."

"How would you falling off a horse be faster?"

"I wouldn't necessarily fall off. Besides . . ." She turned far enough to wave at the smoke rising from the chimneys of Herdon, still not very far behind them. ". . . it has to be faster than walking."

"It really doesn't. We'll walk for fifty paces, run for fifty paces. It's what the volunteers do . . ." More dead in the pause. ". . . when they have to cover ground. Can you run?"

She followed his line of sight down to her feet, dust from the road already sticking to damp skin. At least the dried blood was gone. "Who walks to a rescue? I can manage fifty paces."

It wasn't just her feet that hurt. Ankles, knees, hips, calves, thighs . . . she felt like one of the labeled anatomy posters at the front of the Healer Hall. Personally, she'd have called the first fifty paces of running *limping quickly*. Eyes on the road to avoid the occasional loose stone on the packed clay, Mirian was peripherally aware of Tomas running easily beside her, and a quick glance showed none of the resentment that had hovered around his four-legged form yesterday like a particularly acrid smoke.

By the third set, her muscles had loosened up and running came easier.

By the tenth, fifty paces walking wasn't enough for her to catch her breath.

Tomas, who'd started to run on fifty, circled back beside her when she didn't. "It's all right. We'll walk a while longer."

Mirian found enough breath to mutter, "Told you. Should've stolen a horse."

He had dimples when he grinned. She hadn't noticed that before.

They passed a set of cart tracks that led east to a small farm, the stubble of last year's crops still filling the field nearest the road. They passed a trail leading west, and Tomas pointed out the tracks of the deer that had made it.

Then they ran.

Forty-nine. Fifty.

And stopped.

"Do you know where this road goes?"

"Does it matter? I know the Mage-pack is at the end of it."

"It can't be one road from Herdon to Karis. We're the width of two conquered duchies away from the old Imperial border." When Tomas lowered heavy brows, Mirian sighed. "Too sensible?"

"A little."

And they ran again.

Forty-nine. Fifty.

Shrugging out of the too-small jacket, Tomas twitched inside the confines of his remaining clothes.

"What's wrong?"

"The trousers are itchy."

Mirian managed to keep from laughing but only just. "I think they're made to have small clothes under them."

"Why not make them so they don't itch?"

"I honestly don't know."

An enormous ox patty, still damp enough to suggest war hadn't stopped lumber from the mill heading toward buyers, blocked her path and she jumped it rather than go around. The sun was shining, birds were singing, and, while she didn't have much breath to spare and they were heading to a fight with the emperor himself, walking along a country road with Tomas Hagen was almost pleasant. Her mother would be . . .

. . . appalled. Mirian fought the urge to talk about the weather and ask Tomas his opinion on the new higher collars for evening jackets.

They were running when they passed tracks leading to a farm tucked into a hollow not far from the road. One of the farm's outbuildings had recently burned down, a pair of charred timbers rising out of the ruin like blackened bones, the smell of damp ash heavy on the air. A girl out in the garden froze, hoe half raised, and watched them pass. The distance was too great to see her expression, but from the way she stood, curled in on herself, it looked like she was afraid. A pig in a pen by the garden watched warily as well.

Mirian slowed to a walk, then she stopped and turned up the track.

"Where are you going?"

"To trade apples for . . . not apples. Stay there, I'll be quick." She pulled two from the pouch as she walked. They looked so red against her hand she felt like she was in a fairy story. The girl looked at the apples, looked at Mirian, and finally limped to the edge of the garden.

It wasn't the fruit that had convinced her to approach, Mirian realized. It was the bruising on her face that matched the bruising on the girl's. When the girl glanced at Tomas, Mirian shook her head. "No, it wasn't him."

She took two apples with trembling fingers, then two more. "How?"

Even Mirian knew apples didn't look like that after having been stored all winter, not without help. "Earth-mage."

Still holding the apples, the girl jerked back, searching for mage marks. Mirian opened her eyes wider. After an extended search, the girl's shoulders sagged, and Mirian was just as glad she didn't have to tell her she had no time to help.

A glance down at the apples. "Trade? We got sausage they didn't find." Pyrahn wasn't that different a language from Aydori, although accent dragged the girl's words sideways.

The pig watched her as the girl ran to the cottage. Mirian wondered if there'd recently been a second. The cottage door hung crookedly from the frame, inexpertly repaired, and through the gap she heard voices but not words. Saw a pale face at the front window, features too distorted through the tiny panes of thick green glass for her to tell if it was a man or a woman. Then girl returned with a length of cooked sausage as big around as two of Mirian's fingers. She handed it over silently.

"Thank you."

Mirian had gone three steps back toward the road when she heard, "Where you going?"

Right now? Eventually? "To get back something the Imperials took from us."

Arms wrapped around her torso, the girl's mouth twisted. The war had paused here on its way to Herdon and the sawmill. "In them carriages?"

The road had been empty all morning. Three coaches careening past this farm at full speed would be noted, day or night. "Yes."

"You won't catch 'em."

"Not today. But we will."

After a long moment, the girl nodded. "All right then."

It sounded like a benediction. Mirian nodded in turn and joined Tomas on the road. "We can do this," she said as she handed him half the sausage. "We can run and walk and find food and . . ." To her surprise, he held the piece of sausage to his nose and took a deep breath.

"You were upwind," he told her, eyes watering. "And these trousers are itchy enough."

Concentrating on putting one foot in front of the other, Mirian bounced off Tomas' arm, grabbed it, stopped. "What?"

"There's a horse coming."

"With a rider?" She was too tired to be embarrassed by his expression. "Right. Of course." After a moment, she realized she still held his arm and released it. The fields on both sides of the road were dead grass and small cedars and a low evergreen Mirian didn't know the name of. *Not relevant*, she told herself and then aloud: "Should we hide?"

Tomas moved around to put himself between her and the approaching rider. "No time. If you see an enemy run, you can't stop yourself from giving chase."

"You're going to chase the horse?"

"What?" He threw a confused glance back over his shoulder. "No. If we run now, the rider will chase us. Because we're running."

Not entirely certain that applied to those without the option of having four legs, Mirian was about to protest when the horse appeared around a curve, disappeared into a dip in the road, and suddenly reappeared impossibly close. Quickly buttoning her jacket, she tried to look as though she'd been displaced by war rather than like an active enemy of the empire. She watched the road in front of her feet, concentrated on the swing of her skirt against her legs, and looked up at the last minute, unable to help herself.

The rider wore a familiar uniform, Imperial purple jacket over black trousers and boots, bicorn crammed down on his head. Tomas had said the empire would have taken over the mill. The destruction at the farm was proof soldiers had gone to Herdon, so, on this road, the mill was the only logical destination. Horse and rider had nothing to do with the two of them.

If the soldiers who'd taken the Mage-pack were worried Tomas had survived, they'd set up an ambush. Captain Reiter and his men hadn't had time to get far enough in front of them to send a courier back. All very logical, but Mirian's palms were wet, and her heart pounded in time with the horse's hooves anyway.

As the rider passed, he looked up, saw her, slid his gaze down to

Tomas, frowned, began to straighten in the saddle, pulling back on the reins . . .

Tomas snarled.

Without breaking stride, the horse moved to the far side of the road. Mirian had no idea horses could move sideways like that. The rider swore, grabbed a double handful of mane, and hung in midair for a moment, one foot in the stirrup the other hooked on the far edge of the saddle, trying desperately to keep from falling. Bit in its teeth, the horse ignored both words and reins, equally desperate to put as much distance as possible between itself and the predator. By the time the courier got himself seated again, he'd gone far enough past that he kept going.

Mirian released a breath she couldn't remember holding. "I wonder what he thought he saw."

"Pack," Tomas grunted as he moved back to her right.

The horse certainly had, but the rider? Unlike some Pack, unlike Jaspyr, Tomas on two legs wasn't obvious. He was young enough to have no facial scarring and his fur not only covered the points of his ears but was a solid black that passed for hair. Even in Aydori, it might take a second look from non Pack. Armin hadn't realized and Tomas had been naked; usually a dead giveaway. "But the courier was Imperial."

"There's Pack in the empire."

Surprised, she had to take three quick steps to catch up. Thirty-seven. Thirty-eight. Thirty-nine. Almost time to run again. "I didn't know that."

"We don't talk about it much. Sometimes people can't find their place in the Pack they're born into and they wander. Sometimes they go higher up into the mountains, to Orin or to Ural where it's nearly all Pack." He snorted. "Rough wood, raw meat, and hearty beer."

"You've been?"

"Not likely, but sometimes people wander out. And sometimes the wanderers end up in the empire. Or somewhere that then becomes the empire," he growled.

And neither said, *like Aydori* although Mirian knew they were both thinking it. "Will they help us?"

"They might, if we can find them. But interactions between small isolated Packs without direct family ties can be . . ." His hand cut the air in a gesture that suggested *violent* or *bloody*. ". . . difficult."

Between Packs? Mirian wondered as they started to run. *Are we a Pack?* But she didn't know how to ask without seeming stupid or arrogant or both.

By late afternoon, they began passing more farms and, without discussion, stopped running even the short distances Mirian could manage. She didn't know Tomas' reasons, but she found herself hobbled by the knowledge that young ladies did not run regardless of how little the rules for young ladies applied to the present situation. It was one thing to run unseen out in the country and another entirely to do it approaching civilization. It helped a little when she reminded herself it would be a very bad idea to attract too much attention.

The road made a long sloping curve to the left, past fields with herds of black-and-white cows, and disappeared under a sprawl of red roofs that rapidly became larger buildings packed close, haze obscuring details in the distance.

"Is it smoke from the war?"

Tomas lifted his head, nostrils flared. "The war was over in Pyrahn the minute the duke rabbited for the border, and Imperials don't burn down the emperor's property."

"A rebellion?" They couldn't be the only people in Pyrahn fighting back.

"I think it's factories."

"Factories?" Mirian squinted, trying to get a better look. "Then this has to be Abyek." The road they'd been following, the road the coaches had taken the Mage-pack down must have turned almost due north and brought them out to the Aydori Road. Schoolhouse geography taught that Abyek was the largest city in Pyrahn, larger than the Duke's Seat. The current duke's great grandmother had built it to take advantage of new trade with Aydori. The Pack Leader at the time had insisted it be built a full day's travel from the border so that the Pack would never have to deal with the stink of manufacturing should there ever be a shift in the prevailing winds. Most of Bercarit had been built of Abyek bricks fired with Aydori coal and other industry had soon joined the brickworks. "I'm fairly certain Mother bought my sister a set of dishes from Abyek."

"They must've changed horses here."

It took Mirian a moment to separate the horses from the dishes. "Are we going in?"

Tomas nodded toward their shadows, stretching out to the right. "It's too late to figure out how to go around. It'll be nearly dark by the time we get there, and I bet this road will take us right . . ."

"Looky, looky, looky."

Attention on Abyek, Mirian hadn't noticed the five farm workers coming down a lane toward the road until the largest spoke, and by then they were nearly on top of them. She didn't know if Tomas hadn't seen them or merely believed they were beneath his attention as Pack. Or believed they wouldn't be stupid enough to approach Pack.

In Aydori, they wouldn't have been. Before she could remind Tomas that not only were they not in Aydori but no one knew him as Pack, they were blocked by a belligerent half circle of men in dirty smocks with dirtier scarves tied round their necks.

"Ignore them," the memory of her mother said. *"We do not acknowledge the existence of ruffians."*

Clearly her mother's advice worked better when applied to bricklayers in the city.

"I'm guessin' you two don't know there's a toll on this road. Bin a war, you know. We all gotta pay." Not much of the largest man's breadth was fat and he was easily a head taller than Tomas. Mirian had never understood the phrase *fists like hams* before. She did now.

Tomas let the bedroll with his jacket slung over it slide off his shoulder as he stepped forward. Mirian caught it before it hit the ground. "Move aside."

"Move aside?" His beefy face flushed red when he laughed and the other four laughed as well, a beat behind the leader. "You look like the gutter all barefoot and rags, but you talk like you think your shit don't stink. Get thrown out of your fancy house on your fancy ass when the Imperials come through, did you? Well, I don't give a rat's ass what you were, there's a toll on this road for the likes of what you are now. And since I doubt you got coin to pay it, I'll take a little time with your girl." There were two teeth missing on the right side of his mouth when he smiled, and he looked at her the way Best had, like she was a thing not a person; only without Best's minimal excuse of being the enemy.

Experience had definitively proven she didn't need mage marks to set his trousers on fire.

The memory of cooking meat and blisters rising up under where a ginger eyebrow had been stopped her.

"One more chance . . ." Tomas bit each word off in a way that should have been a warning. ". . . to move aside."

"You filthy . . ."

Tomas stripped with the efficiency of long practice. Aydori fashions would have made it easier, but he was still impressively fast. As his trousers hit the road, Mirian found herself surprised by the difference between seeing him take off his clothes and seeing him without them. The latter meant he was Pack, just changed, the former that he was . . . well, undressing. It was a subtle distinction she really wished she could talk over with her sister.

And one she shouldn't be thinking of now.

Astonishment held the farm workers in place as Tomas folded forward, enormous front paws slamming down on the road. Then his hackles rose, and he snarled. In the firelight, he'd passed as a very large dog. These men weren't given the choice of mistaking what he was.

Four of the five men turned and ran back up the lane. One left a tumbled pair of wooden clogs behind.

Their leader paled but held his ground. Or froze in place, too terrified to move; Mirian wasn't sure.

Tomas stepped forward, stiff-legged, and snarled again.

A dark stain spread on the front of homespun trousers. He turned, fell, scrambled to his feet, and ran after his friends, keening in fear.

"If you see an enemy run, you can't stop yourself from giving chase."

Mirian grabbed a handful of Tomas' fur, imagined a candle on the end of his nose, imagined blowing it out with air warmed by her body and hoped that would be enough to direct her scent over Tomas' face. A handful of fur wouldn't stop him. "Tomas! He's not worth the delay."

He jerked free of her grip, took two steps, and changed. "My clothes," he said, reaching back without turning. His voice sounded rough. Given the snarling, Mirian wasn't surprised.

She scooped his shirt and trousers off the ground and pressed them into his hand. He had a scar just under his left shoulder blade, enough muscle that his spine was in a shallow valley of pale flesh, and dimples . . . She jerked her gaze back up to the scar. "Why aren't they in the Pyrahnian army? They seem like they'd enjoy shooting people."

"If they were in the army, they'd have retreated to Aydori."

"You're right. We don't want them there." She twitched her jacket into place, smoothed her skirt with both hands, checked that the bedroll was still, well, rolled, patted at her hair . . .

"Mirian?"

He'd turned without her noticing and was staring at her, one hand clutching the hem of his shirt. There was a dusting of fine black hair on the back of his knuckles. She hadn't noticed that before. "What?"

"Are you all right?"

"Of course. She let the bedroll slide off her shoulder, hitched it back up, and smoothed her skirt.

"You're shaking."

"I'm fine. If we were staying around here, I'd be worried. Big-and-ugly doesn't strike me as the sort who takes embarrassment well." Her laugh sounded a little stretched, even to her. "And that's all that happened. You scared him. He ran. They all ran. Fortunately, we're just passing through. But he had a point. Well, not really a point." Words slipped from her mouth like beads sliding off a string; unstoppable now they'd started to fall. All she seemed to be able to do was send other words after them. She followed the bedroll to the ground. "People judge you if you're barefoot, don't they? Shoes seem to be the dividing line between worthwhile and wretched." One boot already out and in her hand, she looked up. Tomas had moved closer. "Not if you're Pack, at least not in Aydori. If you see a well-dressed person without shoes in Aydori, you know they're Pack. And even in shoes, Pack wouldn't wear these." She waved the boots. "Too slow to get on and off. But we're not in Aydori, are we? They saw your feet and didn't know you were Pack. This will keep happening." The leather had dried and stiffened, but she sat back, skirt billowing around her, and worked the boot open, one foot stretched out, ready to receive it.

"Mirian?" Tomas' hand closed around her wrist. She needed to pay more attention; she hadn't seen him drop to one knee. Then his other hand gently cupped the unbruised side of her jaw. "Tell me what to do to make it better."

"You don't . . . It isn't . . ." Mirian pressed into his touch, chasing the warmth, then pulled away and watched his hand fall slowly back to rest on his knee. She clenched her teeth against the spill of words, breathing through her nose while she forced herself to recognize that nothing had happened. Nothing they couldn't deal with. After a moment, she swallowed, took a deep breath, and met Tomas' worried gaze. "It didn't occur to me that we couldn't just rescue the Mage-pack. That we'd have to deal with all sorts of other people on our way to defeating the Imperial army. Stupid, right?"

Tomas thought about it for a moment, then shrugged. "How would you know? We've never done it before."

To his surprise, she started to laugh. He'd said the only comforting thing he could think of. He didn't think it was funny.

"We've never done it before?"

Maybe it was a little funny.

"You have a place on a wagon heading out tomorrow afternoon, Captain Reiter. It will take you to the garrison at Lyonne where these orders will procure a seat on the first available mail couch. If all goes well, you'll be in Karis in a week."

"Thank you, Sergeant." Reiter accepted the paperwork, nodded, and left the office. He'd learned not to argue with military bureaucracy years ago. A ride on a nearly empty supply wagon had taken him from the battlefield to Abyek—a dawn-to-dark trip that suggested even the old Duke of Pyrahn hadn't wanted his cities too close to the Aydori border and the beastmen who were his allies. He then cooled his heels for twelve hours while his orders were processed. Reminding the most officious major he'd ever met that they came directly from his Imperial Highness the Emperor Leopald by way of General Loreau had no effect. The major had merely sniffed and pointed out in return that this was the Imperial army and all their orders came from the emperor.

There were days, Reiter thought, when hurry up and wait should be made the army's official motto. Not that he was in a hurry to get back to Karis. While his loss of the sixth mage was a direct result of the artifact malfunctioning, facts often were ignored when it came time to place blame. And Lieutenant Lord Geurin would have placed plenty of it before Reiter caught up.

His time was his own for another twenty-four hours, so he settled his bicorn as he stepped out of the only permanent building the garrison yet boasted and crossed between the geometrically precise lines of tents, past the garrison work detail toiling at the perimeter wall. Men, women, and children of Abyek and the surrounding countryside hauled bricks and mixed mortar under the command of an Imperial mason and a guard made up of those not quite functional enough to return to the front lines but not so broken they could be discharged. After a hundred years of expansion, it was an easy position to fill.

The prisoners wore hobbles, their time on the work detail determined by the severity of their crime against the empire. He'd been uneasy the first time he ever saw children hobbled, but after he saw a soldier's head crushed by a piece of masonry pushed from the roof of a building by a pair of ten year olds, days after the actual battle was over, he learned to just walk by.

Today, he walked by and across the Aydori Road and into Abyek.

Shadows had started to gather by the time they reached the outskirts of the city. Tomas chafed at their pace—Mirian's insistence on wearing her boots, on needing the social standing they provided, had slowed them considerably. She still limped as they passed between a double line of houses spreading out from the city to meet the farms, but at least she limped faster, the heat and pressure of her feet having softened the leather.

She had also taken the time to retrieve the farm worker's abandoned clogs, and Tomas had finally, reluctantly, put them on when his own feet had started attracting attention from men and women hurrying home from work at the end of the day. Not the attention he was used to as Pack, but sideways glances that lifted the hair off the back of his neck and kept a low growl rumbling intermittently in his throat.

"They don't look frightened, exactly," Mirian murmured, moving close enough they could speak without being overheard. "More like they're not comfortable in their own skin."

He'd almost gotten used to his world having been divided into the scent of Mirian and the scent of everything else. Under scents layered on by work and time, the sweat of the people passing by them smelled sharp. Strained. "There'll be Imperials here. This is the new edge of the empire, so they'll be building a garrison. I guess it takes a while to get used to being conquered."

The road split and split again, the houses built closer together until they became long rows of two-story brick built tight to the road. The people on these streets kept their eyes to themselves. Scent crowded on top of scent and Tomas breathed shallowly through his mouth to keep from being overwhelmed. It was no more crowded than parts of Bercarit or even the old, non-Pack parts of Trouge, so he knew he'd eventually be able to push most of what flooded his nose to the background. It didn't help that the scent of the coaches had been buried, and he couldn't stop himself from casting about for them even though he knew—at least his head had known—he wouldn't be able to track them all the way to Karis.

As the road they followed came out from between two five-story tenements and into a market square, four Imperials entered from the opposite direction. They were the first he'd seen since the bullet had shattered his shoulder. The blind rage he thought he'd overcome pulled his lips back off his teeth and one arm out of his jacket . . .

"Stop it." Mirian stepped between him and the soldiers, both hands trying to tug his jacket back up onto his shoulder. "You can kill those four, but what about the twenty after them?"

"They won't have silver." His fingers sank into her upper arms, but instead of shoving her out of his way, he hung on.

"And the hundred after them? You said there was a garrison here. Enough damage will kill you even without silver. Then how do I free the Mage-pack? Tomas, stop reacting and think!"

"They killed . . ."

"I know. If not these men, then others like them."

Muscles knotted across his back with the effort it took to keep from charging across the square. Mirian had moved so close—or he'd pulled her so close, he wasn't sure which—that the only air for him to breathe in was air she'd already breathed out. He closed his eyes and matched his breathing to hers; as hers slowed, his slowed. After a moment he nodded. "You're right." When he released her arms, she made a small pained noise and his eyes snapped open. "I hurt you."

"Small price to pay to keep you alive." She smiled, mouth a shallow arc, lips pressed together. If it was supposed to make him feel better, it didn't. "I know how strong you are, and I still stepped in front of you. I'm fully capable of taking responsibility for my own actions. Besides . . ." This smile actually did make him feel a little better. ". . . it was the first time for miles I haven't been thinking about my feet."

He couldn't stop himself from smiling back. "I guess I'm happy to have been a distraction. But I'm still sorry I hurt you."

"I know."

It wasn't exactly forgiveness. When she stepped away and he dragged his jacket up into place, he realized the whole thing had happened in a matter of minutes; the four Imperials had only just reached the center of the square.

It had been a market day although only one stall remained open, the owner hurrying to finish a final sale, splitting his attention between the soldiers and his customer and the sky. While three of the Imperials stood scanning the doors and windows facing into the square, muskets cradled loosely across their left arms, right hands purposefully cupping the trigger guards, the fourth pushed past a small group of older children waiting to use the well—young enough to still be at home, but old enough to be helpful—and stepped up onto the housing.

He took a deep breath, squared his shoulders and bellowed, "This is to remind the citizens of Abyek that curfew is in place from dark until dawn. Anyone appre . . . appre . . ."

One of the children giggled and the soldier flushed.

"Anyone *breaking* curfew will be added to the garrison work detail. No exceptions." Brows drawn in, he stepped off the housing directly into the group of children. When they scrambled to get out of his way, he shoved the slowest hard enough to knock her down, stepped over her legs, and joined his waiting squad. As the children hauled their fallen companion up onto her feet, the body language of every one of them was as much anger as fear. Sooner or later one of them would challenge Imperial authority and probably get shot.

"We can't get through the city before dark," Mirian said softly.

Tomas glanced at the sky. "We might not be able to get out of this square before dark." The square was empty of everyone but them and the children, waiting for one last bucket to fill. The stall owner had disappeared down an alley, pushing his barrow before him, and the soldiers were heading out of the square to the north. "It's all right, though. Once everyone's off the streets, I can keep us away from the patrols."

"We have to eat and sleep."

Because that was the sensible thing to do. "As the coaches get farther away."

"And Karis stays right where it is."

He'd pretty much decided that her certainty was equal parts reassuring and irritating.

"The children have noticed us."

He turned in time to see a whispered conversation, hidden more by accent than by volume. As the others scattered with their water, their ambassador clomped across the cobblestones toward them. Only her scent gave away gender. Her hair cropped short like Mage-pack hair, she was dressed in faded brown trousers, a fraying sweater, and the same type of wooden clogs he wore. Hers were *also* a little too large and she nearly kicked out of them with every step. A split lip, almost healed, and scabs across her knuckles only just visible under too long sleeves marked her as a fighter. If she were Pack, she'd grow up with scars and try for the Alpha three or four times before she was actually ready.

"If you don't got nowhere to go," she said, glancing toward where the Imperials had disappeared, "the Sisters of Starlight, they got a place that way." A grubby finger pointed east. "Two streets. They painted it white." Her eye roll reminded Tomas of Mirian. "I hear they feed you, too, but you gotta listen to them talk."

"And what are the Sisters of Starlight?" Mirian asked.

"Dunno." The shrug was dismissive. "They come along behind the army. My da says it's some stupid Imperial religion."

"Thank you."

She swept a shrewd gaze over Mirian from boots to hair and snorted a nonverbal *you don't belong here* before she glanced up at the sky. "Better hurry," then she spun around and ran, the clogs ringing out her progress until she disappeared into one of the buildings across the square.

Lights were already showing in a couple of upper windows.

Tomas slipped his feet out of the clogs, no point announcing their position to Imperial patrols. "If it's the Sisters of Starlight, we'll have to run to beat curfew."

It was the Sisters or the street.

Mirian took a deep breath. "We run."

Running the edges would attract less attention; right across the middle of the square would be faster. When Mirian stumbled halfway, Tomas tucked both clogs under his right arm and grabbed her hand in time to keep her on her feet. To his surprise, she hung on, fingers wrapped tightly around his.

A white house in a row of dirty brick was easy to find even as dusk turned to dark.

The door was still open a crack when they reached it, Tomas nearly dragging Mirian the last few feet. A middle-aged woman dressed all in white who he assumed had to be one of the Sisters opened it the rest of the way, peering out into the street. "I saw you come. Hurry, hurry." Her accent was different yet again, and she smelled strongly of lavender. Tomas shoved Mirian over the threshold and followed. As the door closed emphatically behind them, he checked her forward motion and slid past her. If it was too dangerous to stay, he needed to know before they were any farther in. Before the door was locked.

There were eleven other people in the room. Seven men and four women who all looked older than they smelled. Ten of them looked down quickly rather than meet his gaze, the eleventh looked hopeful for a moment, then sighed and closed his eyes. There were two obvious couples and a woman who sat alone, as far from the others as she could get and still be in the same room. She wore trousers and one sleeve of her heavy workman's jacket had recently been soaked in gin. There was no furniture, nothing anyone could use as a weapon, only what looked like layers of worn rugs. The glass in the single window in the front wall had been painted black. Besides the gin, the room smelled of old blood and urine and stale sweat.

And lavender.

Behind him, a steel bolt slid home. Bolts were easy enough to open from the inside. He could do it in fur if he had to.

"Is safe. Is safe." The Sister pushed by him. Tomas' eyes watered a little as the scent of lavender grew momentarily stronger. "No soldiers get in. No abominations get in."

Mirian wrapped her hand around his and pushed up against his side. "Abominations?"

Distracted by the contact, Tomas managed to pull himself together enough to wonder why she bothered asking. Who knew and who cared what Imperial Starry Sisters thought were abomination.

The Sister turned back to face them, hands tucked under the loose fall of cloth that made up the top layer of her costume. "The new Prelate of the Church of the Sun," she said, as though that was enough to make everything she was about to say the absolute truth, "has declared the beastmen abomination."

"What does that mean?" Mirian asked pushing closer to him. He could feel himself sinking into softer parts.

"That they are not been cleansed by the fire."

Mirian's grip on his hand tightened enough it started to hurt. "But what does that *mean*?"

The Sister looked confused for a moment, then her face cleared and she smiled. "Oh, for the abominations. That they are not given the protections of the law and in their death, they will not be reborn in the fire. Now go, take your young man to sit. There will be food."

It took Tomas a moment to realize what *the beastmen* meant. Took him a moment to realize it meant him.

The Sister had started through a door in the back wall before he put it together. *He* had been declared an abomination by someone who'd never met him and knew nothing about him. How could a church declare a whole people abomination? It didn't make sense. He'd begun to form a protest when Mirian used her entire body to shift him to an open bit of carpet against the wall no more than three feet from the front door. He snapped his mouth closed and tried to pull away, but was too afraid of hurting her again to use the effort necessary.

She smelled better than everything else in the room combined, but he really *was* afraid of hurting her. When she tried to maneuver him down to the floor, he locked his knees.

"We can't stay." He breathed the words into the curve of her neck and tried not to inhale.

Mirian curled one arm up over his shoulder, stroking her fingers through his hair. He started to jerk away until he realized the sudden familiarity was to cover his ears. "If we're caught after curfew, the soldiers will find out." The words were warm against his cheek.

"They won't catch *me*. Not in the dark. Not on four legs. I'll go. You stay."

"I can't walk another step, and you will not leave me with these people! They smell terrible and they're filthy."

Tomas pulled back. There were dark circles under her eyes and a crazy gleam in them. Nothing about the way she held onto him said seduction. She clutched at him the way a much younger Mirian would have clutched at a rag doll. "*We're* filthy."

"Not the point!"

A hand clutched at his trouser leg and he looked down into a hopeful dark-eyed gaze. "You got a drink?"

"No."

"I need a drink."

Mirian leaned past his shoulder and showed teeth. "He said *no*."

They suddenly had a larger area of open carpet around them.

"Sit, sit, new people. There is food."

There were three Sisters now. One carried a large pot, the other two bowls and spoons.

"Sit," Mirian repeated. So he sat. And put the clogs back on.

The food was nominally stew, although it was mostly potatoes and smelled a little like lavender.

The Sister who'd let them in spoke as they ate of how science had found that the stars were also suns, were also life-givers, and as there were a thousand small suns in the sky so there would one day be a thousand Sisters ministering to those abused by war.

Leaning sideways, he breathed, "A thousand? I think her math is off."

Mirian snickered, turned it into a cough, but he felt like he'd accomplished something.

After the food, there was an opportunity to use the privy at the end of the tiny back garden then, when everyone had reclaimed their bits of carpet, the Sisters intoned a long blessing in Imperial, mostly about the burning away of sins. Two of the men, half propped against the wall and half against each other were obviously asleep before they finished.

When the Sisters took the lamps away into the kitchen and closed the door, Tomas noticed that bits of the black paint on the window had been scratched away to make star patterns. As his eyes grew more accustomed to the dark, he could make out what he thought were supposed to be the Stag and the River, both only barely visible in the minimal spill of light in from the street.

"At least they're consistently crazy," Mirian muttered against his ear. Sat up. Rummaged in the bedroll and pulled out the telescope— he recognized the whisper of its chain as she tucked it under her jacket—then pushed the bedroll back toward him. "You should sleep on this so no one tries to take it."

"Sleep on it?"

"Use it as a pillow."

"Why don't you use it as a pillow?"

"They can't sneak up on you."

Tomas wasn't sure who *they* were, but since no one could sneak up on him—at least no one in the shelter with them—he tucked it up against the wall. Without the hard ridge of the telescope, it wasn't entirely uncomfortable.

"I think there's bugs in the carpet."

"There were bugs in the straw."

"It's not the *same*."

"Risking the curfew's looking better, isn't it?"

She shot him a look of such exaggerated disdain that he snickered. The Sisters were a little crazy, but it could be worse. They had food and shelter. They were a day closer to Karis and while he could have played hide and seek with the Imperials all night, Mirian couldn't.

People were muttering and shuffling into different positions all over the room. Someone growled a profanity. Someone answered with a louder one. The air was fresher than he'd expected by the floor, less stagnant, and he wondered if Mirian had anything to do with that. Did she think about blowing out a circle of candles?

Mirian was . . .

Still sitting. And not looking as though she were about to lie down any time soon. Tomas pushed himself up on his elbows. "What?"

"I'm not putting my head on that carpet."

How was he supposed to sleep if she sat there looking disgusted all night? He couldn't change, so there seemed to be only one solution. Lying down again, Tomas patted his right shoulder.

Her brows went up.

She'd had no difficulty sleeping next to him in fur. Even though he was exactly the same person, she'd been willing to trade society's opinion for warmth and comfort. If it came to it, he'd rather be in fur. In fur, he was content with physical contact. In skin he could only hope the surrounding scents would prevent any embarrassing reactions.

Of course that wouldn't matter if Mirian kept acting like she'd been out shopping with her mother when they were introduced instead of tied to a tree. Wait . . . was it because there were people around them tonight? First, how could the opinion of these people matter? And second, given Mirian's earlier behavior, they'd no doubt already assumed the worst.

Tomas suspected neither point would provide a winning argument. He had to be . . .

. . . sensible.

Pushing himself back up again, he leaned in and whispered, "If you don't get enough sleep, you'll slow us down tomorrow."

She looked annoyed, probably because he was right, but a moment after he lay down, she settled her head on his shoulder, one hand gripping the edge of his jacket. Her sigh had a certain sound of surrender to it.

He wouldn't have been able to stop himself from pressing his lips against the top of her head had her hair not been so disgusting.

Chapter Eight

"WAKE! WAKE AS THE STARLIGHT fades and we are given over into the care of the one Sun!"

Mirian jerked her head up off Tomas' shoulder and stared blearily across the room at one of the Sisters. She thought it might be the Sister who'd let them, in but they'd done such a good job of making themselves "*. . . as similar as the stars in the sky . . .*" that she couldn't be certain.

"Wake!" the Sister declared again. "And bid the stars farewell!" Overdress flapping, she hung a lamp on the brass hook by the door and disappeared back into the kitchen.

Surrounded by grumbling and wet, hacking coughs, Mirian sat up and yawned. Even as exhausted as she'd been, the sounds coming from the people around her had chased sleep off four or five times in the night. Creaking. Snoring. Moaning. Muttering. Once she'd woken to the sound of wet, ragged breathing moving closer. Tomas had growled, a low rumble deep in his chest she felt as much as heard, and the breathing had moved away.

Tomas didn't seem to want to meet her gaze as he stiff-armed himself into a sitting position, shoulder blades against the wall, knees up. While he'd offered his shoulder as a pillow, two nights had been enough for her to grow used to the liberties fur allowed. She had a horrible feeling, given the position she'd woken in, she'd crossed the line between keeping her head off the carpet and cuddling.

"I'm very sorry for not allowing you personal space," she murmured, already so close she didn't need to lean in or raise her voice.

His cheeks flushed, and he pulled the bedroll out from behind him onto his lap. "You couldn't put your head on the carpet. I understood."

"It's different when you're in fur. You're more . . ." Perhaps *more* wasn't the right word. "Or you're less . . ." No, that wasn't right either. She sighed, gathered her skirt up out of her way, and rolled up onto her knees. Assuming that *bidding the stars farewell* meant it was dawn, the curfew had ended. Only a single bolt secured the door. "We should go."

"Go?" Tomas looked startled. His head whipped around toward the kitchen door as it opened. "Porridge!" And back to her. "I smell porridge. We should eat."

Ignoring, for the moment, that it was a long walk to Karis, Mirian couldn't understand why he'd want to stay. "We can eat while we walk."

"Eat what? Hunt Pack rules, eat when you can. This is free porridge, Mirian. Porridge doesn't grow on trees." He sounded as though he were babbling even though individual words were clipped off short.

"Their church says you're an abomination," she hissed under the rise in noise as the three Sisters and their cauldron appeared. "It's dangerous to stay."

"It's stupid to starve!"

Her stomach growled and she sat back down. "If they drag you off to the fire, I'm not going to rescue you."

"I don't need you to rescue me."

"Fine!"

The porridge was terrible. Plain boiled oats with no honey or cream and given the amount of grit, Mirian suspected the Sisters had bought the last sweepings off the millstone. But Tomas was right, it was stupid to starve, and the only money they had to buy food was in the purse taken from the dead soldier. She tried to swallow without tasting, mushing the lumps against the roof of her mouth to save her teeth. Across the room, a man with a long stained beard coughed and splattered porridge over the woman next to him; two of the Sisters had to stop praying to break up the fight.

Four days ago, she'd been eating eggs and kidneys and toast in the breakfast room, wondering how anyone could think of going to the opera when the Imperial army was marching on the border. Her father had already left for the bank and she could hear her mother's voice in the distance demanding to know where her green silk shawl had gone. The very next morning her mother had called her an unnatural child, and maybe she was because she missed the comfort, but not her parents.

She missed the chaos of the university dining room more than her parents. Or at least the porridge in the university dining room. She'd never been fond of the chaos.

Tomas ate with the bowl balanced on his raised knees, head down, and it wasn't until he finished that he sagged back against the wall, sighed in what sounded like relief, set the bowl and bedroll aside and stood. "We should go."

"Go?" If he recognized his tone echoed back to him, he gave no indication. Mirian was tempted to just sit there. To ask the Sisters for seconds. To make a privy run.

Actually . . .

She took his hand, let him pull her to her feet, and handed him the bedroll. "I'll be right back."

To his credit, it only took him a moment to work out where she was going. "What's wrong with . . . ?"

"It has a door I can close. Bushes don't." She had to curl her toes inside her boots to keep the leather from rubbing against abraded skin. Every step over and around other people in the room felt as though she had hot coals pressed against her heels. By the time she reached the privy, she was breathing short and sharp through her nose, in too much pain to appreciate morning air only moderately tainted by old sweat and grime. And if she used the privacy of that closed door to let a few tears fall, well, that was the point of privacy.

When she emerged, Tomas was waiting for her outside the door, standing a little apart from a trio of women who also waited, ignoring a fourth who flashed a gap-toothed smile and pushed out breasts

covered in torn cotton as aggressively as any of society's daughters
with all their teeth and clothed in silk. With neither power nor fur,
she didn't stand a chance and Tomas looked bored rather than interested or embarrassed, either of which Mirian could see the woman
would prefer.

Their imaginary, blind, one-legged priest from the woods could
have seen it.

Aggressive flirting would become aggression in a minute—no one
liked being ignored—and aggression directed at Tomas would end
up with him outing himself as Pack.

As Mirian saw it, she had two options. She could claim Tomas as
her own, redirecting the aggression and probably resulting in having
to defend her claim physically, or she could direct the woman's interest elsewhere.

If you can light a candle . . .

No.

Air and water; first levels were useless. Putting the woman to sleep
would cause new problems. She couldn't see a way metal-craft, even
at second level, could be applied. Pushing the tangle of blackberry
canes to bloom and then fruit would require touch and Mirian refused to move closer to the man currently urinating on the garden
in direct contradiction to the Sister's instructions.

Fortunately, before she'd been accepted at the university, she'd
had another teacher.

Closing the distance and raising a hand to keep Tomas quiet, she
murmured, "I heard the man with the green kerchief say your breasts
had to be false. Is that true?"

The woman's eyes were so bloodshot Mirian almost mistook the
red for mage marks. "He said what?"

"That you stuff rags in your bodice."

"That fucking bastard!" In spite of missing teeth, her snarl was
impressive.

"He said they were too perfect to be real."

"That flaming piece of shi . . ." Her eyes widened. "Too perfect?
Did he now . . ." Tomas forgotten, she shoved Mirian aside and strode
across the garden to apply her charms to the man in the green kerchief. Who cowered in the face of the sudden onslaught of smiles and
breasts. He could consider it payback for urinating on the blackberries.

My mother would be so proud.

Tomas merely continued watching her like she was the only thing worthy of his attention in the immediate area. That was so Pack. Arrogant and secure in their power. It seemed she'd have to remind him daily that they weren't in Aydori and that, although he could still invoke terror in fur, in skin he was only a young man who was going to attract attention for his looks and who couldn't let anyone know he was Pack and, honestly, what had he been thinking just standing there looking superior?

"I traded the fire-starter for these," he said, holding up a pair of wooden clogs. When surprise kept her from an immediate reply, he ducked his head and added, "We don't need it and you can't walk in those boots."

Mirian actually felt her mouth open to point out wood didn't go with her outfit, but managed a slightly strangled *thank you* before sinking to the ground and struggling with her boots. Wood didn't go with her outfit? Lord and Lady, that was her punishment for allowing her mother back into her head. Before she could untangle the knots, Tomas knelt at her feet, set the bedroll on the ground, and dealt with them.

"Let me . . ."

As he peeled the first boot off her foot, she clenched her fists so tightly that the broken edges of her nails cut into her palms. The second either hurt less or couldn't possibly hurt more.

Her heels looked like raw meat, the scabs scrapped off, the flesh below red and oozing. They felt as bad as they looked. In a just world, they'd at least distract her from her aching legs, but in a just world it was still too early for the maid to have opened her curtains.

"Can't you . . ." Tomas waved a hand. ". . . fix them?"

They looked a lot worse than they had when she'd first exposed them. "No. That's third level healing."

"Have you ever tried?"

About to remind him one more time of why she hadn't been returning for a second year of university, Mirian frowned. In fairness, she *hadn't* ever tried. She'd been tested for second levels of everything save metal a hundred, a thousand times, to no effect, but she'd claimed sleep on her own. Twice. And she'd called metal to her. So why not a third level in healing? The damage was a little more than the tiny wounds the students learned to heal on themselves, but the principle was the same and she'd be no worse off if she failed.

Logically, her ability to perform the first level body equilibrium meant she knew her body. She knew it whole and undamaged. Water wanted to be water, her professors had said, and her body wanted to be whole. She could, logically, return it to that condition.

Logic, her professors had also said, is not applicable to mage-craft.

In this case, it seemed they were right.

They were alone in the garden when she looked up and shook her head.

Tomas closed a warm hand around her ankle. "It's okay . . ."

She didn't need to be comforted. She was familiar with failure.

". . . the clogs won't touch your heels. And they're easy to kick off if we need to run." He stood and held out his hand. For the second time that morning, she let him pull her up.

The clogs weren't terribly different than last season's summer shoes. Wood, rather than leather, and a lot heavier, but easy to kick off was, after all, fashion forward in Aydori. She wouldn't call them comfortable, but the inside had been worn smooth and, while they were grimy, nothing stuck to her feet. She frowned as she realized the people who took shelter with the Sisters of Starlight had only what they wore and now one of them had even less.

"The fire-starter's worth more than new clogs," Tomas told her, as though he'd heard her thought. "We don't know where to sell it and wouldn't have the time even if we did."

The color of the sky said it was no longer dawn, but early morning.

"Out! Out!" One of the Sisters stood in the doorway and Mirian got her first well-lit look at what they were wearing. In the lamplight, all that white had turned their bodies into featureless blobs. Mirian knew they couldn't possibly be wearing nightgowns under the long white tabards, but the shapeless style was similar. No one would be joining the Sisters of Starlight for the uniform; that was for certain.

The Sister took a step toward them, waving both hands. "You must be gone!"

"Your boots?" Tomas asked, hanging the bedroll over his shoulder.

Mirian glanced down. A pair of well-made boots would no doubt come in handy, but it hurt just thinking of putting them on. "Leave them."

All three Sisters flapped them through the kitchen and into the outer room where the door stood open and the air was distinctly fresher than it had been.

"What about . . . ?" Tomas paused on the threshold, circling his hand.

Mirian had forgotten entirely about having set the air in motion. She'd been nearly asleep when she'd done it, certain that if the assault on her nose was any indication, Tomas must be truly suffering. Air drifted up the first spiral then across into the second where it spiraled back to the floor then crossed back to the beginning. Both spirals rotated slowly around the center of the room. Technically, the mage-craft was nothing more than blowing out a thousand specifically placed candles, but she had to admit she was impressed by the complexity she'd managed while unable to sleep. Except . . . "How did you know?"

Tomas tapped his nose. "Even with the door open, the scent's so strong I can tell when I'm crossing the streams. And the power is unmistakably you."

That made sense. Mirian had half thought *she'd* smelled the spirals while crossing them. "I'll leave it. It'll run down eventually . . ." Everything did. ". . . but until it does, this place needs all the help it can get."

In spite of the early hour, the street outside the Sisters' shelter was empty of everyone but a few stragglers heading toward the northeast. Toward the pall of smoke already building. Toward the factories.

"They're going in the right direction." Mirian turned on the ball of one foot, the clog pivoting easily over the cobblestones. "We could follow them."

"Or we could go back to the market to pick up the road we know goes through the city."

They didn't know it, not for sure, but she had to admit that the odds were higher. Tomas' nose was next to useless in the city, and the factories would have guards, and the coach had very certainly not gone by way of the factories unless factories in Abyek came with livery stables.

Tomas rocked back and forth, his clogs ticking against the cobbles. He shifted, created a different rhythm, and grinned as it became the same song the 2nd had been singing on their way to the border. About to ask what he was doing, Mirian realized he was waiting on her decision.

Still, she'd already acknowledged his nose was next to useless here. "Back to the market, then."

The shelter stood nearly in the center of a long block of two-story houses, white-painted bricks standing out against the red—although most of the red, especially on the upper levels had been blackened by smoke. Mirian hadn't seen a set of stairs in the shelter, so they were probably behind a door in the kitchen. She wondered if the Sisters used the second floor for arcane rituals or rented it out to pay for the cauldrons of food. She could hear babies crying and a man shouting, could smell food cooking and old urine. Three small children sat on a threshold eating porridge from bowls in their laps, a wet stain against the wall next to them. A pair of small dogs standing in one of the upper windows yapped hysterically at the world until Tomas glanced up, then they tumbled over each other in their haste to disappear.

How did people live like this?

"I owe you an apology."

Tomas sounded sincere, but Mirian couldn't think of what he had to apologize for.

"We should have left when you wanted to. Staying . . ." He waved a hand at the sky, or the buildings, or something Mirian wasn't aware of. ". . . that was time we'll never get back."

"Yes, we will."

"First level time travel?"

"What? No!" If he'd been her sister, she'd have poked him for that. As he wasn't, she settled for rolling her eyes. "If we'd left immediately, I'd be in my boots. Because we stayed, you had time to trade for the clogs. They're not exactly comfortable, but I'm not crippled in them, so I can move significantly faster."

"I hadn't thought of it like that." His lips twitched. "That's very sensible of you."

"Thank you." She was rather impressed by how much she made it sound like *shut up*. After a moment, she added, "It wasn't the porridge, though, was it? The reason you wanted to stay."

His cheeks flushed, and he shoved his hands into his trouser pockets.

"And you still don't want to talk about it. That's all right." Some people needed to ease into mornings. Yesterday, he'd been up long enough to steal clothes before she woke. "My father is always difficult before his first cup of coffee." She stepped over a glistening gray lump with no idea of what it was. Or had been.

"Your father drank coffee? That's . . ."

"An insanely expensive import from exotic lands far to the south that the neighbors couldn't possibly afford? That's why my mother insisted on it. And why only my father drank it. I thought it smelled amazing."

Tomas snorted. "You don't know what amazing smells like."

And another chance to mention Jaspyr Hagen passed as they reached the market. The permanent stalls around the edges had already opened, and the first of the barrows were being set up. There were significantly more women around than men. Mirian didn't know if that was because the men had died during the war or because the Pyrahn army had run for Aydori or because more men worked in the factories. The war itself didn't seem to have touched this part of the city at all, but, as the newspaper had reported the Lord Mayor had surrendered with only a few shots fired, that was easily explained. Her mother had gone on about cowardice, but her father had only put down the paper and said, *"Modern cities weren't built to be defended. His Grace and the army were on the way to the border and Emperor Leopald wanted those factories in one piece. Smart thing to do. Saved a lot of lives."*

Strangely, there were more men than women in the group gathered around the well and they were visibly stirred up about something. The distance combined with their excitement and their accents made it impossible to understand what all the shouting was about. They looked rough, although Mirian suspected she might not be the best judge of that. From the way others were watching them, they were trouble; she hoped they weren't fomenting some kind of stupid rebellion because that would draw the soldiers.

"Around or through?" Tomas asked, stepping out in front of her.

Around more than doubled the distance. With the market still almost half empty and the crowd up against the well, they could cross in nearly a straight line. "Through."

"Stay close."

"So no wandering off to shop." When he turned, showing teeth, she raised a hand. "I'm sorry. You didn't say that. You didn't even imply that. Assuming that was what you meant was unfair to you."

"I meant you should stay close."

"I know. It's just, there's people out there. Being out in public, like this . . ." The shirtwaist cuff protruding from beneath her jacket was stained with a thousand shades of dirt. ". . . awake enough to be aware of what people are thinking of me, unwashed, unkempt . . . it's . . . unsettling. It makes me defensive."

"You'll never see them again. Why do you care?"

She could see he honestly didn't understand. But then, he was Pack—in fur, in skin, clean, dirty, nothing changed that. If she were Mage-pack, she'd have that certainty, too.

Lord and Lady, Mother, get out of my head!

She didn't *need* to be Mage-pack to know who she was. Unwashed and unkempt perhaps, but she was Mirian Maylin regardless. She squared her shoulders and lifted her chin. "I *don't* care. It's a long way to Karis; let's go."

His nod held nothing but acceptance.

Of course it was one thing to say she didn't care and another thing entirely not to care. Mirian looked across the square, locked her gaze on the road that would take them out of Abyek, and tried not to think of her appearance. Tried not to think of that old bald man or that woman with the tanned, bared forearms or that gaggle of children watching her and judging. She wasn't very successful until they came they came closer to the well and some of the shouted words grew clearer. Suddenly, she wasn't thinking of her appearance at all.

". . . Imperial courier said . . ."

". . . how it is now!"

"Why shouldn't we get . . . ?"

". . . Imperials don't need the fucking money!"

". . . enough to risk . . ."

"Fuck it, for that much I'd . . ."

". . . abomination!"

Tomas growled low in his throat and Mirian grabbed his hand. "They don't know." She was proud of how steady her voice sounded. "Just keep walking."

But it was already too late.

"There! There it is!" The crowd parted, exposing the man at the well. The farm worker who'd stopped them on the road pointed at Tomas. Still huge and flushed and jowly, but triumphant, not afraid.

Mirian tried to yank Tomas away, but he growled louder, hands going to his jacket.

"Hold him!"

An elbow slammed into the side of Mirian's head. She stumbled back, fell, and from the ground saw the farm worker clamp one enormous hand down on Tomas' shoulder and wrap the other around his face as the men who'd been holding him stepped back. Tomas could change in clothes. He'd be tangled in the fabric, but he'd have teeth and terror . . . and why didn't he change!

"Silver pin!" The farm worker bellowed. "That Imperial courier gived out a handful yesterday!"

"To you, Harn?" one of the other men laughed.

The farm worker's name was Harn. Not that it mattered now.

"No, but I got one anyway, don't I? Shoved it right into him and he's helpless."

Tomas fought and snarled, got an arm free and closed his hand around the front of Harn's throat.

The big man banged their foreheads together, and Tomas sagged. "I should've stuck the pin in your fucking eye!" he bellowed, stepping back and allowing the crowd to take Tomas to the ground.

Mirian threw herself at one of the men holding Tomas' leg, trying to knock him off balance. A hand in her hair threw her back. She landed on her side. Cried out as a boot caught her under the ribs, once, twice.

"Three silver emperors for the pelt! That's what the courier said!"

"Then he has to change, Harn!"

Coughing and crying, Mirian rolled up onto her hands and knees.

"I don't fancy that!"

"Let him change! We kill him and takes his pelt!"

"No, no, I heard the stories! We let him change, we all die."

"He don't need to change!" Harn dropped to one knee and dragged Tomas' head up. Blood from his nose ran down over his lips and teeth. "This here, it ain't hair. It's fur. And the courier says it's good enough!"

Harn waved a knife, the blade long and thin.

"Kill 'em quick, Harn!"

"Kill him?" The big man laughed. "Maybe after!"

Pain stabbing up under her ribs, Mirian didn't have breath enough to scream.

If you can light a candle . . .

Reiter had just swallowed his last mouthful of toasted bread when the screaming started. Unwilling to spend the morning kicking around the garrison, he'd gone back into the city just after dawn looking for an alehouse one of the other officers had mentioned enjoying down in the working class part of town. *"Safe enough,"* he'd said. *"We haven't changed their lives any. At their pay grade, it's all pretty much shit. Why should they care which bastards they work for?"*

In the older cities of the empire, Reiter would have gone to a coffee house. If such a place existed in Abyek, he wouldn't be able to afford it, given the prices of the commonplace out by the new border. Fortunately, he had no problem settling for ale and was pleasantly surprised to find he could have a mug of tea so strong it nearly ate the plating off the spoon. In spite of speaking no Pyrahn and the waiter no Imperial, they'd managed to find enough common ground for him to order and negotiate a price in Imperial coin. Commerce always found a way.

The eggs had been just the way he liked, the sausage a little short of actual meat but still tasty, and if he couldn't get a decent biscuit and gravy, he was reasonably content with the thick slices of toasted bread that replaced that staple in this part of the world. The meal had cost more than he'd normally put down—one way or another that could be tracked back to the war—but his back pay had caught up to him in Abyek and he had nothing else to drop it on. As he cut and chewed and swallowed, he tried not to think of it as a last meal. He wasn't particularly successful. He didn't need to be one of Colonel Korshan's company, smart enough to invent rockets and balloons and whatnot, to know he'd be lucky to survive reporting back without the sixth mage. A smarter man might think about deserting, but he'd given the army his entire adult life; if he couldn't believe they'd give him back a fair chance to be heard, then he'd thrown that life away. Besides, the Soothsayers had tossed him into this pile of shit. There was nothing that said they wouldn't find him if he ran, and that made reporting his failure the smarter thing to do.

Although, he allowed, spreading honey on a fourth slice of toasted bread, that didn't mean he was in a hurry to get it done.

At the first scream, he put his knife and fork down on his empty plate. At the second, he stood, and threw a handful of coin on the table. As three, four, and five heralded a rush of noise blending terror and rage under what sounded like explosions, he ran for the door. People out on the street stared toward the rising smoke, but they'd just lost a war and had learned better than to run toward a battle.

Reiter had been on the winning side.

Three streets down, a new sound had him glance left, and he spotted half a dozen young soldiers coming out of an alehouse somewhat shabbier than one he'd just left.

"Corporal!"

The corporal jerked around to face him, his expression as much guilty as startled. "Sir!"

"With me!" Reiter didn't give a crap what the corporal or his friends were guilty of. They were there.

"We're off duty, sir."

"Did I ask?"

"No, sir!"

He heard their boots hitting the cobblestones behind him, but he didn't look back. If he'd needed to look back, the Imperial army had no business winning so much as a darts tournament.

The road spilled him out into a small market square although he had to shove his way through a small huddle of weeping civilians to actually enter it.

A man burned in the center of the square. Reiter had seen more war than he cared to remember, and men were too wet to burn like man-shaped torches—although as this man *was* burning like a man-shaped torch, Reiter found himself grateful for the presence of the unnatural, masking flame.

Behind the burning man, the well shot a pillar of water up into the air.

Barrows and stalls had collapsed. Every piece of board in the market had grown thorns.

What looked like a small cyclone had just reached the square from one of the narrow side streets.

Whatever was happening, it was centered around the well.

He'd nearly reached it, one arm up over his nose to block the stink, when he recognized a familiar spill of gray skirts. Up on her knees, one hand pressed to her side, she crawled toward a body lying near the feet of the burning man.

Young, dark-haired, male—probably the beastman who'd helped her escape. The abomination. Ignoring for the moment that they were in Abyek, because that made no sense at all, Reiter added up the pieces. Seemed a local tough had tried to collect the emperor's bounty on abominations and had tossed the girl aside as harmless because she had no mage sign in her eyes.

Screaming grew louder all around the market as the cyclone came out from between the buildings and began flinging debris.

Reiter grabbed the girl by the back of the jacket, hauled her up onto her feet, and punched her as hard as he could. Her head snapped back, and he barely caught her before she hit the ground. He'd just had his career, and possibly his life, handed back to him.

The cyclone vanished, white-painted bricks clattered down onto the cobblestones. A piece of charred meat shaped like a man stood for a moment then collapsed and sizzled. The pillar of water pouring from the well dropped to barely six inches high.

"Sir?"

Straightening, he handed the girl into the arms of a large young private staring wild-eyed at the destruction. "Get her back to the garrison. Tell them they're to use that stuff the surgeons use to keep her out. Captain Reiter's orders." He was a Shield. Anyone who could read insignia had known he was there on the emperor's command. His orders would be obeyed. "Take him, too!" The beastman wasn't in pieces. If the stories were true, that meant he was still alive. "Find a barrow that's not been destroyed, pile them both into it. Get them to the garrison, quickly, and keep them both unconscious."

"Yes, sir!"

"Corporal!"

"Captain Reiter, sir!" The state of the corporal's boots declared he'd already lost his breakfast.

Given the smell of burned meat and hair and offal that coated nose and throat, Reiter didn't blame him. Not as long as he followed orders. "Until more troops arrive, we're it."

"Sir! We don't have our weapons!"

"We won't be shooting anyone. You know how to put together a work party?"

Indignation took a shot at replacing horror. "Yes, sir!"

"So put one together. Get people out from under collapsed stalls. Find casualties. Apply field dressings. Can you talk to them?"

"A little, sir!"

"Good. They won't care that we're Imperials. They need someone to pull order out of chaos."

"No, sir! I mean, yes, sir!"

As the corporal barked orders, and the beastman and mage rumbled toward the garrison in a salvaged barrow, Reiter moved to take a closer look at the burned body. His fingers were gone. What could have been a wooden knife hilt had been cooked into the palm of his hand. Reiter slid the toe of his boot between the charred wrist and the pavement and lifted.

Six-inch thorns jutted out through the back of his hand and explained why he hadn't dropped it.

A glint of metal caught Reiter's eye and he splashed through the water back to where he'd found the girl. Radiating out like a sunburst from the place she'd been kneeling, the cracks in the cobblestones were filled with metal. Metal that appeared to have been molten moments before but had already cooled to the touch.

"Did you have any idea of what you were doing?" he wondered, the question unheard amid the surrounding grief and profanities.

The voice of a heavyset woman rose above the rest as she backed a boy into a corner and started beating him with a belt. "You have fire eyes—don't tell me you didn't do it! Don't lie to me! Don't lie to me!"

As Reiter ran to save the boy, he realized this neighborhood was going to become brutal for anyone with even the minimal mage marks found outside Aydori.

Nearly three hours later, the moment Reiter stepped onto land claimed by the garrison, before he'd even got through the gate, a private barely old enough to shave separated himself from where he'd been leaning against the fence and stepped into his path.

"Captain Reiter, sir, Major Halyss wants to see you in his office."

"Tell him I'll be there immediately after checking my prisoners."

"No, sir. Sorry, sir, but he said you're to go right to him."

It had been worth a shot.

The major was on the second floor at the far end of the garrison building from the transport sergeant's office. Reiter hadn't met him, but he knew Major Halyss was Intelligence and had just arrived from Karis. Soldiers' gossip said that General Reed, the garrison commander, had been giving the major as much leeway as wouldn't undermine his command. The major's father was evidently a power at court.

The office was surprisingly bare, the major sitting at a nearly empty desk writing quickly. The boy came to attention, but Reiter fell into parade rest and waited. After filling a third sheet of paper, Halyss tossed his steel-tipped pen back into the inkwell, blew on the last sheet until the ink would take the pressure of his finger, then folded all three and sealed them, pressing his signet into the wax.

"Brendon."

"Sir!"

"Sergeant Pine. For immediate courier."

"Sir!"

Halyss watched the boy leave, then turned a dark-eyed gaze on Reiter. Who came to attention.

"Never mind that, Captain. In fact, sit. It's a borrowed office, I don't plan on staying long, but we might as well make use of it."

He sounded *hail fellow well met*. His eyes said *trust no one*. Reiter sat, but he didn't relax. Expecting another Lieutenant Lord Geurin, he was pleased to see that while the major had all the innate airs and confidence of the aristocracy, he appeared to lack an obvious sense of petulant entitlement. Of course, appearances could be deceiving.

"So, your prisoners." The major leaned back in his chair and smiled. The smile made Reiter think of Aydori. "I hear they were wheeled out of what a very incoherent young private seemed to think was a riot or a sacrifice or flame knows what and into the custody of the Imperial army. They're boxed and drugged. So I was wondering, just out of curiosity, you understand, why you would ask they be drugged with a substance even the surgeons admit is experimental. Useful, definitely," he added, "but experimental."

"It's important they don't wake up, sir."

"I did gather that, yes."

Rather than attempt an explanation, Reiter pulled his orders from inside his tunic, and passed them across the desk. The major's gaze rested a moment on the Imperial seal, then he read the single page quickly and passed it back.

"Clear enough. Creep into Aydori, capture six mages, take them to Karis. While I'm well aware ours is not to question why . . ." Reiter suspected Halyss would question the emperor himself given the opportunity. ". . . I don't suppose you were given a reason for your covert mission?"

"Yes, sir. But I'm not at liberty to say."

"Not even to me?"

"No, sir."

"Something that inexplicable, my guess is Soothsayers." Halyss said *my guess is* like he meant *and I know flaming well*. "Crazy bastards." He made the insult sound personal. "So this girl in the cells . . . ?"

"She's the sixth mage. Lieutenant Geurin is on the way to Karis with the other five. I had her. I lost her." Reiter met the major's gaze. "Now, I have her again."

"Good for you. Given the chaos you pulled her from, I suspected as much—not that she was your mage, of course, but that she was a mage, and so I checked her eyes. As I said, I was curious. Thing is . . ." Halyss leaned forward. ". . . mages have been a bit of a hobby of mine. Why is it mage-craft is dying out in the empire but still strong in the old mountain countries?"

"Science?" Reiter offered when it became clear Halyss actually wanted an answer.

"That's a theory, but I've found no reason science and mage-craft can't coexist. It must be something else, mustn't it? At any event, this hobby of mine has to do with why I've been sent to the front. I'm more useful here." The major's affectations slipped just for a heartbeat. If Reiter hadn't been watching him so closely for his own protection, he'd have missed it. It seemed Halyss wasn't happy about his orders. "Those five women you were to capture, pardon me, six, are not the only mages in Aydori. Their artillery has more Fire-mages than cannon by all reports. Oh, yes . . ." He sat back and raised a hand, as though Reiter, sitting silently, had commented. ". . . her eyes. No mage marks. They're not dependent on consciousness, by the way. No mage marks, not a mage."

"So I've always believed, sir. But this confirmed it." Reiter pulled the tangle from his pocket and set it on the desk. Halyss' eyes widened, surprise evoking an honest response.

"This is from the Archive," he said, confirming the rumors of his previous post. Only someone who'd spent significant time at court would know about the Archive, let alone recognize an artifact taken from it. He reached out, paused, and only continued when Reiter nodded. "You realize, don't you, that this little golden net is probably worth more than everything you and I will ever own in our entire lives?"

"Because of the gold . . ."

"Because it can't be duplicated." Fingers through the weave, Halyss held the tangle up to the light.

"There were six of them, sir."

Halyss stared at him for a long moment. "Not what I meant, Captain." The fine gold chain glittered as he turned it. "We have lost the knowledge and the ability to create more and an attempt to regain even some small part of that knowledge is . . ." He stopped and stared at the tangle, mouth partially open. When Reiter followed his line of sight, the only thought in his head was suddenly, *probably worth more than everything you and I will ever own in our entire lives.*

"Do you know what this looks like, Captain?"

"It was like that when it came off the mage, sir."

"Not what I asked."

"It looks . . . melted?"

"No, it doesn't." Major Halyss tapped the blackened ends of the two broken sections. "Enough heat to melt this would have been enough heat to melt at least another inch or two of the gold. And these links, while elongated, aren't melted. Emperor Leopald has been experimenting with electricity . . ."

And other things, his tone added. Reiter suspected he didn't want to know what those other things were.

". . . and this almost looks as though it had been overloaded. The weak points blew, the rest . . ." He poured the tangle into his hand. "Well, as I said, almost. This happened when she removed it?"

"I can't say for certain, sir. All I know is that she had it on, and when I found it lying on the ground, it was like that."

"That's impossible." As the major seemed to be speaking to himself, Reiter ignored the clearly incorrect statement. "You disagree?"

Apparently, he hadn't been ignoring it completely enough. "It wasn't hit by lightning, sir. That I can say for certain."

Dark brows rose. "You can say for certain it wasn't hit by lightning?"

"Yes, sir."

"All right," Halyss allowed, his slight smile almost an apology, "clearly not impossible." Slipping a finger through one of the unaffected sections, he lifted it and let it dangle. "She was responsible for that disaster in the market."

It wasn't really a question. Reiter answered it anyway. "I believe so, sir." The attacks had stopped after he punched her; that made her involvement hard to argue against.

"It's been reported she used five of six crafts. That's not entirely unusual, you know. There are records in the Archives of powerful mages dabbling in the other disciplines—Air-mages can light a candle, Water can blow it out—but I've never read anything suggesting the level of power witnessed this morning. Although, in fairness, I'd barely got started in the Archive before I was ordered to the front. Who knows what potentially useful information is buried in there." The resentment resurfaced to be quickly buried again. "I don't suppose you observed any evidence of healer-craft this morning, Captain?"

"No, sir."

"No real surprise. From the initial reports, I don't imagine she was very interested in healing anyone."

Had a type of healing magic put Armin to sleep, Reiter wondered. But all he said was, "I expect not, sir."

"The lack of marks concerns me." The dark brows drew in. "If Aydori is breeding stealth mages, that's not going to go well for us."

"But we're winning." The front was outside Bercarit, waiting for artillery.

Halyss waved that off. "We always win. We're *the* empire." He rolled his eyes. "As though there's only ever been one. However, that said, His Imperial Majesty has lost interest in this particular battle.

I suspect, although don't quote me on this . . ." It sounded like a friendly warning. Reiter knew it wasn't. ". . . the battle was a feint to allow you and this . . ." The tangle poured from hand to hand. ". . . to succeed. We may take Bercarit. We may pull back to the border, I don't know."

Yet, the pause said.

"My source believes she was protecting her companion this morning in the market." When Reiter raised his brows, Halyss waved it off. It was none of Reiter's business who he got his reports from. "I made sure the silver pin stayed in his shoulder, by the way. You didn't mention it. He can't change to the wolf form as long as it's there."

That explained why the burned man had dared try and claim the bounty. The fool had thought the more dangerous of the two had been neutralized.

"His Imperial Majesty has been sending pins around the empire with the couriers and the proclamation. Between the pins and all the shot, it makes me wish I'd been paying enough attention to invest in silver a few years ago." He smiled dazzlingly, unconcerned when Reiter didn't return it. "So, you'll be taking the girl—and I imagine as much of the drug as the surgeon will give you—to Karis as ordered by His Imperial Majesty." Fingers half curled around the chain as though he had to force himself to let go, Halyss passed the tangle back. "There are people at the palace who are going to want to have a look at that. What are you going to do with the boy?"

He didn't know. He'd only known he couldn't leave him lying in the square. The thought of having him scalped or skinned for a bounty made him feel sick.

Halyss' expression had gone so neutral, Reiter knew he'd let that show as well. Not safe. Not safe at all. He didn't know how it was among civilians, but in the Imperial army, the emperor's will was not questioned. As his first sergeant had said, *"The emperor decrees; we agree."* The emperor had decreed the beastmen were abominations. Outside even the laws that governed the use of animals. Reiter considered himself as good a liar as anyone who sometimes had to deal with incompetent superiors, but the absolute absence of emotion in the major's level stare suggested he not attempt to lie now. So he said nothing at all.

After a long moment, Halyss nodded, as though he'd heard what he wanted to. "Take him with you. His Imperial Majesty's been collecting them for a while."

"Why? I'm curious," he added when the major's brows went up. The major had, after all, been curious first.

"No idea." Halyss answered flatly, absence of tone a warning. "He could be studying the enemy. He could be having rugs made. The point is, the boy's not covered on your current orders, so I'll write an addendum that'll clear it with transport."

Reiter wondered what he was being warned about. Not to be curious? "Thank you, sir."

"Well, you can't leave him here. They'll skin him for sure." The major grinned, the *hail fellow well met* back in place, but the expression in his eyes unreadable. "It's a long way from here to Karis, Captain, and on a trip that long, *anything* can happen."

The emphasis was slight, but Reiter knew he hadn't imagined it.

Hand in his pocket, Reiter let the tangle's fine gold links slide over his fingers as he watched a nameless private load the girl into the wagon. Her hands and feet were tied and both would be secured to a ring in the wagon's side, but—more importantly—her head lolled against the private's shoulder. Ancient artifacts had failed; time to give science a chance. The work party had been less careful when loading . . .

Major Halyss, Reiter realized, had only ever referred to him as "the boy" not "the abomination" or even "the beastman." When Reiter thought of him as "the boy," he saw he didn't look any older than hundreds of soldiers in the Imperial army. Young men away from home for the first time, determined to fight bravely no matter what because they had no idea of what that could mean. Soldiers Reiter had commanded, led into battle, watched die, watched deal with having killed.

Might be best if he not think of him as *the boy*.

Might be too late.

The work party had been less careful when loading the male prisoner, Reiter amended, having tossed him into the back of the wagon, roughly arranging his limbs only after the surgeon supervising had intervened. When the surgeon turned away, one of the detail had

laughed, lifted the boy's head by a handful of hair, and said something Reiter hadn't caught. There could be no doubt it concerned
the bounty.

"It's five days minimum to Karis even if your orders allow you to
commandeer space in a mail coach as soon as you cross the old border." Surgeon Major Raynold crossed her arms and glared at Reiter,
at the wagon, at the backs of the dismissed work party, at nothing in
particular. "No one's ever been kept under, or even partially under,
that long. I'm telling you again, it isn't safe."

"It won't be safe if they aren't under."

Raynold ignored him. "Let them come out of it as far as possible before you put them under again. Unless you want them to
die on the way, make sure they drink while they're conscious
enough to swallow. Get as much water into them as you can. Oh,
and keep checking that the pulse remains steady. You know how
to do that?"

"I do."

"Not that it matters; if the pulse starts to flutter, your only option
is to hope they throw off the effects of the drug before the heart
stops. And that means your only choice will be to let them die or
take your chances with an angry mage or a furious beastman."

"He can't change with that silver pin in his shoulder."

"Then make sure it remains in his shoulder. I wish I'd had more
time to study him. That hair's fur you know. Teeth are larger, bones
are heavier. I'd like to see one change. I never have."

With them declared abomination, it was unlikely she ever would.

"You're certain the girl's a mage? I examined her eyes and there's
nothing there."

"I'm certain."

"That's a new one on me, then. My mother had a couple of healer
marks. Gold flecks. Couldn't see them unless you knew to look.
Still . . ." A nervous laugh and she pinched the bridge of her nose.
"These two, they're not in great shape, but there's nothing wrong
with them that should kill them before you get them to Karis.
There's bruising on both torsos from the gentle application of boots.
I expected her ribs to be cracked at least, but they're solid. He's got
a recent scar on one shoulder, and she's got fresh scars on her heels.
Oh, and you're lucky you didn't break her jaw when you put her out.

There's new swelling there on top of old." She nodded down at the leather satchel on the ground between them. "Everything you need's in the case, so there's no point in me staying here while you wait for your driver. I've work of my own to do; a dozen wagonloads of wounded came back from the front this morning."

"Did you hear how it's going?"

Surgeon Major Raynold snorted. "People are still getting shot. Bleeding out. Losing arms. Legs. Eyes. More rending and tearing than usual, but, otherwise, that's how it always goes. Remember, water your prisoners every time they wake. If you can convince them to behave without putting them back under, their chances of arriving alive go up, but, for pity's sake, use no more of the drug than I showed you. Too much and they'll not only be dead, but you'll have wasted anesthetic I could have put to better use." She took two strides toward the hospital tents, then she paused and turned. "Oh, and one of the drug's components is flammable. Very flammable. All things considered, you'd best remember that, too."

Reiter considered the man-shaped torch as he watched Raynold disappear between the tents, and he wondered how dangerous it was keeping flammable liquids under canvas, the garrison's hospital being at best about half built. No surprise army bureaucracy had decided the paperwork needed a solid structure before the wounded.

He racked his musket, then tucked the satchel in under the wide seat and pulled out his watch. Half one. The transport sergeant, while not pleased about both circumstances and Major Halyss interfering with his scheduling, had said there'd be a driver available at . . .

"Captain Reiter!"

"Chard?" No mistaking the squint or the grin even if he hadn't recognized the voice before he turned. "I left you at Bercarit." Major Gagnon had been happy to accept three more muskets and the men able to shoot them. *"The Shields don't leave Karis, so they can't be Shields, can they? I was hoping for a little more in the way of reinforcements, but they'll do."*

"Yes, sir, you did, but they were short drivers, so I came with the wounded this morning. I thought I was done with horses when I joined, but I guess not." He glanced into the back of the wagon. "Hey, you caught her again. Why would she come to . . . ?" He squinted across the road at the city, looking confused.

"Abyek," Reiter sighed.

"Yeah, Abyek. Why would she come here instead of going home?"

"I have no idea."

"She dead, Cap?"

"No. Neither of them are," he continued, cutting off Chard's next question. "Stow your pack and let's go."

"Looks dead," Chard noted, reaching in and moving the girl's arm out of the way before dropping his pack in beside her. "Still warm, though. Who's he?"

Abomination. Beastman. Boy. But this was Chard . . . "The dog."

Chard froze, halfway up onto the wagon. "The dog? Wait, from that night? No shit! I mean," he added hurriedly, "no shit, sir. That's my dog? The big black one?" He slid his musket into the rack, sat, and twisted around to take another look. "I can't get over how much they look like people."

. . . gold hoops in her ears.

"Let's go, Private. It's a long way to Karis."

"That's just what Major Halyss said, Cap." Chard unwound the reins from the brake, and slapped them down. "Walk on." The big gelding shook himself, as though he were shaking his harness back into position, and started out of the yard.

"Major Halyss?"

"Yes, sir. Met me down by the hospital tents where I was helping unload the wounded and said you needed a driver. Said you needed someone who wasn't going to get all stupid about mages and that tangle thing and stuff. That he'd made it smooth with transport and I was to meet you here. The horse's name is Thunder because he has wicked bad farts."

"Major Halyss said that?"

"Not the bit about the horse. Found that out on my own from a guy in transport."

With the Duchies of Pyrahn and Traiton now the Imperial Provinces of Pyrahn and Traiton and Imperial governors installed in both Ducal Seats, trade had begun to pick up again. Reiter thought of what he'd said to the young corporal in the square about how people just wanted order made out of chaos. The armies of both duchies, the nobility, the stupidly patriotic had retreated to make a stand in Aydori. Most people—well, not the people who'd been living where the empire wanted to put a garrison, but most people—had just got on with their lives as best they could. After generations of conquest, most people had acquired a certain fatalistic opinion about the empire's advance. Practice allowed Imperial bureaucracy to get things up and running with terrifying efficiency. As Chard passed an enormous wagonload of brick pulled by four huge black horses with feet like dinner plates and feathered ankles—Were there ankles on a horse?—he wondered if trade had even bothered to stop. He did know there were piss-all privately owned horses now in either province since both sides had been drafting them as theirs were shot. Any horse in Pyrahn or Traiton currently either worked for the army or for Imperial interests.

Chard slapped the reins down again, and Thunder confirmed his name before breaking into a trot.

$$\boxed{\textit{Chapter Nine}}$$

THE SUN HAD SLIPPED behind them so that they drove over the edges of their shadow. Reiter had a vague memory, a child's memory, of his gran pulling him aside, fingers pinching the inside flesh of his arm, and telling him to mind his shadow. To not walk in his own darkness. He hadn't thought of his gran or her superstitions in years.

"Pull over to the side, Chard."

Behind them in the wagon box the boy was starting to shake off the drug, tongue flicking out trying to lick his lips, his nostrils flaring. Did he have the senses of a dog even when he looked like a person? Next to him, the mage's eyes moved under her lids. Both their pulses were strong although hers was definitely quicker. The pin was still in place, pushed into the flesh of the boy's shoulder, just past the edge of the recent scarring. With the surgeon's warning in mind, he decided to wait a little longer before giving them another dose.

"Back on the road."

"Yes, sir. Say, Cap? You ever get her name?"

"The enemy doesn't have names. It makes them easier to kill."

Chard flinched and muttered, "Ouch." He spent a few minutes

staring at the swing of Thunder's tail, then he turned. "Is she going to be killed?"

Reiter kept his gaze on a field beside the road, a field plowed and planted, the marks of two armies—infantry, cavalry, artillery, and whatever dangerous shit the engineers had been up to—already erased by the need to feed Abyek's factory workers so they'd keep making the bricks and whatever else those smoking monstrosities turned out.

"Captain Reiter?"

"Just drive, Private."

Mirian knew her hands and feet were tied. She knew her head ached and her jaw throbbed, but she didn't hurt as badly as her last memory of the market insisted she should. Her mouth tasted much as it had after she'd been sent by the family doctor to a surgeon for a toothache, so it seemed they'd been drugged. She knew she was in the back of a wagon, tied to a ring bolted into the side of the box and that Tomas was beside her although too far away to touch, also tied.

Had the Imperials been smart enough to leave the silver pin in his body? She tried to reach out and identify the metal, but her head felt as though it had been stuffed with ash. Too light to move aside, it merely moved around. And ash would explain why her eyes stung, tears welling up with every blink.

She was conscious; Tomas wasn't. They knew what he was, so they might have given him more of the drug. Or, possibly, body equilibrium, first level healing, had helped clear the drug from her system faster.

Common sense told her they were on the Aydori Road traveling east toward Karis. The shadows told her it was afternoon.

She hadn't been surprised to hear Captain Reiter tell Chard to pull over. It seemed the whole empire was allowed to kill Tomas, but who else would want her? The shouting in the market must have brought the soldiers, and the soldiers had brought her to the captain. Brought *them* to the captain because Tomas wasn't dead and he hadn't been skinned.

However bad it was, it could be worse.

The wagon stopped.

She'd barely gotten her eyes closed and her breathing steadied when the captain turned to examine them.

She thought he must really want to believe she was still unconscious to not have noticed she was awake.

She knew they had to escape.

She just didn't know how.

"Pull over, Chard."

"Here, Cap?"

"Here." Reiter twisted around on the seat and dropped down into the wagon box, ignoring Chard's efforts to get Thunder to move to the side of the road. They were nearly to the Duke's Seat, a good-sized city built around an ancient fortress on a hill. The fortress, at least, could have held out indefinitely in an earlier time. As it was, the artillery had brought up the big twelve pounders and bombed the shit out it. One of the officers at Abyek who'd been at the Seat during the bombardment had said he'd had to keep his mouth open in order to stabilize the pressure in his ears from the firing of the guns. Reiter'd been staring at the approaching ruins and thinking about the rebuilding when he'd realized that the soft sounds the boy'd been making for some time had become words.

Words in Aydori. Not words Reiter could understand but definitely words.

What's more, the boy's eyes were open. Whites bloodshot, pupils blown, he flicked them from side to side, gaze not quite focused. His nostrils were widely flared, although he had to struggle to get air in through his nose. His lips were pulled back off his teeth. He wasn't fighting the rope yet, but he would.

Reaching for a canteen, Reiter turned to check the g . . . mage.

Her eyes were also open, an even paler gray than he remembered. Almost silver. She closed them immediately and opened them again an instant later, aware she'd been too late. He hated that she looked afraid, but, realistically, how else would she look? If he hated it that much, he knew what to do about it. Mixed in with her fear was a quiet assessment that reminded him a little of Major Halyss.

He slid a hand behind her shoulders and held the open canteen to her mouth. Although he'd been afraid he might have to force the issue, she drank so willingly, he had to pull back and slow her down. When she'd finished half the water, he laid her flat and did the same for the boy. Still barely aware, he growled and muttered but drank.

Having tossed the empty canteen aside, Reiter pulled the glass bottle and one of the cloth pads from the satchel. Carefully pulling the cork from the bottle, he damped the cloth, stopping before the liquid spread past the marks Major Raynold had drawn.

The boy's growls had grown wilder and he'd begun to fight the rope, but unlike the poor flaming bastard in the market, Reiter knew which of his two prisoners was the more dangerous. When he turned back to the mage, her pale eyes were fixed on the cloth in his hand.

"Don't."

It was as much an exhale as a word, but he heard it. Ignored it. He didn't fault her for trying to escape, but if she hadn't broken the tangle . . .

When he pressed the cloth over her mouth and nose, her eyes narrowed in a silent challenge, and it soon became clear she was holding her breath. From the little he knew of her, she'd pass out before she inhaled. He moved his thumb just far enough to touch the bruise on her jaw, pressed, dimpled the green-yellow swelling, and she gasped. Her eyes watered, her eyelids fluttered. When she could no longer keep her eyes open, he lifted the cloth away and used a dry edge to wipe the snot from her upper lip.

"Uh, Cap?"

"I know."

He had to brace himself as the boy fought the rope hard enough to rock the wagon. Chard muttered nonsense at the suddenly restive horse, trying to keep it still as Reiter prepared a fresh cloth. The major had insisted: one cloth, one dose. He clamped a hand down on the silver pin, and pressed the cloth down on the boy's face. When it was over, he wiped the snot from his lip, too.

Chard watched him climb back into his seat and, at a nod, got Thunder moving again. "So, Cap, I was thinking about the water."

Not what he'd expected. "The water?"

"You're getting them to drink, right? What happens to it?"

"The same thing that always happens to it."

"Well, yeah, Cap, but they're tied in the back of a wagon. What happens if they need to piss?"

"Then they piss." The tone shut Chard up. Reiter knew that if he lost the mage again, he'd better desert. The best he could hope for from the emperor would be years under the whip on a work detail.

They were nearly clear of the Duke's Seat before Chard said, eyes on the road, "We're not stopping at the garrison, Captain?"

"No."

"It's just sun's going down, and Thunder . . ."

"Find a field with some forage for him. We'll spend the night there."

"It's just I heard the 2nd Swords are with the governor, and I got a cousin . . ."

"Find a field, Chard."

"Yes, sir." He chirped at Thunder, then added, "Duke's Seat is a dumbass name for a city, ain't it, Cap. Figure the emperor will rename it?"

Abomination.

The emperor liked renaming things.

"I expect so."

The pond was shallow but declared suitable; the forage a sufficient supplement to the nosebag. The farm buildings were ruins, the farmers killed or driven off, and the land not yet awarded to Imperial soldiers for services rendered. Lack of shelter didn't bother either man, both had campaigned long enough they only cared their beds be dry and not under fire. The prisoners would remain where they were.

Chard dumped an armload of dead wood by the small fire pit, and frowned across it at the wagon. "We could tie them to that tree, Cap."

"She was tied to a tree the last time," Reiter muttered, shoving his fire-starter in among the kindling. Flame smothered by the force he'd used, he had to pull it out and try again.

"Yes, sir, but this time she's on the drugs."

"Then she won't care where she is."

"But . . ."

Reiter raised his head and locked eyes with Chard. "They stay where they are."

Chard proved to be smarter than he looked. "Yes, sir. I'll get more wood."

You won't fight for it, will you? Reiter thought watching him walk away. *You know what you believe, but you're a good soldier, for all your mouth, and you follow orders.*

"Tomas? Tomas, can you hear me?" Hair catching against the floor of the wagon, Mirian struggled to get as close to Tomas as she could. Tied as they were, she couldn't touch him. The drug still controlled him, locked him in his head with his dead, left him muttering about Ryder and Harry and the taste of blood in his mouth. "Tomas, please be quiet!"

She thought she'd regained enough control of her mind that she could get herself free, risk burns by setting fire to the rope, but then what? She couldn't escape without Tomas, and he never quite managed to shake off the delirium before Captain Reiter used the drug again.

The only thing that kept her from sinking into despair was that her rudimentary healer-craft overcame the drug more quickly every time. Soon or later, she'd be aware with time enough to free them both from the ropes and remove the silver before Tomas' mutterings alerted the captain. If she could force Tomas to change, hopefully the change itself would expel the drug as it had healed his shoulder.

Unfortunately, she couldn't start until she could finish. If the captain caught her during the attempt, she had no doubt he'd ensure that it would be the *last* attempt.

Here and now, discomfort had her so distracted, she was afraid she couldn't concentrate long enough to light even an actual candle.

"Ryder!" Tomas rolled his head toward her, eyes focused on the past. "No!"

Reiter was feeding sticks into the small blaze when he heard the boy's raving turn to words. "I'm starting to think I should've had a longer breakfast and minded my own flaming business," he muttered as he used a taper to light a small lantern.

It had been easy to tell Chard that their prisoners would remain in the wagon but less easy to live with that decision when he dropped down off the seat into the box and found the young wo . . . found the mage staring up at him. As the boy's eyes focused only intermittently, Reiter tended to her first.

When he raised the canteen to her mouth, she shook her head. "You have to drink."

She shook her head again. The lantern didn't throw light enough to be sure, but he thought she blushed.

Oh.

He knew what he'd told Chard, and if she'd just pissed herself . . . well, he'd seen people survive much worse. It was a different thing entirely to specifically refuse her.

"Your word you won't try to escape, and I'll take you far enough out of the firelight for a little privacy."

To his surprise, she frowned thoughtfully up at him and, after a long moment's consideration, said, "You have my word."

"Chard!"

"Sir!"

"Get up here and get the boy in your sights. You hear me yell, you shoot him. You hear her yell, you shoot him. She comes back without me, you shoot him. You smell anything burning, you shoot him."

Her frown had changed from thoughtful to annoyed. "I gave you my word."

"You did. It strikes me you're the type to lie if it was practical."

To his greater surprise, she laughed, winced as it pulled the bruise on her jaw, and said, "Sensible."

He found himself wanting to know what her laugh sounded like when it wasn't so bitter.

They didn't speak again and, when she was done, he took the boy as well although he forgot to check the silver pin until both prisoners were once again tied and drugged.

The skin around it was red and a little puffy. When Reiter touched the pin, the boy moaned, sounding even younger than he looked.

At the fire, Reiter sat with his back once again to the wagon and grunted his thanks as Chard handed him a mug of tea.

"I heard a rumor once, Cap, that we took Derbia because Emperor Leopald's da, that being Emperor Armoud . . ."

"I know who the last emperor was, Chard."

"Yeah, 'course you do, Cap."

"You heard a rumor," Reiter prodded after a moment. Under normal circumstances, he wouldn't encourage Chard, but he needed the distraction.

"Right. So this rumor says Emperor Armoud really likes tea and that's why we took Derbia."

"It's possible."

"But you were in Derbia, right, Cap? I mean not then, but the Spears got sent to put down the revolution, and when I got pulled to this . . ." The shadow of his gesture flapped around the fire like a crow over a corpse. ". . . mission back in Karis, I heard you saved the emperor's nephew's life from a mage when you were a sergeant and that's why you got made an officer. And then that's why you got sent on this, because you fought that mage."

He hadn't so much fought the mage as shot him in the back before he got a chance to do much of anything. Very few soldiers in the Imperial army had any experience with mages, and those who did knew only the village healers or gardeners or blacksmiths and didn't believe they were dangerous. It had been dumb luck that the emperor's idiot nephew had been directly in the mage's line of fire and had overreacted to Reiter's shot.

Reiter remembered the man-shaped torch in the market. It seemed there was a chance it hadn't been an overreaction.

"Cap? Is it true?"

"It's true enough."

The army had set up a checkpoint at what had been the border between the Duchies of Pyrahn and Traiton and was now the new provincial border. Reiter doubted there was an actual reason for it as both duchies had been effectively conquered at the same time, but someone in a position to make decisions had thought it was a good idea.

Reiter returned the salute of the fresh-faced lieutenant on the gate, noted two of the three rankers under him were anything but fresh—both too broken to return to the front—and handed over his orders. The lieutenant's eyes widened at the Imperial seal, and his hand shook when he handed the papers back.

"Your prisoners . . ."

"His Imperial Majesty's prisoners."

The boy, and he couldn't have been older than the boy tied in the back, paled under his freckles. "Yes, sir. But she's . . . I mean, she's . . ."

A young woman tied, drugged, bruised clearly made him uncomfortable. Good.

"She's His Imperial Majesty's prisoner," Reiter repeated.

"Yes, sir. What did she . . . ?" His voice trailed off under Reiter's stare. He backed away from the wagon and saluted again. "Very good, sir."

Fraris, the only city of any size in Traiton, was visible from the border. They wouldn't make it across the new province to the old Imperial border by dark, but they'd be there tomorrow.

"You know, Cap, he was a good dog."

It took Reiter a moment to understand what Chard was talking about. "He wasn't a dog."

"Yeah, I know, but . . . I don't see why he's an abomination, either. Best, he said the beastmen are abominations because the church says so, but Best is like crazy religious. I even heard him pray when we weren't under fire. How does the church know?"

The church obeyed the emperor. Or at least the new Prelate did and the church obeyed him. Reiter didn't think he'd tell Chard that. It'd be just like Chard to complain about it in front of the wrong people and make Reiter responsible for him going under the lash.

"Abomination means they're less than animals," Chard muttered, frowning unhappily. "But he was a good dog . . ."

She was startled enough when he climbed down into the wagon, that she said his name.

"Captain Reiter."

"You have the advantage of me." He'd heard Lieutenant Lord Geurin say that once. It seemed more likely to get a response than, *And you are?*

She shook her head, turned it toward the boy who was whining low in his throat. "Tomas?"

He still didn't have her name, but he had the boy's name. The boy had a name. The beastman had a name. Abominations didn't have names.

"It was Soothsayers, wasn't it, Cap?"

"Wasn't what?"

"What sent us into Aydori to get the women. I mean they told us that we were there because if you take their mages they do what you say and not fight, and we were all about not fighting beastmen, and then their mages were all women and that wasn't good, but this . . ." He jerked his head toward the back ". . . this is more than that. It's enough more and it's enough crazy, it's gotta be Soothsayers. 'Cause we got five. Why would we need six so bad?"

"Stop asking, Private. That's an order."

"It's Soothsayers," Chard sighed.

Reiter let it go because he'd just remembered . . .

The baby.

He'd forgotten the prophecy said she was pregnant.

The unborn child begins it all.

Or would be pregnant.

Or was back when they stopped the coaches in Aydori, when and where the Soothsayers had instructed them to.

He should've asked the surgeon to check.

Reiter watched the shadows stretching out in front of them on the road. It looked as though the darkness his gran had warned him not to walk in was in a hurry to get to the empire.

"Long as the weather's holding, we could make a push, Cap."

It took him a moment to understand what Chard meant by a push. Reiter stared at the horse. Thunder, as though aware of the scrutiny, farted twice before pulling the wagon through the cloud. "I don't think he's got a push in him."

"We've barely had him at more than a walk all day, Cap. He's got . . ." Chard's voice trailed off as Reiter turned. "Still," he added slowly as though checking each word for Reiter's reaction, "we bring him in overheated and it'll be my ass the stable-master puts in a sling." He flashed a sudden grin in Reiter's direction. "Thanks for thinking of my ass, Cap."

"Shut up, Chard."

"Yes, sir."

The growing Imperial presence on the road indicated the checkpoint they'd have to pass at the old Imperial border would actually mean something. The first day out of Abyek there'd been only a couple of couriers, and although the road past the Seat had been busy enough—given the building of the governor's complex and its half garrison—the lateness of the hour had meant the road beyond had been nearly empty. Today, after passing Fraris, there'd seldom been a moment when they'd been without Imperial company. Couriers. Soldiers. Wagonloads of goods. A ragged work detail, chivied along by a bored sergeant who saluted with his whip handle. A trio of cavalry officers, one with a bloody pelt tied on behind his saddle. Reiter returned salutes, saluted when it mattered, and was just as glad when the cavalry officers ignored him as they cantered past.

Chard had made a noise, but for a change said nothing. Reiter had seen a muscle jumping in his jaw and from the depths of his frown, obvious even in profile, the younger man seemed to have been thinking deeply. Thinking was fine. He could *think* all he wanted.

There wouldn't be a green lieutenant asking the questions at the old Imperial border, but someone whose balls had actually dropped. A report detailing the wagon, the prisoners, and the orders being followed would be on its way to the Lyonne garrison before the smell of Thunder's passage had faded. By the time they arrived, the garrison's duty officer would know exactly what to expect. Given the prisoners, odds were high a courier would be sent to the emperor before Reiter had time to load them on a mail coach.

"Start looking for a place to camp, Private."

Chard glanced around at the forest on both sides of the road. "Yes, sir." The expected protest about time or location never came.

Major Halyss had been right. On a trip this long, anything could happen. But it would have to happen on this side of the border.

Chard found a place by a creek far enough off the road and under thick enough cover that they wouldn't be seen even before the sun fully set. Wheel ruts and a fire pit made it clear the area had been used as a campsite in the recent past.

By the time Chard had returned from the creek with the horse, Reiter had decided that a small, smokeless fire would be best. He didn't want the attention a larger fire might attract, but neither did he want the attention that might arise from having had no fire at all.

"Hey, Cap!"

He looked up from his small blaze to see Chard emerge into the clearing holding a twelve-pound shell.

"Busted a bunch of trees back there all to ratshit. What do you think they were firing at in here?"

"Given the artillery had to pass by on the road, I'd say a sniper." The crews on the guns could set up and fire surprisingly fast when they had to.

"Just one?"

"If there'd been more than a single sniper, they'd have reduced these woods to kindling before they advanced." The Duke of Traiton, taken by surprise, had rabbited the moment it had become clear that the troops gathering at the Lyonne garrison were not the traditional bi-yearly show of strength but intended to cross the border, diplomatic protests be flamed. He then turned and dug in along the border with Pyrahn, where his much smaller force could count on the Duke of Pyrahn's backing. Reiter acknowledged it was the best the duke could've done. It hadn't changed the ending.

When dusk had settled almost into night, Reiter lit the lantern and climbed up into the wagon. Chard was so emphatically not watching him, he might as well have been staring. The mage's eyes were closed and her breathing shallow, but Reiter could tell she was conscious. Her body practically vibrated with the need for him to go away.

He knelt by her feet, pushed the bottom of her skirt, heavy with dirt, out of the way and untied the rope manacles. Her feet were filthy and cold, so he wrapped his hands around them until they warmed. They weren't tiny, delicate feet. They were sturdy, like the mage herself, strong enough to do what was necessary. When he set them carefully down and looked up, she was staring at him, frowning slightly. He felt his face grow hot as he untied the rope from the metal ring. "Come on."

She glanced at the boy, Tomas—Reiter made himself say the boy's name. The hair—fur—had been pushed up on one side of his head exposing the point on his ear. It wasn't an extreme point. Reiter had known an artillery captain back in the Shields whose ears looked much the same. The artillery captain didn't walk on all fours covered with fur, though. At least, not as far as Reiter knew.

The boy'd begun to shift slightly, small movements against the hold of the ropes, but he hadn't even begun to mutter. They had time.

"Chard."

She flinched although he hadn't raised his voice.

"Get the boy in your sights. Same orders as last night."

"Yes, sir."

He took his musket with him tonight.

He led her away until the fire was a barely visible flicker through the underbrush and turned his back. Shoving his hand into his pocket, he expected the cool slide of the tangle across his fingers, but felt instead the strand of her hair he'd taken from the artifact the night she'd escaped from him. He pulled it out, drew it one last time between thumb and forefinger, settling the memory, then scattered it on the leaf litter. When he heard the rustle of her skirt falling back into place, he asked, "Are you . . ." How did the quality say it? ". . . increasing?"

"What?"

"With child?"

"No!"

Of course she wasn't. She'd never attempted to protect a child. Women did that, didn't they? And if she wasn't with child then she wasn't the sixth mage of the prophecy. She couldn't be. Unless she'd been with child and wasn't now . . .

"Were you?"

"With child? I've never . . ." The lantern, hung on a convenient branch stub, threw shadows over her face, but he got the impression she'd have slapped him had her hands been free.

So she couldn't have been and not known. And the boy . . . Tomas wasn't the father. Reiter tossed his musket aside. Let the evidence show he had it with him, but didn't have time to get a shot off. Heart pounding as though he were going into battle, he stepped closer and began to untie her hands. Eyes wide, she tried to back away. He tugged her close again. After a moment, she stopped struggling and he returned to fighting with the knots.

She asked a question. Remembered. Asked it again in Imperial. "What are you doing?"

"Being overwhelmed by an escaping mage."

"I can't go without . . ."

"I don't expect you to."

He could almost hear her trying to choose her next question. No surprise she cut straight to the point. "Why?"

"I'm a soldier." The light was bad and the coarse fibers of the rope made it difficult to feel how the pattern had twisted. "I have been since I was fifteen. I've fought in pitched battles and skirmishes. I've waited in ambush; been caught in one. Although I've done what I could to adjust the consequences of bad orders, I've still followed them. I honestly don't know how many people I've killed." Threading the dangling length of rope back through a loop unraveled the knot. "But there's a difference between killing and murdering." He unwound the rope, stroked a thumb over the unmarked skin on her inner wrist just once, then backed away. "If you cross the border with me, you don't have a chance. Tomas has less of one." Major Halyss had called him "the boy," and when he'd flatly said the emperor might be making rugs, he'd meant the emperor might be making rugs. Not a metaphor. Tomas couldn't be left at the Abyek garrison, and Reiter'd been warned what would happen to him if he was taken to Karis. When the mage stared at him, confused, he sighed. "Look, it's never just one thing that changes a man's mind. It's a hundred small things adding up. I know you have no reason to think good of me, but I'd appreciate it if you didn't kill me when you take me out."

"When I what?"

"If I just let you go, I'm a dead man. Too many people know I have you. Too many people know what my orders were. You have to escape."

She glanced down at her hands, then up. "I have to make it look like I . . . we escaped. How?"

Was he going to have to knock himself out, Reiter wondered. "You're the mage."

"Not much of one."

"Not much . . . The scene in the market says different." He frowned as she frowned, clearly not understanding what he referred to. "You don't know about what happened in the market?" He'd wondered at the time if she'd known what she was doing; it hadn't occurred to him she had no memory of it.

"That farm worker was going to skin Tomas. I took hold of a man in a leather vest, and he threw me back. He kicked me. I think . . ." She pressed a hand against her side. "I *thought* he broke my ribs. And then I woke up in the garrison next to Tomas, and that woman drugged us. I thought the solders had come because of all the shouting." Her pale eyes widened. "You came. That's why Tomas isn't dead. Isn't skinned."

"You think I wouldn't have allowed that to happen?"

She spread her hands and looked at him like he was a little slow. "You *didn't*."

No, he didn't. Hadn't.

Chard would wonder soon what was taking them so long, so Reiter told her quickly what he'd seen when he entered the market. Her face showed horror when he briefly described the burning man, but not regret. As he sketched out the rest, she looked confused, listened without asking questions, then twisted her foot into the light and stared down at the back of her heel. "He had a knife. I wasn't thinking . . ."

"You have to start."

"Funny." Her smile held no humor. "Usually people tell me I think too much."

Reiter wanted to see her smile, her actual smile. He knew he never would, but he wanted it so much it sat like a rock in his chest. "Chard doesn't know about this . . . escape. He can't lie for shit. Try not to hurt him. He runs on at the mouth, but he's a good kid." Chard still hadn't called out to ask if there was a problem. What the fuck did he think they were doing out here? "A fire of any size," he added, "will draw attention from the border. And you want as much of a head start as you can get."

"We'll be . . ."

"Don't tell me! I'm a very good liar," he explained. "But they won't ask nicely."

She drew in a deep breath and let it out slowly. In spite of shadows, he could actually see her thinking of what she was going to do. There was still a chance she could kill both him and Chard. He'd gambled she didn't have it in her. If he got in her way, yes, but not coldly and deliberately after he'd released her and armed her with what she was capable of. She'd slept Armin and walked away when she had less reason to think kindly of him.

He could tell the moment she came to a decision. It hadn't taken her long and there'd only be one way to find out if that worked in his favor.

She squared her shoulders, paused as though something had just occurred to her, and said, "You asked earlier; my name is Mirian."

"Sleep." The captain's forehead felt warm and dry under her fingers and Mirian watched him crumple to the ground, feeling confused as much as anything. Her ribs were whole, her heels unbloodied, and, when it came down to it, Captain Reiter had no reason to lie about what he'd seen in the market. She had tested very high, multiple times, so perhaps that meant low levels at very high power. But in every craft? She'd never heard of that happening.

Still, whatever it meant, it didn't matter now. What mattered now was making the most of this opportunity. Somehow. Perhaps she should have used the captain's experience in strategy and tactics rather than put him to sleep, but she couldn't think while he was watching her.

First, she had to deal with Chard.

Leaving the lantern where the captain had hung it, she picked her way carefully through the underbrush. The firelight showed Chard sitting on the side of the wagon box. From the angle of the musket, he had it pointed up under Tomas' chin. He was staring at Tomas, not watching for them to come out of the woods, and he didn't look happy.

If she emerged alone, he'd shoot Tomas. If she called to him, he'd shoot Tomas. He might not want to and he'd likely feel guilty about it, but he'd do it. Bottom line, that was all that mattered.

Captain Reiter was right. She had to start thinking like a mage.

Raising a hand into the breeze, she sent a puff of it toward the wagon, into the wagon box, over Tomas, and out to where the horse grazed on the end of a rope tied to a wagon wheel. In the end, it was nothing more than blowing out a long, curving line of candles. . . .

Military horses might be the most phlegmatic known—and given that this horse had been transporting one of the Pack for two days suggested *might* wasn't entirely accurate—but Mirian suspected that the fresh, immediate scent of predator had to be entirely different than a faint scent woven into the other scents of the road.

The horse half reared and tried to run, dragging the wagon forward and throwing Chard off the side into the box. He popped up again almost immediately and leaped to the ground, stumbled, grabbed for the rope, and murmured a long string of calming nonsense as the horse reared and plunged around him. He was brave, Mirian would give him that. She couldn't have stood so close to those hooves.

Whether it was because the scent wasn't repeated or because the horse found Chard reassuring, he calmed fairly quickly. Snorting and blowing, he allowed Chard to get one hand on his bridle and the other up under his mane.

"There now, you stupid git. What were you all up in yourself for, huh? You catch scent of . . ."

When he turned, Mirian put him to sleep.

Chard dropped and rolled between the horse's legs.

The horse looked down, looked at Mirian, and shook his head hard enough the wagon creaked.

Tomas moaned.

If the horse got another less deliberate nose full of Pack . . . Mirian untied the end of his lead rope from the wagon and started around to the other side of the fire. The horse watched her go, stretched out his neck as the rope came up taut, and refused to move. Pulling didn't help. Coaxing didn't help.

Tomas moaned again.

"Fine. Have it your way." As she sidled in close, he rolled his eyes but continued to stand right where he was. "I'm not going to hurt you, okay?" The clip attaching the rope to the bridle was too stiff for her too open. What difference did it make if he dragged the rope with him? So what if it got caught; he was huge. Someone would find him. Except . . .

She couldn't leave him tied. Not having been tied.

The clip was brass. Brass felt bright. Sharp. The taste of vinegar across her tongue and she held a cooling sphere in her hand. The rope dropped to the ground. Another moment to drag Chard away, then she was up in the wagon, murmuring much the same calming nonsense as Tomas began to thrash.

One hand gripping his hip, Mirian burned the rope securing Tomas to the side of the wagon. He lay panting but still, so she jumped down to get the lantern and Chard's knife. It would be safer to cut the ropes around his wrists and ankles. The knife was sharp, but the ropes were thick . . .

"I'm sorry! Oh, Tomas, I'm so sorry." Blood dripped onto the wagon as she pulled the pieces of rope away from skin rubbed raw and red. His ankles were no better than his wrists except that she'd managed not to cut him while freeing them. Although she'd been tied the same way, her own skin—wrists and ankles—had been completely unmarked. She stared at her wrist and pushed the memory of Reiter's touch to the back of her mind. Evidently, she could heal herself. That didn't mean she should experiment on Tomas. The hole in his shoulder had closed when he changed, and these injuries were nothing in comparison.

When he changed . . .

The skin around the silver pin felt red and puffy. He keened as she hooked her fingernails under the head and yanked it out.

"Tomas? Tomas, can you hear me?"

No. Though his eyes moved back and forth under closed lids, the muttering hadn't yet become words.

Thrusting the pin through a fold in her skirt, she wondered if he'd change as he began to shake off the drug. Would his body recognize what it needed? Mirian had no idea. She stripped him out of his shirt and stopped, hands on the waistband of his trousers. Tomas wouldn't care. Would, in fact, prefer to be out of all clothing when he changed. Depending on how much or how little of his mind had returned, he might even be panicked by the feeling of being trapped in the cloth.

Mirian managed to get both sides of the flap unbuttoned without touching anything but the buttons. Leaving it lying closed, she took the lantern down to his feet, grabbed his trousers and pulled only to find Tomas' weight held them in place.

"Fine."

She'd been nearly drowned, captured by the Imperial army—twice—tied, drugged, and she'd killed two men. She wasn't going to be recaptured because she was too missish to take off a man's trousers, particularly when she'd seen that man naked on more than one occasion. Tugging the rough wool over damp skin, she clenched her teeth and kept her eyes locked on her hands. There was, after all, a difference between seeing and looking.

Like between killing and murdering.

Hysteria began bubbling up through the cracks. Mirian shoved it back down.

Untied and unclothed, Tomas began to thrash in earnest, arms and legs flung wide. Mirian rescued the lantern and slid back to the very end of the wagon. Mouth open, Tomas panted, every exhale a small cry that sounded equal parts pain and anger. He rocked up until he was half sitting, his eyes so wide they showed white all around—Mirian doubted he saw her—then he fell onto his side and changed.

He continued to pant in fur form, whining, still under the control of the drug.

Leaving the lantern where it was, Mirian crawled up beside him and lifted his head onto her lap. "Change again, Tomas. Please. One more time." Curling forward, she pressed her face to his, breathing with him then slowing the rhythm. He slowed with her. They were breathing the same air. From her mouth into his. "Change, Tomas."

A paw pushed at her leg, then a hand grabbed her skirt. "Mirian?"

Forehead to forehead, she kept breathing with him. "I'm here."

"Head hurts."

"I know."

"Hungry."

Her stomach growled and she straightened. "Me, too." How long since they'd eaten? "Stay here. I'll go get food."

He started a protest but didn't manage to finish it. While no longer under the control of the drug, he hadn't managed to quite make it back to himself. By the time Mirian returned with a hunk of salt pork and half a loaf of dark bread, he'd changed again and gone to sleep. His tail twitched, but he didn't wake when she stroked his shoulder.

She brought the lantern closer.

His fur now had a silver streak over the place the pin had been for the last two and a half days. The silver that had shattered his shoulder hadn't left a mark, so this must have been the result of time.

"Tomas?"

His nose twitched when she waved the pork in front of it, but he didn't wake. He'd slept after the last time he'd healed himself, so she stroked his head and backed away.

She was a little worried about the food. If she could purify water, could she purify pork? Would it be like water because it was being purified, or would it be healing because it was meat?

"Maybe they teach something useful in second year," she muttered, leaving most of the meat and half the bread for Tomas. She emptied a canteen, set the last full one by the meat, and gathered up the rest.

The horse snorted, tail sweeping great arcs, as she moved upwind of him. He danced sideways until he was as far from the creek as he could get and remain in the clearing. Fine. They didn't need to be friends. She filled the canteens, purifying the water, and left them by the wagon. The packs turned up two bedrolls, another fire-starter, and more money. A lot more money. As she slipped the worn leather purse into her jacket pocket, she touched the edge of something hard and had to bite her lip to keep from giggling. She'd tucked the telescope into her jacket that night in the shelter. The Imperials took everything else, took their clogs, tied her up and drugged her, and had carefully tucked the telescope she'd taken from a dead Imperial soldier back where they found it. And they *had* found it. She'd been half aware as a frowning woman had pressed careful hands against her ribs.

The world was strange and getting stranger.

She found the oil in time to refill the lantern, then almost couldn't find Captain Reiter out in the woods. He was lying where and how she left him; legs bent, one arm by his side, the other thrown wide. She thought about taking his watch, but that seemed unnecessarily rude when she'd been left her stolen telescope. His chest rose and fell. She prodded him with her foot. He didn't wake. *I woke and they were gone* wasn't much of an excuse. She knew the feel of silver, so she pulled the shot from his ammo pouch and sent it down into the ground.

Still not enough.

Standing so close she could slide her toes under the edge of his thigh, she reached into herself the way they'd taught her and thought of blowing out a thousand candles burning in a circle around them.

Trees shattered.

Dirt under his paws. Hackles up. Heart pounding. Lips drawn back off his teeth. His nose said power. Familiar power. Tomas ran toward it.

Past a narrow band of woods, he found Mirian standing in a circle of downed trees, everything from oaks to underbrush flattened to the ground, the man he'd helped her escape from once before, lying at her feet.

And it all came back. The market, the garrison, the wagon, trapped in his head by the drugs, held to two legs by silver, Mirian waking him . . .

He staggered a bit as he changed. Would have stayed on four legs except he needed his voice. "What did you do?"

Her fingers went white around the handle of the lantern and he thought for a moment she might drop it. "I blew out a candle."

"A candle?"

"Maybe a few." Stepping over the captain's body, she picked her way carefully toward him, wincing as she stepped on shards of branches. As she reached him, he ducked his face into the curve where her neck met her shoulder and took a deep breath. Her hand felt like ice against his chest as she pushed him away. "The food, money, and bedrolls go with us. Everything else we leave."

He tipped his head to the side, caught sight of the Imperial on the ground, and, reminded, growled.

Mirian grabbed his arm before he could change. "Leave the captain alone. He released me."

"Why?"

"Because there's a difference between killing and murdering. Come on."

He had no idea what she was talking about, but he couldn't decide if that was because of the drugs or her scent or because it didn't make any sense. He followed her anyway. When she stumbled as she stepped out into the clearing, he got his arm around her waist before she fell. "Are you hurt?"

"Tired." As she sagged back against him, he twisted a little to keep his reaction from rubbing against the wool of her skirt. "The horse is gone."

Tomas inhaled and coughed. "Smells like you scared the crap out of him."

Mirian half giggled, the noise not quite escaping although he felt her body shake. Stepping out of his hold, she hurried toward the embers of a small fire, her movements a combination of fragile and frantic he didn't much like. She looked as though she might break herself into pieces at any moment. "We have to hurry. If the horse has bolted along the road, the Imperials will look for where he came from." She threw a wool blanket to the ground and began tossing things onto it. "There's not much food, but we'll take what there is. Did you eat the pork I left in the wagon?"

His stomach growled and his nose twitched and the pork smelled good enough that he went over the sleeping body of another Imperial without pausing on his way into the wagon. Mirian's scent was on the meat, so he had to assume she'd eaten. He barely stopped himself from swallowing it whole. By the time he jumped back to the ground, she had the bedroll tied and hanging from her shoulder. He could smell the clothes he'd been wearing, biscuits and dried meat and . . .

"Stop it." She pushed his head away. "The captain said we're close to the old Imperial border."

Tomas rose up on two legs. "And you trust him?"

"Yes. No. But he wasn't lying."

"That makes no sense."

"Probably not. We don't need all six . . ." She stared at the canteens hanging from her hand and dropped four. ". . . I don't know why I filled them all. Why would I . . . No, never mind."

"Mirian?"

"We need to head east. There's no point in taking the lantern, they could track the light. You'll have to get us across the border and find us somewhere safe. As soon as you can."

If they were that close to the old Imperial border, the enemy would know the ground. "We should keep moving."

"We should." Her eyes were enormous, her cheeks pale. Nearly overwhelmed by her scent, he hadn't really looked at her face. Her lips trembled slightly as she spoke. "But we won't be able to. One thing I learned as a banker's daughter; bills always come due."

Most of Mirian's weight hung off his back by the time he found the overhang. With one side open to the elements, it wasn't a proper cave, but it was deep enough that it was dry in spite of the rain. Slabs of rock thrown up by artillery practice made it nearly impossible to see from any distance. The surrounding scars from repeated shelling made it obvious why no animal had chosen to den here. He'd have preferred to be farther from the border, but he no longer had a choice.

He felt her slip, changed as she fell, and went down with her, managing to keep her head from hitting the rock—although collapsing beside her seemed like a better idea. "You still with me?"

Her fingers moved against his arm.

"All right. We're almost there. I'll just carry you for the last bit, okay?"

Except she wasn't small or delicate like the beauties Harry and the other men of the 1st had exclaimed over and the rain had slicked his skin and weighted down her clothes. He settled for half carrying, half dragging her in under the overhang, then leaving her just out of the rain while he opened the bedrolls and spread the blankets in the back. They were thick enough wool that the parts folded to the inside were still dry. He ate two of the biscuits that spilled out before he realized he'd done it.

He changed on the way back. It was easier to move on four legs, although his shoulders scraped the roof, and when he figured he was far enough away from both Mirian and the blankets he tried to shake some of the water out of his fur without knocking himself over.

When he got back to Mirian, her teeth were chattering.

"I thought you could keep yourself warm!"

She didn't answer. Apparently, that was one of the bills coming due.

"Think of her like she's Harry," he muttered, breathing shallowly through his mouth as he unbuttoned her jacket. He set the telescope aside, a little surprised she was still carrying it. The tiny pearl buttons on the shirtwaist were rounded, so they slipped free with no trouble. The tie inside confused him for a moment before he realized it was part of the extra fabric holding her breasts in place. Once he worked that out, he could slide the jacket and shirtwaist off together. The skirt and the petticoat were held on by a buckle, a button, and a tie and were easy to remove. He paused, one hand resting on the curve of her waist and tried to decide the best way to hold her. He could think of her like she was Harry all he wanted, but his nose and his body knew better.

He scraped his knees carrying her back to the blankets—nothing another change couldn't heal—and narrowly missed cracking his head when he bent forward to lay her down. Breathing heavily, resting his forehead against hers, he wrapped her in the blankets and changed as he collapsed beside her far enough away he wouldn't get the blankets damp.

She whimpered, freed a hand, and grabbed a handful of fur. Her grip was barely strong enough to hold on, but when she tugged him toward her, he went. Later, he told himself, jaws cracking as he yawned, when she was able to keep herself warm again, he'd go hunting for something to . . .

Danika's first sight of Karis was as a blaze of light though the small window in the mail coach door as they rounded a curve approaching the Vone River Valley. At first she thought it was a fire on the horizon and then, as the angle changed, she realized the lights were too regular to be anything but gaslights along the major avenues and shining out the windows of the homes of the wealthy. As they drew closer and the angle changed again, she saw there was so much light it couldn't just be from the homes of the wealthy unless Karis forced its shopkeepers and skilled workers to live elsewhere. Ryder had planned for gaslights on the streets of Bercarit—and later Trouge once the more conservative population saw how useful they were— but she'd never heard him speak of running the lines into private homes.

It was beautiful, in an extravagant way, and she found herself sharing it with Tagget who shifted forward nearly onto her lap to see what she was looking at, and grinned. "I gotta say, I'm glad to be home."

Carlsan, propped in the far corner, didn't bother opening his eyes. "Shut the fuck up."

Kirstin's eyes were closed as well although Danika knew she wasn't asleep.

"You're from Karis?"

He scratched at his stubble and grinned. "Born and bred. We were all stationed there though. Shields never leave the . . ."

"Shut the fuck up," Carlsan repeated, this time with an emphasis Tagget couldn't ignore.

He settled back in his seat, glared across at her as if his indiscretion had been her fault, and closed his eyes looking more petulant than repentant.

Danika sighed. *I want to go home.* She saw Tagget shift uncomfortably, reached over to touch Kirstin's knee although she knew the other woman wouldn't acknowledge the contact, and watched the lights of the city grow closer.

The drivers, or the soldiers up with them, Danika didn't know who, sounded the horns as they approached and clattered through the outskirts of the capital without slowing significantly. Finally, as buildings closed in on every side, the horses slowed to a trot. And then a walk.

The lieutenant banged on the roof. "Shades down!"

Although it might have been because she could no longer see, the city seemed larger than Danika imagined possible. She heard people cursing the coaches. Once she heard people laughing. She heard music four or five times. The lights grew brighter again, turning the paper shade from brown to amber. Then darker. Then so dark she wondered how the horses, let alone the driver, could see.

The coach stopped.

She heard the lieutenant climb down. Knew it was him because he was the only one who kicked the wagon edge as he searched for the last step. She heard him challenged, but couldn't hear his answer although she strained hard enough the net sent a pulse of pain for the first time in hours.

Metal creaked and dragged across stone as gates opened. The coach moved forward, slowly.

Stopped again.

More voices.

Carlsan, his eyes open now, straightened but stayed where he was. Tagget lifted the edge of the shade and peered out.

Someone shouted orders. She didn't catch what was said because the door was thrown open and they were ordered out.

Kirstin opened her eyes as Tagget reached for her arm. Just for a moment, she looked to be in such pain that he froze and Danika reached for her instead. Then she blinked, and the blank expression she'd worn since leaving Aydori returned.

"Come on, move." Down on the pavement, Carlsan stretched an arm into the coach and grabbed Danika's sleeve. Once he had her attention, he let go and stepped back. When she stumbled a little on the small step, Tagget caught her elbow from behind until she steadied.

"Thank you."

He mumbled something that might have been *no problem*.

When only Kirstin remained, Danika leaned back inside and took her hands, tugging her gently to her feet and out the door.

They looked to be in a courtyard behind the palace. Dark and small, it had room for only one coach at a time and, unlike at the posting houses when they were allowed to mingle, Lieutenant Geurin gave orders to keep them separate. Tagget and Carlsan moved them over by the wall. Danika watched from between their shoulders as a few minutes later Jesine and Annalyse emerged from their coach. Annalyse looked as though she were barely holding it together, but Jesine, although she wasn't much older, held her back straight and her head high, sweeping the assembled company with aristocratic disdain, the net glinting within auburn curls like a crown. Before her marriage, her family had been as high in Aydori society as it was possible to get and not be Pack, and she intended everyone in this courtyard to know it. When she glanced her way, Danika smiled.

To her surprise, Murphy helped Stina down from the third coach, the two of them laughing like they shared a joke. Which would be impressive as Stina spoke next to no Imperial.

Now they were all on the ground, Danika ducked her head, found a breeze, and murmured, *"Calm. Stay calm."*

Lieutenant Geurin pinched her chin and lifted her head. "What are you doing?"

"Praying."

He smiled. "Good."

There were suddenly a great many more men in the courtyard. Orders were shouted and the soldiers who'd taken them from Aydori were replaced by clean-shaven, unsmiling men in spotless charcoal-gray uniforms, with low brimmed caps instead of the familiar bicorns. Lieutenant Geurin was assured General Loreau would see him in the morning, and then their soldiers—the soldiers who'd been with them since Aydori—were gone.

Eleven strangers watched them with cold eyes as though they

were lesser beings. No curiosity. No sympathy. Two soldiers—no, two guards for each of them.

Although they wore no visible rank insignia, she assumed the man standing apart had to be their officer.

He gestured and the heavier of her two guards shoved Danika toward the open door.

She stumbled, caught herself, and turned to glare. "There is no need to be . . ."

"Silence." The officer held up what looked like balls on leather cord. "Or be silenced."

Another time she might have argued, accepted the consequences, but she was tired and sore and hungry and her bladder was full and there were a hundred excuses available if she needed them.

The building looked new. Something about the hard edges made her think it had been built purposefully for them.

When she saw the six doors opening into the windowless hall, she knew it had been.

But the guards kept them moving past those doors too fast for their exhaustion to be able to command their legs, stumbling, half-dragged at times, the lamps set high along the long wall flickering with their passing. At the end of the hall, a seventh door opened into a vestibule. Danika had almost no time to see it as one of the soldiers tightened his grip on her arm and dragged her through another door and down a flight of stairs. Heart pounding so loudly it was all she could hear, she started to struggle.

It wasn't the stairs that terrified, they were as new and sterile as the hall they'd just left, but the smells that coiled up them spoke of an older, darker part of the palace. Ryder used to tease her because her nose was so limited, but she'd have given anything right now to be able to smell even less.

Blood. Offal. Rot. A dark patina layered onto the stone by centuries of pain and fear.

Stone all around them now, huge ancient blocks. Almost no light. The shadows told stories of desperation and the death of hope.

Danika's shoes barely touched the ground as her guards half carried, half dragged her forward. She begged, pleaded, fought . . .

Then Jesine, who'd been so strong, so sure since they were taken, keened. The sound rose up and spread, the closest she could come to a howl. It was cut off short by an open-handed blow, too hard to be named a mere slap, and Danika remembered she was Alpha.

Her feet found the floor and she walked, head up, past six low iron doors, dark and stained and a cruel parody of the doors they'd first seen. Those doors had said shelter; these said prison. Her lips drew back. She twisted as far as she could and through bared teeth breathed, *Calm. Stay calm. Be water. Be earth. Be air. Be life. Be strong.* She was Alpha. They'd find their strength in her.

When the thinner of the two guards moved around in front of her and pulled a knife, she didn't flinch. When he cut the cord holding her hands together, she managed a heartfelt, "Thank you." Close enough the words brushed his face, she saw his eyes widen in confusion. He barely managed to step aside in time as the guard still behind her shoved her into the cell.

She landed on her knees, her hands sliding along the damp floor. She saw rusty steel rings on the wall in front of her, dark rot softening the corners.

The door slammed shut and Danika froze.

The darkness was complete. No window. No light around the edges of the door.

She sat back on her knees and wiped her hands against her skirt. She wasn't afraid of the dark.

But she hadn't seen the whole cell.

Was she alone?

Had they thrown her in with someone . . . something . . . ?

Breath held back behind her teeth she listened. Heard nothing. Nothing at all. They could have taken the rest of the Mage-pack away and she wouldn't know. They could leave her. Forget her. Alone . . .

No.

Her hand dropped to the curve of her belly.

Not alone.

Her child. Ryder's child.

A reason to survive.

Chapter Ten

DANIKA HAD NO IDEA how long they left her in the dark. She tried to keep track of the passing time, but couldn't do it. She relieved herself in the far corner because she had to. She found the small bucket of water by tripping over it and spilling half. She settled against the wall opposite the door. She wasn't afraid of the dark and at least the cell wasn't moving. If she ever had to get in a coach again, it would be too soon.

She slept. She woke. She slept. Nothing changed.

The water was gone.

No one came.

She slept. She woke. Relieved herself again. Maybe again.

She thought that maybe she'd screamed because her throat felt like she'd been swallowing broken glass, but she had no memory of doing it.

When the door finally opened, the dim light spilling in hurt her eyes so badly she flinched away and they had to drag her out. Out into an empty corridor. Empty. Silent. Where were the others?

She was afraid to ask. Afraid they'd throw her back in the dark. Hated herself a little for that fear.

At the top of the stairs, were four doors—two facing her, one beside her, one to the right. They all had identical brass locks. Big brass locks. Locks. She had no keys. But the door to the right was open and the soldiers dragged her to it.

Inside the door was . . .

Danika had no idea.

It was a small, narrow room, tiled, pipes running along the ceiling at the far end, and a grate in the floor. Her heart slammed against her ribs as she realized it would be an easy room to clean. The guards shoved her forward. She shook her head and resisted. She couldn't be brave about this. Not when all she could think of were knives and her baby and pain and . . .

There was a woman in the room.

Danika squinted, trying to bring the woman's features into focus. It was too bright. But she was tall. As tall as Annalyse and large. Not softly rounded like Stina but squared. Competent.

The door slammed closed. She heard the key turn and the woman say in accented Aydori, "Clothes off. Now."

When Danika moved too slowly, she was efficiently stripped, handled as though she were an object not a person, and shoved toward the grate where she could smell . . .

Soap?

She turned and looked past the woman to see a large piece of unbleached linen toweling and a robe of the same fabric hanging on the back of the door. Frowning, Danika stared up at the pipes as the woman muttered and pulled a wooden plumb on the end of a chain.

Oh.

The guards took her back down the hallway with the six wooden doors. It had to be the same hallway Danika had seen before, but the door they'd entered the palace by no longer existed. Concrete blocks a very little bit lighter than the rest filled in the space as though there'd never been an opening in the wall. The guards yanked her to a stop at the second-to-last door, and she assumed the last door was for the missing sixth mage.

Her shadow went through the door before her, so she turned to see a lamp behind a sheet of glass above the door. The room had no window. There would be light only when their captors allowed them light. Given where she'd just been, the threat was implicit. Both hands clutching the robe, tiled floor cold against her bare feet, Danika saw a bed made up with sheets and blankets along one long wall, in the far corner a commode and next to it a basin on a small washstand. Beside the basin were a tin mug and a plate of bread and cheese.

She cried out and spun around when the door slammed behind her, but the light stayed on.

This was it. This was . . .

This was . . .

This was a room with food.

She ripped chunks off the bread and shoved them in her mouth, coughed, caught the wet mass in one hand and forced herself to eat it slowly. Then the cheese. It was mild and almost tasteless and the best thing she could remember eating. When the food was gone, she gulped down the warm barley water in the mug, then staggered to the bed and collapsed more than sat.

This wasn't a cell; it was a room. She could smell nothing but the soap she'd washed her hair with. She could see into all the corners. A nightgown had been thrown across the end of the bed. Scooped neck, long sleeves, unbleached muslin. A nightgown.

Then . . .

A sound . . .

A sound so faint only an Air-mage could have heard it.

There was a crack, not quite the width of her baby finger under the door. Lying on her side, Danika could feel the air moving down the corridor and hear the door to the room beside her close. She heard two pairs of booted feet move away and the door at the end of the corridor by the water room open and shut.

She might have slept, her body surrendering to relative safety, because it seemed like no time had passed when she heard the door at the end of the corridor open again. Two pairs of booted feet moved closer, but this time she could hear the soft sound of bare feet beside them.

The door to the room beside the room beside hers closed.

They were bringing the others up.

The guilt that had come with being clean and out of that horrid darkness faded.

Feeling almost lightheaded from the loss, she got to her feet, slipped out of the robe, and slipped on the nightgown. It was large on her, would be tight on Stina, short on Annalyse, swamp Kirstin, but fit Jesine if the gowns were all the same size.

She hadn't worn a nightgown since she married Ryder.

Wearing the fabric like a shield, she was back on the floor in time to hear the fourth door close.

And then, in time, the fifth.

They were safe. They were all safe.

Rolling onto her back, Danika took a deep, cleansing breath. She listened to multiple boots moving about in the hall. Froze as they stopped outside her door. Stifled a scream as the lamp went out.

Clung to the sound of the boots moving away.

Remembered the sound of the doors closing. Four doors had closed. She wasn't alone. They were all here.

The room was dark. As much of a cell as those ancient stone holes for all it smelled better.

She wasn't afraid of the dark. Not this time. She had her crack under the door.

And then . . .

. . . in the distance, so faint she thought she heard it because she wanted to hear it, a howl.

Rolling back up onto her side, Danika pressed as close to the crack as she could. Nothing. Nothing but the barely perceptible movement of the air against her cheek. Just when she'd begun to think she'd been imagining it, she heard the howl again.

Young. Male. Terrified more than defiant.

"Hush. I'm here now. We'll fix this." Danika blew the words out under the door and waited, sending her presence on every exhale. When the howling finally stopped, she hoped it was because he'd heard.

Rolling over on her back, she wrapped a hand around the curve of her belly. It seemed there were more Pack here to save than those she'd come with.

The roses in the border had clearly needed deadheading for some time. Danika had no idea why she'd left it so long. She pulled the faded blossoms toward her, one by one, barely managing to snip them off the canes before the next rose wilted and then the next. This was rapidly becoming more complicated than her small gardening ability could deal with. She'd have sent a message to Tylor, the second level Earth-mage who oversaw the estate's flower gardens, but the air was so completely still she was afraid to disturb it.

The air was never that still naturally.

Turning to call, she realized that the house had moved again and she was staring down the west lawn toward the pond and the rough land beyond it. She heard a bird and then Ryder came over the hill, running toward the pond. Highlights danced over his fur and his tail looked unnaturally fluffy. He changed as he dove in, and stayed on two legs as he climbed out of the water, having swum across to the nearer side. His dark hair hung down into his eyes, the water made the muscles of his arms and shoulders gleam. She drew her gaze down the line of hair on his chest, over the flat planes of his stomach, between his legs . . . He'd obviously caught her scent.

She smiled and stepped forward.

He ran toward her, but ended up farther away.

The light behind him grew brighter until she had to raise a hand to shield her eyes . . .

Staring up at the tiled ceiling, Danika blinked and remembered. When the distant howling had finally stopped, she'd made her way to the bed. It had been comfortable enough, certainly more comfortable than anything she'd slept on since being taken, and her body had almost convinced her she could die of tiredness. But her mind hadn't allowed her to rest. Fear for the others had chased its own tail around and around her head. Jesine and Stina would manage, but Annalyse was very young and something had been broken in Kirstin. She'd suddenly realized warm water and food and a bed did not translate into her ever seeing the other women again. This was a better prison—and the thought of going back into the dark, into that hole with its patina of old death and fear made her feel like throwing up—but it was still a prison. They should have fought. Screamed. Struggled.

Died free?

No. As clichéd as it was, where there was life there was hope.

Eventually, her body had won and she'd slept.

Her body had won because it was no longer only her body. She could feel tears prickling behind her eyelids and wished she could give in to a prolonged bout of sobbing but was afraid that if she started, she wouldn't be able to stop.

Taken from her husband. Taken from her home. Her family would be frantic. *All* their families would be frantic and, for all that their families were high in the leadership of Aydori, Danika doubted they'd be able to count on anything as civilized as diplomatic recourse. There was no one country left in this part of the world strong enough to stand against Leopald's armies. Should the news of their kidnapping reach the international community, the action would be weighed against the chance of losing Imperial trade and then ignored. Leopald, she'd told Ryder at dinner nearly a year ago, had begun to conquer with his purchasing power as much as with his armies—and although Ryder had laughed to hear it put that way, he'd had to agree she was right.

The five of them would have to free themselves.

Danika rubbed at the tears running into her ears and then scrubbed her nose with the sleeve of the nightgown. She had no idea how long she'd been in Karis. How long in the hole in the dark. How long asleep in a bed. No idea if it was day or night.

"RISE!"

The voice filled the room and pressed against her as if it needed the space she filled as well. The nightgown twisted around her legs, Danika nearly fell out of the bed but managed to get a foot free at the last moment. An Air-mage could have sent such a message, shoved it in under the door as she'd slipped her messages out under the door last night, but Danika would have recognized the use of the craft. The voice had *not* come from an Air-mage. Trolls and giants were creatures of myth. Therefore, in order to achieve that volume, the voice had come from a machine. She searched for a speaker and found a small circular grill set almost invisibly into the tiles of the ceiling. Without the net she could have followed the air currents back, if not to the speaker at least to the machine. As she understood it, machines were delicate. She wouldn't have to be.

A thought occurred and she searched again, finding no lenses. They might be listening, but they weren't watching.

"Use the commode!"

Not quite so loud this time and identifiable as a woman's voice. Older. Embarrassed by her failure to use the machine properly the first time. Angry at those who'd made her feel embarrassed. She was trying to hide both, but words were air given form and Danika had been . . . *was* the most powerful Air-mage in Aydori. It could have been the woman from the wet room.

Why would their captors believe they needed to tell five expectant women to use the commode?

Danika had barely finished when the sound of the bolts slamming back announced the opening of the door.

Perhaps it had been a time warning rather than a command.

She didn't recognize the two guards who stepped into the room. They weren't the two who'd taken her to the cell, but they might have been the two who'd taken her from it. The uniform, the hair cut short, the cap pulled low on the forehead, all worked to obscure individuality.

They reminded Danika of a line in *The Governing of Reason* by Gregor Mertait, a politician from Talatia in the Southern Alliance. *Safe within the obscurity of the mob, many deeds are performed that would not be countenanced by the individual.* If Leopald had read the book, she could only assume he thought no one else had because Mertait went on to say: *The mob cannot be reasoned with and will sweep all before it, but divide the mob back into individuals and it loses its power.*

The guard on the left had a mole under his right ear. The other man had a black thumbnail, the edges still red and swollen enough the accident had likely just happened.

They both held pistols pointed at her and black batons thrust through loops on their belts. Clearly, Leopald was taking no chances on two grown men being unable to physically overpower one pregnant woman. More evidence that Leopald didn't trust the net. Nor did he know exactly what he'd taken. If the net failed this moment, this very instant, they'd have no time to pull the trigger before they were slammed against the far wall of the corridor hard enough to splatter their brains over the stone!

Danika took a deep breath and let it out slowly, knowing they'd see the trembling of her hands as fear rather than reaction to the sudden violence of her thoughts. She'd killed once. She didn't *want* to do it again.

She would.

Want had nothing to do with the situation she found herself in.

Mole-under-ear gestured with his free hand, indicating she should move forward into the hall. He moved with her, backing up as she advanced. Bruised-thumb stayed where he was. As she passed him, she murmured a polite, "Excuse me."

Manners, her mother had taught her, could be a shield in troubled times. And she remembered the confusion of the guard she'd thanked. Given the insults from the soldiers who'd taken them, the guards had very probably been taught the mages of Aydori lay with beasts and were therefore less than beasts themselves. Confusing the guards was a place to start.

Once in the hall, the guards . . .

No, as portentous as using the descriptions might be, she needed to always think of the guards as individuals.

Once in the hall, Mole-under-ear and Bruised-thumb fell in on either side of her. Mole-under-ear on her left, was left-handed. Bruised-thumb on her right, was right-handed. As they stood beside her, their weapons were in their outside hands, making it all but impossible for her to grab one—had she decided to do something so incredibly stupid. Either the more over-the-top stories about the Pack had not only been believed but applied erroneously to the Mage-pack, or Leopald *really* didn't trust the net.

Or, she reluctantly admitted, it was coincidence.

The lamps were on over the other doors, but the doors remained closed. Wherever they were taking her, she was going there alone.

She could feel the weight of their attention. She didn't dare try and send a message.

The door at the end of the hall opened into the vestibule . . .

. . . and she froze.

Not back to the darkness. To the stone and the damp and the smells and the hunger. She couldn't. She wouldn't . . .

They dragged her out of the hall. Closed and locked the door behind them.

Danika knew herself a heartbeat away from begging when they turned her toward the open door on the right—the door to the water room.

She found her feet, shook off their hands, and walked in.

No woman waited inside this time, but, this time, she knew what to do. After days in the same clothes, in the woods, in the mail coaches, in the hole, hot water was the next best thing to freedom.

Back in her room—no, her cell. No matter how comfortable it seemed in comparison, it was still a cell. Back in her *cell*, the commode had been emptied and cleaned, the bed made, and the robe hung from a hook that hadn't been there previously. A wide-toothed comb had been left on the small table, and a high-waisted, long-sleeved dress of blue cotton had been laid out on the end of the bed.

Danika turned as the bolts slammed into place behind her and dropped to the floor, listening to discover if the other women were to be treated the same way. She heard the bolts pulled back on the door next to hers. Heard the door opened. Heard Annalyse's voice, young and frightened, heard her bare feet against the slate floor in the hall, not moving freely but shoved along. Heard the door open at the end of the hall.

As Annalyse entered the water room—Danika couldn't hear either Annalyse or water, but she had to believe that was where the younger mage had been taken—much lighter footsteps—leather shoes not boots—hurried down the hall and turned into Annalyse's empty room. The sounds from the room were the familiar sounds of a maid at work.

Danika dressed while she waited for Annalyse to return. The fabric was coarser than any she'd ever worn, but the style was Aydori. The front panels of the dress crossed over themselves, support built into the bodice, a double panel of fabric down the center front. Undoing the two buttons in the band tucked up under her breasts would allow her to step out of it. Lady Berin had been wearing a nearly identical style in the carriage, although Lady Berin's dress had been of significantly better quality. She wondered if Leopald realized the Mage-pack was not actually Pack and couldn't change.

When Annalyse was returned to her cell, she thanked the guards in stiff Imperial before they closed and bolted her door. Danika smiled. The shield of manners.

Kirstin, next to Annalyse, refused to leave her cell. To Danika's surprise, the guards left her and moved on.

Jesine and Stina went with the guards in turn. Stina was unusually quiet, but neither of them sounded as though they had to be forced. The maid attended to their housekeeping while their cells were empty.

When Stina returned, the boots marched down the hall to Danika's door, and she scrambled up onto her feet as the bolts were thrown. Bruised-thumb beckoned her out into the hall. Mole-under-ear stood with his pistol aimed into Kirstin's cell. Without waiting for instruction, Danika hurried down the hall.

Still in the robe, Kirstin had curled into a nest of bedding in the far corner of the room between the bed and the wall. The room smelled like vomit. No, not quite vomit. Like bile that remained when there was nothing left to throw up. Wishing she had Jesine with her, Danika stepped farther into the room and softly called Kirstin's name.

Kirstin looked up, her eyes widened, and any fear Danika had that she'd been injured fled as she suddenly found herself with an armful of her ex-rival. Danika sank to her knees, holding on as Kirstin crumpled with her, sobbing over and over against her shoulder. "I thought I was alone." There were bruises wrapped purple and green around pale wrists and another that looked like a handprint just visible where the robe pulled away from her shoulder.

I am Alpha, Danika reminded herself, and somehow kept her voice from wobbling. She would lend Kirstin her certainty because that was all she had right now to offer. "No, dearling, no. We're all here. You're not alone." When one of the guards made an impatient noise behind her, she freed an arm and gently lifted Kirstin's head so that blue-flecked dark eyes met hers. There was more of Kirstin in them now than there had been at any time since they'd been taken. "The guards are here to escort you to the water room. And that's all they want. When you return, your cell will have been cleaned and there'll be clean clothes left for you. Granted, not clothes even approaching fashionable, but . . ."

"Where we lead, fashion follows." Kirstin found the strength for a half smile and Danika mirrored it.

"Exactly, and fashion *will* follow." It was as close as she could get to declaring they'd find a way to escape. It was unlikely the guards spoke Aydori, but they already had evidence that it was spoken here, so they had to assume every word would be overheard. Except . . .

Heard you in the coach. Kirstin exhaled the words. Sniffed, pulled back a little, and added, *Only one dead. Sad.* She frowned when she felt Danika tense, but there was no way Danika could explain how that one death had made her feel with the guards in the room.

Shielded by Danika's body, Kirstin took a moment to slide on an approximation of her best society face, then she stepped away and said in broken but passable Imperial, "My apologies for the delay. I found myself indisposed timely." Hopefully, only Danika heard how brittle her voice was. How easy it would be to break her again.

Bruised-thumb raised a hand and held Kirstin in place, while Mole-under-ear beckoned Danika out into the hall and escorted her back to her room. *Cell*, she corrected herself again. Not a house, not a dorm, not a hotel: a prison.

As her door began to close, she heard Kirstin say, "That is a Deni pistol, yes? The brass work is very distinct. Sloppy action on old style. Single shot, yes? Too bad."

Kirstin's uncle was a Metals-mage who developed weapons for the army. Officers among the volunteers carried a double shot pistol, and Danika remembered either Ryder or Jaspyr saying he was working on a rotating something or other that would shoot up to six rounds.

She dropped to the floor, mouth to the crack under the door. *Harmless.* Only Kirstin, she sighed to herself, as she rolled onto her back and stared up at the ceiling, could go from heartbreaking mess to making enemies so quickly. None of the others had spoken to the guards. None of the others had insulted their weaponry. She didn't even want to think about why, among her limited vocabulary, Kirstin knew the Imperial word for *sloppy*.

While she waited for Kirstin to return, Danika used the comb to tug her hair into some kind of order, although she had a feeling she'd left it too long and it was now sticking up in an irredeemable spiky mess. Both Kirstin with her thick, dark waves, and Jesine with her auburn curls, had hair more suited to the short style of the Mage-pack After a moment's reflection, she took a deep breath, hooked a few teeth under the net, and pulled.

She was still dry heaving into the commode when her door opened. She straightened and wiped her mouth on a corner of the robe as a new guard came into the room. He beckoned, the gesture already familiar. By the time she reached the hall, Danika'd decided to call him Mouth-breather and his partner, Hairy-knuckles. It seemed Mole-under-ear and Bruised-thumb had been assigned exclusively to water room duty.

They took her back into the vestibule and through the door in the opposite wall.

It led to a large, high-ceilinged room. Danika's gaze skipped over the table set with five places, over the guards standing along two walls, and locked on the other four women of her Mage-pack. They stood a little apart from each other. Not talking. Not touching. Waiting.

Danika spread her arms.

The next few minutes were a frenzy of touch and tears. Everyone's cheeks were wet, and Annalyse was still crying when they finally pulled a little apart. Kirstin wasn't the only one with new bruises, but none of them were badly hurt and, more importantly, they were together.

Although too conscious of the guards to say much.

Kirstin swept a disdainful gaze along the walls. "I've never really liked those households that keep too many footmen," she sighed. "It's pretentious."

Jesine shot Danika a look that clearly stated, *"She's back."*

Danika smiled and, when no one objected to Kirstin's declaration, added, "They're well trained, though. Seen but not heard."

"Only the best," Jesine agreed, and directed her smile at the line of uniformed men. Jesine was beautiful. Unless they were guarded only by men who solely enjoyed men, that had to have caused a reaction—even in the plain, deep yellow dress that she'd somehow managed to make look better than the identical piece of clothing worn by all of the others.

Danika and Kirstin were in blue, Annalyse in green, Stina in brown, Jesine in yellow. They'd been color coded to match their mage marks, a style that went in and out of fashion in Aydori, usually among the young and the not terribly powerful.

"Who came up with the theory that simple and comfortable has to be unattractive?" Stina pulled a bit of heavy brown cotton away from her body and sighed with exaggerated frustration. "A little embroidery would have killed them?"

Annalyse stared at her for a long moment, then sputtered with laughter.

"That's my chick." She put her arm around the younger woman's shoulders and pulled her in for a hug. "Don't give them the gift of your grieving."

As Stina clearly had Annalyse in hand, Danika turned her attention back to Jesine and Kirstin, hoping Kirstin hadn't made it *all* the way back to her old self. Fighting among themselves would help only Leopald.

"I'm better," Kirstin was saying. "The pain from trying to remove the net has faded, I promise." The white lines still marked her fingers, but she pulled them from Jesine's grip a little impatiently. "They don't hurt. I just couldn't cope for a while, so I went away. I'm sorry if I frightened you."

She sounded sincere, but Danika couldn't shake the feeling that when it came to Kirstin, nothing was that simple. Unfortunately, her stomach chose that moment to growl.

Annalyse giggled and covered her mouth when it started to get out of control. "What do we do about the food, Lady . . . I mean, Danika?"

They all had to be hungry.

"We eat."

"Is it safe?"

She didn't blame Kirstin for being suspicious. "Yes, it's safe. We've had the stick. This is the carrot."

The porridge had grown cold, but that didn't matter. There was honey to put on it and butter and cream. There were large, fluffy biscuits warm in a napkin cocoon, with more honey and butter and jam to put on them. There was no tea, but there was water that didn't taste of rust.

Danika caught Annalyse's gaze and nodded, ever so slightly, toward the pitcher.

The younger woman reached for it and frowned over at Stina who'd kicked her under the table. Her green-flecked eyes widened as she realized what was expected of her. She lifted the pitcher with shaking hands and took a deep breath, braced for pain as she poured the first glass. "Oh. It doesn't . . . look like there's anything but water," she amended hurriedly, cheeks flushed. "I'd very much love a cup of tea."

"So would I." Reaching across the table, Danika squeezed her hand. Annalyse clearly hadn't used any low-level mage-craft since being netted but had still been willing to try and purify the water. How could Leopald hold them with such women as these?

"This is a banana." Jesine waved a long yellow fruit. "Sirin and I . . ."

Sirin Hagen was Ryder's third cousin, silver-furred like Jaspyr and at forty, eighteen years older than Jesine. Danika had seen them together, and it was clear Sirin's nose had known what it was about. Ryder had sent Sirin and Kirstin's husband Neils to the front with the 2nd. Annalyse's husband Geoffrey was Hunt Pack and Torvin Menkyzck, Stina's husband was a senior officer. Tomas had said the Hunt Pack was dead. Annalyse was a widow at twenty. Stina at thirty-seven, her three children left in Aydori without a father.

But they couldn't all be dead. Looking around the table, Danika saw every woman there thinking, *He can't be dead.*

"Sirin and I," Jesine repeated defiantly, "had them on that trade trip Ryder sent him on to Abyek last spring. You eat them like this." She peeled the thick skin down, pushed her chair away from the table, and slid the end of the fruit into the perfect circle of plush lips.

Not one of the guards made a sound, but over half of them shifted in place.

Annalyse turned her giggle into a cough and hid it in a napkin.

"It's an interesting sort of prison." Stina pushed back from the table, one hand gently stroking circles over her stomach. "Someone has put a lot of thought into it. We've seen the worst, we've seen the best, and they can control us by sliding us up and down the scale depending on how we behave."

"Shut up," Kirstin snapped.

"The voice this morning, it spoke Aydori." Annalyse twisted the napkin with both hands. "Are they listening to us?"

"Count on it."

"Then I imagine," Stina said calmly, "that they'll be pleased we understand what's going on. It'll save them a lot of time."

"And we will be model prisoners." Danika cut off Kirstin's response. "We have more than ourselves to think about." She dropped her hand to mirror Stina's and glared at Kirstin, exhaling. *Lull to false security!*

Escape!

Absolutely.

Kirstin's cheeks were dark as she dropped her head, but Danika knew her well enough to recognize it as anger not embarrassment. She swept a gaze around the table, breathing *Lull to false security* directly at each woman, aware that Kirstin would hear it each time. The reemphasis couldn't hurt. From the outside, it would seem that she was demanding compliance with her call to be model prisoners and as she was, in a way, she had no fear of discovery.

The sound of trumpets filled the room. Danika barely stopped herself from searching for speakers in the ceiling and kicked Kirstin under the table when her chin started to rise. Credit where credit was due, Kirstin wasn't stupid and she followed Danika's lead, searching *around* for the source of the noise rather than up.

No need to let their watchers know they'd found the speakers in their rooms.

The guards snapped to attention.

Danika had seen more military reviews over the last year than in the rest of her life combined, but she'd never seen anyone come to attention with such fervent precision.

High on the inside wall, a double section of wallboard swung open to lie flat, exposing a small chamber lined in flowing panels of Imperial purple fabric. The chamber contained only a single high-backed chair positioned close enough to the edge of the wall that when the man sitting in it shifted his foot where it was resting on what looked like a roll of carpet, the toe of one highly polished boot jutted out into the room. Above the boots, he wore cream-colored pantaloons, and a dark coat cut in a military style, gold cord looped over and around one shoulder, gold buttons gleaming. He wasn't a large man, but, as far as the angle allowed, Danika thought he filled out both pantaloons and coat without resorting to padding. He had thick brown hair, eyes so blue they seemed mage marked, and his full lips were surprisingly red against his pale skin. His age was common knowledge, even in Aydori, and he looked to be a full decade younger than his thirty-four years.

One last flurry of trumpets, then: "His Imperial Majesty, Leopald. By the light of the Sun and the strength of his people, Exalted Ruler of the Kresentian Empire, Commander in Truth of the Imperial army, Supreme Protector of the Holy Church of the One True Sun."

That was new. The Prelate had always been the Church of the Sun's highest office.

Smiling, eyes shining, Leopald leaned forward. "I know, the sixth mage hasn't arrived yet, has she, but I couldn't wait. I needed to see you. You'll just have to tell her everything when she arrives tomorrow, or the next day at the latest. You know how Soothsayers are. It's so hard to get an exact time out of them."

Danika was reminded how professors sounded when students they were mentoring did something clever. Friendly and proprietary sounded dangerously similar. And she *still* had no idea who this sixth mage could be. For all his smiles, she very much doubted Leopald would tell her if she asked.

"It's unfortunate that you're not all capable of understanding Imperial, but I'm sure that those of you who are will explain to the rest when I'm done. You're fascinating, all of you, actual high-level mages, and I wish I could trust you enough to discover what you're capable of, as our records concerning mages could definitely use updating, but, regretfully, no." He sounded as though he did honestly regret the lost opportunity for study. "Let me explain why you're here. When wild and mage together come, one in six or six in one. Empires rise or empires fall, the unborn child begins it all. Soothsayers, obviously." His smile was a friendly request to share a common reaction to such ridiculous poetry. "There were also a lot of numbers, eventually determined to refer to time and location, but that needn't concern you. The prophecy suggests that one of your offspring will bring the empire down, so, for purely nationalistic reasons, I should have you killed before you whelp. Now, I would honestly hate to have to do that because that same prophecy also suggests that one of your offspring will make the empire greater than it is. That interpretation argues for your lives. As it happens . . ." Sitting back, he crossed his feet at the ankle, leaving them still propped on the rolled carpet. ". . . one doesn't rule the world's greatest empire by leaving things to chance, does one? If I control the offspring of the prophecy, I control the effect they have on the empire. It's simple really. If your offspring is a beast, it will be a favored pet and trained to kill at my command. Eventually, if things go well, I'll have the last of the abominations under my control. If your offspring is a mage, it will learn to use its powers to my benefit. They'll live useful lives, unable to move against me or the empire." Leopald had a strong, reassuring voice. He spoke as though what he said was so obviously inarguable that any reasonable person would have to agree with him. "But what of you, the bearers of these offspring? Neutered as you are by ancient technology, you'll live quietly here until your offspring are whelped. Fed. Exercised. Kept clean. All your needs seen to. However, a bitch can whelp in any kennel and, as you've discovered, there are less pleasant places prepared for you." Still smiling, he uncrossed his legs and kicked the roll of carpet at his feet.

No. Not a carpet.

A wolf's head and front paws flopped down over the wall.

No. Not a wolf.

"I was amazed by how long he lived, even given the silver knives. He changed twice after they had the skin off him, you know, and then continued to twitch for some time."

Danika could hear Kirstin and Jesine throwing up. Stina's heavy breathing. Annalyse sobbing. But she was Alpha. She straightened her back, clenched her teeth, and swore that Leopald would die before any of the children were born.

The smell of cooking meat pulled Mirian up out of a dream of flying. She opened her eyes, blinked several times to little effect, and finally had to grind the heels of her hands against the lids to bring the rock overhead into focus. Rolling onto her side, she peered out of the overhang at a brilliantly sunny day, at the ground beyond that rose and fell in such a random pattern it looked as though it had been stirred by a giant hand, and—although she had to squint to bring it into focus—in the shelter of a flat rock rising nearly half her height into the sky, at a smokeless fire with a carcass roasting over it on a skewer of green wood.

Her mouth watered. She threw off the blanket, crawled two steps toward the food, realized she was naked, and dragged the blanket back over herself again. Cheeks hot, she vaguely remembered wet clothes being removed and a warm body pressed tight to keep her from freezing. The memory of the body flipped between fur and skin.

"Tomas?"

He was there so fast he must have been just out of sight. Toenails skidding against the rock, he bowled her over and then pushed his cold, wet nose against every bit of exposed skin he could find, as though he'd forgotten what she smelled like.

Giggling—cold and wet tickled—Mirian grabbed two handfuls of fur and dragged his head up so she could see his face. "I'm fine. Really. Except that you're heavy!" Releasing her grip and stroking the fur smooth, she added, "How late is it?"

Tomas' body rippled, changed, his forearms pushing up under her shoulders, his weight on his elbows just under her armpits. He stared down at her, eyes wild. "Two days. You were asleep for over two days."

"No . . ."

"Yes." He dropped his head and sniffed a bit frantically along the edge of her ear. "I couldn't wake you. I didn't want to leave you, but I had to make sure the search parties weren't on our trail. The Imperials can't track for shit, and this area's never been hunted so there's lots of small game, but you wouldn't wake up." He growled the last bit with his mouth against her shoulder, and Mirian shivered although she wasn't at all cold.

No point in apologizing since it hadn't been her fault, but she tucked his hair back behind his ears and let her finger linger over the points. "How did you know I was only asleep?"

"What?"

"You said I was asleep. How did you know?"

She felt as much as heard him swallow, then he raised his head and grinned. "You snore."

"I do not."

"You do." His grin broadened. "I was terrified the Imperials would come close enough to hear you. Actually, I was terrified they'd hear you back in Aydori."

He'd been frightened; she could still see the fear lurking behind the laughter in his eyes. No excuse. "You brat! I don't . . ." Her laughter escaped before she got the last word out and, an instant later, he joined her. It didn't take long before she ran out of breath although that was more likely due to the solid weight of the idiot roaring with laughter on top of her than to any lingering effects of the drug that had put her to sleep for so long.

"Come on, stop!" She poked his side, just above his lowest rib.

"Ow!" He snapped his teeth by her ear, so she poked him again. "All right! Bully." Eyes bright, he smiled down at her, and she suddenly became aware that there was only a blanket between them. Not even a blanket in places. Skin to skin.

"Tomas . . ."

"You smell amazing." He wasn't laughing now.

"So I've heard."

"I want . . . We could . . ."

They could. And she wanted to. At least part of her wanted to. Wanted the comfort. Wanted the closeness. Wanted the distraction. None of those were bad reasons, and another time they might be all the reasons she needed—but not this time. Here and now, they couldn't use the excuse that they'd been overwhelmed by circumstances. This would be a decision they'd both have to live with when the comfort and the closeness and the distraction was over, and she wasn't ready for that. She wasn't sure Tomas was ready for that either, in spite of his evident arousal.

But *no* seemed too final after everything they'd been through together, so she took as deep a breath as their positions allowed and said, "Not now."

"Not *now*?"

"Tomas, I just woke up. I've been asleep for two days."

"I know!"

"And I really have to . . ." She bit her lip and thought, *Seriously? He's naked. You're naked. At this point you're missish?* "I really have to pee."

"You have to pee?"

She gritted her teeth and stared up at him.

After a long moment, he snickered. "You have to pee."

"Stop repeating it!"

"Sorry." For a moment, she thought he was going to say something else, but instead he rolled off her, changed, ran out from under the overhang, and disappeared off to the right.

Mirian crawled after him, wrapped the blanket more securely around her body, then, once clear of the overhang went in the other direction.

Soaked in rain then dried in the sun didn't make her clothes clean, but it made them significantly cleaner than they had been. Mirian dressed quickly in skirt and shirtwaist and applied herself to the rabbit. When Tomas finally returned, he changed, pulled on his trousers and shirt, and declined the meat she'd left for him.

"I've had plenty. Thank you. There's lots of rabbits around here."

He seemed embarrassed, more formal with her than he'd ever been.

"Tomas!"

He glanced up as the leg bone bounced off the top of his head.

"You weren't being led by your nose. It was the right reaction, just the wrong time." Jaspyr Hagen had been no part of her decision. Mirian opened her hand and let the last of that possibility go. When she looked up from brushing her empty palm against her skirt, she realized Tomas was staring at her, brows drawn in, confused by her mime. "When it's the right time, we'll both know."

"When?"

"If!"

His teeth flashed white and very pointy, and he snatched the rib out of the air before it hit him. "So you're saying we may later?"

"I'm saying you're an idiot. What do you think 'not now' means?" She rolled her eyes as he looked more cheerful and began cracking the bones to get at the marrow. Something told her that would have been an easier conversation if the Imperial army had left her the collar instead of the telescope, but she had no intention of examining that *something* too closely. "Is the Imperial army still searching for us?"

"No. As frightening as it was not being able to wake you, going to ground for a couple of days was probably the best thing we could have done. You can't track someone if there's no tracks to follow. Not," he added thoughtfully, "that they can track for shit." His eyes widened. "Language. Sorry. Sometimes I forget you're not Harry. I mean, I know you're not Harry, I just forget you're not . . ." He caught the third bone, too. "Stop that."

"Stop being an idiot. I'm honored that you sometimes forget I'm not Harry."

"He died."

She stretched out her leg and pushed against his knee with her toes. The Pack was tactile. Not all of her mother's advice was bad. "I wish I could have met him."

"You'd have liked him. He'd have liked you." Tomas closed his hand around her bare foot and squeezed gently. Then he exhaled emphatically and said, "Unless they had a problem on the road, the Mage-pack reached Karis about the time you went to sleep. Maybe before." He squinted up at the sky. "We'll be three days behind by full dark."

"Then we'd better get moving."

There was a lot of money in the pouch she'd taken from Captain Reiter and more than she expected in Chard's. Perhaps enough to pay for a seat on a mail coach and . . .

. . . arrive in Karis drugged, chained, or locked in a small box. Or all three. Captain Reiter seemed like the type who didn't take unnecessary chances.

Or hadn't taken unnecessary chances.

Mirian let the coins spill over her fingers, absently noting the metals that made up each, and wondered why Captain Reiter had freed her. It wasn't one thing that had changed his mind, he said. He hadn't done it on the spur of the moment. He'd planned it. Had set it up to look as though a powerful mage had overcome every possible precaution. She thought of the circle of trees blown flat and wondered if perhaps she couldn't have freed herself.

"Mirian?"

"Coming." Sliding the coins back into the purse, she tied the bedroll, and draped the rope over her shoulder—although she held the whole thing against her body as she crawled out from under the overhang.

"Ow!"

Tried to crawl out from under the overhang.

"Are you all right?"

"I'm fine." She touched her forehead and then stared down at the drop of blood on her finger. "I didn't see the rock."

"Really? I'd assumed you smacked into it on purpose."

"I'm going to smack you," she muttered, but accepted his hand, allowing him to pull her to her feet. "You're going to stay in skin for a while?"

He shrugged. "I thought you might want someone to talk to."

Or he might. He'd been more than two days on his own. But all she said was, "I would."

Following him away from the overhang, she marveled at the slabs of rock surrounding them . . . "Ow!"

"You all right?"

"Fine." . . . and at the shards of rock underfoot. There were enough edged, broken pieces that she locked her eyes on the ground, careful where she put her feet. They were going to have to go through the whole shoe thing again. And trade her clothes for clothes more likely to be worn wandering about with someone wearing what Tomas was wearing. Suddenly stepping out into the open, Tomas grabbed her arm as she teetered on the edge of an enormous crater.

It wasn't so deep the bottom looked blurry, but it was deep enough for all that. It looked like a giant's footprint. "What is this place?"

"An artillery range. This close to the border, it's the empire showing off."

Mirian didn't know if Tomas knew a lot about artillery or just a lot more than she did. The explanation he began seemed *thorough*. After a while, as they found themselves back under the cover of a second-growth forest, she glanced up at the sun and interrupted, "Are you sure we're going in the right direction?"

"We have to swing north to make sure we don't pass too close to the garrison."

That made sense. "I should have searched the captain's pack for a map."

"To Karis?"

"Good point." Once in the empire, all roads led to Karis. A captain in the Imperial army wouldn't need a map to find the capital.

Tomas stepped up and over a fallen tree, waiting for her on the other side. "My grandfather told me once that Earth-mages never get lost."

Mirian thought of Bernard walking the promenade with her at the opera and hoped he was alive. "Always knowing where you are doesn't necessarily mean you know where you're going."

"Do you . . ."

"I'm not an Earth-mage."

She wasn't an Earth-mage, but she'd grown apples out of season. She wasn't a Healer-mage, but she'd thrown off the Imperial drug, and the cut she'd got leaving the overhang had already closed. Tomas doubted she'd even noticed. She wasn't an Air-mage, but she'd flattened a circle of trees.

"Mirian . . ."

"Yes, I think it would be a good idea for me to practice some mage-craft before we get to Karis."

"How did you know that's what I was thinking?"

She grinned, and he had to fight the urge to lean over and kiss the corner of her mouth. "It was all there in the way you said my name."

"Really?"

"No." She leaned sideways far enough to bounce her shoulder off his. Like Harry would have.

Reiter settled back against the barely padded seat in the mail coach and braced himself as the driver sprung the horses. Chard, who'd been staring out the window, would've fallen to the floor had there been room. As it was, he barely managed to stop himself from landing in Reiter's lap, legs tangled with his musket.

As Reiter shoved him back to his own side of the coach, he flushed and muttered, "Sorry, Cap."

"You might want to pay more attention. It's still a long way to Karis."

Although, for a while, it had begun to seem like he wouldn't be leaving the Lyonne garrison. No one had doubted his story, not when they'd backtracked Thunder to the camp and found the two of them still out and a perfect circle of shattered trees, but no one had been too willing to believe it either. The moment Reiter had woken, he'd been pulled from the infirmary into a meeting with the garrison commander who'd tapped the two sets of orders on his desk and informed him that he'd already sent a courier to Major Halyss.

"You're questioning an Imperial seal, sir?"

The colonel had smiled tightly. *"Given the way you were found, I'm questioning every flaming thing about this mess. Your report, Captain."*

The report jumped from *". . . gave her a little privacy to relieve herself . . ."* to *". . . opened my eyes in the infirmary with no idea how I'd got there."* but was, otherwise, complete. While the colonel chewed at it, Reiter marveled at how much difference leaving out a single sentence made. A single sentence: *I let her go.* And a name. Mirian.

"How did she knock those trees down?"

"She's a mage, sir. Other than that I can't say. I wasn't conscious when it happened."

"Mage-craft is a dying art, Captain. There isn't a mage in the empire who could do half—no a tenth—that damage."

Depending on how the battle at Bercarit was going, that might no longer be true. If the empire tried absorbing Aydori, they'd find themselves suddenly in possession of any number of powerful mages. For a while.

"Did she have a weapon?"

"Just her mage-craft, sir."

"Impossible."

It hadn't been difficult to see why the colonel had been left behind in Lyonne rather than given a role in the winter campaign or the spring advance.

Fortunately, Major Halyss had confirmed Reiter's identity and supported his report as far as he'd been able.

"Can't say I'm not happy to be leaving," Chard muttered, finally turning from the window. He pulled his stained and nearly shapeless bicorn down over his forehead, then slapped the barrel of his musket back and forth between his palms. "You get taken out by a girl and they look at you funny, you know?"

"She was a mage."

"Still a girl, Cap." Chard grinned across the coach at him as though that, at least, was undeniable.

Reiter didn't plan on denying it.

He'd tried to leave Chard behind, the way he'd left Armand and

Best in Aydori, at least partially because what was waiting for him in Karis was likely to be unpleasant, but Chard been surprisingly stubborn.

"You're an officer and you can leave me where you like, sir, but I think I need to go with you to Karis. I was there. You might need me to back you up."

Reiter knew flaming well that Chard's word would carry no weight at all with the men who'd sent them out chasing prophecy's tail, but he was selfish enough not to want to face them alone.

Chapter Eleven

THE CEILING OF THE ROOM was too high for Danika to get a good read on the air currents. Words she set loose might go anywhere, so she had to choose those first words carefully. Hands over her face, as though to block the memory of the dangling pelt, she stared up at the piece of wall once again covering Leopald's rathole and breathed out through the crack between her hands, *Talk to me.*

To me not *to us.* Her position meant she'd played more power games than the rest even if some of those games had been against Kirstin.

The wall fit snugly; Leopald might never hear her. He certainly wouldn't if she didn't try.

"*Why?*" Mouth partially covered by a napkin, Kirstin seemed to be listening to Stina's low murmur of comfort, but her voice brushed past Danika's ear.

"*He likes to talk, we need information. Knowledge is power.*"

Kirstin rubbed her thumb over the white lines the net had etched into her fingertips. "*Power is power.*"

Without the net, the five of them had power enough to free themselves and while they'd never used that power aggressively, Leopald had ensured they'd be willing to. Telling Kirstin to leave the net alone would only annoy her, and, in all honesty, with the lingering headache from her own attempt pressing needles behind her eyes, Danika didn't feel she had the right. *"Remember, we're terrified."*

Horrified. Furious. Not terrified. Annalyse, still weeping silently in the circle of Jesine's arms, her knuckles white around a fistful of her skirt, was grieving for the dead, not terrified or submissive. Marrying into the Pack required power, but it also required the ability to stand up to teeth and strength and instincts and face them down. Submitting in Aydori came with more layers of power and politics than Leopald could imagine.

"Stand!"

It was the voice from her cell, speaking first in Imperial and then in Aydori.

Four sets of mage-flecked eyes turned to Danika. Who stood.

"If we behave, we're treated well. If we don't, we go back into the dark." She hoped the rage that kept her lips back off her teeth couldn't be heard. "It seems simple enough. We have more than merely ourselves to think of." Then, sweeping her gaze around the circle, she breathed, *Lull them.*

Jesine stood first and gifted the guards with a tentative glance from under long, gold-tipped lashes. It was the kind of look that would have evoked protective instincts in a stone. It wasn't sexual. It spoke to the best part of men, the part that wanted to protect, that wanted, sometimes in spite of themselves, to be a hero.

The other three stood at the same time. Stina wore her most placid expression. Annalyse looked young and frightened. Kirstin smiled, and Danika hoped she'd heard *lull*. She hated herself for thinking it, but the barely present Kirstin who traveled from Aydori to Karis had caused her less concern.

"Go with your guards!" Again in Imperial and then Aydori.

The guards broke into pairs, and pointed.

Danika breathed *harmless* at Mouth-breather and Hairy-knuckles and walked down the hall to her cell as gracefully as she could manage. She hadn't been one of the season's beauties, but Ryder had told her the first time they'd met that she walked like she was dancing.

Two new guards, Crooked-finger and Pocked-chin, arrived to

take Danika back to the big room before she had time to get hungry or tired. She was almost certain they were the pair who'd escorted Stina to breakfast. It seemed the guards were working a variation of the way the soldiers had shifted in and out of the coaches.

Good. It wouldn't be long before all twelve were convinced they were harmless. Guards who believed their prisoners were harmless grew careless. Their reaction time slowed.

In the big room, the debris of their meal and the two puddles of vomit had been cleared away. The room smelled of strong soap and held what looked like a Healer-mage's examination table and a lectern with an inkwell and an open ledger. Standing between them was the woman who'd been waiting in the water room when they'd been brought up out of the dark. Danika guessed she was in her late thirties, early forties, light brown hair going gray and twisted up into a knot on the back of her head. Had they both been barefoot or both in shoes, Danika figured there'd have been no difference in their height. She was slightly stocky and wore a dark green bib apron over lighter green clothes so plain they had to be a uniform. Her hands and bare forearms looked strong. She wore a neutral expression like a shield, but it didn't quite hide the resentment in the gaze that swept over Danika from head to foot and back again.

"On the table."

It was the voice from the speakers. The voice who'd told them to rise and use the commode. It made sense. She'd spoken Aydori in the water room. Her accent had been twisted by Imperial and . . . Danika wasn't sure, but she assumed Pyrahn. As the woman opened her mouth to repeat the instruction, Danika moved toward the table, having taken enough time to establish she moved because she chose to, not because she instinctively followed a superior's command.

"Who," she breathed, *"are you?"* The table was high enough, her feet dangled above the floor. She tensed as the woman pressed her hand against the swell of her belly, but there was no cruelty in the contact, only a familiar efficiency.

"How far along?" This close, she smelled of the same soap as the room.

"Who? Almost four months." Closer to three.

The noncommittal noise could have been acceptance or disbelief. She crossed back to the lectern and dipped the pen and wrote a notation on the first page of the ledger. Her handwriting was also efficient, dark and blocky enough to see even from where Danika sat. "Any problems?"

"*Who?* Problems as a result of being kidnapped, exposed to an unknown and ancient artifact, dragged across three countries . . ." Danika touched the fading bruise on her face. ". . . beaten, and unlawfully confined, not to mention the emotional effect of not knowing what has happened to my husband, my family, and my country?" Pulled around by Danika's words, the woman turned away from the ledger, brows drawn in, but before she could speak, Danika added, hands spread. "I don't know."

"You don't know if you're having problems?"

That tone Danika knew. The beautiful are stupid. The rich are useless. The powerful have no common sense. It was, in its own way, as uncaring as Leopald's belief they were animals but more familiar and easy enough to work with. She smiled and answered with the same gentle reproach she'd have used on a young Pack member being too aggressive. "I don't know if the baby is having problems. It's all happening on the inside, isn't it?"

Given their relative ages, the reproach both was and wasn't patronizing. The woman took a deep annoyed breath before responding. "Any problems on the outside, then."

"Beyond the obvious?" Danika glanced over at the guards. "No."

"First child?"

"Do I have children in Aydori crying for their mother? No."

"Yes or no. I don't care about the rest."

Danika inclined her head in a gracious, silent apology and hid a smile as the woman spun on a heel back to the ledger. She made another notation, the pen's metal nib digging into the paper, then pulled a watch from her apron pocket. Cradling it in the cup of her palm, she gently flipped it open. She cared about the watch. That might be useful.

When she turned to note Danika's pulse, Danika breathed, *Who?* at her a fourth time.

"My name is Adeline Curtin. I'm a midwife. You'll be in my . . . care."

The slight pause before the last word made Danika think she'd only just stopped herself from saying something else. Custody? Control?

"How do you come to speak Aydori."

Adeline's eyes narrowed. "Answer when spoken to."

Danika inclined her head again.

Before she left the room, she sent another suggestion toward Leopald's rathole that he speak to her. On the way back to her cell, she breathed *Adeline Curtin, midwife* onto the air that found its way under the doors, knowing Kirstin at least would hear it, and one more *harmless* at Crooked-finger and Pocked-chin.

She pulled the pillow off the bed and waited on the floor for Kirstin to return.

"She was born in Pyrahn. Came to the empire with her husband." Kirstin's voice drifted down the hall and in under Danika's door. *"She doesn't want to be here."*

"Who does? She can't be angry at Leopald, so she's angry at us."

"She's angry at the world. If you push, she'll attack."

That sounded familiar. *"She wants to be Alpha, but every time she's challenged, she's lost the fight."*

After a long moment, long enough Danika thought the other Airmage might not answer at all, Kirstin said, *"We know how to work with that."*

If Adeline learned Aydori in Pyrahn, she had to have been born into one of the trading families. Her accent was too rough for negotiations, so probably carting; either learning the language when the drivers practiced at home or traveling back and forth across the border on the wagons.

I don't know you yet, Adeline Curtin, Danika thought, curled by the door listening for Stina's return. *But I will.*

Just as she began to get hungry, she heard the guards escorting the other women from their cells. Three of the other women . . . When Danika finally reached the big room where another meal had been laid out, Jesine wasn't there.

They waited.

"They brought her back after she saw the midwife," Kirstin murmured, "and I didn't hear them take her away again."

"She asked too many questions." When they all turned to look at her, Stina shrugged. "She's a Healer-mage in a room with a midwife. You know she'd have assumed they'd share information."

Adeline, as they knew her, would have resented that assumption.

Kirstin shot a narrow-eyed glance at the guards. "Do we demand to know what happened to her?"

"We know what happened to her," Danika answered. "She's locked in her cell for asking too many questions."

"Sent to her room without supper," Stina added.

"Treating us like children," Kirstin snarled. When Stina sent a bland look toward the guards and another toward Kirstin, Kirstin reluctantly smiled. "Fine. Like potentially dangerous children."

"Danika? What do we do?"

"We eat," Danika told Annalyse, pulling out a chair and sitting down. "We stay strong." There was a tureen of chicken stew with potatoes, carrots . . . She wrinkled her nose. . . . and parsnips in the center of the table. Next to it, a large basket of rolls. "Annalyse, you serve." When Annalyse frowned, she added, "I thought it might help steady you, if you had something to do."

The frown deepened.

Putting the serving spoon into the tureen, Danika stirred it once then pointed the handle at the younger woman. Annalyse flushed and took it, stirring twice more before she began to serve. Danika wasn't certain purifying water would have any effect on possible drugs in chicken stew, but Annalyse was a powerful Water-mage and it certainly couldn't hurt.

Without Jesine, they were quieter than they'd been at the last meal.

"Kirstin, talk to Stina. Need distraction."

As Kirstin held forth about how bored she was alone in her cell, Danika set up communication tests with Stina and Annalyse, kicking Annalyse once in the ankle when the younger woman nearly replied to a question no one watching would have heard asked.

Leopald didn't make an appearance. That didn't mean he wasn't up there in his rathole, watching.

"Creepy stalker," Kirstin muttered.

Danika leaned back in her chair, stretched as though she was working the kinks out of her neck and breathed at the wall. *"Talk to me."*

On the way back to her cell, she breathed *harmless* at Gouge-in-boot and Crooked-front-tooth.

Although they'd just eaten, there was bread and cheese and barley water in the cell as well as a clean nightgown across the end of the bed. Danika glanced up at the lamp, still burning brightly, then lay by the door.

"Me?" Stina was speaking quietly, mouth pressed as instructed to the crack under her door, but it was still dangerous if those listening heard her.

"*Stina, I hear you.*" Kirstin's voice rode the air currents. "*Can you hear me?*"

No answer.

"*Stina, I hear you.*" Danika took her turn. "*Can you hear me?*"

No answer.

Danika recited the first three verses of the ancient epic *The Hunt*, memorized and dreaded by every Aydori schoolchild and took comfort from knowing Annalyse was doing the same.

"Me?" If Stina had nearly breathed it, Annalyse hummed. Smart. Hide the word in singing done to keep up failing spirits.

Like Stina, both Air-mages could hear her but couldn't make themselves heard.

"*It's not much, but it's something.*"

"*It's nothing much,*" Kirstin snarled. "*We should tell the guards to free us.*"

"*We can't convince them to do anything they don't want to do.*"

"*Berger didn't want to die.*" Before Danika could answer, before she knew what she was going to say, Kirstin added, "*We have to escape!*"

"*We'll only get one chance. I'll listen to any plan that allows us all to survive the attempt!*"

It was a higher-stakes version of an argument they'd had before. Being Alpha was as much about knowing when to be cautious as when to attack. Kirstin had never been good at either caution or compromise.

Singing, as it turned out, was also a way to stave off boredom. Danika had a nap. Grew hungry. Ate the bread and cheese and drank the barley water. Had another nap. Made plans. Threw those plans away. Made more plans.

The door at the end of the hall opened. The movement of the air changed.

"*Annalyse?*"

And just barely, over the sound of boots against tile, a joyful, "Yes."

The lamp went out.

Heart pounding, Danika reminded herself that the same thing had happened last night. Although she had no idea if it was night. It was dark at least. She put on the nightgown, threw her pillow back down by the door, and waited for a howl that never came.

She hoped it was because he'd heard her and had been comforted, not because he'd been killed and skinned.

The next day began almost exactly the same way.

Different guards. Chipped-tooth and Dry-lips.

Jesine was there at breakfast. "I kept asking questions when told to be quiet. That's what the voice in the room . . ."

"Cell," Danika corrected quietly. "They're cells."

Jesine's gold-flecked eyes narrowed thoughtfully and she nodded. "That's what the voice in the cell said. I'm really hungry."

While Jesine talked, a normal enough reaction given her taste of isolation, Danika told Stina to work at the wood of her cell door. They had no Metal-mage among them, but Stina had once brought a rosewood sideboard into bloom. If she could weaken the wood enough to break it free of the hinges, the latch, and the bolt, then she could open all the other cells.

It would be slow work at the level the nets allowed, but it was a start.

The guards had taken her to the shower first but brought her to any communal time in the large room last. Danika thought if she could figure out why, she might be able to put the information toward their escape plan.

This morning, she was returned to the room to find the breakfast debris gone and the other four women standing in a line facing the wall where Leopald had appeared, their guards behind them close enough to grab them, far enough away to use their batons if necessary.

As she was herded toward the line, she noticed the other two guards standing at the base of the wall on either side of a large pile of multicolored fabric. The room smelled of . . . coriander.

The moment she stopped in the place left for her—Mole-under-ear and Dry-lips in the place left for them—the sections of the wall folded back, the guards all snapped to attention, and Leopald smiled down at them, leaning forward in the high-backed chair. The pelt he'd rolled out was still there but had been rolled back. Although they could no longer convince themselves it was a carpet, that helped. A little.

"Just so you know . . ." He actually looked a little sheepish although Danika assumed the expression was as false as their compliance. ". . . the Soothsayer's Voice objected to me taking Terlyn out of his room. He hasn't left it for thirteen years, so you'll have to excuse him if he's a little shy."

Terlyn? Danika turned her attention to the pile of fabric. It seemed to be undulating in response to Leopald's voice.

"Now, what I want you all to do is, one at a time, go forward and touch his hand. If you can't find his hand, any exposed skin will suffice, but do be brief. He's precious to me. He doesn't See very far ahead, so there are days when he's almost coherent and you have no idea how much I appreciate that. You start."

The hand shoving her forward seemed to indicate Leopald had been speaking to her. Searching the pile of fabric for the flesh within, Danika walked toward the Imperial Soothsayer, telling herself she wasn't doing it for Leopald, she was doing it to satisfy her own curiosity. She'd met two Soothsayers. One had to be kept in restraints to keep from harming himself and the other had walked out into a lake with a concrete block tied around her neck barely a month after Danika had met her. Their families tended to keep them out of sight—there'd never been a Soothsayer in the Pack—and they certainly had no place in Aydori politics.

Lifting her dress, Danika dropped to one knee at the edge of the fabric. If Terlyn was an adult, he was sitting on the floor under what appeared to be layers of scarves. There were fewer layers at the top where the faint outline of a face was just barely visible and an impressive number of layers farther down. Danika moved one. Then another. An undulation slid a third scarf aside, exposing a hand so pale it made Kirstin's milky skin look ruddy. The Soothsayer had bitten his fingernails short and ragged.

When Danika touched him, his skin felt warm, almost feverish. He shivered.

But he said nothing. He sat unmoving as Annalyse, Jesine, Kirstin, and Stina came up to him in turn and briefly pressed a finger to the back of his exposed hand, wiping the finger off against their skirts as they left him.

"Well," Leopald sighed as Stina returned to her place in line. "That was a disappointment. Terlyn has been quite vocal about how the sixth mage is being pulled toward the palace. I had hoped with you all together he might . . ."

"Two, two, two, zero, three." Terlyn slapped the floor. "Sixth! Two, two, two, zero, three." Slap. "Sixth!"

"Ah, confirmation that she's on her way." For a moment, Danika thought Leopald was going to applaud. "The numbers are new. Are they dates? They could be, couldn't they? Or measurements. Or coordinates. It's always fascinating to hear what they'll come up with, isn't it?"

"Bag of nothing." Terlyn's voice was surprisingly deep.

"Not that it's always immediately useful."

"White light!"

Leopald leaned forward far enough to smile indulgently down at him. "I'm sure the Interpreters will eventually discover where these particular puzzle pieces fit into the larger rhyme. And can you believe the Voice said he'd be too frightened to speak outside his usual environment?"

They left the room as Terlyn repeated the list of numbers, over and over. The skin between Danika's shoulder blades tightened. Although his face remained covered, she could feel the Soothsayer's gaze on her back.

"Remove your garment."

Danika smiled and unbuttoned the dress, slipping it off her shoulders and laying it neatly across the examination table. The room was cool enough her nipples hardened, but it wasn't uncomfortable.

Eyes narrowed, ignoring the new guards, Dimples and Freckles, so vehemently she might as well have been pointing at them, Adeline took measurements. Not only height and weight, but every possible measurement—length of fingers, width of nose, circumference of head. Danika cooperated so graciously, it appeared she was doing the midwife a favor.

Adeline took her time, clearly waiting for Danika to be embarrassed by her nudity.

Danika resisted the temptation to box the midwife's ears, so often so perfectly in position, and considered Terlyn's prophecy. *Bag of nothing* could mean he Saw empty cells and *white light* could stand for freedom. Of course, it could also mean he Saw an empty bag—there had to be a few around the palace—and a beam of moonlight through his window, if he had a window. *That* was the problem with Soothsayers.

Finally, after entering the distance between navel and hips in the ledger, Adeline growled, "You lay with beasts and you have no shame."

"I've done nothing to be ashamed of," Danika chided gently, but she spoke Imperial because she doubted the watching guards spoke Aydori.

"Talk to me."

On the way back to her cell, she breathed *harmless* at Dimples and Freckles.

No one missed the second meal. The emperor did not join them.

Talk to me.

Later, lying on the floor by the door, Danika dug her fingernails into the wood as the young male howled.

"Can you hear him?"

"Yes."

"Race you to the tree!" Holding the bedroll tight against her side so it wouldn't bounce, Mirian took off running. They ran at least half the time now and every day she ran farther and faster. Her skirt felt looser where it moved over her hips, and her feet had become so callused she doubted any of her old shoes would fit.

A black wolf ran by, bundle of clothes gripped in his teeth, a dangling sleeve dragging through last year's grass.

"Tomas, you cheater!"

He dropped the clothes at the base of the tree, circled it, and changed. "You didn't say anything about staying on two legs."

"It's not much of a race if you're on four!" she panted, throwing an arm around the trunk to stop herself.

Tomas grinned. "You only say that because you lost. If you want to rest here for a minute, I'll go make sure we're still on track."

"Be careful." The words were habit more than anything. Without a map, the road was their only way to Karis; the compass she'd taken

from Captain Reiter, no good without a heading. She watched Tomas run off to the south, then sank crossed-legged to the ground.
Circling a breeze around the tree about ten feet out so she'd know
when he returned, she settled in to practice.

By the time Tomas broke through her circle, she'd blown down
three dead cedars, tipping their roots up out of the ground, pulled a
scattering of old bird shot out of the tree behind her, re-formed it
into a small lead bar, and had lifted a trio of fallen leaves about fifteen feet above the ground. She set the leaves on fire—one, two,
three—and scattered the ash as Tomas settled beside her, the silver
streak at his shoulder glittering in the first strong sunlight they'd had
for a couple of days.

"It's not silver like a standard silver wolf, is it?" The fur felt both
coarser and sleeker under her fingers. "I mean, Jaspyr was really
more a pale gray. This is almost a metallic silver. Very elega . . ."

"When did you meet Jaspyr?"

Mirian sighed and pulled her hand away. Tomas almost never
changed when she was touching him now. She suspected it had to do
with what they'd almost done. "At the opera."

"In fur?"

"No, that was the next day."

He stared at her for a long moment. Mirian lifted her chin and
stared back. "You were the mage he had up his nose."

It wasn't a question, but she answered it anyway. "Yes." It didn't
hurt anymore. Apparently, she wasn't quite sensible enough to not
miss the ache.

"Why didn't you tell me before?"

Only one possible answer to that. "It wasn't any of your business."

"Wasn't it? And now?"

She shrugged and sent another half dozen dead leaves up into the
air, far enough she had to squint to bring them into focus. *Far enough*
seemed to be getting closer every day, living rough doing her vision
no favors. She split the breeze carrying the leaves and danced them
around each other before igniting the odd numbered and letting the
evens fall back to the ground.

Tomas picked up one of the fallen leaves, crushed it, then reached
for his trousers. "You promised you'd take it easy."

In fairness, she didn't want to talk about what was or wasn't his business either, so she let him change the subject. "Practice won't cause another collapse. The last time, I'd expended a lot of energy in the market . . ." She still hadn't told Tomas the details; that she'd killed another man to keep him safe. She wondered if she ever would. ". . . plus gone through two days of constant healing from the drug . . ." Tomas told her he'd had to change multiple times while she was out to completely clear his system. Had they not been who they were, Mirian suspected they'd both have died before reaching the empire, let alone Karis. ". . . and then I did that final thing with the trees. This . . ." Another half dozen leaves danced into the air and ignited one by one as they reached the highest point in the dance. ". . . is just playing around. It's all basic levels just . . . extended a bit by circumstances. What?" she demanded as he made a face.

"Extended quite a bit." He pulled his shirt on over his head and added as he emerged, "Harry was a second level Fire-mage and he couldn't do that thing you're doing with the leaves."

"Of course he could, it's just lighting candles. Only they're leaves." She took Tomas' offered hand and let him pull her to her feet. "And once you can blow a candle out, and you blow it . . . Ow!" With her attention on Tomas, she lost track of the last burning leaf and a piece of it landed on the back of her free hand, the blister healing almost before it formed.

"That's not basic."

"It really is. It wouldn't be basic if I healed you. Which I won't do," she added hurriedly, pulling free of his grip. Healers practiced on themselves for almost a year before they were taught to heal others and she had no one to teach her. The drug had forced first level body equilibrium to perform more efficiently, and she didn't remember healing herself in the market so that couldn't count. What's more, she didn't need to know how to heal someone else. When they found the Mage-pack, Mirian would remove the nets and Jesine Hagen could heal any injuries they'd taken.

She pulled Captain Reiter's compass out of her jacket pocket, flicked it open, and squinted down at the dial. "Same heading?"

"Adjust about five degrees south."

"All right." Moving around the tree, Mirian lined up the compass needle and pointed. "We're aiming for that big tree at the edge of the woods, the one that's been topped off."

Tomas frowned. "That's not very far."

"So you won't mind running it on two legs."

She blew a path through the grass in front of her as she ran, exposing the ground. Being able to heal whatever she might jab into her foot didn't mean she wanted to deal with the pain.

Tomas scooped up the bedroll and followed, allowing Mirian to set the pace.

Jaspyr.

That explained a lot.

But Jaspyr wasn't here with Mirian; he was.

Four strides took her across the cell. Touch the wall. Turn. Four strides back. Touch the wall. Turn. Five shorter steps. Touch the wall. Turn. Five shorter steps back. Touch the wall. Turn. She couldn't lie in front of the door all day.

As Danika heard the bolt thrown back, she turned, biting her lips to give them a little color.

Dimples and Bruised-thumb.

"*Harmless.*"

And when she got closer, she glanced down to see the bruising had faded, glanced up and smiled at him, pleased to see he was healing.

You're an individual and I see you, but I'm harmless so it doesn't matter.

Adeline wasn't waiting in the big room.

The emperor's rathole had been opened again. This time the head and front paws of the pelt—of someone's father, husband, brother, son—hung down over the wall.

"Come closer!"

The guards stayed by the back wall, standing rigidly at attention. Danika walked forward until the lower edge of the rathole began to cut off her sight line.

Leopald smiled and stared down at her, elbows braced on his thighs, his chin resting on linked fingers.

Danika stared back. The Pack were predators and she was an Alpha. She'd been stared at with a lot more intent. At the last minute, she remembered this was a power struggle she needed to lose, tipped her head to one side, and looked down at the floor in a ritual submission.

"You seem to be settling in well, no hysterics, no self harm, no pointless attacks on those you can't hope to beat. Although," he added, and she could hear the smile in his voice, "those last two points are essentially the same thing, aren't they? I suspected your instinctive need to protect the unborn would temper your reaction once you were shown the alternatives, and I'm happy you've proven me right. Does it hurt?"

That last question, Danika realized, was more than mere noise. He was asking her directly and he sounded as though he cared. That surprised her enough, she looked up.

He straightened and spread his hands. "Look, I know you're able to understand me—does the artifact hurt?"

"A little, Your Imperial Majesty." She spoke to him as though she wasn't his prisoner. As though this were a social situation where Lady Danika Hagen and Emperor Leopald had been forced by proximity to make small talk.

He seemed pleased she'd used his full title, as though she'd done an unexpected trick. "When you say a little, what do you mean, precisely? The mages it was tested on were depressingly inarticulate, although, in fairness, the available mages were just generally depressing. Poor. Superstitious. Uneducated."

Danika had a feeling that anyone with money or education or social standing would deny even basic mage ability in Leopald's empire. "It causes . . ." About to say *our*, Danika changed her mind. Better he thought of them as isolated rather than as a group. ". . . my head to ache, Your Majesty."

"Constantly?"

"Yes, Your Majesty."

"On a scale of one to ten?"

She considered that for a moment. The pain was background noise most of the time. On a scale of one to ten, a two or a three. "A four, Majesty. Sometimes a five." Was he expecting her to tell him the truth?

"Fascinating. And if you attempt to use your powers?" He smiled and shook a finger at her. "Come now, you don't expect me to believe you haven't tried?"

"Any use of power causes the pain to increase, Your Majesty."

"Of course. Of course. I'd love a demonstration, for scientific purposes, but I've been informed it would be bad for your whelp. Puppy? Cub? What would you call it?"

"A baby, Your Imperial Majesty."

"Yes, I suppose you would," he said thoughtfully as though this had never occurred to him. He tapped a finger by his left eye. "You have blue flecks. If you weren't wearing the artifact, what could you do?"

What do I control when I control you? He might as well have whispered it on a breeze.

"Air, your Imperial Majesty. Without the net, I could send a scent . . ."

His lip curled.

". . . my voice," she corrected, "across distances."

"How far?"

"Majesty?"

"Precisely how far?"

"I've never tested the exact distance, Your Majesty."

"Why not?"

"There was no need." She'd fulfilled the criteria the university required for her level and had never needed to send her voice farther than she'd been able.

Leopold shook his head, almost pityingly. "It's lack of curiosity that sets the lesser races apart. Can you fly?"

Social manners, Danika reminded herself. "No mage can fly, Your Majesty."

"No, not now, but in my Archive are documents that tell of mages who could fly. I have ancient journals that suggest even the mages of Aydori are powerless in comparison to the mages of old. Who were," he leaned forward and dropped his voice slightly, "completely insane as far as I can tell and more trouble than they were worth. But still, flying . . ." He settled back in his chair. "I can fly. Science has given me the sky. I have balloons to take me above the earth. I can send my voice over a distance; I can split my voice into multiple destinations over short distances. My people have fire-starters and surgeons who can cut into bodies and pull out diseases. Science gives freely to all, not just the few. Mage-craft is done."

"I wonder . . ." She bit her lower lip and stared off at nothing.

When she refocused on the emperor, he was staring down at her, red lips curved in a mocking smile.

"You wonder if mage-craft is done?"

"I wonder . . ." She smiled and shook her head, as though overwhelmed by the thought. "I wonder what science and mage-craft could accomplish if they worked together."

"Science and mage-craft don't work together."

Danika dipped her head, reluctantly correcting him. "*Haven't* worked together, Majesty."

Back in her cell, she tossed the pillow by the door, stretched out, and shared the details of the conversation with Kirstin.

"He dismissed me after that, but I could almost smell him thinking."

"You think he'll remove your net?"

"Not without taking every precaution, but then we'll know how it comes off."

"Lord and Lady, Danika, it's like you think we have all the time in the world to get out of here."

She pressed a hand against her belly. Stina was the furthest along at nearly six months. *"I know exactly how much time we have."*

"Tomas, that rabbit isn't dead." Not dead but clearly terrified, staring up at her from where it dangled from huge black jaws.

Tomas set it on the ground, not opening his mouth and releasing it until it was securely held between his front paws. He changed and spent a moment crouched adjusting his grip although Mirian noted that he didn't lift the frightened rabbit off the ground. Rather than straighten, he sat, the rabbit between his knees but outside the curve of his crossed legs. "It's injured. I thought you could practice healing on it."

"What?" Mirian, who'd returned her attention to their small fire the moment Tomas had lost his fur, turned to stare at him. "You want me to heal a rabbit?"

He shrugged. "You won't practice on me, and we need to know what you're capable of before we engage the enemy."

"So you want me to try and heal our evening meal?" The thought of healing something, then killing and eating it was a little creepy.

Actually . . . She shook her head as though trying to shake the thought free. . . . it was a lot creepy.

Tomas snickered and Mirian wondered how much of that had shown on her face. "If you heal the rabbit, we won't eat it. It'll live long and have baby rabbits. I'll catch something else for us to eat."

"That's not . . ."

Actually, it wasn't a bad idea. It was a sensible idea even. She *couldn't* practice on Tomas, and it *was* best they knew what she could do. It was sitting quietly within the cage of his hands. Mirian suspected *quietly* meant *too terrified to move*. If it could move . . . "How badly is it injured?"

"Not badly. A couple of puncture wounds on the back of its neck."

She laid another stick on the fire and watched it start to burn without her help. "What if I can't heal it? And it's not that I want to fail," she added hurriedly, "because I'm still thinking of it as food."

"It's not injured so badly it couldn't heal on its own. If you can't heal it, I'll let it go."

"All right." Mirian shuffled around until she sat facing him, her knees touching his, the rabbit corralled between them. When Tomas tensed to lift his hands away, she shook her head. "No, you keep holding it. I can't be distracted by worrying that it'll get away from me."

Its fur was soft, plush. She'd left a rabbit fur hat and muff back in her room in Bercarit, but this fur had more substance. The rabbit flinched as she touched it, in fear not pain, not that it mattered beyond how much it hurt her heart because she had to have contact. Although not the usual contact. Tomas hunted to keep them fed and they mostly ate rabbit.

Don't think of the rabbit as food.

Logically, she reminded herself, an injury was an injury, whether on her or on a small animal. She could heal herself, so healing another would merely be extending that outward. An examination showed the rabbit's skin had been pierced in two places by Tomas' teeth. Blood had dampened the fur around the bites, clumping it into dark triangular points. She couldn't put the blood back, so all she could do was close the holes.

Close the holes . . .

Close . . .

The rabbit writhed, twisting out of Tomas' grip, and Mirian snatched her hand away staring down at the animal in horror. Every thing that might be considered a hole on its body had closed. Unbroken fur covered its eyes, nose, mouth, ears . . . anus although she wouldn't, couldn't check.

Scrambling onto her knees, she twisted to the side and threw up. Threw up again when she heard the crack as Tomas broke the struggling rabbit's neck. Her stomach spasmed over and over until only bitter bile dribbled out of her mouth.

She couldn't stop crying.

She could destroy. Two men were dead by her hand. But she couldn't heal.

When Tomas wrapped his arms around her, she didn't fight him. She collapsed against his chest and cried until she had no tears left. Cried for the rabbit and the Mage-pack and Ryder Hagen and Jaspyr Hagen and the two men she'd killed and for Tomas and for her because they were going to rescue the Mage-pack and they didn't have the faintest idea of how and for the first time since hearing gunshots that morning on the Trouge Road, she missed the bland certainty her life had been.

"Bland would drive you crazy," murmured a quiet voice against her hair.

Mirian sniffed and rubbed her sleeve over her face. "I didn't mean to say that out loud."

"I know."

"I got you wet." She pulled away from his chest and dried that cheek as well. "I'm sorry."

He loosened his hold, a little, and shrugged. "Skin dries."

"I'd have made a mess of your fur."

"And that's what I was worried about. Here." One arm released her, stretched out to the right, and came back with a canteen. "Rinse your mouth."

She sloshed a mouthful of water around and had to poke him so she could get enough clearance to spit. The fire had burned down to embers, the last of the daylight had faded, and she couldn't see the puddle of vomit, but she could smell it. "What happened to the . . . to the body?"

"I got rid of it."

"You didn't . . ."

"Eat it?" She might have felt him shudder. "No."

"All right." Another mouthful of water. "Good. I'm all right. Thank you. Let me go now."

He released her reluctantly. "I could hunt . . ."

"No. I mean, yes, for you." She crawled to fire pit and began piling the smallest twigs in the pile against the coals. "I couldn't eat."

"You need to eat."

"I said I can't!" The fire flared and she froze, refusing to back away. If she'd actually been able to advance beyond first level while at university . . . If she'd attempted to heal another student . . .

"Mirian. . . ."

"Just don't!" She slapped away the hand reaching out for her. "Leave me alone!"

But when she woke up screaming in the middle of the night, he was there, arms pulling her close, murmuring comfort against the top of her head, as if he'd known she'd been dreaming of his fur covering eyes, nose, mouth . . .

"Your orders, Captain Reiter, were to bring back six mages. I know, because those were the orders I gave to General Loreau. One in six or six in one. Not a single Soothsayer said anything about five."

Reiter stared over Emperor Leopald's head, gaze locked on what looked to be a blue drawing of a shepherdess playing a flute, a recurring image on what he considered to be entirely inappropriate wallpaper. Of course, wallpaper wasn't something he'd given much thought to previously, so for all he knew it might be exactly correct for a debriefing that would probably turn into a court-martial that would, in turn, turn into an execution. Reiter doubted the emperor would allow wallpaper to delay an official court-martial should he decide a mere captain's action had been treasonable.

"Lieutenant Lord Geurin, as his uncle persists in informing me, returned with five of the mages, leaving the sixth mage for you. Although, as you were his commanding officer, and as I have had the unfortunate privilege of meeting Lieutenant Geurin, I rather suspect you ordered him to Karis with the mages already secured as you considered him incapable of finishing the job."

Was he supposed to answer that, Reiter wondered. Would anything he said matter if he were already marked to die?

Apparently not, as the emperor barely paused for breath. "I have read your report. I have read the report written by the garrison commander at Lyonne. I have read the letter written to the garrison commander from Major Halyss at Abyek. You may not know that Major Halyss was, until recently, a highly regarded member of my staff and I continue to value his opinion. Captain Reiter . . ." The emperor sighed his name. ". . . would you please look at me. That staring at the wall thing you military men do is annoying."

"Sir!" Reiter forced himself to drop his eyes and found the emperor gazing up at him, shaking his head.

"All that emphatic agreement is a bit annoying, too."

But he was smiling, so Reiter managed to breathe almost normally in spite of the fact he was looking at the emperor. Or the emperor was looking at him. Had been looking at him. The emperor. Reiter had been in the army for two years when Emperor Leopald had risen to the Starburst Throne. He'd taken part in the pageantry with the rest of his company, he'd drunk to the young emperor's health, he'd sworn new oaths to His Imperial Majesty Leopald, Commander in Truth. When he'd been transferred to the Shields, he'd realized he might be given a chance to see the emperor from a distance, then he'd been given orders carrying an Imperial seal, and, now, the emperor was looking at him. Smiling at him.

"The evidence suggests you made every attempt to carry out my orders."

His shoulders straightened. His body reacted to Imperial attention as though it had a mind of its own.

"Under normal circumstances, I honestly wouldn't care about how hard you tried. I care about results. That's how one builds and maintains an empire after all, isn't it?"

His shoulders slumped, just a little. Reiter wasn't sure he liked feeling even so minimally out of control.

"However, the Soothsayers have Seen the sixth mage here, at the palace, which somewhat negates your failure. More importantly, at least as far as you're concerned, last fall two Soothsayers Saw you at the palace standing by my side in a square of purple. Two of them." From the emperor's tone, visions by multiple Soothsayers seemed to be important. "Although," he added, "it wasn't until recently that the Interpreters were able to identify you. I will not bore you with the reams of bad poetry."

The pause extended almost long enough Reiter thought of throwing in another *sir*, but the emperor began talking again before he could.

"I had assumed you'd be here, with me, as a reward for successfully completing your mission. Apparently not, and, yet, here you are. So, as blame must be placed, if I am not placing it on you, where do I place it?" He raised a hand. "Don't answer that. It seems to me you performed as expected; the artifact did not."

"Your Imperial Majesty, all six of the artifacts were tested multiple times." The voice came from just behind Reiter's left shoulder, from one of the two civilians who'd accompanied him and General Loreau into the Imperial presence. They were courtiers, both self-important and simpering, but, other than that, Reiter had no idea of who they were or what their function was. Courtiers were not introduced to captains. "I performed the tests myself, as you requested, rather than leave them to a lesser researcher. The mage should not have been able to remove the artifact!"

"And yet she did." The gold net dangled from the emperor's finger, the broken links with their blackened ends obvious. "I believe you stated at the conclusion of your research that attempting to remove this artifact without the proper tool destroyed not only mage ability, but all cognitive ability as well."

"Those were the results we obtained during testing, but in fairness, Majesty, we never tested it on a mage as strong as the mage the captain lost."

If the narrow-eyed reaction was any indication, the emperor didn't appreciate this attempt to pass the blame back. Neither did Reiter, but he had to admit the emperor's opinion counted for more. "Lieutenant Geurin reported that when one of the other five merely tugged at the artifact, she scarred her fingers and was all but unresponsive for the rest of the journey."

"Again, Majesty, we have no data on comparative power between the two mages."

The emperor's wide-eyed gaze shifted left. "Lord Warder of the Archive."

"Your Imperial Majesty?"

The reply came not from the man who'd been talking, but from the older of the two civilians. Actually, Reiter would have been willing to bet he'd be the older of *any* two civilians. He looked like a turtle in fancy dress, his face and neck a cascade of wrinkles and his clothing at least a generation out of style.

"What was the condition of the artifacts when you removed them from the vault?"

"All six artifacts were in the same condition, Majesty. That was why I removed those six. While gold does not decay as baser metals may, there is a certain delicacy to the construction of these artifacts in particular, and I was, therefore, careful to check for any physical differences."

"So no broken links, Lord Warder?"

"Not so much as a weak link, Majesty."

"Interesting." Elbow propped on the arm of his high-backed chair, the emperor dropped his chin onto the heel of the hand not holding the artifact, two fingers curled by his mouth, two resting on his temple. He looked as though he were considering nothing more important than if he should have another drink before he left the officer's mess for the night. "As the sixth mage removed the artifact with no apparent damage to herself, I can only assume the artifact was, in fact, defective. Not physically, as has been stated by the Lord Warder of the Archive, so, therefore, the testing had to have been defective. Do you have anything to say in your defense, Lord Master of Discovery?"

"I can only repeat, Majesty, that the mage should not have been able to remove the artifact."

"And yet she did. Six mages, Lord Master. Six. The Soothsayers were specific and now, thanks to your incompetence, I have five. Yes, the sixth is on her way, but that's not the point. General Loreau."

"Sir!"

The emperor rolled his eyes. "Have him taken to the north wing. I'll decide what to do with him later."

"Majesty!"

The artifact glittered in the lamplight, swinging from the emperor's finger. "The evidence speaks against you, Lord Master."

"Your Imperial Majesty, no! I beg of you . . ."

He kept begging while soldiers dragged him from the room. He was still at it when the door closed behind him. Reiter stared at another shepherdess, sweat sticking his uniform to his back. Locked in position in front of the emperor, he'd seen none of what had just happened. That should have made it less affecting. It didn't.

"Tavert."

The conservatively dressed young woman sitting on a stool just behind the emperor's chair taking notes on a lap desk, looked up. "Majesty?"

"We'll try Doctor Lord Camberton as the new Lord Master. It should make him happy. He's wanted the job long enough." The emperor's smile made him look almost too young for his responsibilities. "Try to make it clear that I'd rather he not *overshare* his happiness with me."

"Yes, Majesty."

The emperor straightened, the languid posturing gone, and Reiter found himself back under the regard of a piercing blue gaze. He made a mental note to ignore the affectations.

"You showed initiative, Captain Reiter, using the drug to keep the mage under control. I like that." The corners of the Imperial mouth flicked up into a quick smile. "I'd have liked it better had it been successful, but still, initiative. I've had an opening on my staff since Major Halyss left—somehow his father convinced me that the major's knowledge of mage-craft would be of more use on the front, given what the Swords are fighting in Aydori—and I'd like you to fill it."

Well aware he wasn't being asked if he wanted the job, Reiter managed a fairly neutral, "Sir?"

"I found Major Halyss' study of mage-craft to be of use in my own research. You don't have his academic background, but you've certainly had more exposure in the field and that might be of equal, albeit different, use. Also, your appointment should stop Lieutenant Geurin's uncle from petitioning me on his behalf. The man's an idiot. Actually, both men are idiots. It's a family trait." Reiter came to attention as the emperor stood. "Walk with me, Captain."

A small door at the back of the room led to an empty hall—the walls the first without wallpaper he'd seen since arriving in the palace. When the emperor beckoned him forward, Reiter fell in behind his right shoulder. When His Imperial Majesty, Exalted ruler of the

Kresentian Empire, Commander in Truth of the Imperial army, said *walk*, there was only one option. Reiter suspected his legs would have obeyed regardless.

"When my father redesigned the palace, he added a way to get to the public rooms without having to deal with the public. Why should the servants have all the privacy?"

The emperor wasn't particularly tall. The top of his head just cleared Reiter's shoulder. Had he been a soldier not the emperor, Reiter would have described him as just over tit high on the average whore.

"I find myself with a decision to make, Captain. You're aware of the reason you were in Aydori?"

"The Soothsayers' prophecy, Majesty."

"You don't approve."

Reiter thought he'd kept that from his voice.

"Of my using Soothsayers in general—and I'm sure I don't need to tell you how different your circumstances would be had the Soothsayers not Seen you—or of this prophecy in particular?" The question sounded conversational, but then every word out of the emperor's mouth had *sounded* conversational.

Reiter couldn't lie to the emperor. He was *the emperor.* "I think combat requires initiative that might be stifled by Soothsayers, Majesty."

"Ah, yes, a soldier's opinion." He didn't sound as though he disapproved. "I, however, need to maintain a wider perspective. Soothsayers are useful for that. One in six or six in one. Empires rise or empires fall, the unborn child begins it all. Clearly, I intend to see the empire rise. It's in the nature of doing my job. Unfortunately, although the Soothsayers are quite emphatic about the sixth mage eventually arriving at the palace, they've Seen nothing about how she gets here. Is she captured again? Do you think that's likely, Captain."

"Not easily, Majesty."

"Not easily." The emperor frowned. "Well, then, let's hope she's being drawn by the power of the prophecy. However, in case the prophecy could use a little help . . . Tavert."

"Majesty."

"I want the army in Traiton and Pyrahn on high alert. Have Major Halyss pulled from the front and put in charge of making very certain my sixth mage is heading in the right direction. Major Halyss is more of a thinker than a fighter. I'm sure he'll be pleased to have something less dangerous to do."

"I'm not sure she's less dangerous," Reiter said without thinking.

The emperor actually stopped walking long enough to stare into his face. As a drop of sweat rolled down his side, Reiter figured it wouldn't hurt to show a few nerves. After a long moment, the emperor smiled. "I like you, Captain."

There didn't seem to be anything to say to that but, "Thank you, Majesty."

Although the area next to the road became more built up as they moved deeper into the empire, it took a while to find what they needed. A skirt snatched off one line then later, a belt to cinch it tight. A shawl taken off another line. While Mirian might have no understanding of the whys and whens of laundry, she trusted her ability to judge price. And she thanked the Lord and Lady when they finally found a shirt. From a distance, she now looked like any lower class woman of the empire. Up close, however . . .

"This thing has no support!"

Head cocked, Tomas frowned as she twitched the unbleached muslin back and forth. "Why does it matter?"

"It tells anyone with eyes, I don't belong here. Also, it hurts when I run."

On the list of things Mirian thought she'd never do, shopping for Imperial undergarments off village clotheslines had to be right at the top. Running across the empire with Tomas Hagen to rescue the Mage-pack was an unlikely, but possible, childish daydream. Stumbling around in the dark, avoiding houses with geese, to find the ridiculous number of items Imperial fashion required to replace a simple set of banding, would never have occurred to her. She missed the simplicity of Aydori clothing.

In spite of Tomas' protests that they were merely living off the enemy, which was perfectly legitimate in a time of war, they left a little money at every house they took clothing from.

Seedlings pulled from the edges of gardens, she assumed no one would miss. They all looked the same to her, a darker blur in the shadows of the night, so maturing them was always a surprise. They grew a lot of cabbage in this part of the empire. And onions.

Turning into the breeze, Mirian pulled the shawl tighter around her shoulders and tried to figure out why she'd been feeling anxious all morning. "It's like I can *almost* hear something. Something important."

"Danika?"

It was possible, but she'd heard Lady Hagen's voice on the breeze and this didn't sound the same. "I don't think so." It sounded less . . . directed. "If there's Pack in the empire, are there mages here, too?"

Tomas shrugged. "There's mages all over. But Ryder says . . . said, Imperial mages aren't much. First and second levels if that."

Maybe that was it. Maybe it was nothing more than a mage without enough power to be understood. But flinching at a shadow, her reaction not her own, Mirian didn't think so.

Midafternoon, Tomas stopped running so suddenly she nearly tripped over him. His head went up, nose into the breeze. His ears flattened, his hackles rose.

"Tomas?"

He growled, and took off running toward the northeast, angling away from the road.

"Tomas!"

Even running as fast as she could, she lost sight of him fairly quickly, but he was following his nose, so she followed the breeze.

The sun had nearly reached the horizon when she started to smell smoke.

Sweet, greasy, almost familiar smoke . . .

A moment later she could see multiple strands of dark gray rising over the trees, writhing against the sky.

Breathing through her mouth, she came out of a hollow, pushed through the masking trees, and stared down a long slope at a burned-out compound tucked against the side of a small valley. A fairly large cottage, a well, a garden, a low shed half open for wood and half closed in for livestock . . . all destroyed. Recently destroyed. The blackened shells of the buildings and a small dark pile in the center of the garden still smoldered. She couldn't make out the details of the pile no matter how she squinted or how hard she rubbed her eyes.

She couldn't see Tomas, although this had to have been what he'd caught scent of.

Heart pounding, she slowly walked forward until she wasn't only looking at the destruction, she was in the midst of it.

Only two walls of the cottage stood, less of the shed, and it looked like they'd burned it down with the chickens inside. Even the well-head had been destroyed, stones smashed away and tossed aside, the destruction more evidence of viciousness than even the fires.

Boots had pounded the garden hard, bootprints crossing and re-crossing crushed seedlings and stained earth.

They'd killed the chickens in the shed. Why had they dragged the rest of the livestock here?

Even staring directly at the blackened pile, Mirian couldn't figure out what the bodies had been although through the unmistakable smell of lamp oil, she thought she smelled pork. She thought, at first, it was her eyes, then she saw the foreleg slightly off to one side, far enough away from the heart of the fire its shape had survived in spite of how small it was.

After that, it wasn't hard to pick out skulls, shoulders, bones cracked and black.

There were Pack in the empire. Small family groups. Children.

Fur stank when it burned.

She couldn't smell fur.

Killed. Skinned. Dismembered. Burned.

She only hoped it had been in that order.

"They can't have gone far." Black against the burned wood, she hadn't been able to see Tomas until he rose to his feet. She could hear a whine and a snarl both in his voice. "I wanted to track them, but I knew you were following and . . ." He dropped again to four feet, threw back his head and howled.

Mirian felt something break inside. She backed up, nearly tripped as her heels sank into a patch of softer earth, didn't stop until she reached Tomas' side. With his howl sounding inside her, replacing the horror with rage, she pointed at the pile of smoldering bodies and then pulled her clasped hands apart.

If water could be parted, so could earth.

When the last body had tumbled out sight into the cleft, she brought her hands together again.

Knelt and laid her palms flat against the ground.

The bare earth turned green and wildflowers bloomed, covering the grave in a thick carpet of color, covering the ruins in a tangle of vines.

Mirian glanced toward the sunset as she stood. "Don't get so far ahead I can't find you."

Snarling, Tomas took off to the south.

He was out of sight almost immediately, but somehow she never lost his trail.

She caught up to him just after full dark on the outskirts of a village. Together, they watched six men strutting down the road. They carried pelts, and they were laughing. Talking. Bragging. Two of them planned to head straight home. The other four were going to the pub to celebrate.

It turned out it didn't matter if they still had silver shot remaining. They had no chance to use their guns.

The breezes stole their screams away.

And Mirian buried the bodies too deep to ever be found.

Chapter Twelve

I T WAS ALMOST MIDNIGHT when a sleepy page led Reiter to a room off another nondescript corridor, set the lamp he carried on the small shelf just inside the door, yawned, and said, "This is yours now, sir."

Left alone, Reiter discovered everything he owned had already been brought over from the garrison and stored neatly—uniforms hung in the large wardrobe, small clothes folded in the drawers underneath, and his shaving kit set out on the washstand under the mirror. No musket. No pistol. No knife. Only the soldiers on guard carried weapons in the palace. He hoped his were still in the garrison armory.

After a day standing silent in a fluctuating cluster of distant relatives, sycophants, and courtiers—Tavert, the emperor's mobile secretary had been the other person with him the entire day—Reiter was almost certain he'd rather have been court-martialed. Not to the point of execution, but a few years of hard labor had started to look good. If he'd been given Major Halyss' old job, he was clearly missing something. But then, Major Halyss was Intelligence and he was Infantry, so that didn't surprise him.

The room was about twice the size of his room back in the garrison's officer quarters but shabbier, the furniture both worn and mismatched, probably salvaged when the rooms of those with higher rank were renovated. Besides the bed and wardrobe, there was a desk with a filled inkwell, three iron-nibbed pens and a pad of paper, and a fairly comfortable chair. The heavy brocade drapes covered a tiny window, the thick glass beaded with rain. Given the hour and the weather, he couldn't tell what the window overlooked although he doubted he'd been given a room with a view. Too small to fit through, he supposed he should be thankful that if he couldn't climb out, no one wandering the roof could climb in. On the wall across from the bed, a scuffed door led to a water closet so narrow his shoulders brushed the walls on either side.

Giving thanks the room was painted, not papered—in one day he'd seen enough appalling wallpaper to last the rest of his life—he wondered if this had been Major Halyss' room. Probably not. Halyss' birth no doubt rated him a repeating pattern of bright green fishermen.

The door didn't lock, but Reiter had spent his entire adult life in the army and had long since lost any need for privacy. More importantly, the bed was comfortable and he was exhausted from keeping his mouth shut. He'd never suspected running an empire could be so inane—although given Lieutenant Lord Geurin, he supposed he should've had a clue. His last conscious thought involved the whorehouse he'd planned on visiting had he survived this morning's debriefing . . .

"Captain Reiter."

His eyes snapped opened, and by the time he'd focused on the private standing just inside the door, his hand had closed around empty air where his pistol should have been. "Who . . . ?"

"Linnit, sir. I've been assigned to you." He crossed the room, threw open the drapes, then returned to the door and picked up a pitcher. "I'll deal with your boots while you shave, sir." Distant bells sounded six. "Breakfast in the guard mess in half an hour. I'll be back."

Reiter missed waking under artillery fire. At least then he knew what the flaming fuck was going on. Hopefully, the emperor wouldn't take long to tire of him and he could go back to the safer prospect of being shot at. He sighed and got up.

His window looked due east, directly into the rising sun. If he'd been a religious man, he'd have seen that as a blessing. As it was, he blinked away the sunspots, noted a maze of roofs and chimneys, and in the distance, rising above the edge of the building, an arc of gold almost glowing in the sunshine. At first he thought it was the roof of some kind of garden pavilion, then he recognized it as a balloon although it was larger than what they used for reconnaissance in the field and more oval than round. Had General Loreau demanded the Shields have their own balloon corps just because the other two divisions did?

He was shrugging into his tunic when Linnit returned with his boots.

"I'd best lead you to the mess, sir. It's your first morning and this place is a rabbit warren."

"Country boy?"

"Yes, sir."

Until the emperor said differently, he was to be housed and paid like a captain of the guard. The largest difference being he took his orders directly from the emperor and when the 6th Shields—currently the company on Palace duty—rotated out, he wouldn't.

"Breakfast here, all other meals with the emperor's staff unless you're released, then do what you flaming well please." Major Meritin swallowed his last mouthful of coffee and set the mug aside. "You get lost in the palace, and you will, ask a page, that's what they're hanging around for. Don't bother the servants. And don't piss the servants off because they'll make your life shit. You're going to need at least one full court dress uniform, probably two. Court dress," he added when Reiter opened his mouth. "If you were an officer of the guard, you'd be fine in the kit you've got on." It was, differences of rank insignia aside, identical to the dress uniform the major had on. "But you're not. The field gear in your room fit you?"

"Yes, sir."

"I'll have Linnit deal with it, then. You won't be given time to see a tailor." He paused, a piece of gravy-soaked biscuit halfway to his mouth. "You okay with half shares on Linnit or you want to bring over your own ranker? He'll have to be vetted if you do."

Reiter thought about Chard, if only to have a familiar face around, but he doubted the private would be able to keep his mouth shut—on any number of sensitive topics. Best the boy be free of this clusterfuck like Armin and Best. "Linnit's fine."

"Good. Emperor's staff gathers in the staff room at eight and goes over his schedule for the day."

"Do you know what I'll be doing, sir?"

"Other than whatever His Imperial Majesty tells you to, I haven't the faintest flaming idea, Captain. The only information they sent me is that the staff gathers at eight, and you can thank Tavert for that. That one's got her head out of her ass, but I can't say as much for the rest of the hangers-on."

Even with limited exposure, Reiter could have said a number of things about the rest of the hangers-on, but he knew better than to open his mouth. The palace was just a better-dressed, better-fed version of a garrison town, and in a closed system, words always found their way to the wrong ears.

Although he left in plenty of time, he was almost late when he finally found the staff room. Linnit was right; the palace was a rabbit warren and the rabbits who'd built it had been insane. No wonder the emperor's father had added a few hidden straight lines. The page he'd finally managed to grab had slipped behind a tapestry—"It's just a copy made by the new machines, so don't worry about touching it or anything. It's not historical."—and out through a small door into the empty room next to the staff room.

Reiter slipped into the last vacant seat at the table, recognizing most, if not all of the men and women who'd surrounded the emperor on his first day. Half of them, he wouldn't trust at his back in a bar fight—they'd still be smiling when they stabbed the knife in. The whole lot of them ignored him. He studied them in return, paying particular attention to those he seemed to have most annoyed.

At eight thirty, Tavert stood, slipped her arms through the shoulder straps of her desk and led the way out of the room. About half the pack peeled off on assignment, the rest jostled for position as they joined the emperor in his morning assembly room. Reiter practiced being invisible. He followed and stood and kept his mouth shut. He started a mental map of the halls behind the halls. At noon, he ate a surprisingly bland meal at the lowest table in the Imperial dining room. In midafternoon, he heard the emperor say, "Captain Reiter, you're with me."

Reiter glanced at the sunlight spilling out through a window at the far end of the corridor, adjusted the map in his head, and realized they were, if not entering the north wing where the disgraced Lord Master of Discovery had been sent, heading to the north side of the palace. He followed the emperor behind yet another machine-made tapestry—although this one didn't seem to be a historic copy; Reiter thought he recognized the Battle for Nirport as he ducked under the stiff fall of fabric.

The short hall behind the tapestry led to a narrow flight of stairs that ended in a small room draped in Imperial purple. The room contained only a high-backed chair and a wolfskin rug.

The emperor paused, turned to face Reiter who stood between the two rear fabric panels, and spread his arms. "You were Seen standing beside me in a purple square. And here we are." He smiled and lowered his arms. "Fascinating how accurate they can be, isn't it? Especially when you consider how their prophecy starts out sounding like mad babbling. This room, it hadn't even been built when we were Seen in it."

So a purple square had been built after it was Seen. Did that count as assisting a prophecy? Where would they have stood together had the emperor built a yellow square instead?

"You're thinking about the implications of prophecy, aren't you?" The emperor looked pleased.

No, not just pleased, pleased with him, and Reiter felt himself respond—his shoulders straightening, his chin rising slightly. It was another unconscious reaction to Imperial approval. This time, he was certain he didn't much like it.

"Was this Seen because it happened or did it happen because it was Seen?" the emperor continued. "Everyone does ask those questions, Captain, but speaking as someone who has been around Soothsayers for his entire life and who now has the largest collection of anyone in the known world, I advise you to let it go. Someday, possibly someday soon, Imperial scientists will work out a rational explanation for how the Soothsayers function, but until then, leave prophecy to the Interpreters and the Voice. You'll be happier. Unless . . ." He leaned forward and Reiter had to stop himself from leaning away, pushed by Imperial intensity. ". . . you're familiar with the latest research into electromagnetism?"

"No, sir."

"Of course not, you're a soldier." He sounded as though he understood but, just for an instant, looked so disappointed Reiter vowed to find someone who could explain it to him. "And discussing the cutting edge of scientific discovery is not why we're here, is it?" Smile back in place, the emperor moved past the chair to the far wall and . . .

. . . pressed his forehead against it?

"Captain."

Reiter moved forward and found himself standing close enough to His Imperial Majesty that he could smell a soft, pleasant scent rising from the other man's hair.

Stepping away from the wall, the emperor tapped the edge of a small brass ring set into the plaster. "Go ahead, Captain. They can't see the lens from the other side."

He had to bend to bring his eye to it, he was that much taller, and, after a moment adjusting his position, found himself looking down into a large windowless room. Ten men in dark gray uniforms stood in pairs along two of the walls. It looked like a military uniform, but it wasn't one Reiter had ever seen and he couldn't make out insignia. They carried pistols. Not holstered; the weapons were in their hands, ready for immediate use. Seated around the round table in the center of the room, were five women who looked vaguely familiar.

"My mages."

He turned to see the emperor beaming at him, his blue eyes wide, pupils enormous. Another glance down into the room and Reiter realized why the women seemed familiar. The last time he'd seen them, they'd been kneeling on the Trouge Road. These were the five mages he'd left with Lieutenant Geurin while he'd chased down the sixth. The blonde had been the woman who spoke Imperial fluently, spoke to him as though she weren't kneeling in the dirt, captured by the enemy. The tall, very young woman with the light brown hair had been sick and the gorgeous redhead was the Healer-mage who'd gone to her. He had no specific memory of the other two.

A soft clank, metal against metal, pulled his attention back to the emperor in time to see one of the panels of fabric fall back into place. Reiter heard a woman's voice ask a question—obvious from tone even without understanding the content—and another voice answer.

"Do you speak Aydori, Captain?"

"No, Majesty." At least half of these women spoke Imperial, but surely the emperor didn't need Reiter to tell him that.

"Pity. I have transcribers and translators working on everything they say, but it's mostly been fairly innocuous. They complain, particularly the small, dark-haired one, then the blonde, who is clearly their leader, calms them down. She reminds them of how much worse it could be . . ."

How much worse had it been? Reiter wondered.

". . . and she reminds them that they have more than only themselves to think of. She's much more intelligent than I anticipated, and I'm certain it's been due to her influence that they've settled into captivity so easily. Although, it is also an understanding of how to use their own biological imperatives against them. The abominations rule by strength of tooth and claw, and I've proven to them that my strength is much greater than anything they've left behind."

"But they're not . . ."

"Abominations?" The emperor smiled as though Reiter had said something particularly clever. "You haven't the background to understand their physiognomy, not yet, but you must admit that the abominations define the socialization these women come from. And they carry abominations in their bodies. Well, some of them carry abominations. Some may carry mages." He frowned thoughtfully. "It's a pity they don't whelp litters actually, although, if it were possible, that would certainly change the interpretation of the prophecy. Mages are dying off in the empire, Captain, although not in Aydori. Fascinating place, Aydori: outwardly civilized, inwardly bestial and clearly unable to stand against science and technology. I know what you're thinking," he added, his smile broadening. "You're a military man and you're thinking science, technology, and several thousand highly trained soldiers armed with silver shot. You're right, of course. All the science and technology in the world is useless without strong hearts to wield it. The guards in there are part of my personal security force and have been trained for my specific needs. I'm very cognizant about bringing this threat . . ." He waved toward the spyhole. ". . . into the heart of the empire. I've read the old texts and . . . You can read, Captain? My apologies, of course you can," he answered his own question. "Or you'd never have been promoted out of the ranks.

Well, as you can read, I'd appreciate it if you could familiarize your-self with some of the mage histories. Another set of eyes, particularly eyes that have faced mages in the field, could be useful. And speaking of eyes, take another look at my mages and tell me if you see any weakening of the artifacts. I'd rather not have a repeat of what happened with your sixth mage happen here. I have every faith that we could contain it, but best to not have it occur at all."

Reiter saw women eating, smiling, looking sad. He saw Mirian's pale gray eyes and hoped the Soothsayers were wrong. Or that their babbling had been interpreted incorrectly. Why would she come here when he'd freed her?

Why had she gone to Abyek after she'd escaped? He should have asked.

"This is their first meal of the day," the emperor continued. "They haven't seen the outside world since they arrived and I'm experimenting with their sense of day and night to keep them off balance. Not excessively, of course, given their conditions. Still, the midwife attending them assures me that the lower orders are remarkably persistent when it comes to reproduction."

Remarkably persistent?

"So, Captain Reiter, do you see any evidence they're able to use mage-craft?"

"No, Majesty." As he spoke, he saw the blonde woman, the leader, look up, almost directly at him. He stepped back, nearly tripped on the rug, and had to catch himself on the arm of the chair, suddenly wanting to speak with her alone.

The emperor laughed. "Oh, they know this observation booth is up here, but they can't see the lens and don't know when it's occupied. Also, just in case, I've acquired protection charms from the Archive for the four represented crafts. All tested, of course." He reached back behind the fabric and the sound of voices from below stopped. "I was looking forward to sharing my research with Major Halyss—he was the only person at court interested in mages—but never imagine I'm not pleased to have you here in his stead."

It seemed to Reiter that the emperor would be happy with any pair of ears—Halyss' interest in mages or his own experience was incidental to the emperor loving the sound of his own voice. And he could only hope none of that showed on his face. "Thank you, Majesty."

"Fascinating, aren't they? I can't spend as much time observing them as I'd like, but I try to be here for meals. Unfortunately, other duties call." His sigh held equal parts regret and acknowledgment of the inevitable. "As they do now."

Following the emperor out of the room, Reiter tripped again on the rug. In his own defense, parts of it had buckled up, too large for the space. He glanced down and heard Major Halyss say, *"He's been collecting them for a while now. He could be studying the enemy. He could be having rugs made."*

"Magnificent, isn't it?" Out past the hanging fabric, two steps down the stairs, the emperor turned and looked proudly at the pelt. "They're larger than actual wolves, you know, so even trimmed up, they cover a more useful area. You attempted to bring me an abomination as well as the mage, didn't you, Captain Reiter? How did you find him to be?"

"He was mostly unconscious, Majesty . . ."

The emperor laughed. "Safest way to keep them."

". . . but he seemed to be . . . a person."

"It's a fascinating camouflage, isn't it? Spend a little more time with them and you'll see that slough off fairly quickly. Their response to stimulus is distinctly bestial."

To Reiter's surprise, the emperor remembered to tell Tavert he was to be given access to the Archive. He'd begun to suspect that words poured out of His Imperial Majesty's mouth without His Imperial Majesty being aware of them, but it seemed he actually paid attention to what he said. Reiter watched a little more closely as the emperor interacted with the people around him—a smile here, a touch there, the right word said at the right moment. He made people want to please him. Walking through workshops clustered against the south side of the palace, he spoke to men who wore heavy leather gloves and goggles, the dusters over their clothing speckled with small burns. He didn't seem to mind shouting over the noise of welding and pistons and any number of small roaring machines Reiter couldn't identify, and those men—and women, Reiter amended, although the protective clothing made it hard to tell—spoke back, not to their emperor but to someone who understood what they were saying.

He was smart.

And so excited about the possibilities technology offered, it was almost impossible not to share that excitement.

He had as little to do with the day-to-day running of the empire as General Loreau had to do with the day-to-day running of the Shields, but Reiter had been a soldier long enough to know that generals put their marks on their divisions, their prejudices and bigotry trickling down to the lowest rankers.

Emperor Leopald considered the beastmen of Aydori abominations, so regardless of what they'd been, that's what they'd become within the empire.

The Empress Ileena and Everin, Leopald's seven-year-old son and heir joined the court for dinner. Even from where Reiter sat, well below the salt with the unimportant and unranked, he could see the emperor make his wife blush with pleasure. His son stared at him adoringly. Happy families.

The mages, the women at the round table had families.

Every soldier he'd ever fought had a family.

The women at the round table weren't soldiers.

"This one's had pups."

"It's a pity they can't whelp litters actually."

After the tables were cleared away, Reiter put his back to a wall and stood quietly watching the ebb and flow of the court as though he were watching the advance and retreat of a battlefield—although he was smart enough to know that was far too simple an analogy. The people who followed the emperor during the day were not the people around him now. These men and women were older, powers in their own right. These were the officers who actually saw to it that battles were won.

It wasn't hard to pretend he had no place in the court; that he was merely an officer of the guard, unseen until needed. Playing guard was a welcome relief after a day spent feeling like he'd been swimming with all his strength and barely keeping his head above water.

Camouflaged by his uniform, he overheard more than one person complain that the silver needed for the Aydori campaign was well on its way to bankrupting the empire. Although they complained the way people complained about the weather or the traffic in Karis or the stink in the summer. They didn't like it, but they couldn't do a flaming thing about it. They didn't blame the emperor—even though it became clear Aydori had been the emperor's private project—

they blamed the Soothsayers. The emperors had always used Imperial Soothsayers and the empire had thrived. It was just how it was.

They were, Reiter realized, a convenient Imperial scapegoat.

No one could leave the room until the emperor did. While Reiter suspected it'd be useful to see how the currents in the room changed without Imperial attention to court, he didn't get the chance. The emperor beckoned, and they left together. He could almost feel the impact of the daggers glared at his back.

The five captured women were eating another meal. The emperor had him look briefly then surrender the spyhole.

"When I have the leverage of their offspring to protect my people, I think I'll remove one of the artifacts and try a few simple experiments before I breed them again." His face was so close to the wall, his voice was slightly muffled. "Have you ever thought of mage-craft and technology working together, Captain?"

"No, Majesty." He'd never thought of mage-craft at all until the mission to Aydori, and his musings on technology had started and finished with wondering where the hell the artillery had got to and how fast he'd have to move if Colonel Korshan's rockets headed back toward Imperial lines.

"I know, who would? But it's a fascinating thought and you'll never guess who gave me the idea. Pity I'll have to wait so long to attempt anything."

"Wouldn't you be able to begin sooner if you made a treaty with them?"

"Them?"

"The mages, Majesty."

"Yes, of course," the emperor laughed. "If they were people."

"You're early," Tavert said the next morning when he entered the staff room to find only her and one of the other workers there. She seemed pleased—as much as she seemed anything that wasn't professionally neutral.

"I have a good sense of direction." It had been one of the reasons he'd been sent to Aydori in the first place. Although, just to be certain, Reiter had given himself extra time in case he took a wrong turn in the hidden halls.

"The emperor is in the north wing this morning observing a procedure. He'd like you to go to the Archive. The Lord Warder is to show you the scroll."

"*The* scroll?"

"The Lord Warder will know."

No one in their little group was to accompany the emperor to the north wing. No one complained about it. Besides the mages, what else did the emperor *have* in the north wing?

"Take him with you. His Imperial Majesty's been collecting them for a while."

Stupid question. Even unasked.

Directions to the Archive were reasonably straightforward. Reiter waved off the offered assistance of a page and headed into the oldest part of the palace. The Archive was on a lower level, a level that had been a second floor before the third emperor had earth built up around the building and more stories added.

The closer Reiter came to the Archive, the emptier the halls became. By the time he approached the Archive's double doors, he was entirely alone. As he reached for the curved steel handle, the door opened, the lamps that hung down the center of the corridor flickered, and Reiter found himself face-to-face with an elderly courtier. Not the Lord Warder of the Archive, but one of the stern-faced men who he'd seen move in and out of the emperor's orbit yesterday evening. One of the "officers."

Reiter stepped back out of the way and instinct brought him more-or-less to attention.

"You're Captain Reiter."

"Sir." It probably should be *my lord*, but without knowing the specifics, Reiter figured *sir* was as good a general purpose title as any.

"My son wrote to me of you."

"Your son, sir?"

"You would know him as Major Halyss. He said he met you at the Abyek garrison. That you shared his interests." Dark eyes searched his face, pale lips within the gray beard pressed into a thin line. After a long moment, he punctuated the examination with an emphatic exhale. "I have been informed you've taken my son's place on the emperor's staff as someone His Imperial Majesty can speak to about mages."

"Yes, sir."

For an instant, Reiter thought he saw concern in the dark eyes. "Be careful."

As he walked away, Reiter wondered what interests Major Halyss had said they shared. And what, exactly, he was to be careful of.

They'd moved too far from the road to take the time to move back, but Mirian never hesitated in picking their path. While she occasionally pulled out the telescope, she'd stopped using the captain's compass. Tomas didn't know if she followed air or earth or something else again. Nor did he care.

He followed her.

"Wait."

She glanced down at the arm he'd stretched across in front of her, but when she turned to face him, he thought for just a moment that in spite of how close they were standing she didn't see him. It had been happening more and more often lately, but lots of mages got lost in the craft. Even Harry had used it as an excuse although, in Harry's case, it had actually *been* an excuse. He stood silently until her eyes focused on his face and she began to look impatient.

He checked the breeze again, picked up the scent, then pointed north. "Pack."

Tomas was half out of his shirt before Mirian realized what he'd said. "Alive? Tomas!" She grabbed the waistband of his trousers as he started to pull them down. "Are they alive?"

"Yes. And heading this way." He glanced down at her hand then back up at her face. "He's moving pretty fast."

"He?" The trousers dropped as she released them. Just one, then. That changed things. "Are you going to fight?"

"No!" He frowned, face half furred, and added, his voice slurred by the changing shape of his jaw. "Maybe."

Then he was on four feet and, given the way his hackles had risen, Mirian suspected *maybe* was a distinct probably. They'd both been on edge for the last couple of days. Grieving for their dead. Snappish and uncertain about the way they'd dealt with it. The men who'd brutalized and murdered the family deserved to die, they agreed on that. What they couldn't seem to settle on is how they were supposed to feel about what they'd done. Triumphant. Disgusted. Guilty. Justified. Nothing was clear anymore so Mirian, who could now feel the weight of Karis on the earth, kept them moving, clinging to the idea of rescuing the Mage-pack. At night she clung to Tomas; in the daylight, they didn't talk about it.

And now, more Pack.

Alive.

She started after Tomas just as a huge dark gray wolf suddenly appeared out of a dip in the land. Between his color and his speed she had to squint to bring him into focus and then squint again, unable to believe his size. She'd thought Jaspyr Hagen had been a small silver pony when she'd seen him running toward her back in Bercarit. On that scale, what she saw now was closer to a full-sized horse. The stranger was the biggest Pack she'd ever seen. He made Tomas look small.

Mirian began to run as Tomas sped up.

She couldn't hear either of them snarling. That had to be good. She hoped.

The first impact happened in the air, all eight paws off the ground. They landed, spun around each other, charged in again. Tomas hit the ground on his side, rolled, and was snarling by the time he'd reached his feet.

If this wolf was a wanderer, he'd want to establish dominance. If he was defending his family, he'd want to establish dominance. Tomas either thought he was protecting her or he needed to bleed off the emotional impact from killing those men or he was just reacting to the other male. And he was trying to establish dominance.

Mirian didn't have the patience to put up with it.

"Enough!" She used the wind to whip the word between the two of them, then, as they scrambled apart, put herself there bodily. "We're no threat to you," she told the stranger, "and you're no threat to us, so just stop it! Tomas!" The growling behind her stopped.

The stranger stared at her for a long moment, then he opened his mouth, tongue lolling out, and Mirian suspected he was laughing at her. She folded her arms and glared. To her surprise, he sobered, nodded once, as to an equal, and changed. Mirian watched him rise, and rise, and rise. The top of her head came to his shoulder and she was not, to her mother's very vocal dismay, small. His shoulders were broad, heavily muscled, and scarred, his arms as big around as her thighs.

Look at his face. Look at his face. Look at his . . . Lord and Lady!

She snapped her gaze back up to his face. He was old enough the gray fur he kept on two legs passed as hair. Although he looked nothing like him, he reminded Mirian of her first impression of Ryder Hagen that night at the opera—the same barely contained energy, the same potential for danger barely harnessed.

He smiled, eyes crinkling at the corners. "We've been expecting you."

"We?"

"Me and Jake. He Saw you here yesterday and sent me out to find you."

"Saw?"

"Aye. He's a Soothsayer, sure enough, and mad as they come. Still, he's mine and I'm his and we manage. I'll wait for your lad . . ."

"Tomas Hagen," Mirian told him. Even without turning, she knew Tomas was still in fur, unwilling to admit the fight was over.

"He's a Hagen, is he? Well, I expect we'll talk of that as well, but, for now, he needs to get his clothes." The callused end of an enormous finger gently touched Mirian's cheek and dark eyes looked into hers. "I don't like leaving Jake for long on his own, so we'd best be on our way."

"We don't have time. We have to . . ."

The stranger cut her off. "You have to come with me. There's things Jake's Seen me tell you that you need to hear, little mage."

"How did you know she was a mage?" Tomas demanded, gripping Mirian's shoulder. Mirian leaned back toward him, a little afraid he was going to try and drag her out of danger and fully aware there'd be no danger unless Tomas started something. "She didn't do anything and she has no mage marks."

"She put words on the wind." The big man glanced over Mirian's head. "And I have a nose, don't I? Besides, Jake Saw it." Then back at Mirian. "My Jake's quite taken by you, little mage."

"He's never met me."

"He sort of met you yesterday. He's in tomorrow now, and you still seem to be around."

"That's . . ." Mirian frowned. The Mage-pack had been at the palace for days. They had no time to follow this man home to his crazy Soothsayer. They had to get to Karis and rescue the Mage-pack without having any of idea of what they were up against—beside the entire Imperial army—and no idea of how to get them out of the palace after they somehow managed to find them. But Jake had Seen the big man tell her things she needed to hear. "Can't you tell me . . . ?"

"No. He Saw us at our table, sitting down when I told you."

She sighed. "Tomas, maybe you'd better go and get your clothes."

"We don't even know his name," Tomas growled.

"You have my scent, but if you need something to call me, Gryham will do."

"Just Gryham?"

"Never had need of another." He folded his arms and his brows rose.

Mirian flushed. "Mirian Maylin. Tomas . . ."

He got his clothes, but didn't put them on, taking the bedroll from Mirian and draping them over the top. Mirian could sort of see his point in remaining naked. If Gryham was in skin and Tomas was in trousers, Gryham would have the distinct advantage if it came to a fight, able to change faster. It seemed wisest to ignore that Gryham would have the distinct advantage if Tomas were already in fur and Gryham was dressed for the theater.

Over the last few days, Mirian had gotten very good at looking Tomas in the face. It shouldn't have been so hard to apply the same discipline to looking at Gryham.

"We've got a bit of a walk," Gryham explained as they headed east. "Jake Sees accurate, but he's not always so convenient. This was as close to home as you came on your own."

His accent put a different rhythm on familiar words. "You speak very good Imperial."

He laughed. "Very good, is it? Well, I live in the empire, don't I? Have for years."

"How do you know my name?" Tomas demanded, his shoulder bumping against Mirian's as they walked.

"I knew Dominic Hagen briefly when I was no older than you are now. He'd be . . ."

"My uncle."

Not just Tomas' uncle but the Pack Leader before Ryder. Mirian's father had called him the man who'd brought Aydori into the modern world.

"I wandered down into Aydori from Orin looking to see a bit of the world, but when you're an Alpha my size, people expect you to challenge. I might've won, who knows, but I didn't want Aydori, did I, and your uncle was smart enough to see that." Gryham ran a hand down his thigh. Mirian watched the blur against the sky that meant a passing bird. "Scar's nearly faded now. You've a bit of his look about you—color of fur, length of leg. That silver streak, that's where the pin was?"

Tomas rubbed the scar. "How did you know?"

"Jake Saw it. He's been Seeing you two off and on for some days now. He seems to think that silver color's important. Means something. Doesn't know why or what it means though. Just keeps repeating *find the silvered.* Soothsayers." But he said it fondly.

Mirian remembered the Soothsayer in Herdon. How he'd grabbed her ankle and yelled, *"White light."* Given that Gryham had managed to find them, Jake must have been a little less annoyingly obscure.

Gryham's low stone cottage was on the other side of a fast-moving stream. There was no well, but a shed and a garden, and it both did and didn't look familiar. Mirian stood at the edge of the rough bridge and made herself step onto it.

"Something wrong, little mage?"

"It just . . ." She gripped a handful of her skirt so tightly her hand ached. "There was a family, Pack, and they were killed . . ."

"Aye. Jake Saw you find them."

If she had to call his expression anything, she'd say he looked sad. "Why aren't you angry?"

"I'm angry. But he also Saw you deal with those who did the killing. It's good they paid."

"It doesn't change anything."

He shrugged. "They won't do it again."

"You're still considered an abomination."

"You think I haven't been called names before, little mage? Since I came out of the mountains, I've been called many names."

"But this name can get you killed!"

"Yes. But most that know we're out here don't know I'm Pack. Besides, Jake'll give us a full day's warning. That's all he Sees, a full day into tomorrow. It's why he's not crazier than he is, I expect. Also, I'm large."

"I noticed."

"Most do. Now . . ." He changed, leaped the stream, and changed again. ". . . come on."

Tomas changed and jumped the stream as well. "You could always part the water," he called from the other side.

"There's a bridge," Mirian sighed. And crossed it.

Jake was a short man with dark hair and dark stubble. The dim light inside the cottage made it hard for Mirian to see the details of his face. "You want one rabbit to do for four people," he shouted as they came into the cabin, "it's going to have to be stew. We'll use the last of the parsnips. Sure they look like limp dicks, but you won't notice after they're cooked."

From the smell, he was frying fish. And fiddleheads.

"Rabbit's for tomorrow night, then. Guess I'm hunting." Gryham crossed the cabin, wrapped both enormous hands around the smaller man's face and kissed him on the mouth. It wasn't a fond kiss, it was more an *if we didn't have company I'd do you right here on the floor* kiss. "Come back, love. We're here."

"I think I'll get dressed," Tomas muttered behind her, dragging his clothes off the bedroll. When Mirian glanced back at him, he shrugged. "There's only so much the scent of fish can cover."

"Have them set the table up outside." His mouth finally free, Jake grinned up at Gryham. "And put some flaming trousers on before I burn supper."

"We don't have time for supper." Although her mouth was watering, Mirian felt she had to make the protest. Supper wouldn't bring them closer to the Mage-pack. When Jake turned toward her and raised a brow, she sighed. "Fine.

"Furs, fish, fortunes sometimes." Jake grinned over the edge of his mug. "For those who don't need to see too far. We find enough to trade for what we can't make on our own. Flour, cheese, decent tea."

Mirian frowned, smoothing the tangled fringe on her shawl. "And no one in the village looks at you differently since the church declared the Pack abominations?"

"Most of the village thinks Gryham's my keeper, assigned by the emperor himself."

"Why would they think that?" Tomas asked.

Jake's grin broadened. "Everyone knows the emperor loves his Soothsayers.

"You lied to them." Mirian shook her head as Jake laughed. "But Soothsayers can't lie."

"Not in vision," Gryham grunted. "The rest of the time, there's nothing stopping them. Except maybe basic decency."

"It was for your own good."

"So you keep saying." Gryham lifted the hand he'd been holding since they sat down and kissed the back of it. "Liar."

Sometimes it seemed as if the two of them spoke their own private language. Mirian wondered if her parents had ever been like that and doubted it almost immediately. "There's a course on Soothsayers at the university, but I've never heard of visions being prevented by touch."

"I'll bet there's plenty you haven't heard of, little mage."

Tomas growled. "Stop calling her that!"

Gryham stared across the table at him. "When she tells me to."

"I don't mind." Mirian shifted sideways on the bench so she and Tomas were touching. Pressed their shoulders together. Dropped her nearer hand to his thigh. Wound her bare foot around his under the table. Felt him relax. When the corners of Gryham's mouth twitched, she glared them still and turned to Jake. "Do you remember what you see in vision when you're not in vision?"

"Not until it happens. This university of yours, does it have a name?"

"Officially it's the Aydori Institute for the Identification and Instruction of Mage-craft but no one ever calls it that. It's just the university."

"Like it's the only one," he snorted. "Why not call it The Institute?"

"That never quite caught on."

Gryham beamed at her when Jake laughed. "It's where they taught you to be a mage?"

"It's where they teach mages," Mirian allowed. "They didn't have a lot of luck teaching me."

"Good."

"Good? It's not good! All I know is basic level mage-craft. First and second and maybe I can fake a few third levels just from over-hearing them spoken about, but that's it!"

"Good."

"Stop saying that! It's not good, it's pathetic!" Under the edge of the table, Tomas closed his hand around hers and squeezed. Mirian took a deep breath. "All right. Fine. Tell me why you think it's good."

"I can't."

"You can't. I thought we were here because . . ."

"I can't." Jake nodded at Gryham. "But he can. I Saw him do it."

"Inside first." Gryham stood up and stretched. "It still gets cold after the sun sets."

"Fucking rain. This keeps up, the garden will flood."

Mirian looked up at a clear sky and the first evening stars, down at Jake, then back up at Gryham.

Who shrugged. "I can't be touching him all the time. And now we know why you don't leave tomorrow."

"The Packs came out of the mountains; Orin and Ural beyond that. Lines on maps mostly; it's still wild land up there. Pack lands. Aydori was the closest to non Pack lands and so non Pack started to move in. They're like rats. *Some* of them are like rats," Gryham grunted as Jake drove an elbow into his side. "Pack Leaders in Aydori had to decide whether to drive them out or learn to rule them. Decided the latter, didn't they, and Aydori got civilized."

"What's wrong with civilization?" Tomas demanded. "Orin is all raw meat and beer."

"There's nothing wrong with raw meat and beer, and while I don't give a half-eaten rat's ass about civilization's opinion, things are simpler in the mountains. The mage-craft isn't so tied up in rules and levels and shit. Less of it comes from here . . ." He leaned forward and tapped Mirian's forehead. ". . . and more of it comes from here."

He tapped her breastbone, as far from her breasts as he could get and still be touching her chest.

Tomas growled.

"Stop it," Mirian said absently, leaning back against his arm. "When you say more, you don't just mean *more*, do you?"

"It's a good thing I've spent the last seventeen years translating for Jake," Gryham sighed. "I mean, if you're a Water-mage, how much healing do you learn?"

"Healing isn't part of being a Water-mage."

"And that, right there, that's the problem. Used to be, everyone had to do a bit of everything to survive, but civilization means specialists because suddenly everything's so bleeding complicated with foundries and gaslights and brass buttons, it takes all a person has to learn how to do just one thing, and if everything's that complicated, then mage-craft can't be simple. So mages in Aydori started making rules. And enforcing them. Soon enough, the rules started enforcing themselves. Go far enough up into the old country, and those rules don't mean shit. There's no Air-mages and Water-mages and all that one-color mage marks. There's mages. You're a mage."

Mirian rolled her eyes. "I don't have mage marks. Of any color."

"And yet . . ." Jake spread his hands.

"You've got power. I don't need Jake to tell me that. I've got a nose and you smell . . ." This time when Tomas growled, Gryham acknowledged it with a dip of his head, somehow making the small movement look patronizing. "You smell powerful. Too powerful to be confined by the dams and channels these made-up rules have put around what it is to be a mage."

"I'm a river?"

Gryham smiled. "If you want, you could put it that way. River pulls water from all around—from runoff, from rain, from springs—power works the same way. You need to be a river, not a bucket. I'm thinking you're already halfway there."

"I'm not . . ."

"You're not an athlete, you never did jack shit to build your strength, but you've run from Aydori into the empire. How do you think a pampered society girl . . . ?"

Mirian felt her lip curl. "My father is a banker."

"How do you think a pampered banker's daughter got this far? Your mage-craft has been rebuilding your body."

"That's not . . ." Except body equilibrium had thrown off the sleeping drug without her consciously guiding it. Logically, it could be making adjustments to help her run.

"Not to say you couldn't use a couple of days' rest, mind. A little natural healing to wipe those circles out from under your eyes, a few decent meals. Anyway," he continued before she could respond, "way I heard it, the power is everywhere, but the mage has to open herself and say fuck these bullshit rules."

"Only less bluntly," Jake muttered.

"Just as fucking bluntly." Gryham kissed the top of Jake's head.

Mirian frowned. "I tested high."

"There you go."

She shook her head. "But the more powerful you are, the more you need rules."

"The more powerful you are, the more you need responsibility." When everyone turned to stare at him, Mirian twisting around so she was almost on his lap, Tomas flushed. "It was something Ryder used to say."

"And Ryder is?"

"My brother. My Pack Leader. He died. In the Imperial attack." To Mirian's surprise, he looked away from Gryham, caught up her hand in his, and added, "Jaspyr died with him."

She tried to pull free, but Tomas hung on tighter. "Let go."

"If you're waiting for h . . . Ow! Why did you pinch me?"

"She pinched you because you were being an ass," Gryham told him quietly as Mirian got to her feet.

When Tomas tried to stand as well, she glared him back onto the bench, considered explaining, decided it was no one's business, and left the cottage. It was too warm and too close and too full of men.

The night was clear—no sign of the rain Jake had Seen coming, and the grass was cold and wet underfoot. Mirian walked over to the chopping block, finding it more by the way it disrupted the air currents than by sight. If her mage-craft had been rebuilding her body, it seemed to have forgotten to fix her vision. There were moments when it seemed no worse than it had ever been and more and more moments when she felt like she was looking through a veil. And not a cute net veil, either.

She sat, pulled her feet up under her skirt, heard her mother say, *You're not a child anymore, Mirian,* and wanted to laugh. Or cry. Or scream. No, howl. She wanted to throw back her head and fill the night with sound, to bleed off some of the pressure she could feel building behind her bones. To consciously decide to let go instead of having the release controlled by circumstance.

When the cottage door opened, she expected Tomas, but she knew the space he filled in her world and, even in the dark, she could tell it wasn't him. It wasn't only that Gryham was so much larger, it was more that he didn't fill a space in her world so much as push against it.

He circled the chopping block, rubbed up against her knee almost hard enough to knock her over, and changed. "You can't blame him for trying to piss a circle around you. Lines need to be clear when two Alphas share space."

She sighed. Tomas had no reason to be jealous of Gryham, not the way he and Jake were all over each other. "I understand."

"No, you don't."

He was laughing at her. "Stop it."

"Tomas isn't the Alpha in your little Pack, little mage. You are."

"That's not . . ."

Gryham stood silently, waiting predator patient while she went back over every interaction she'd had with Tomas since he walked into the firelight pretending to be a dog. In spite of instinctive physical reactions, he'd barely tolerated her until . . .

Until she'd put him to sleep on the road to Herdon.

She must have made a noise or moved because Gryham was done waiting. "You put his ass back on that bench with a look. Pack's not complicated; someone's in charge, that someone's you."

"But I'm not Pack!"

"Pack, Mage-pack." She could feel Gryham shrug. "Not saying you'd still be in charge if there were more than just the two of you. Not saying you wouldn't be either. Just telling you what it is right now. Who's Jaspyr? He the reason you and young Tomas haven't shared skin?"

Startled, Mirian answered without thinking. "You can *smell* that?"

He snorted. "I can see that. You're easy with him 'cause you're not thinking of him that way and he doesn't know what to do with his hands."

"Jaspyr's not . . ." He wasn't a lot of things. But what was he? "Jaspyr was a moment that passed days ago."

"Woke you up, though, didn't he? You'd better let Tomas know this Jaspyr's not the reason you two aren't going at it like mink."

"I don't know what mink . . ." And then she parsed the tone, rather than the words, and stiffened. "That's none of your business."

"Like as not." He held out a hand. "Have to admit, the boy's got serious self-control because you smell bloody amazing."

Mirian sighed and put her hand in his, allowing him to pull her to her feet. "So I've heard."

"So what did you think of my Archive, Captain?"

Reiter watched the emperor watch the women down in the room. "It's impressive, Majesty." The large room had been lined with shelves and half a dozen huge scarred tables filled the center space. Junk covered every flat surface—old bits and pieces of tarnished jewelry, carved wood worn smooth from handling, stones with holes through them or runes etched into them. The whole room smelled as if generations of rats had died out of sight and slowly rotted, the smell too pervasive for one rat alone but too faint for it to be a problem solvable by a bringing in a terrier. Or a fan. Had Reiter not seen the tangles in action, he wouldn't have given the whole lot a second thought.

The Lord Warder of the Archive had assured him that every item was rigorously tested using the most modern scientific criteria, and while they might not know exactly how every piece functioned, they would in time. The old man had either been impressed that the Soothsayers had prophesied Reiter's presence, or lonely, or slightly crazy, because he'd been helpful above and beyond orders from the emperor.

"Did you see the scroll?"

"I did, Majesty." There were hundreds of scrolls, but Tavert had been right, the Lord Warder had known exactly what he'd meant when he'd said he was to see *the scroll*. The original wasn't paper, but finely tanned skin; the Lord Warder had called it vellum as he'd smoothed out the surface, his fingers encased in a pair of fine kid gloves. A good portion of it had rotted away and what writing remained was faded and in a language that had been long dead when the empire was founded. Reiter had only a vague idea how they'd managed to translate it even after the old man's explanation. Soothsayers had figured prominently, so it was no surprise the explanation made little sense.

"Did you read the translation?"

"I did, Majesty."

"And what did you learn?"

"The Pack was created by mage-craft." He decided to keep the whole *if the translators weren't blowing smoke out of their asses* to himself.

"And now you understand why they're abominations. Unnatural. An ancient construct by a blind mage so powerful he or she could pervert the rules governing life itself. The really fascinating extrapolation is that the origin of the abominations explains why mage-craft is dying out in the empire. As science and technology push the abominations back into the wild, where they're most comfortable . . ."

She had gold rings in her ears.

". . . the bloodlines die out. Abominations need to be bred back into the bloodlines of the mages in order for mage-craft to remain powerful. I guarantee you, Captain, that if we knew how to test for it, we'd find the abominations in the blood of these women as well as in their bodies."

The boy, Tomas, had a slight point to his ears. Reiter had known a man in the army with three balls. He knew what he thought was stranger.

"Just think what I could accomplish if one of these five throw a mage of that caliber. Empires rise . . ."

It took Reiter a moment of puzzled silence to realize the emperor had been quoting the Soothsayer's prophecy. "Or fall, Majesty."

For the first time since he'd come into the tiny room, the emperor turned from the spyhole, his blue eyes narrowed. "What did you say, Captain?"

"The prophecy, Majesty. Empires rise or empires fall." Reiter could feel sweat beginning to bead along his spine. The emperor's expression made him feel a certain kinship to the pelt they stood on. "If the Soothsayers are concerned . . ."

And just like that, the bayonet was withdrawn and the emperor shook his head indulgently. "The Soothsayers aren't so much concerned as they are open to all possibilities." He pushed his hair back off his face and smiled. "It's up to us, as reasoning people, to apply those possibilities. Thanks, in part, to you, I control five of the six possibilities and the sixth is on her way."

Reiter didn't want the responsibility the emperor seemed willing to grant him.

"Did you know that science keeps us alive fifteen years longer than in our grandfathers' generation?"

"No, Majesty."

"It does. I've been thinking, since I first read the scroll, what mage-craft strong enough to create a whole new species could do. If I controlled that mage, if that mage had been trained from birth to obey me, if I could trust their mage-craft, then I could live forever. I'd have the time I need to make the empire great. And when the abominations are gone, wiped out in the wild, mage-craft will die out in the wild. I will control the only remaining mages. Worth the losses in Aydori, don't you think, Captain?"

Fortunately, before Reiter could answer, before Reiter could decide what to answer, the emperor kept talking.

"And now this new possibility of science and mage-craft working together . . ." He rubbed his hands together, rings whispering over each other, and grinned. "I can't wait. If you could move back behind the rear draperies, Captain."

As the emperor settled into the chair, Reiter backed through the two panels of fabric, until he was suddenly teetering on the edge of the stairs. Weighing the chance of a fall against missing what was about to happen, he decided to balance right where he was. Shuffling left on the balls of his feet, heels suspended over nothing, lined him up with the narrow gap between the pieces of fabric. When the emperor reached down to the side of the chair, Reiter noticed a brass-bound lever built into the base.

Long, pale fingers closed around the lever and shoved it forward. The floor vibrated and the front of the room opened, splitting in two and folding back. On the one hand, the emperor formed policy based on the insane ramblings of Soothsayers interpreted through bad poetry. On the other, his engineers were superb. The man was a mass of contradictions.

Reiter was tall enough he could see the faces of the women around the table as they stood and turned to face the emperor. He didn't know how the emperor saw it—it was all theory to the emperor, and he believed he'd proven his strength, so he probably saw it as respect—but Reiter thought they stood because it was a better position for fighting than sitting down.

"It has occurred to me," the emperor said, "that I have very little personal experience with mage-craft." Reiter could hear the smile in his voice. "While I'm considering a certain proposal . . ." His tone was an unpleasant mix of coy and patronizing. ". . . I require more data points in order to make an informed decision. If the net were removed and you could give me one small demonstration of your power, what would it be?"

The largest woman said something under her breath.

"Ah, yes, you're the one who speaks so little Imperial. Louder please, so it can be translated."

"She said she would make a rose bloom, Your Imperial Majesty." It was the blonde who'd spoken on the road. Something about her tone reminded Reiter of Major Halyss' father, and he wondered what the other woman had actually said.

"Fascinating, but not very useful. You."

The youngest woman started, glanced at the blonde, who nodded. "I part water, Majestied."

"You're part water . . . oh, you can part water."

She visibly relaxed when the emperor laughed—even kidnapped and imprisoned, that was the effect he had on people. Reiter found it one of the more disturbing things he'd ever seen.

"A lot of water?" he asked. "Lakes? Rivers?"

She shook her head. "Not know amount, Majestied."

"Oh." She actually looked disappointed when he sounded disappointed. "No matter. I'm sure it'll be fascinating discovering how much water you can part. Eventually, of course. You."

The tiny dark-haired woman stared at the finger pointing at her. "I send you smells."

"Not very useful, I'm afraid, although I could see sending smells away as being of some benefit. Still that's what we have fans for. And you," he pointed at the blonde, the other woman in blue, "you'd do the same. So what would you do?"

Even frowning slightly, the redhead was gorgeous. Reiter hoped Sergeant Black had kept the men under control on the way back to Karis.

"I'm a Healer, Majesty. If you want a demonstration, I'll heal."

"Excellent." He pulled the lever back.

Reiter watched the women watching the emperor until the wall closed and he was grateful for the extra moment the fabric screening him provided when the emperor threw himself up out of the chair and turned.

"I knew, of course, what each of my mages could do. I had Lieutenant Geurin courier me the color of their eyes as soon as he reached civilization, thus the color-coded clothing so each craft could be identified from a distance. I've researched each of the six crafts. You're wondering why I asked then, aren't you? I was curious," he continued without giving Reiter a chance to answer. Reiter closed his mouth and moved aside, to give the emperor room to get past him and down the stairs. "Curiosity, according to my priest, is my greatest failing. I wanted to know if they'd lie. I can't abide liars and, more importantly, I don't trust liars. This kind of cooperation indicates they can be taught, and I'm so very pleased that they answered the question as asked instead of spouting foolish defiance." He chuckled, a warm, almost fond sound. "I suspect that I'll find when I read the translation that the first to speak wasn't going to make the rosebush bloom, but rather do something rude with it."

Reiter suspected the same.

"If there's to be a test, I will, of course, use the Healer-mage. Easiest to control and absolutely safest for bystanders." He turned and smiled as he reached the bottom of the stairs. "Given that I'd be one of the bystanders. I know I told you that I wear protections, but in all the years I've been searching, the best I've been able to find is a charm to protect against being put to sleep but nothing that protects from healing as a whole." Reiter fell in behind his left shoulder and they walked toward the main corridor where Tavert would be waiting. "I've never found even so much as a scrap of writing that suggests such a thing exists. Do you know why, Captain?"

The pause suggested that this time the emperor wanted an answer. "Because healing can't be used to harm, Majesty?"

"That's it exactly. And, credit where credit is due, the Soothsayers spoke of the Aydori mages ten, no just over eleven years ago, so I've had plenty of time to prepare. In your report, didn't you say you suspected your mage was healing herself, forcing the drug out of her system?"

"Yes, Majesty."

"You must observe the experiment, then." He seemed so energized by the prospect, Reiter had to hurry to keep up, in spite of his longer stride. "For comparison's sake. Tavert!"

She was waiting with half a dozen others when he emerged. "Majesty."

"Paper and pen!" He scribbled a note, smeared a little ink on his cuff, blew on the paper to dry it, folded it, and handed it back to her. "North wing."

Tavert handed it back over her shoulder where it seemed for an instant no one would take it. Finally, a skinny man Reiter thought was a distant Imperial cousin stepped forward and bowed.

"It would be my pleasure to do your bidding, Majesty."

The emperor ignored him. "Captain, you'll have just enough time to go back to the Archive and ask the Lord Warder for the fork."

Chapter Thirteen

DANIKA HAD ASSUMED she was being taken from her
cell for either another unnecessary session with the midwife—clearly designed to teach them they were livestock
with no self-determination—or to another conversation with Leopald. When she saw Jesine already standing next to the examination
table, she hid a smile.

Leopald had taken the bait sooner than she'd anticipated. He was
clearly used to getting what he wanted when he wanted it. She
couldn't influence him to do something he didn't already want to do,
so she should've assumed that once the idea of combining mage-craft
and technology took hold, he'd immediately act on it. His questions
had identified Jesine as a Healer-mage, the only craft with no aggressive potential, which made her the safest of the five were he to remove
one of the nets.

In order to escape, they needed to know how to get the nets off
safely

Leopald was about to show them.

Jesine held out her hands, and Danika walked into her embrace.

The wall was already open, the emperor smiling down at them, apparently pleased to see them together, his foot still propped on the pelt of a father, brother, son. When Danika prayed to the Lord and Lady, and she prayed more frequently here than she ever had at home, she prayed for a few moments alone with Leopald as they left the palace. Just long enough to move the air from his lungs.

"It has recently occurred to me that I've no need to wait until you've whelped before I begin doing simple tests." Eyes gleaming, he leaned forward. His lips were dark enough that Danika wondered, not for the first time, if he stained them. "You . . ." He pointed at Jesine. ". . . will be freed from the suppression artifact and then you'll be given an opportunity to use your mage-craft to heal a wound. Not a major wound, of course, but a wound serious enough that I'll gain some idea of your ability. A baseline, as it were, that I can use to create further tests. You . . ." His pointing finger moved from Jesine to Danika. ". . . are here for two reasons. One, as the leader of this small Pack, it's useful to me that you know what's happening. That way, you'll be able to explain my position in the face of uninformed reactions from the others and maintain the calm that's so essential to your comfort. Two, it occurred to me that I needed a way to control the healing. To know that the maximum effort was being applied."

How would her presence control . . .

Adeline closed one hand around her upper arm and reached across with the other, slashing the edge of a narrow blade across Danika's chest just above the neckline of the dress. Danika had realized what was about to happen the moment Adeline's fingers had dug in—not in time to move, or to try and defend herself, but in time to grit her teeth and refuse to scream.

The edge must have been very sharp. For a moment nothing happened and all three of them stood frozen in place, staring at the path of the blade. Then the flesh separated and blood welled up and the pain hit.

"Get her on the table." Jesine's voice had lost all languid and ladylike overtones. "And remove the net at once!"

It hurt. It hurt. It hurt.

The room spun. Then the fingers digging into her arm grounded her with a blunter pain and Danika managed to help lift herself up onto the table. Lying down hurt in a whole new way and the blood shifted, pouring back over her throat rather than down over her breasts. She felt careful hands opening the dress and moving it away and forced herself to focus. Leopald wanted a demonstration. The net would be coming off now.

Adeline pulled something from her apron pocket, something small. She poked it into the mass of Jesine's copper curls, and twisted. Jesine sucked back a pained cry. Danika kept her eyes locked on Adeline's hand. When Adeline tugged and the first bit of net cleared Jesine's hair, Danika could see pinched between the midwife's fingers . . .

Wood?

A strand of the gold net was tangled around and between a double prong made of wood.

Jesine spread her hands over the wound. The heat radiating from them was almost enough to burn. "Shh, it's all right. It'll be all right. Just a little pain and then it'll be all over, you'll see. I promise."

Adeline had shuffled to the left—Danika assumed to get a better look at what Jesine was doing, bringing the hand holding the artifact closer. Danika let her head drop to the side. This close, the new artifact looked like a small fork. She had forks at home with ivory handles that looked much the same. Adeline had no mage-craft so mage-craft wasn't necessary to remove the net. Only the wooden fork . . .

. . . snatched from her line of sight so quickly Danika thought Adeline might have realized she was staring. As a distraction, she screamed.

Not *only* as a distraction.

"That was fascinating, wasn't it, Captain?" The emperor started down the stairs without waiting for an answer. "You can read about mage-craft until your eyes bleed, but there's nothing like seeing it work to remind you that science can't explain everything. Well, not yet, anyway. Hard to believe I'd planned on waiting until they gave birth before I began testing. The healer can work right up until the whelp drops. Of course, the problem with Healer-mages, as I'm sure you've seen, is that at the level we were just shown there's not a lot of gain to be made in combining their craft with technology. Now, if they can heal sickness as well as injuries, then that's a different matter. As diagnostics improve and we learn more about diseases, then, with practice, Healer-mages alone could keep people alive indefinitely."

Practice. Reiter thought of blood pouring from a gaping wound in pale skin and wondered how the emperor would have the Healer-mage practice on disease.

"My physician told me that going to a Healer-mage is equivalent to drinking one of the those vile herbal teas old women force on you. I believed him, of course, because he's a man of science, but I now begin to think that's just because he's never seen an actual Healer-mage in action. I'd bring him in to see mine, but he'd most likely die of professional jealousy, unimaginative old coot." He giggled and Reiter was glad to be behind the emperor's shoulder because he really hated grown men who giggled and he doubted he'd survive the emperor seeing his expression. "What we need to do now is determine parameters . . . and I'm an idiot! I should have timed the healing! I don't suppose you checked your watch as it began and ended?"

Reiter schooled his expression as the emperor turned. "Sorry, Majesty, but no."

"I forgot, so I'm not surprised you did. Perhaps Adeline Curtin noted the time. She used to be the matron in Darkbin."

"The women's prison?"

"Yes, that's the place. Horrible in there, they tell me, but then it's a prison, so horrible is rather the point, I expect. The more relevant point is that she doesn't want to go back which is good because it's surprisingly difficult to find an Aydori-speaking midwife whose loyalty you can count on. Although, between you and me, I find her mildly disquieting."

She'd taken a scalpel and cut a woman under her care. Reiter found the idea of her as a midwife in a women's prison more than *mildly* disquieting.

"Ah, well, if we didn't record a time today, we have to make sure we record one the next time. And I've just now thought of a way we can use your background to our advantage. Write up a list for me, Captain, of all the various injuries you've seen on a battlefield." At the tapestry, he waited for Reiter to lift the fabric, and murmured as he passed, "I wonder what would happen if we cut a finger off? Would a Healer-mage be able to regrow it?"

"Majesty, a page brought this from the north wing." Outside in the larger corridor, Tavert offered the emperor the fork. The emperor redirected it to Reiter.

"See that gets put away safely, Captain."

"Yes, Majesty." As he walked away, he heard Tavert reminding the emperor of a tailor's appointment. Apparently Her Imperial Majesty wanted him in a new jacket for the upcoming public festival.

It was funny how everything inside the palace was connected to everything else. Until today, Reiter had never realized that fresh blood soaking into blue fabric created Imperial purple.

Curled on the floor, pressed tight to the crack under her door, Danika rubbed at the thin scar on her chest and took long, careful breaths. Inhaled slowly. Exhaled slowly. Fought the urge to pant. To whine. To keep screaming. She knew she'd lived a fairly sheltered life. Everyone she knew had lived a fairly sheltered life. Before Aydori was attacked, even the soldiers in her family or among her extended acquaintance were more about showing off their uniforms for pretty girls than they were about danger and pain. Her brother had fallen off the roof when he was ten and broken his arm, and the more dominant members of the Pack had scars, but she'd gone from being a slightly bored schoolgirl, to excelling at the university, to a loving marriage without ever being hurt badly enough for her to remember it now.

Kirstin had heard her scream. Her words on the air had not only been frantic but forceful enough to reach all of the others, and the net had clamped down. She was probably in more pain now than Danika, who had only the memory of pain.

Murmuring comfort to the others, Danika made plans. They had to find out if Adeline Curtin was the keeper of the second artifact and, if not, where it was kept. Stina had to finish freeing the hinges on her door. And they had to escape before Leopald took his testing to its logical conclusion and injured one of them—injured her—in a way Jesine couldn't heal.

"Well, you'll never fucking fit in his, but I might be able to help."

Mirian stopped trying to lay words onto the breeze—she'd been practicing all day, and couldn't figure out how Lady Hagen had made it seem so effortless—and waited to see if Jake would speak again. Gryham and Tomas had gone out hunting, disdaining the downpour that had held them at the cottage for a second day, and she'd been told to remember anything Jake said.

"What did you See?" she asked when he picked another potato out of the basket she'd matured and began to peel it.

He raised his head, gaze unfocused, and Mirian realized he still stared into the future. "Hurry."

The knife slipped and he swore, back in the present as blood dripped on the floor.

"So, Captain Reiter, is it true there's captured Aydori mages in the north wing?"

Reiter turned, surprising the woman seated next to him, who'd been leaning in, her breath warm and wine-scented against his cheek.

Her name was Onnyle Cobb. Her family was minor nobility. She did something at the treasury and wanted to do something more important. He had no idea who most of the people sitting down every evening at the formal dinner were, but over the last few days, he'd managed a reasonably thorough threat assessment of those he ate with.

Ate beside.

Over the last four meals, there'd been a bare exchange of common civility—he still wore his old dress uniform, making him the only one in the room except the guard not in court dress—but it seemed he'd been assessed in turn.

Cobb waited for him to answer, still pressed a little too close, her eyes lying about how interesting she found him. Reiter found himself suddenly thinking of pale gray eyes, narrowed in scorn, and how he preferred their honesty.

He turned his attention back to his chicken. He'd never been told not to speak of the mages, but, given that he alone accompanied the emperor to his observation booth, it didn't take a genius to realize that the Aydori mages weren't common knowledge. In order for a thing to remain uncommon knowledge, those who knew of it had to keep their mouths shut.

"Is it true, Captain?"

Ignoring her didn't seem to be an option. "I can't say."

A warm hand closed around his arm. "Ah, but rumor says you accompany His Imperial Majesty when he goes to visit them."

Most of the men who'd been sent into Aydori had been reassigned to the other divisions. No surprise that one of them had bragged about a successful mission before he'd left Karis. Less surprise if it had been Lieutenant Lord Geurin; that ass would brag about taking a successful shit.

"People talk about you, you know. You were Seen by the Soothsayers. That's impressive. Important. And now, because of the Soothsayers, you have the ear of the emperor."

Reiter considered telling her that the emperor had his ear, that the emperor talked and he listened, but that would only extend the conversation, so he cut to the chase. "What do you want?"

She started but recovered quickly, allowing the flirtation to become business. "I'm wasted where I am. I have ideas that could revolutionize tax collecting. I want you to put a word in the Imperial ear."

"No."

She opened her mouth, closed it again. Reiter had sent soldiers to kill and he'd sent them to die and he knew how to draw a line in the sand. When Cobb turned her attention back to her meal, so did he.

"Head for the cleft . . ." Gryham put a hand on her shoulder and turned her slightly to the left. ". . . and that'll take you to the Tardford Bridge."

"Karis is this way." Mirian turned herself back, squinting into the morning sun.

"And if you go that way, you'll have to cross at the Vone at Chamon. Small town, everyone knows everyone, and they're all suspicious as shit of strangers. No, you want to cross at Tardford. Second largest city in the old empire, shitload of people, and it's easier to hide in a crowd. Lots of people wander into big cities looking for work. No one goes to a small town unless they got friends or relatives there. You go to Tardford, you avoid the kind what think a uniform or a piece of paper gives them power they've no right to . . ."

"Bureaucrats, soldiers, priests," Jake put in from Gryham's other side.

". . . and you'll be fine. You move your ass," Gryham continued, wrapping an arm around Jake's shoulder and pulling him in close, "you get to Tardford tomorrow. You take Old Capital Street right through town, then strike off straight for Karis. The road follows the river, but you don't have to. It'll take a day off your run."

"We could get a ride."

"Could you?" Gryham snickered. "You're going to put a wolf in a wagon behind a horse?"

"We went from Abyek to the border in a wagon."

"Flat on your back and sweating out drugs. You get into a wagon now and you better be sure you stay downwind of anything pulling it."

"I could . . ." Mirian began, chin up, glaring at Gryham, but Jake cut her off.

"Ignore him. He's missing the point. Horses are fine if you're carrying shit or if you need to cover a short distance fast. You . . ." He nodded at Tomas. ". . . can run for longer than any horse. Not as fast, but longer. Can probably run longer than Master Musclebound here . . . ow! You . . ." He turned his slightly manic grin on Mirian. ". . . are rebuilding yourself to keep up to him. Why the fuck would you slow yourselves down by bouncing along behind a horse?"

Tomas stared out toward the cleft—although Mirian couldn't see anything cleftlike, it was possible he could—and kicked at a clump of dead grass. "Tardford, Chamon; why don't we just avoid people entirely?"

"And walk across the Vone?" Jake snorted. "They put towns where bridges are."

"Mirian could part it."

"You sure?"

"No," Mirian answered before Tomas could. "I'm all about bridges!"

"You need to be around people or you'll be screwed in Karis," Gryham told them. Mirian didn't appreciate the whole *you're idiots* subtext, but he wasn't wrong. "You've gone wild last few days. Can't say I blame you, but the capital's not going to empty out when you walk in, is it? You need to practice being civilized."

Tomas kicked at another clump of grass, looked down at his foot, then up at Gryham in triumph. "We need shoes to go into a town."

"Well, you'll never fucking fit in his," Jake pointed out, smacking Gryham on the chest, "but I might be able to help."

Mirian leaned around Gryham. "You said that . . . Saw that yesterday."

"Did I? Well, now we know what I meant. Fucking yay. Stay here. Gryham . . ."

Gryham rolled his eyes, but allowed the smaller man to pull him back to the cottage. As they disappeared inside, Mirian untied the bedroll and pulled out the telescope. Aim for the cleft was all very well, but she couldn't even see the cleft. She pointed herself at Karis, then moved as much as she thought Gryham had moved her, shut one eye, and held the telescope up to the other. The brass eye-piece warmed quickly.

"It's right there." Tomas moved in and shifted the telescope a little farther. "Can't you see it?"

Without the telescope, the triangular cut in the distant hills blended into the landscape. With the telescope, she could just make it out, although the edges were fuzzy. "You've got good eyes."

"It's right there!"

"I can see it *now*." More or less. "It's hazy by the river."

"No, it isn't. Mirian . . ."

"I don't want to talk about it." Because if they talked about it, she'd have to acknowledge what was happening. That wasn't sensible, but she didn't care. Mirian lowered the telescope as Gryham and Jake returned, and slid it away as Jake dumped the carpetbag he carried out onto the ground. "Why do you have so many pairs of old shoes?"

"I live in the middle of nowhere. I don't get rid of shit." He tossed a pair of work boots, tied by their laces, at Tomas who ducked. "Try these. They're big on me and you lot have small feet for your size. I think it's a paw thing."

Mirian had never noticed Tomas' feet.

"Now these . . ." Jack handed Mirian a pair of leather house shoes.

". . . are soft enough the laces might pull them tight enough to fit you. You're not what I'd call delicate."

"Thank you."

He grinned. "Any time."

The shoes fit well enough, as much too big on her as the boots were too small on Tomas. They wouldn't be comfortable, but if they had to rejoin civilization, they needed shoes.

"I never thought I'd say this," Tomas murmured as Mirian packed them into the bedroll, "but I miss those wooden clogs."

"Definitely easier to get out of," Mirian agreed. "And not . . ."

"Just keep to the right, you'll be . . . Your right, you idiot, not their right! Good *night*!"

They turned to see Jake staring toward the east, one hand holding a slipper, Gryham a step away.

"And now," Gryham grinned. ". . . you know what to do tomorrow." He reached for Jake's free hand, but Jake snatched it away and stiffened.

"Hurry!"

Mirian felt as though someone had just stroked a cold finger down the center of her back. "Gryham. He Saw that yesterday, too."

"About keeping to the right?"

"No. He said, 'Hurry.'"

"Did he?" Graham wrapped his arms around the smaller man and pulled him close. "Then you'd better be getting a move on."

Reiter stared at the jacket Linnit had laid out on his bed, at the gold braid on the epaulets, the double strands of gold cord hanging down under his left arm, and the gold frogging across the front and around the cuffs. "Tell me this is a joke."

"It's court dress, sir."

He knew it was court dress. He saw officers in court dress every day. But, like many things, it looked a lot worse when it was applied to him personally. The only thing that made it even remotely acceptable was that the gold was a color only and at that he'd be paying for the color out of his next half dozen pay packets—real gold would take the rest of his flaming life.

Linnit approached, fabric draped over his hands. "The sash has to go on before the jacket."

The sash had fringe. Reiter felt like an idiot. He took what comfort he could in the plainness of the black trousers and that his dress boots had been deemed suitable. Wearing this mockery of a military uniform, he'd be less noticeable within the court but unable to hide should he want to step to the side.

One of the officers whistled as he entered the guards' mess. He hadn't made any friends, he wasn't around enough for that, but they'd ignored him the way they'd have ignored any new man posted to the unit. That easy neutrality was gone. He wasn't just another military man doing a job; court dress in that room was about equal to bragging that he'd been mentioned by the Soothsayers and he had the emperor's ear.

Except he didn't have the emperor's ear. Not today. The emperor was closeted with policy makers, Tavert informed him, and had left no instructions, so he had the morning to himself.

All that braid pulled him into an inane conversation with the Imperial cousin and one of the other hangers-on, neither of whom had spoken a word to him before. Reiter declined an invitation to a race meeting and was less polite when they expressed a stupidly uninformed opinion about how the Swords were fighting in Aydori. They'd no need to be as extreme in their advance as Onnyle Cobb—they had the ear of the emperor as well—they just wanted him on their side. Another voice lobbing their desires at the emperor's defenses.

He finally freed himself, feeling grimier than he did after months of campaigning, and went to find the balloon he'd seen from his window. Got lost twice, surrendered, and asked a page.

"People used to be all around it all the time, back when it first went up. His Imperial Majesty, he went up in it every day. Well, maybe not every day, but every other day for sure. And the prince, too. But His Majesty doesn't go to it much anymore, so nobody really does, Until his Majesty tells them to take it down, though, they've got to keep it ready in case His Majesty wants to go up."

Even the pages were talking to the braid. They'd been as disdainful of his old uniform in the way only boys who knew they were essential to the running of an Imperial palace could be. What did they care for the guard? The guard was like furniture that just happened to move on its own.

"This is as far as you can go behind things." The shortcut ended in a false wall a foot in from the ubiquitous tapestry. "From here," the page pointed as they stepped out into a broad corridor in what was clearly a high traffic part of the palace, "you go straight to the Sun Gallery and turn left. There's doors out into the courtyard." He smiled up at Reiter expectantly.

In his old uniform, the pages hadn't expected "gifts" for doing their flaming jobs.

The Sun Gallery had a wall of glass facing east. The other walls were a deep gold, and from the way they were glittering, Reiter guessed there was real gold in the square tiles. He thought of the times men had died because the artillery had fired everything it had and it hadn't been enough and wondered how many shells one of those tiles could buy. The room was warm and bright and there was a priest murmuring prayers to a small group at the far end by a golden sunburst. The priest's robes glittered as well.

Although, in fairness, Reiter had to admit the tiles and the robe were the first overt signs of wasted wealth he'd seen. The emperor wasn't the type to have golden statues of himself scattered around the place. He had five pregnant mages hidden away in private rooms instead. And each mage had two guards with drawn guns. And their "midwife" had a knife she was willing to use.

Reiter would have preferred golden statues.

The balloon in the courtyard was also gold—a huge, egg-shaped bubble of silk, tied by silk cords to an Imperial purple basket heavily adorned with the Imperial crest. Even the sandbags were stamped with the Imperial crest. A ridiculous number of tassels dripped from the whole thing—balloon, basket, bags. It didn't look anything like the efficient one-man balloons the army used for recon.

"It represents the Sun taking His Imperial Majesty up into the sky," one of the young women told him as he frowned at the unexpected gaudiness. The six in charge of the balloon, young men and women both, dressed in uniforms of high-laced boots, leather breeches, leather vests—"Our flight jackets are stored in the balloon."—were bored and happy to have someone to talk to. Reiter spent a surprisingly enjoyable morning—once he got them to ignore his *personal* gaudiness, learning about balloons.

The men who rode the recon balloons were never willing to answer questions.

Although all the seats at the table were full, Onnyle Cobb wasn't at lunch.

"But you're sure you're all right?"

"I'm fine, Annalyse." It took almost everything Danika had left to force her fingers away from the scar. They'd replaced the dress while she was in the water room, so the pale line she could just see with her chin tucked in as far as it would go, was the only evidence of the wound.

The younger woman met her gaze for a long moment, then nodded and turned to Jesine. "And are you all right?"

"For the first time in my life," Jesine ground out through clenched teeth, "I want to harm someone."

"That's right . . ." Danika stirred a spoonful of honey into her tea. ". . . you have no younger brothers."

Annalyse laughed and clapped a hand over her mouth as though the sound had surprised her.

Jesine smiled and shook her head. "Please, only children have problems, too. I never had anyone to blame." She picked up a biscuit and ripped it in half. "At least it's over. He's seen what I can do."

It wasn't over. Danika had suggested Leopald scientifically test the parameters of mage-craft and, as her professors used to say, one test did not establish a parameter. Leopald would keep going until he caused an injury Jesine couldn't heal. Kirstin, immersed as she was in politics, would have realized exactly where these tests were headed. Stina would have been suspicious. But neither Kirstin nor Stina were at breakfast, no doubt being punished for rudeness to the emperor and Danika couldn't tell Jesine she was wrong. Not when the shadows under the Healer-mage's eyes said she hadn't slept. Not when Annalyse already believed laughter forbidden.

Danika drank her tea, and dropped her other hand to curl into her lap so they couldn't see her fingers tremble.

"Speak to me alone."

She'd influenced Leopald once, and as much as she might personally wish it had gone differently, they now knew what they needed in order to get the nets off. He had no idea of what any of them were capable of. Of what she was capable of. While Stina continued to destabilize the wood of her door, the first step of the more conventional escape, Danika would try and convince His Imperial Majesty to take the net off her.

Healers might not be able to cause damage; she could.

"It was fascinating to observe how unaffected she is, wasn't it, Captain? It certainly seems to indicate that the lesser orders can shrug off pain that would flatten the rest of us."

Even with very little time granted him at the spyhole, Reiter had recognized faking it for an audience. Not only for the emperor—and he'd bet his pretty new uniform the blonde knew the emperor was watching—but for the other two women at the table. "Have you considered speaking to her about it, Majesty?" He had no idea where that had come from, but it wasn't a bad idea. If he were talking to her, the emperor wouldn't be ordering her cut. Probably.

"Yes, I have." The blue eyes actually twinkled as the emperor smiled up at him from the lower step. "I'll speak to her alone after our evening meal. You're anticipating me now, Captain. Well done. I like that in my staff."

Danika's skin crawled as Adeline examined her, pressing a brass bell gently against her belly, a nipple on the hose attached to the narrow end of the bell tucked into the midwife's ear.

"No bleeding?"

"Other than the obvious?" Danika smiled at Adeline's scowl. "No."

"Where fork?" In a just world, Adeline would be keeping the artifact in her apron pocket. Who wouldn't want to brag about that?

"No pain?"

"You were there for the pain."

"No *other* pain?"

"No."

"Where fork?"

"Don't start thinking you can lift the wooden thing from my pocket. It's back in the emperor's hands."

And Leopald was unlikely to just hand it over, no matter how often or how loudly Danika asked.

Onnyle Cobb wasn't at dinner either.

When Reiter asked about her, the young priest who'd sat at her other side for all the meals Reiter had taken in the formal dining room patted at the ludicrous golden sunburst ruff he wore around his skinny neck and frowned in exaggerated confusion. "Who?"

"The young woman from the treasury who's been sitting between us."

"I'm sure I don't know who you're talking about." The frown turned into an equally exaggerated smile. "More bread?"

Reiter had told no one that Cobb had asked him about the captured mages.

It seemed he hadn't needed to.

Ask about the captured mages . . . disappear.

It seemed people disappeared from court often enough that those who sat at the lowest ranking table weren't surprised.

Gryham had been right about them disappearing into the crowd. They'd entered Tardford at dawn with the wagons arriving from the country. The crates of squealing piglets squealed louder when they caught Tomas' scent, but as it was only a matter of degree, Mirian doubted anyone else noticed. When their country escorts turned left toward their waiting buyers, they stayed on Old Capital Street as instructed, keeping to the right when given the choice.

They walked like they knew where they were going, quickly, purposefully, her hand in the crook of his elbow, with their heads slightly down so as not to give offense to their betters.

"Our betters?" Tomas asked after Mirian explained it. "Where are you getting this stuff?"

"It's how Joy Miller, an innocent country girl, walked through town unseen on her way to confront her real father. It's a novel," she added impatiently when Tomas' brows went up. "It's not like either of us have real world experience in walking around unseen."

"I was a scout in the Hunt Pack."

"On four legs. And we're dressed like country people . . ."

"In stolen clothes."

"Fine, we're not innocent."

"Or in a novel."

Mirian stopped, grabbed the front of his jacket and dragged him around to face her. "Don't make eye contact," she growled. "The way you do it, people will think it's a challenge and we can't attract attention. Clear?"

He held up both hands. "Clear."

"They will *skin* you!"

"I know."

"Fine." As she let him go and they started walking again, an elderly woman smoking a pipe and leaning on the sill of a second-floor window across the street, gave her an approving thumbs up.

Most of Tardford was north of Old Capital Street and the street itself remained working class enough they never felt terribly out of place. Mirian kept up a constant murmur of *don't notice us, don't notice us* although she had no idea—and no confidence—it was doing any good. The practicing she'd done at Gryham and Jake's had been inconclusive. Pack could hear her no matter how quietly she spoke and Jake was so used to hearing what no one else could he paid no attention. Outside of town, just before they reached the road, she'd rubbed dirt into Tomas' hair, making it look less like fur and adding enough weight only a stiff gust of wind would knock it askew, exposing his ears, but she still kept part of her attention on his head. She didn't really care what the people around them thought as long as they didn't think *abomination*.

At midday, she rummaged in the bedroll hanging off Tomas' shoulder and finally opened the purse she'd stolen from Captain Reiter, using his money to buy them four skewers of grilled meat off a street cart on *the right side* of the street. Tomas assured her that he could only smell pork. She was a little surprised by how many bills were in with the coin. Aydori had only recently—and reluctantly—changed to paper money. The empire had used it for decades. Did army captains usually carry that much cash? Did they have to buy their own bullets? Pay their own men? Her parents had been fairly generous with her pin money, but if she'd correctly converted the value from Imperial to Aydori, this was more money than she'd seen in one place outside her father's bank.

"It's not that much," Tomas told her, licking grease off his fingers.

"It is."

"Bills were sent to your parents, right? You never carried more than a few coins. The captain's pay packet probably caught up to him in Abyek. He could have a month or more back pay in there."

"He snuck into Aydori and captured the Mage-pack!"

Tomas snickered and started on his third skewer. "I'm not saying he deserved to get paid for that, I'm saying he was doing his job. First time Harry and me got paid, we . . ." He flushed. "Never mind."

She supposed it made sense that a country couple heading to Karis to seek their fortune would have their life savings with them. So, logically, it made sense for thieves to look for couples heading to Karis to seek their fortune in order to rob them. She put a little more emphasis on her *don't notice us*, then had to stop when Tomas pointed out the eddies chasing after them against the prevailing wind.

By midafternoon they'd only the East Gate Market and a few cross streets of increasingly rural houses to get through before Old Capital Street joined up with the new Capital Street and started following the curves of the Vone River to Karis.

"The East Gate Market marks the place where the old east gate used to be when there was a city wall." When Tomas turned to glare, Mirian pointed at the wall. "There's a plaque."

"And we've got so much time to stop and read."

"Because charging right through town doesn't look suspicious at all!" Mirian snapped. Watching out for an entire city as well as Tomas' ears left her feeling as though she were being pulled to pieces. "Forgive me for needing a moment to collect myself."

"These boots are too tight and my feet are killing me. Why are you such a . . . Never mind. Not important." He went to run a hand up through his hair, caught himself when her eyes widened, and muttered something she didn't catch. Pivoting on one heel, he headed away from the building. "Come on."

Mirian grabbed his arm and pulled him to a stop. "The last time we tried crossing a market, it didn't work out so well. You almost died." *I killed someone.*

She still hadn't told him how Harn the farm worker had burned. Didn't want him to think differently of her. Had no idea of what he saw on her face, but his expression gentled.

"That won't happen this time." He adjusted her grip, tucking her hand into the bend of his elbow, and tugging her forward. "We'll stay to the right just like Jake told us to."

By midafternoon the market should have been emptying out, but banners had been strung across the small square, there was a distinct scent of toffee in the air, and a stage was being set up near an inn called . . .

"The Cock and Bottle," Tomas told her. "If you keep squinting like that, you'll have lines."

She elbowed him in the side. She'd always been nearsighted, but this wasn't a tiny cleft in a set of foggy hills off in the distance. She should have been able to read the sign. Rubbing her eyes didn't help. If she were being sensible about it, she'd admit her vision had been getting worse since she'd left Aydori, but—all things considered—denial seemed the better option.

She studied the market as though she could still see into the corners.

It was warm enough that men and women drank at tables set up outside. Young children and dogs chased each other around the small square—although the dogs stayed away from Tomas—and older children lingered in groups. There weren't a lot of men between fifteen and thirty.

"The empire went to war this winter, and the army always recruits heavily from the working class." Tomas shrugged when Mirian looked up at him. "I'm Hunt Pack, but Harry was an officer in the 1st. He liked to share what he'd learned even if I didn't give a rat's . . . if I didn't care."

"I wish I'd met him."

After a moment, Tomas smiled. "He'd have liked you."

With Tomas' arm warm under her hand and his shoulder bumping hers as they walked, it felt like they'd crossed a line. Just for a moment, they might have been walking out in Bercarit. They might have met each other the usual way. Her mother would be having joyful hysterics in the background. Then one of the children shrieked and a heated argument started up as they passed a cheese shop, and the moment ended. They weren't those people anymore.

Those people would never have bought cheese for later and, next door, the last round loaf of dark rye bread over Tomas' protest.

"It's solid," Mirian sighed, stuffing the purse back in the bedroll. "It won't get crushed."

"Rocks are solid," Tomas muttered.

Those people, the people they'd been, they had people who bought food for them. Bought it. Prepared it. Served it to them. As much as Mirian didn't really want to be those people anymore, it certainly wasn't all bad. Most of it—like food and clothes and beds and privilege and a total lack of terror—was wonderful.

"Tomas . . ."

There were four young men, more noticeable because of the lack of young men, watching them from across the square. Mirian's mother would have called them toughs and, secure in her social standing, loudly wondered why they were permitted to linger in the same places as their betters. They were unshaven, in jackets heavier than the weather required. Jackets heavy enough to hide things in and under. Stolen things and things used to steal things.

"I see them. Remember what Jake said. We stay to the right." Tomas caught her hand and pulled her back beside him. "That's not your right."

"What is it about men in groups?" Something squished under her foot. She flinched and kept walking. "Individually, they may be perfectly tolerable, but get a group of men together and they become insufferable. Give them guns and they're an army." One of the toughs blew her a kiss.

"Stop looking at them. They'll wait until we're out of the market to attack. There's too many witnesses here. We'll lead them somewhere isolated, and I'll take care of it."

"Somewhere isolated enough no one will scream abomination."

"Absolutely."

"If they're just going to rob us, don't kill them."

"Mirian . . ."

"I know. Try not to kill them."

"I'll do my best."

Smiling, laughing, the toughs changed the angle of their approach.

"Tomas . . ."

He stiffened. "Okay, I was wrong. They're not going to wait until we're in a dark alley to attack, they're going to make their move right here. Jostle around us, intimidate us. Rob us without a fight. Probably threaten you, to make me give in."

"What if we yell for help?"

"I can take them. I'm not going to . . . Ow." He glared at her. "You pinched me!"

"You can't *take them* here. You'll give yourself away!"

"I'm going to have to because there's no point in yelling for help. The way people are deliberately ignoring them, they've been terrorizing this neighborhood for years."

They were at the far right of the market already and couldn't go any farther right. Soothsayers were useless! Still, they could always go back . . .

"For this to work, there has to be more of them, probably two more behind us."

"Would that be the sensible thing to do?" Tomas muttered.

Mirian only barely resisted the urge to pinch him again. "For them."

They could let themselves get robbed. After all, she'd stolen the money in the first place.

But the chances were too high that a gang of young men looking for trouble would discover what Tomas was. They weren't expecting him, they wouldn't be carrying silver, but his changing and their dying in the middle of the afternoon during some kind of festival with people drinking beer and watching like they were at the theater would set a hunt after them. And the hunters would have silver.

If she waited until they got close enough and put one of the toughs to sleep, what would the others do? Stupid question. They'd fight. Just looking at them, Mirian could see that would be their reaction. And fighting brought them back around to Tomas being found out. She'd have to sleep them all at the same time. But she needed to touch them to sleep them and there was no way she could touch them all at the same time.

No. Technically, the mage-craft needed to touch them.

She had to stop them while they were still far enough away no one would know what had happened and who'd been responsible.

A breeze lifted her hair.

Air-mages laid words on breezes all the time.

Words had power.

She'd moved scent on a breeze that first night in the cave.

She'd slept that soldier without even thinking. It was second level healer-craft.

All she had to do was lay the power on the air and deliver it to the toughs the same way she'd made the leaves dance.

Logically, she could do this.

The breeze swept around her, small whirlwinds gathering up debris. She had seconds before someone noticed.

"*Sleep!*"

Tomas got Mirian out of the square and down one of the side streets with no direct line of sight to the market, hoping he'd bought them enough time. They didn't run, but he kept them moving as fast as wouldn't attract attention. Not only Pack chased when prey ran. Mirian's hand was tucked back in the angle of his elbow, his hand clamped over it, and it felt like ice with fingers. She stumbled as she walked, pressed up against his side.

He turned them down a lane between two silent houses, saw a cat asleep in the sun . . .

"How far did it spread?"

"What?" She twisted and stared up at him, squinting like she couldn't see his face even though he wasn't that much taller than she was. Just for a moment, it looked as though her eyes had gone to pieces, bits of the gray floating around over her pupils. Then she blinked and the moment passed. "Tomas?"

He'd probably been brushed by the mage-craft and it had affected his vision. He blinked his own eyes and said, "It's starting to look like you put the whole city to sleep."

The four jackasses who'd planned to rob them had fallen first. They'd crumpled to the ground as the breeze whipped past, then men, women, children, dogs, even pigeons, everyone in the market went to sleep. Everyone but Tomas and Mirian. Given her lack of control, he'd been thankful for that at the time, but now he wondered if they were the only two standing in all of Tardford.

And if Healer-mages could do this, why weren't they standing on the front line? A sleeping army wouldn't have killed Harry. And if this was something Mirian had made up, because she'd never been taught the rules Gryham said mages had made for themselves, then the rules needed to be changed.

A dog, out of sight behind a garden wall began to bark and a voice yelled at it to shut up.

"Okay, it didn't go this far. That's good to know." He steadied her as she tripped, but kept them moving. "Are you all right?"

Mirian dug the heel of her free hand into her eyes. "I didn't mean for everyone . . ."

"I know." He twisted one ear back the way they'd come, that silence suddenly shattered by a single raised voice although he couldn't make out the words. Time was running out. "Come on."

They left the city on a footpath, north of where Old Capital Street joined the broader, newer Capital Street. Tomas could smell horses and oxen and see a cloud of dust rising behind a carriage down near the river, but this section of the road was empty. He got them across it and immediately down another lane. The low building to the right was a dairy; in spite of lunch, the smell of cow was almost overwhelming.

"When we're past and we're upwind, you'll have to keep my scent from reaching the cattle, or they'll panic and lead anyone following right to us. Can you do that?"

"Of course I can."

"Of course you can? You blew a bunch of trees down and passed out for two days. There's no 'of course' about it."

She shifted so less of her weight was hanging off his arm. "I did it that first night in the cave. I can do it."

And she did.

At least he assumed she did. Nothing blew down or over or away, but the cattle didn't panic, and that was all Tomas cared about. If the two women whitewashing one of the outbuildings, or the man with the manure fork noticed them, well, it stood to reason that strangers had to walk out of cities as often as they walked in.

They began to pass farm lanes, then fields, and as the sun began to set the lane they followed ended at a pond where geese hissed a warning from the opposite shore. To the south, the land sloped down toward the river.

"Karis is that way." Mirian pointed to the northeast, then knelt and began tugging at the laces of Jake's old shoes. "We have enough light to run for a while."

Tomas heard *I need to run* and began to undress.

His feet stopped hurting after he changed, but he still sat down to spend a minute or two chewing his pads.

"Come on." Mirian was standing now, her own feet bare. She took a step and he saw the grass part, opening a path in front of her. When she ran, she ran with her whole body. He almost didn't recognize the girl he'd resented, who'd stumbled and limped and winced her way to the forest road that first day. This Mirian ran like . . .

. . . like she was trying to outrun something.

Her scent was too strong for him to run behind her, so he ran beside her until it grew dark, then he lengthened his stride and cut her off.

She slammed into his side, caught herself with two handfuls of fur, and laughed. "My feet know where they're going."

There was something hiding behind that laugh. He changed so quickly, she still had one hand on his shoulder, and he stepped back before he could close the distance. "Your feet need to sleep."

"My feet," she began, yawned, and surrendered.

They tucked in under the low branches of an evergreen. Mirian pulled the branches closer to the ground on one side and rooted them, creating a living cave. They shared the food and then, when Tomas would have normally changed to sleep he stayed in skin and poked at the dirt with a piece of stick. "If you need to talk . . ."

Girls needed to talk. He'd heard Danika yell it at Ryder. *We have to talk about it! You never want to talk about it!*

He thought Mirian wasn't going to answer, was about to thank the Lord and Lady for small mercies, when he heard her shift and take a deep breath.

"I think . . ." Her voice had a quaver he'd never heard in it before. He didn't like it. "I think I'm going blind."

"It's dark."

"Not right now!" So much for the quaver. "My eyes have been getting worse ever since this started."

"This?"

"Since the Mage-pack was taken. This last time, when I . . ."

"Put half of Tardford to sleep?" The stick broke. He found another.

"You're exaggerating, it wasn't even close to half. That aside, yes, when you were getting us out of the market, I could barely see at all and then it got cloudy and by the time we reached the pond it was mostly better, but the ducks were fuzzy . . ."

"Feathery," he said without thinking. "Sorry. And they were geese."

She poked his shoulder. "I started thinking about when I'd noticed it before and the only logical conclusion is that it's the magecraft."

"Is hurting your eyes?" Tomas knew a Fire-mage in the artillery who wore spectacles, and his grandfather also wore them . . . but his grandfather was old.

"Maybe it's because I have no mage marks. Maybe mage marks protect a mage's eyes from damage. So without them, every time I do something—and according to Gryham I'm doing something all the time—my vision gets worse."

Tomas thought about telling her what he'd seen in Tardford and didn't because she already sounded so upset. "Did Gryham tell you anything about mage marks?"

"No."

"So you could be wrong. It might be lack of sleep or lack of vegetables." He knew non-Pack needed more vegetables than Pack and they'd been mostly living on rabbit. "Or the air is different here."

"I'm not wrong. I went over and over and over it while we ran. Using mage-craft is blinding me. It's the only logical conclusion."

"So what do we do?" He couldn't make out her expression, but then he already knew what it was. He knew her shoulders had squared and her chin had gone up.

"We'll do what we set out to do. Save the Mage-pack."

"But if you can't use mage-craft . . ." He paused, suddenly aware of the breeze clearing her scent from their shelter so he could function. She was *using* mage-craft even while she talked about it blinding her.

"I didn't say I couldn't use it. Or that I wouldn't."

"But if it's . . ." He stopped when he felt her hand close around his.

"We've come too far. And when you weigh squinting and tripping against saving Lady Hagen and the rest . . . it's not even worth considering."

Shifted his grip, Tomas ran his thumb up the inside of her wrist. He could feel her pulse racing under the thin layer of soft skin. "Unfortunately, you're right."

The way she sighed, he realized at least part of her had wanted him to disagree. "Stay in skin."

"What?"

"Don't change tonight."

The only time since this started that he hadn't slept beside her in fur, there'd been a roomful of very fragrant people to help his control. "I don't think . . ."

"So don't think. I don't want to hold you," she continued. "I need you to hold me."

She was asking for comfort. Tomas had to breathe for a moment, the air smelling of sap and earth and Mirian—in spite of her breeze—before he could trust his voice. "I need to put my trousers on, then."

"You don't *need* to."

The emperor was scheduled to spend the morning being briefed on the results of several recent international trade agreements and, as Reiter was not on the list of staff he wanted to attend him, he had another morning off. This time, he stripped off his court uniform, regained his anonymity as just another Shield officer, and left the palace. He had money enough to visit a barber or a coffee shop but not both, so he chose the barber. After, as he hadn't been in Karis with the Shields long enough to make friends, he walked for a while, enjoying the noise and the smells and the complete lack of manners. He reflected on how unfortunate it was no one went to a whorehouse before noon, and reminded himself it didn't matter as Mirian had taken his purse.

When he returned to the palace to dress for the midday meal, he felt almost normal and more like himself than he had since he walked into that Imperial debriefing. The emperor's attention was intoxicating, but he'd been in the army long enough to know what followed extended intoxication.

That the emperor clearly intended to enslave—burn it, had enslaved—the Aydori mages made Reiter feel sick. He wondered what the emperor would say if he told him how he felt. It wouldn't change the mages' situation, whatever it was, although it would undoubtedly change his and not for the better.

And that young priest would have another dinner companion to forget.

Assembling after the meal with the rest of those who followed the emperor in case he needed facts about the noble families, opinions on what his courtiers were wearing, his mood lifted, or to hold a conversation about something no one else was permitted to talk about, Reiter stepped aside as a running page approached. Breathing heavily, the girl handed a folded piece of paper to Tavert who checked the seal and handed it immediately to the emperor.

"From the north wing, Majesty."

"Really? Lord Hyde, what time is it?"

The young man next to Reiter started and pulled out a pocket watch. "Half one, Majesty."

"That's early."

There was a murmur from those around him agreeing it was indeed early.

The emperor ignored them with what Reiter assumed had to be the ease of long practice and cracked the seal, flipping the single sheet open. It wasn't good news; that much was obvious.

"Tell me when it is two, Lord Hyde." The emperor usually made requests to his little pack of hangers-on. That was a command. His boot heels slammed against the floor as he turned and Reiter got the impression he wasn't hurrying to the foundry because he wanted to be there but because he wanted it done with.

The last time Reiter had seen the emperor dealing with new technology, he'd been enthusiastic. This time he was agitated and kept brushing the foreman off, giving only a cursory glance at the machinery he'd come to see.

As the clock on the foundry wall began to chime two, a miniature brass canon firing twice, Lord Hyde stepped forward. Redundant or not, he'd been given an order. "Majesty, it's two."

"Tavert! Cancel the rest of my afternoon."

"Yes, Majesty."

"Captain Reiter!"

"Sir!" It was a hard habit to break.

"You're with me."

Stina thought she was five or six days from being able to push her door off the bits of metal that held it in place. That meant Danika had five or six days to figure out what to do if Leopald had a guard stationed in the corridor outside their cells at night. No, not guard, *guards*, they were always in pairs. And always the same twelve although they shuffled the pairings around. Unless there were specific night guards, that suggested their guards slept when they did. They already believed their captives harmless, merely going through the motions of guarding them into and out of the large communal room, but that would change if they saw one of the cell doors slammed out into the corridor. Or even falling to pieces.

"Kirstin, what's wrong?"

Danika stopped her hand from rising to touch her scar, as Jesine's voice pulled her attention across the table. Kirstin didn't look good. There were dark circles under her eyes and her skin, always pale, looked clammy. She wasn't eating.

"It's nothing."

"It's clearly something." When Kirstin ignored her, Jesine drew herself up, but before she could speak, Danika stepped on her foot.

"*Stina.*"

Stina was the most stable of the lot of them at this point, probably because she was the only one able to actively work toward their escape. "I hate to think what my lot have been up to since I've been gone. Their father lets them run wild . . ."

As Stina launched into an involved story about her three children and the day they tied up the nursery maid with strips of torn sheet, Danika lifted her foot.

Jesine reached out, fingers closing around Kirstin's wrist. "Let me help. Is it the baby?"

Lips drawn back, Kirstin snatched her hand away. "There is no baby!"

'But the prophecy . . . ?"

"Soothsayers are insane. Everyone but His Imperial Majesty seems to know that."

"Are you sure?"

"That Soothsayers are insane?" Kirstin's laugh lifted the hair on the back of Danika's neck. There was no way anyone listening would think she was laughing at Stina's story no matter that Annalyse tried to laugh with her. "Pretty sure, yes."

"Kirstin . . ."

"My blood came last night."

Jesine shook her head. "There could be many reasons for blood. You could be . . ."

"Miscarrying? Had three. I know what a miscarriage is like. I know because I had one just before the Imperial army decided to destroy our lives."

"Yes, but . . ."

"Jesine." Danika cut the Healer-mage off. "She's known all along there was no baby. She was still mourning her last miscarriage when we were taken." That explained . . . well, everything. "That's why she dared try to remove the net." Kirstin's expression suggested she was an idiot for taking so long to figure it out. Maybe she was. "They go into our cells when we're in the water room and they go in while we're here. Will they find anything?"

"Like blood?" Kirstin snorted. "What difference does it make? Like the golden girl says, there could be many reasons for blood."

She was terrified and trying to hide it. Danika could see fear in every brittle movement and hear it on the edge of her tongue. There'd been enough blood then that no one could mistake it. "Why didn't you tell us?"

"I heard the prophecy when you did, Alpha . . ."

Kirstin made the title an insult. Danika let it pass.

". . . and Leopald needs six mages expecting children. There were already only five of us. What were their orders if they came up short? Would they kill us all and start again if they found out?"

"You're talking about your unfortunate stains on the bed, aren't you?"

Danika snapped her gaze up to Leopald's little rathole so fast she felt the movement in her neck. She'd been so intent on Kirstin, she hadn't noticed it open.

"I admit, I was angry at first." Leopald frowned in an overly false and concerned way. "But then I realized I should consider the misrepresentation of your condition as an opportunity."

"An opportunity?" Danika repeated, switching to Imperial. Eyes locked on Leopald's face, she got slowly to her feet, hearing the others do the same.

"Exactly. An opportunity I thought I wouldn't get for some months now." He leaned forward, hands on his knees, eyes shining as though he was about to share wonderful news. "I'm not going to kill your little friend, I'm going to start building the future of the empire now. I'm going to breed her."

Danika actually felt her mouth fall open. He'd mentioned breeding before, but she hadn't . . . because he couldn't . . .

Straightening, he beckoned to the guards. "Take the small dark one to the door into the research wing."

"You're insane!" Danika moved around to Kirstin's side as Mole-under-ear and Poked-chin came away from the wall. She shoved Mole-under-the-ear back, her attention on Leopald, peripherally aware that both the other women and the other guards were also moving. "You are certifiably insane!"

"And you are abomination," Leopald snapped. "Which puts you in no position to judge." The guards' hands closed around Danika's upper arms as he added, "Take her, too."

Chapter Fourteen

THE EMPEROR PUSHED through the curtains at the back of the observation booth before the wall had finished closing, paused and stared up at Reiter, cheeks flushed, eyes narrowed. "Something bothering you, Captain?"

There were so many things bothering him, Reiter didn't know where to start. Particularly as he'd like to stay alive after the telling. It wasn't that the mage had called the emperor insane; it was that the moment the word had been spoken he'd realized it was true. One moment he saw *the emperor*, the next moment he saw a man. A man who kept pregnant women captive, not as an act of war or to keep the empire safe as Seen in prophecy, but for his own *insane* reasons.

"Yes, Majesty."

The emperor barked out a surprised laugh. "Credit where credit is due, Captain. At least you're not a liar." He patted a bit of Reiter's ridiculous gold braid and started down the stairs. "The dark-haired mage has lied to me since she arrived."

His shoulders were right there, right by Reiter's boot, and the stairs were narrow and high. Unfortunately, there was no guarantee of a broken neck and, given that he was alone with the emperor, fairly high odds he'd die regardless of how successful the attempt.

"I despise liars." Most of the anger had faded from the emperor's voice, leaving it tired and slightly betrayed. "Well, anyone would who spent as much time as I do with politicians, wouldn't they? Still, the sixth mage hasn't yet arrived, and I expect as long as I have them all pregnant at once, I'll have fulfilled the prophecy in good faith."

"Uh . . . breeding the mage, Majesty, right now . . . is it . . . that is . . ." This was not a conversation Reiter ever expected to have, but maybe he could buy the mages some time. "Will she catch during her . . . bleeding, Majesty?"

"A very good question, Captain." The emperor sounded intrigued. "I don't suppose you discussed fertility with your mage?"

"No, sir."

"It's hard to know what information will end up being important, isn't it?"

"Yes, sir. But with other bleeding . . ." Flame it! He was not using the word animals. ". . . females, their bodies aren't receptive."

"They aren't?"

"No, sir." Reiter found himself hoping the emperor had never had a dog.

"I expect I'd have known that if I'd kept a few female abominations. There didn't seem to be much point at the time as all my high-powered mages were—or were about to be according to the Soothsayers—female, and breeding my own was the ultimate point of the exercise. Still, that's why we have the scientific method: observation, measurement, testing, and experimentation to modify the hypothesis. And nothing else remotely like the abominations exist, you know. They're unique." Instead of moving down the narrow corridor back toward the palace, the emperor turned, and pointed at the lantern hanging to the right of the stairs. "If you could remove that, please."

The gaslines that had been brought in to light most of the newer parts of the palace hadn't been extended into the north wing. Or at least they hadn't been brought into the hidden corridor leading into the north wing. Was it because the gas was a type of flammable air and an Air-mage would be able to work with it? Wondering who filled the oil lamps and how much they knew, Reiter lifted the lantern off the ornate brass bracket and stepped back, giving the emperor room to reach up and pull the bracket down.

A piece of the wall folded back, exposing a corridor that ran parallel to the room the mages were in. Had been in. *Were* being dragged out of by pairs of guards. The lever on the inside of the wall was in full sight, the works themselves were exposed—polished steel gears and chains and parts Reiter didn't recognize. The emperor patted a brass curve fondly before closing the door and leading the way to the right along the hidden corridor, past another set of gears and levers, under a line of old-fashioned oil lamps.

Reiter could do nothing but follow. He clenched his teeth so hard a muscle in his jaw began to spasm. He was impotent; considering where they were going, the word was darkly apt.

"I hadn't intended to take you any farther with me into the north wing. The work I'm doing there has only peripheral connection to the mages, after all, and it was with the mages that the Soothsayers Saw you'd be useful; however, two things have changed. Do you know what they are, Captain?"

"The mage . . ."

"Yes, of course, the dark-haired liar. That was a little obvious, wasn't it? Actually, now I consider it, the second point is fairly obvious as well."

Reiter had no . . . "Cobb."

"Well done!"

He despised himself for his involuntary flush of pleasure at the Imperial praise.

"I choose my staff for, among other things, their ability to not speak out of turn. So much of my life is public, I like to maintain the minimal amount of privacy I have. To keep it, as it were, private."

"So Cobb was a test, Majesty?"

"Of course. You were Seen by the Soothsayers, and I had certainly hoped you could take the place Major Halyss was to fulfill, but that doesn't necessarily mean you could be trusted."

Reiter's knees actually felt a little weak, his relief out proportion to the amount of time he'd spent with Cobb. "So she wasn't . . . removed."

"Of course, she was removed. As I said, Captain, I like to keep what's private, private, and the north wing is mine alone—the guards are mine, the scientists are mine, the experiments are mine. Although no one will ever know the effort I've put in, I fully intend to use the results of my research to benefit the empire. If you'll recall, I mentioned how the discovery that abominations are necessary to create mages will eventually leave us with the only truly functional mages in this part of the world. The Imperial armies will be unstoppable. More than they are now, of course," he added with a smile that suggested he didn't want to hurt Reiter's feelings, Reiter being in the army.

Telling even a sane emperor to shut up would be suicidal, but Reiter wanted him to stop talking almost enough to risk it. He didn't sound crazy when he talked. He sounded rational. Scientific. Smart. He sounded a lot saner than half the brass Reiter had served under. When he talked, it was hard to remember what he *meant*.

At the end of the corridor, the emperor waved Reiter forward to open a normal door—no iron bars or massive locks to warn of the horrors it hid—then stepped through and smiled his thanks. "Although my observation booth is technically part of the north wing, we're in the north wing proper now. That door . . ." He pointed to the right between two guards in the same uniform as the men who guarded the mages. ". . . leads out into an antechamber where the pages wait. They don't come any farther. While I'm all for expanding the scientific curiosity of the young, there are some things the youthful mind is just not flexible enough to experience. Science is not always pleasant, and the search for enlightenment can take dark paths. Beyond the antechamber is the palace. Well, the rest of the palace, of course, as this is also the palace. It's huge, you know. Of course you do; you've probably spent the last few days trying to find your way around it. Now this way . . ." He turned to the left, indicating Reiter should fall in behind him. ". . . is the way to the testing rooms. I suspect we'll have arrived first."

Constant repetition of *harmless* may have ensured no shots were fired as they fought the guards to keep from being separated, but it changed nothing in the end. Securely held between two large men, Danika saw Stina, Jesine, and Annalyse dragged back to their cells while she and Kirstin were forced down the stairs into the dark.

Panic rising, Danika reminded herself that Leopald had ordered them taken to the north wing, not the cells. Not the cells. The north wing. She laughed, unable to stop the awful sound from escaping at the thought of preferring new horrors to old. Chipped-tooth wrapped an arm around her waist, his new hold gentler if just as secure.

Weight hanging off her guards' hands, Kirstin braced both feet against the wall and pushed. She wasn't very large, but she'd never been weak. Bruised-thumb stumbled off the edge of a step. Swayed. Began to fall. He'd have fallen alone if he'd just let go of Kirstin's arm. Dimples could have saved himself if he'd let go. They both hung on. The three of them landed in a heap at the bottom of the stairs, Kirstin somehow, amazingly, on the top of the pile. She scrambled to her feet and limped past the line of dark cells to the rough wall at the far end where they cornered and recaptured her.

Three steps higher, Danika watched it all.

The fall, the landing, the chase—all done in silence. Dimples cried out when he landed. Bruised-thumb made no sound.

The guards had been ordered not to talk to the prisoners. That had been obvious from the beginning.

That there were men willing to follow orders so exactly was as terrifying as anything that had yet happened.

Danika knew she was both taller and heavier than Kirstin. She could get better leverage and do significantly more damage if she landed on either of her guards.

She was also pregnant. Risking the baby in a fall she couldn't control would bring freedom no closer. Once again, she wished she knew *how* to fight. She knew how to dance, how to speak to her housekeeper, how to entertain politicians, how to dress well, how to lie charmingly, and how to struggle but have no effect on two large men trained to use their bodies for violence.

Just past the last cell there was a full-sized steel door; like the stairs, incongruously new.

On the other side of the door, another row of dark cells. The moment Danika's guard pulled the door closed behind them, the prisoners began to howl.

Pain and anger and fear and anger and hunger and anger.

Danika stumbled and was hauled back onto her feet, fingers gouging bruises into her arms. The floor was sticky. She could smell shit and urine and blood and rot. How much more overpowering must it be to Pack senses?

Kirstin's guards were carrying her now. Danika could see her mouth moving.

Freedom. Freedom. Freedom.

The howling grew louder, anger drowning out the rest.

Danika felt Chipped-tooth shudder and she twisted, mouth near his ear. She couldn't convince him to do anything he didn't already want to do. *"I know you. Let me go."*

His grip loosened.

"I know you. Let me go."

Loosened.

"I know you. Let me go."

Then Gouge-in-boot nearly jerked her out of Chipped-tooth's grip, and he tightened his hold again.

It didn't matter, she realized. If they let her go, she'd follow Kirstin regardless.

She couldn't think of a single thing to say to the captured Pack that would give them comfort.

At the other end of the cells, Kirstin's guards carried her up another flight of stairs although these were old and worn and probably the original access to the cells.

Danika wrapped the anger in the air around her like high fashion, like silk and lace and velvet, and climbed, head up, back straight, teeth bared.

In an antechamber, identical to the one that led to the water room and the big room and their hall, they were handed over to four other guards. They looked harder, more confident—these were men who'd already proven themselves. As they made the transfer, Bruised-thumb swore and jerked back, blood running down his cheek. Blood on Kirstin's mouth. If he hadn't moved in time, he'd have lost the end of his nose.

One of the new guards laughed. "All abominations bite, kid." As he grabbed Danika's arm, she saw familiar scars. She knew the teeth that made those scars. These guards dealt with Pack. If Dimples and Chipped-tooth proved themselves with netted mages, would they be promoted to torturing Pack? Were they looking forward to it?

The door closed behind them, and the howling faded. When the door opened in front of them, a woman wearing a white coat over sensible clothes looked up from a mess of paper on a high desk and said, "Take the dark-haired mage to testing. Blonde to the cage on the deck."

The guards began to drag them apart.

Danika let herself go limp, her unexpected weight pulling her arms from her guards' grip. She dropped to one knee, pushed forward and back up onto her feet, throwing her arms around Kirstin's waist. "Where she goes, I go."

She'd spoken Imperial, but the woman in the white coat only pulled her spectacles off and polished them as though she hadn't heard. "Get them separated, or the abomination will be there before she is."

"Don't ignore . . ." Danika's head snapped back. Her mouth filled with blood. She had to swallow or spit. Only her grip on Kirstin kept her from falling. Another blow and they were yanked apart, Danika clutching fistfuls of Kirstin's clothes, refusing to let go, grunting in pain as blows pounded against her ribs.

"Danika! Think of the baby!"

Danika blinked away tears and tried to focus on Kirstin's face. Wrapped her fear and anger around the Aydori words. "You know what they're going to do to you!"

Blue-flecked eyes narrowed, and Kirstin's upper lip curled. "I know what they think they're going to do. I make my own choices, Lady Hagen. Like I always have."

"Stubborn . . ."

One of the guards jabbed his thumb into the back of Danika's hand, driving it deep between the small bones. Her fingers spasmed, opened, and she lost her hold. As they dragged her along the slick floor, she thrashed and fought. She couldn't get free, but she would not have them say she left her Pack willingly.

Rounding a corner, they planted their boots and threw her forward. Sliding across the glossy tiles on her knees, she slammed up against metal bars and spun around in time to see a cage door shut and barred.

"This mage is the first female abomination we've allowed on the deck over the testing room. I'm looking forward to her reactions. They should be fascinating."

Breathing heavily, Danika rose to her feet and turned to face Leopald, snarling, lips drawn back off her teeth. It seemed at first as though he was in a cage of his own, but there were only bars between them and in front of him. One set separated him from the room below, one from her.

He stood far enough away, she couldn't reach him. Arm thrust through the bars, her fingers clawed at the air.

He shook his head. "Fascinating. They all attempt that. It must be due to some commonality in their blood."

The man standing behind him, wearing a parody of a uniform, stared at the back of Leopald's head in disbelief.

Danika knew him.

Reiter saw the mage's blue-flecked eyes widen and knew she'd recognized him.

"You did this," she snarled, touching two fingers to the blood at the corner of her mouth.

The emperor turned to face him and Reiter barely managed to control his reaction in time. After a moment of study, Reiter maintaining as neutral an expression as possible, he turned back to face the mage. "You remember Captain Reiter, do you? How wonderful. But when it comes right down to it, it's unkind to blame him for the situation you're in. Your current situation is entirely a result of what you are, isn't it? The captain was merely following my orders."

Reiter could see her answer in her eyes—the anger, the terror— and he braced himself. He'd taken prisoners before. While he was still a ranker, he'd been on work details throwing prisoners' bodies into pits. On the other side, in other armies, he knew enemy soldiers did the same. It wasn't personal. It was war.

This wasn't war.

This specifically wasn't even about trying to prevent a danger to the empire the Soothsayers had warned about.

This was, as she had said, insane.

And he'd helped make it possible.

Before the mage could speak, throw accusations or curses—both justified—a door opened. She shot him one last disgusted look, then spun around to throw herself at the bars separating her from the room below.

The deck stretched along one side of a square room. Longer and higher than the small box where the emperor spied on the mages, it was much the same idea without the Imperial trappings or the secrecy. The floor and the walls of the room had been covered in the same large white tiles he stood on. The ceiling had been entirely mirrored, brass rings marking the holes where a dozen lamps had been lowered down from above. At first glance the room looked featureless in the brilliant gleam of the reflected light. At second glance, Reiter saw the rings and clamps where any manner of things could be attached to the walls and the floors.

Through the open door in the west wall, Reiter could see the small, dark-haired mage. Although her guards attempted to throw her into the room, she twisted free and limped through the door under her own power. Rolled her eyes when the door slammed behind her. Glanced up. Curtsied mockingly at the emperor.

She tried to hide it, but Reiter had seen that expression before. Had passed soldiers lying wounded on the battlefield, looked into their faces and seen dead men look back. Men who were breathing and making jokes, but who knew they were dead.

He didn't understand. She'd lain with beastmen in the past and they were, when it came down to it, only another kind of men.

This would be public and unwanted, but she'd survive the experience. The emperor's plan to control the only mages and beastmen in this part of the world meant he needed these mages alive.

What did she know he didn't?

"Kirstin!"

Reiter silently repeated the name the blonde mage had called out. People had names. Abominations didn't.

Kirstin raised a hand in acknowledgment, but didn't look up.

What didn't she want her friend to know?

"We're putting the big tricolor in with her." Nothing in the emperor's voice gave any indication he was aware he was about to destroy a life. Nothing suggested he was about to enjoy the pain and humiliation he'd ordered to happen. "He's been restless, and they tell me he keeps setting the others off. Hopefully, this will calm him a little. The volume they can achieve may be scientifically amazing, but it's still annoyingly loud for the poor people who have to care for them."

"Big tricolor," Reiter repeated. He remembered his grandfather talking the same way about the pigeons he kept.

The emperor laughed. The gleaming toes of his boots were pressed right up against the bars. *Against*, Reiter noted, not through although there was room enough. "Big tricolor rather than the small- or medium-sized tricolor. It's completely unnatural, so it's the easiest to spot when the abominations try to hide among people. I have a number of them. I know it's foolish, but I'm hoping I can get some other colors when these five . . . no, four whelp. Unfortunately, the result of this . . ." He waved a hand toward the room. ". . . will likely be another tricolor."

The door seemed to open again on a wave of sound: snarling, howling, claws and teeth ringing against steel. In the open doorway, a cage. In the cage, an enormous wolf; black and gray and tan fur blended in a way that made it . . . Him, Reiter corrected. Made *him* hard to see in the shadows beyond the door.

The silver collar around his neck glinted in the spill of light from the room as he fought to get free.

"Kirstin!"

"They were very chatty when they brought me around, Danika. I know what to expect." She spoke Imperial so that everyone could understand her—making it harder for the enemy to consider her a beast, Reiter assumed—but she still didn't look up. She backed slowly away until she stood against the wall opposite the door. She twitched invisible wrinkles out of her skirt, folded her hands, and waited.

Metal screamed as the front of the cage rose. The wolf charged out onto the tile.

He was huge. Gaunt. Starving, if Reiter was any judge. His hips jutted up and his ribs hung down like another cage under loose patchy fur.

The mage watching—Danika, he reminded himself. Danika made a soft, pained noise that had Reiter curling his hands into fists, nails pressed into his palms.

Silver spikes lined the inside of the collar, the ends driven into the flesh all around the wolf's throat. Silver poisoned the beastmen. Every soldier in the Imperial army knew that now. What must silver constantly digging into a wound be doing?

The wolf walked carefully, his nails skidding on the slick floor. As the door swung shut behind him, he lifted his head, stared at the emperor with deep-sunk, mad eyes, and charged forward.

One paw nearly reached the emperor's boot. Reiter winced as the wasted body slammed down onto the floor, bones barely covered with flesh and fur rattling against the tile.

The emperor shook his head and sighed. "Every time. They just don't learn. Well, every time they're not tied down," he added thoughtfully.

"He can't change with the collar on!" Danika's cry was loud enough Reiter knew the dark-haired . . . Kirstin had to have heard it. She didn't react. She didn't look up. She didn't take her eyes off the wolf. She wasn't surprised.

"That is the point of the collar," the emperor agreed.

When Reiter turned toward her, Danika stood pressed against the bars, her knuckles white where she clutched at the steel. The cheek he could see, glistened in the harsh light. "How long has he been kept like that? How long since he's been allowed to change?"

"He's permitted to change when we need him to heal." Staring down at the wolf, the emperor shrugged. "He's fine."

"He's barely there!" She took a deep breath, stepped back, and turned toward the emperor. Reiter watched her swallow her pride and her fear and keep her voice calm and level. In a lifetime spent under Imperial banners, he'd never known anyone with that kind of strength. "Your Imperial Majesty, please listen. If the balance between fur and skin is not kept, if there's too long spent in one form over the other, then that form begins to dominate. If this man has been forced to remain in fur, tortured in fur, starved, he won't be responsible for his actions. You still have only five of the six mages the Soothsayers prophesied. If you allow this to continue, you'll have four."

"He's not a man." When she made a noise, as though she couldn't believe *that* was what he chose to respond to, the emperor turned to face her. Standing behind him, Reiter couldn't see his expression, but he knew he was smiling. He even knew the smile. The pleased smile of a teacher who enjoyed sharing his knowledge. "As the abominations are attracted to power regardless of form, I don't see the problem."

Reiter forced his voice to work. "Majesty, I think she's saying there's a good chance the wolf has gone insane."

"I know what she's saying, Captain. Given the way she's throwing the accusation around, I don't think she knows what the word means. Oh, good. He's spotted her."

The wolf had lowered his head, his nose almost to the floor, his shoulder blades rising up above the line of his spine like paddles. There was so little meat on his bones, Reiter wasn't sure how he could even stand. This is what he would have brought Tomas to.

Both of them to, he amended, looking at Kirstin. He'd have brought both Tomas and Mirian to this.

Kirstin's eyes were locked on the wolf, and her mouth was moving. Not begging, nor pleading. She looked determined. He couldn't hear what she was saying.

The wolf could.

His ears went up. Down. He shook his head and whined.

Kirstin kept talking, convincing him to do . . . what?

He shook his head again, and his lips drew back exposing impossibly large, white teeth. His head swung slowly back and forth as he sniffed the air. Then he stilled, nose pointed directly at the mage. He growled and saliva splattered on the floor.

Nothing about his reaction looked sexual.

"Majesty, how long since he was fed?"

"He ate recently. Probably not as much as he would have liked, given his size, but the food is divided evenly among them."

What did he eat? Reiter wanted to ask. Didn't have the courage to ask. Was afraid the question wasn't what, but *who.*

"And when he last ate makes no difference, Captain. The mages both attract and control the wolves with their power."

Reiter closed a hand around the bars, his knuckles white. "She has no power, Majesty. The tangle has suppressed it!"

"Suppressed it. Not removed it."

Kirstin raised her head and looked directly at Danika, ignoring the two men so completely, Reiter felt invisible. Under the cap of dark hair, she had a pair of gold hoops in her ears. "It would have happened anyway," she said. "Better fast than slow, yes? This is my choice, Danika. I cannot suffer as you can, and suffering is all the future holds. We are none of us getting out of here."

She unfastened her dress and let it drop to the ground, a puddle of blue cloth around her feet.

"My choice."

"Good girl," the emperor murmured.

Reiter had barely enough time to notice the smear of blood, dark against the pale skin of an inner thigh before toenails skittered against tile.

Blood.

And a starving wolf.

Kirstin raised her chin. "I wish I could have said good-bye to my boys."

Red spattered against white. It sounded like rain. And branches breaking in a storm.

"No!" The emperor actually sounded surprised.

As the wolf bent his head to feed, ripping the belly open for the organs, Reiter shuddered, clenched his teeth, and looked to Danika who watched . . . no, witnessed, silently. As though aware of his gaze, she turned her head, tears running down her cheeks, and said, "He didn't want to. She convinced him to do it, to take her strength, to survive."

Then she closed her eyes, drew in a deep breath, and threw up. Half-digested porridge and biscuit spattered out through the bars.

Reiter looked at a slender leg and a pale foot against the blue fabric of the discarded robe and remembered that he'd once believed science could do anything mage-craft could do. Science couldn't have done this.

Down below, the door opened and two guards charged in, boots slamming against the tile. They wore packs and carried metal staffs, thick rubber handles gripped in heavy leather gloves. Wires ran from the staffs to the packs and sparks jumped from the staffs' blackened upper ends.

Two steps.

Three.

They stopped in tandem.

Apparently, guards who were able to torture a man who looked like an animal drew the line at approaching while he tore bloody chunks of meat off a woman's body. They hesitated long enough for him rip off an arm and gulp it back, fingers fluttering as her hand disappeared between his jaws, larger bones cracking, smaller crunching. One guard took a step back, the other jackknifed forward and spewed vomit all over the tile. The end of his staff hit the wall.

A tile smashed, and a drift of smoke that smelled almost like gunpowder momentarily covered the scent of blood and guts and puke.

Perhaps these guards had never handed out the wolves' food. Perhaps Cobb had only been removed from the palace. Perhaps the old man sent to the north wing back on Reiter's first day in the palace had been sent to scrub tiles. Those tiles were going to *need* scrubbing.

I should do something. I need to do something. He couldn't save the dead mage. He couldn't even save the live one.

Neither of them had screamed.

"Just a reminder, Captain . . ."

Reiter looked down to see the emperor staring up at him.

". . . that what happens in the north wing is not spoken of. My privacy is very important to me."

"Of course, Your Majesty." Who could he tell?

Reiter had hoped he'd be dismissed when they returned to the palace, but the emperor kept him close for the rest of the day. He stood behind the emperor's chair—behind Tavert and the distant cousins and whoever the flame else those people were—and wore the expression officers wore when they knew a battle had gone to shit but they didn't have the rank to stop it, and all they could do was send more solders out to die.

Fortunately, those officers allowed into the emperor's presence had been trapped in the palace for so long it wasn't an expression they recognized.

At supper, Reiter found he'd been moved to a higher status table. His new companions were more obsequious, but better at it. He pushed his food around on his plate and drank more than he should have. It didn't help.

As the platters emptied of fruit and nuts were cleared away, it was announced there would be dancing in one of the smaller ballrooms. The appropriate pleased response ran through the crowd.

"Her Imperial Majesty loves to dance," the woman seated next to Reiter gushed. "I'm sure tonight's affair is to welcome back the Talatian ambassador, whom she adores and missed greatly while he was gone."

A quick glance at the head table showed Her Imperial Majesty laughing with a dark-skinned man in a deep green uniform.

"The ambassador always seems to enjoy these small *family* gatherings."

"Family?" Whatever he was now, Reiter wasn't family.

She smiled, hand over her mouth to cover a bad tooth. "All of us, of course."

Those who ate with the emperor, regardless of how far away they sat, were expected . . . required to attend.

Waiting with the others in the anteroom outside Their Imperial Majesties' apartments while the emperor changed into evening wear, Reiter wondered if he'd been looking forward to dancing with his wife while watching a young woman torn apart by a starved wolf.

Reiter didn't dance. He stood. He stared at nothing. He kept his thoughts from showing on his face.

"Walk with me, Captain."

It took a moment to pull himself out of his thoughts and focus on the man beside him. Reiter blinked at Major Halyss' father, realized that hadn't been a request, and unlocked his knees. Given that he'd taken Major Halyss' rather specific position at the emperor's side, it had been a moment's work to discover the major's father was Lord Coving, Duke of Barryns, and one of the ten most powerful politicians in the empire.

"His Imperial Majesty prefers you to circulate so Her Imperial Majesty doesn't ask him later why you weren't having a good time." Lord Coving's mouth curved into an approximation of a smile as they began to make their way around the edges of the room. "Her Imperial Majesty would prefer you to dance, but realizes not everyone is as skilled as she is."

"Her Imperial Majesty is a very accomplished dancer."

"Yes, she is." He waved off a clump of approaching courtiers, and they continued uninterrupted. "If you're going to remain at court, you'll have to learn."

"I'd rather be returned to the front. I'm a soldier, sir. This isn't for me."

"Dancing?"

"Court."

"Ah."

It was a simple, noncommittal sound that managed to express solidarity while admitting nothing. It was so noncommittal, Lord Coving had to be aware of what was happening in the north wing. Maybe not the exact particulars but enough. After all, the wing had to be built and equipped. Guards and scientists paid. Reiter had no idea where the money came from, but the emperor definitely didn't dole it out himself. Coving knew and had arranged to have his son sent away before the mages arrived. Before something like today happened and the major, who was a gentleman and not just a soldier, protested too vehemently and got himself killed.

The small orchestra at the end of the room played loudly and enthusiastically. Those not currently dancing talked and laughed. Lord Coving commanded enough space around them to ensure they wouldn't be overheard.

"How can you?"

To his credit, and right now that and getting his son out might be the *only* thing to his credit, Coving didn't pretend to misunderstand. "We give him this and, for the most part, he lets us run the empire."

"For the most part?" The wine that had been nearly too much at dinner suddenly wasn't nearly enough.

Again, the approximation of a smile. "For the most part."

"Would one of *his* parts be declaring an entire people abomination?"

Lord Coving nodded genially, as though they weren't talking about genocide. "He has the right as the head of the church to appoint a new Prelate more sympathetic to his beliefs."

"And attacking Aydori?"

"No, the Prelate had . . ."

"Was attacking Aydori another of his parts?"

"Yes. And it would have been significantly more cost-effective to have placed an army on their border and made treaties for the contents of their mines and their forests rather than spend the silver to kill enough of them to allow us to take the country. Of course, you and I both know the attack was as much to cover the Soothsayers' requirements and your activities as it was to attempt to acquire resources, but we don't spread that information around. Still, the Prelate and Aydori aside, for the most part, His Majesty doesn't interfere and things get done. Trade is negotiated. Borders are secured. Roads are built. Children are educated. There are hospitals and poor laws. You could travel from Karis to the border in only three days should you need to. Well, it might take slightly longer now that the border has shifted, but life in the empire is good and every day we work at making it better. And safer. It's a small price to pay."

Fingernails pressed into his palms again, Reiter growled, "You're not paying the price."

"They're not like us."

He remembered gray eyes and a wide mouth pressed into a thin, disapproving line. He remembered a stubborn glare. Blood. Bruises. Tears. A boy who cried out for his brother. A woman who gave her strength to a starving . . . man. To a starving *man*. He stepped forward enough that he could turn and see Lord Coving's face. "When he's done with them, what differences will he want to study next?"

The orchestra started a new piece, and the emperor laughed as he led the ambassador's wife out onto the floor.

"I don't . . ." There were shadows under the old man's eyes. In his eyes. "He won't be done with them for a long time."

Coving had agreed to ignore the emperor's insanity in order to be one of those few who ran the empire. To Reiter, that seemed unnecessarily complicated. "Why can't you run things without him?"

"Don't be naive, Captain. Someone has to be at the top. If not him, who? His Imperial Highness? Then who guides the prince until he's old enough to take the throne? And who chooses who guides the prince? No, the emperor is essential to the smooth running of the empire." Before Reiter could speak again, Lord Coving caught the attention of a woman about his age who sat wrapped in at least three layers of brilliantly colored shawls, tapping her foot to the music. "Lady Clarin, have you met Captain Reiter? He served with my son and we were just catching up. The captain is on the emperor's staff now and a trusted confidant."

And that was the end of the conversation. Reiter had been told in no uncertain terms that the north wing was part of how it was in the empire and he would just have to accept that.

Finally dismissed at nearly midnight, he returned to his room and stripped. Walked to the wet room through empty halls, past rooms of sleeping soldiers who didn't know how it was in the empire, and stood under the shower until the water ran cold. Then he lay down on his bed and stared at the ceiling, water from his hair soaking into his pillow. When he finally slept, he dreamed of white tiles and red blood.

And screaming.

Danika lay curled on the floor, face pressed to the crack under the door, layering Kirstin's story onto the air. She didn't know if the others would hear or if it would just circle their prison endlessly, but she didn't stop talking until her voice had gone rough and hoarse.

There was no second meal.

No chance to see, to touch, to know that the others were alive.

No chance to find out how much more time Stina needed to destroy her door.

They could see the lights of Karis painting the night sky even though they were still some distance away. The contrast was distinct enough that even Mirian could make out the yellow glow against the black.

Tomas paced, finally settling close enough she could feel the air warming between them. "Do we sleep or do we keep moving?"

"The sensible thing to do would be to sleep. If we keep going, we'll be tired and careless when we arrive. We'll still have to find where the Mage-pack are being held, and we don't have a lot of luck with cities."

"We should definitely avoid markets," he muttered. Then, a little louder, "So I should find us a safe place to sleep."

"No."

"But you said the sensible thing . . ."

"I know." Mirian pushed one bare foot forward, feeling the path to Karis. "I don't think we have time to be sensible. You'll have to be my eyes tonight." Air currents shifted and without looking, she put her hand down to stroke the fur between Tomas' ears. "I can feel when I go off the path, but I can't see to stay on it."

She slipped the belt he wore in skin out of the bedroll then shortened up the ropes so the roll pressed snug against her back, too tight to bounce when she ran. The belt was made of braided straw and as she buckled it around Tomas' neck, she thought of the collar they'd lost in Abyek, suddenly wanting the more formal touch of leather, but not really sure why. "I'm trusting you not to run me through puddles or gorse bushes."

He gave a soft woof, and she shoved at him with her leg.

"Oh, sure, you say that now." She could tell him she trusted him, but he knew that so all she said was, "Jake was right." She closed her fingers around the loose loop of belt, then closed her eyes so as not to be distracted by things she couldn't quite see. "We need to hurry."

The emperor beckoned Reiter up to walk beside him as they made their way to . . . actually Reiter had paid no attention at Tavert's morning briefing and had no idea where they were going. He only knew that wherever it was—north wing, west wing—he didn't want to be there.

He particularly didn't want to be alone with the emperor, but Tavert and the rest had been instructed to fall back, so clearly it didn't matter what he wanted.

"The mage who escaped from you," the emperor murmured, grinning broadly, "my sixth mage. I have word that she's on her way to Karis."

It took Reiter a moment to find his voice and at that he only managed a neutral, "Majesty?"

"Half of Lower Tardford was put to sleep by a nondescript young woman of about twenty with brown hair, accompanied by a young man of about the same age with black hair. They were wearing country clothing. Sound familiar?"

He thought about lying. He thought about strangling the emperor and dying a moment later. "Yes, Majesty."

"That's what I thought. Given what happened in Abyek, it's obviously her."

"It could be another . . ."

"No, no, the prophecy is pulling at her, Captain. Remember what the Soothsayer Saw: The sixth mage in the room with the others. She can no more resist fulfilling the prophecy than I can resist those sugar cookies with the jam centers. I am curious, though, what could she possibly have against markets?"

"Markets are where people are, Majesty."

The emperor beamed up at him. "That was remarkably insightful, Captain. Well done."

His skin crawled under the emperor's approval.

"I can't weaken the door any further until we're ready to go, or it'll fall off its hinges the next time the guards open or close it."

Danika clutched Stina's hand below the edge of the table. Their quiet conversation hopefully looked as much like comfort as the words Jesine murmured into Annalyse' hair, arms around her, rocking her back and forth. There had already been weeping and wailing enough to satisfy their captors, and Stina had spoken only for Danika to hear.

Only Danika remained to hear.

Kirstin was dead.

She winced as Stina tightened her grip. Nodded, although she wasn't sure at what. "Can you finish tonight?" Would Kirstin still be alive if she'd asked that two days ago? Should she have pushed harder?

"No."

"No?"

"I couldn't have gotten through the door before Kirstin died. The question was all over your face, Danika. This wasn't your fault. Or mine, although we'll both blame ourselves. If I work the night through, I can have the door in pieces before morning. But I can't guarantee how much time we'll have to get clear of the palace after that."

"Then we'll have to use the time we have."

"The nets . . ."

"Our mage-craft isn't all we are." Danika drew in a deep breath and let it out slowly. "It never has been. We get out of this prison, we disappear into the city. It's a very large city. We worry about the nets later."

"The Pack?"

The Pack locked in small dark cells, howling, starved, tortured.

"With the nets on, with them nearly mad with pain and unable to change, none of us are strong enough to control them. It'd be a massacre. Which I'm not against," she added as Stina's gaze darkened, "provided the right people die, but wearing the nets we can't ensure that. We'll come back for them."

"Your word, Alpha."

"My word." She hadn't realized she'd raised her free hand to touch her chest until she felt the ridge of the scar under her fingertips. "Right now, I'm worried about what happens if there's a guard in the hall when your door comes down."

"He'll be right outside my door, won't he? And, thanks to you and Kirstin, he thinks I'm harmless. That should slow him down considerably." Stina's lips drew back off her teeth. "Our mage-craft isn't all we are. It never has been. I'll deal with him."

Two or three Tardfords would have fit into Karis with room left over for Bercarit. Lessons on the Kresentian Empire taught that the capital had originally been built within a loop of the Vone River, but over the years that loop had been entirely enclosed by the city. When the sun rose, the yellow glow of the lights had been replaced by a yellow pall of smoke, hanging thickest over the closely packed buildings nearest the water.

"The Mage-pack has to be in the palace," Mirian muttered, trying and failing to pick out individual buildings. "They were taken because of Emperor Leopald's Soothsayers, so he'd want to keep them close."

"The palace is on the east side of the river. The only direct way in from the west is by the Palace Bridge, but it's heavily guarded and there's an old portcullis gate that's still fully functional on the palace end. Rumor has it the bridge itself was designed to break away and that the mechanics are so precise even a child could operate it. The empire is always the enemy," Tomas explained when Mirian turned to stare at him. "Junior officers work out ways to defeat it. According to Harry, you can't take the palace by force; it has to be subterfuge. He suggested once that we could get the entire Hunt Pack in by pretending to be a dog show. Not one of Harry's better ideas," he admitted after a moment.

There were two other ways across the river—the Bridge of the Sun, south of the palace, passing directly in front of the Grand Temple of the Sun, or the Citizens' Bridge to the north.

"We'd need to cross over two thirds of the south city to get to the Citizens' Bridge. It's too far, and these boots hurt my feet."

"Forgive me if I'm weighing your feet against having you skinned at the last minute," Mirian told him, stepping around a section of broken cobblestone. The puddle filling the hole was green and bubbling intermittently in the sun. "We're taking the north bridge and staying away from anything that looks like it might be or had ever been a market."

They stuck to narrow residential streets of narrow red brick houses older, dirtier, and at least two stories taller than the houses in Abyek. The first floor started half a story up, and they learned they could judge the neighborhoods by the seven steps leading up to heavy wooden doors. On those blocks where the steps were whitewashed to a gleaming contrast with the brick, every trace of coal dust removed, stern-faced women with their sleeves rolled up, watched them pass from first-floor windows or from the tops of the steps themselves. While they didn't seem likely to scream abomination, they weren't pleased about strangers. Children too young for school played quietly.

"Alphas by committee," Tomas bent to murmur in her ear.

Mirian laughed, able to feel the weight of their gazes even if she couldn't see their faces.

On blocks where the whitewash was worn or the steps were so close to the same dirty color as the brick that Mirian could barely make them out, babies screamed behind open windows, children ran happily up and down the street with balls or hoops, and the dogs quieted only as they passed.

On some streets, the spaces between the steps had been filled in with small shops—tailors, seamstresses, shoemakers, cabinet makers, ironmongers, undertakers, coffee houses, bakeries, taverns. Once a small school where a dozen children around five or six repeated the

Imperial alphabet. Every now and then the bricks gave way to a wrought-iron fence and small courtyard and a Temple of the Sun. A few of the temples were old enough they'd clearly been built for other gods, before Leopald's grandfather had brought the empire out of the darkness and under the Sun.

"How can they live like this? All crammed in so close together?" Tomas muttered as they turned sideways to slide past a knife grinder's cart. "It's like that room in the shelter, only with more smoke and way too much cabbage. I think my nose has gone numb. There's no air; the buildings are too high and the streets are too narrow and . . . Horse."

It took Mirian a moment to figure out what he meant. Then she heard the clop, clop of hooves against the cobblestones, squinted down a street to the right, and saw an elderly bay not much larger than the ponies at home, pulling a cart full of coal. When the cart stopped, the driver rang a bell and people swarmed out of houses and shops carrying metal buckets as the driver moved from the seat back into the box. The horse lowered its head until its nose nearly touched the road. Mirian thought it looked more bored than exhausted.

It certainly didn't look like it cared there was a predator standing on the corner.

"We're downwind, if she even has a sense of smell left. But we need to be careful. If a horse panics in these kind of close quarters, people will get hurt and we'll be blamed."

"They won't know," Mirian began, then remembered the women on the steps. They'd be blamed because they were strangers and *then* Tomas would be found out. They were so close. Too close to be caught again.

Not close enough.

"*Hurry*," Jake said. Not once but twice. Maybe a dozen more times since they'd left.

Hurry. They were moving as fast as they could without arousing suspicion.

Not fast enough.

They'd been walking for hours when the street they followed spat them out onto a broad boulevard, the buildings made of pale limestone rather than brick. At first Mirian thought the stone new enough it hadn't had a chance to be stained by the smoke and then she made out scaffolding and heard people shouting about water and hats.

"Are they washing that building?"

"If you ask me, they should wash the whole city," Tomas snorted. "But yes."

A raised footway ran along their side of the road—and she assumed the other side as well—allowing pedestrians to move comfortably in front of hotels and theaters and cafés. It was the first part of Karis that felt a bit like Bercarit. Had Mirian been in her own clothing, she wouldn't have felt out of place. As it was, clutching the bedroll and staring, she felt every bit the country yokel she was dressed as.

A double line of steel tracks ran down the center of the road. As they watched, an open, bright yellow-and-red carriage, little more than six rows of empty benches, came to a stop at a yellow post. A small crowd got on.

"This is Citizens' Avenue," Tomas announced.

"How do you know?"

"Says so on the plaque on the corner of that building." Hands on her shoulders, he turned her to face the plaque, much as she'd done to him back in Tardford. "If Citizens' Avenue goes straight through to the Citizens' Bridge—like in any normal city where they haven't destroyed their brains with stink—we could ride. You have money."

Mirian watched the carriage move up the road, a group of young officers waiting until the last minute to get out of the way of the horses, shouting genial insults back at the driver. "We could walk faster. We need to hurry."

"I know, but we can't *run* and my feet are killing me in these boots." He sighed. "Riding would be a more sensible thing to do than crippling me."

He had been limping a little—although, for all his whining, he clearly hadn't wanted her to notice. "What about panicking the horses?"

"Why wouldn't the whirlwind thing work? You started up a whirlwind the moment you saw the number of horses on the street," he added when she frowned.

Cabs. Delivery vans. Private carriages. Riders. All with horses.

Although she hadn't as much seen the individual horses as known they were there.

A quick check of their immediate surroundings and she discovered she'd wrapped Tomas in a spiral of air that rose straight up as it passed his head, dissipating high enough to prevent panic.

"You did start it, didn't you?" he asked, grip tightening on her shoulder. "Tell me it's not happening without your control."

"I'm controlling it." And that was the truth, although she hadn't consciously started it. The moving air pulled a bit of dust up off the footway, but given the amount kicked up by both people and horses, Mirian doubted anyone would notice. The risk of discovery—and yes, lack of control—was preferable to the disaster that would follow if even one of those horses caught scent of Tomas. She didn't care so much about the people—any one of them would skin Tomas for the bounty—but she hated the thought of the animals being injured. "It doesn't matter anyway." She nodded toward the middle of the road where the carriage had disappeared in the traffic. "It's gone."

He turned her to face the other way. "There's another carriage coming."

She couldn't actually pick it out in the traffic, but she could see another crowd already gathering at the yellow post even if she couldn't make out the individual people. "Fine." Truth be told, she was tired of walking, too. Tired of Jake's shoes that didn't fit right. Tired of being either stared at because they were strangers or ignored because they looked poor. She'd gotten used to the feel of the earth under bare feet, of feeling the connection to where she was going. Of having no one watching what she did except Tomas, who never judged.

Maybe the urge to run would ease if she sat down.

Under the dirt and manure, the road seemed to be crushed gravel pounded into tar. Barely able to separate the traffic into individual pieces, Mirian held Tomas' arm as they crossed to the post. The post seemed to be nothing more than a post, so the word *TROLLEY* painted vertically down it most likely referred to the carriage. Or it was an Imperial word she didn't know that meant: *gather here and complain about how long you've been waiting.*

Mirian met the eyes of a stout woman who looked as though she wanted to be left alone and would therefore, logically, not want to chat with strangers. "Excuse me, does this go over the bridge?"

"It does."

"For how much?"

"Havmo from here to the southside. Each." The way she said it, she didn't believe they had it. She didn't care, but she didn't believe.

Mirian slipped her hand into the bedroll and into the purse. She didn't pull it out, they had far too much money for the clothes they were wearing, just slipped the knot and removed a few coins by touch. Fortunately, the coppers with the half moon on the side opposite Emperor Leopald's profile were larger than the rest. She could see which coins were copper but not the image stamped on them.

"Hey." Tomas' breath brushed against her ear. "You all right?"

"Just thinking about . . ." Going blind. ". . . words." Thinking about words was infinitely preferable to thinking about going blind. Halfmoon to havmo. Language moved. Shifted. Changed. The Pack had been named abomination. If it could be changed, it could be changed back although Mirian didn't know how.

First, the Mage-pack.

Her control over the whirlwind slipped a little as she passed over their fare and climbed up onto the trolley, sliding across to the far edge of the last bench, but she got it back before a passing chestnut did more than kick at the traces.

Theaters and hotels gave way to private clubs to banks to construction to what looked like new government buildings on the last few blocks before the river. Which smelled as bad as Mirian had suspected it would.

The tracks extended right across the bridge although the trolley had to keep stopping and starting because of workers hanging Imperial purple banners on overhead wires.

"Flaming Soothsayers and their flaming public days," the middle-aged man on the bench next to Mirian muttered, folding his newspaper and slapping it down on his lap. His coloring suggested his family had originally come from the Southern Alliance although he spoke Imperial like he'd never spoken anything else. In spite of Gryham, she hadn't expected that; people who'd moved to the empire from countries it hadn't absorbed. The empire was the enemy. "Citizens' Square'll be a madhouse tomorrow," her neighbor continued. "How's anyone supposed to get any flaming work done?"

A madhouse might be useful. They could hide in a madhouse.

They got off at the first stop on the other side of the bridge, the yellow post obvious at the edge of what Mirian assumed was Citizens' Square. To the east was the river and the road the trolley continued to travel along. To the north were blurry rows of shops and taverns. To the west just blur. And to the south, the palace wall and the north gate.

"Looks like the Shields' garrison to the west. They never leave Karis; they're here to defend the city. Well, really the emperor. Although Harry figured the rankers and junior officers were rotated out fairly regularly to keep them from getting fat and stupid. I bet there's another way inside the palace wall from the garrison."

Mirian stopped trying to see across the square and focused on Tomas' face. "Are you suggesting we stop to take out a division of the Imperial army on the way?"

He grinned. "Why not?"

He was waiting for her to come up with a plan. She could see well enough to see that on his face. They were here, in Karis. What now?

Mirian had no idea. Her entire plan had been to get to Karis and rescue the Mage-pack.

A ridiculously ornate fountain topped with a large statue of an emperor on a rearing horse—maybe Leopold, maybe not—anchored the center of the square. It was, thankfully, the only horse Mirian could see, although there were a lot of people in the square. Sitting around the base of the fountain. Buying meat pies from a cart. Enjoying a beautiful spring day. Mirian had never seen a priest of the sun before, but the trio of men in yellow robes under white tabards were fairly easy to identify even given her vision problems. She could hear music and assumed it came from the cluster of people over by the garrison. When she heard yelling and the swoosh of falling fabric, she turned to see workers—well, dark shapes—on the top of the palace wall hanging yet more banners.

She and Tomas weren't even the only people in the square clutching bundles and looking lost.

But mostly, there were soldiers. Which made sense if an entire garrison made up the western boundary of the square. Where else would the soldiers go to . . . ?

Tomas' hand closed around her arm. "Mirian, don't look, but I think that's the soldier we escaped from."

"Captain Reiter."

"No, he's no captain."

Mirian frowned, trying to remember the other man. "Blond? About your height? Kind of squinty-eyed?"

"Pretty much, yeah."

"Chard."

"I don't know his name, but he's seen us."

Chapter Fifteen

F OR THE FIRST TIME since the Soothsayers had placed
him at the emperor's elbow, dinner was not served in the
Imperial dining room. The palace staff—as opposed to the
emperor's staff—were preparing for the festival.

"On public festivals, the palace is opened up to the citizens of
the empire and anyone can wander around as if they have a right to
be there." Major Meritin pushed a pile of paper across his desk
toward the corporal waiting for it, leaned back, and continued as
the corporal left the room. "Their Imperial Majesties appear off
and on throughout the day and have, in the past, gone so far as to
interact with random persons in the crowd. It's a security nightmare."

Tavert had already explained what happened at a public festival,
up to and including the phrase: *it's a security nightmare*. That wasn't
why Reiter was in Major Meritin's office. "So you'll have to deploy
more Shields within the palace."

"I tend to think of it as more of a reassignment than a deploy-
ment, Captain, but yes, I will. More than a few. You won't be one of
them. I know," the major raised a hand before Reiter could argue.

"You're bored spitless playing politics, but, honestly, all you can hope for at this point is for the flaming Soothsayers to announce you'll be better off at the border. You're not under my command; I can't reassign you. Even temporarily. Enjoy your freedom."

If the major saw him wince at the word, he didn't mention it.

He had the rest of the day and most of tomorrow until he was required to dance attendance on the emperor again although, as Tavert had reminded him, he could be recalled to the palace at any time.

The guards at the north gate took his name, and he stepped out into Citizens' Square.

A band practiced for the festival to the west by the garrison wall. Half a dozen or so people sat around the base of the fountain. Three kids chased the pigeons. Two old women were arguing loudly about . . . cheese? It sounded like cheese. There were soldiers walking toward the garrison gates. And soldiers walking away from the garrison gates. There were soldiers gathered around the meat pie cart, so old Duff was probably selling off the last of the day's stock.

Out of his braid, Reiter looked like any other soldier killing time in Citizens' Square.

He didn't look like he knew the sound bones made cracked between teeth, or the smell of burnt fur when a charged staff finally came into play, or the look of hate in eyes that were not an animal's eyes. He didn't look like the man the Soothsayers had given to the emperor. He didn't look like he knew what he knew and had seen what he'd seen.

He wanted to take that anonymity to the Blue Goose, the least disreputable tavern his rank would allow him into, eat greasy food, drink cheap liquor, and start a fight where he could use his fists to pound out his anger and frustration. He wanted to. He wouldn't. He couldn't guarantee his tongue if he got drunk, wouldn't recognize one of the emperor's *special* guards if the ass bought him a drink, and while he hated the thought of the beastmen starving, he had no desire to be the next to feed them.

So he'd find a coffee shop and eat, find a whorehouse and fuck, buy a bottle and take it back to his room and empty it where no one could overhear what the liquor let loose. If he were very lucky, he'd be called to the emperor while he was drunk and get bounced back to private and sent to one of the southern colonies to fight natives, disease, and heat.

Halfway across the square toward the shops fronting the north side, Reiter saw Chard talking to a young couple obviously in from the country for the festival. No one from Karis wore that much homespun.

He walked another three steps before he recognized them.

"The mage who escaped from you, my sixth mage; I have word that she's on her way to Karis."

Not only Mirian, but Tomas.

He'd freed them, burn it! Freed them and here they were, ready to play a part in the emperor's horror story.

And Chard was talking to them. The one person in the entire flaming city who'd recognize them on sight.

But Chard hadn't given the alarm. Did he not know who they were?

Reiter angled west. No one would suspect one soldier talking to another. No one should suspect . . . anything if he talked to Chard. They'd spent days together on the road before he'd disappeared into the palace.

"Private Chard."

"Captain Reiter!" Chard spun around and smiled so broadly Reiter could see a missing back tooth. "You're not in an oubliette!"

Behind Chard, Mirian put her hand on Tomas' arm. Just a touch, but it closed his mouth and held him in place. They were both wound so tightly—eyes a little wild, breathing fast and shallow—he was amazed at their control.

"Do you even know what an oubliette is, Chard?"

"Sure, Cap, it's like a dungeon. Sergeant Black said you were probably in one." Chard pushed an obviously new bicorn up off his forehead and scratched at the red line where the leather binding had pressed into his skin. "I think he was kidding, but I bet there's bits in that palace no one knows about, right? The sarge got sent north to the Spears and that trouble in the port. They're wanting rights about something, I dunno. Pretty near everyone that went into Aydori got reassigned out of Karis. Just me and Corporal Selven and Hare, and now you, left as Shields. And you disappeared. I heard some guy named Linnit cleared your stuff out of quarters."

He took a deep breath and flushed. "I'm glad you're not court-martialed or dead."

"Why would I be dead?"

"'Cause, you know, it was a special mission and we lost them, but you were in charge and . . ."

Every time Reiter saw her, her eyes were paler than he remembered. Here and now, they truly seemed more silver than gray. The barest gleam of color between the white and black. When Chard's voice trailed off, finally realizing no one was listening, he said, "So, what's going on here?"

"This is my . . . uh, sister and her . . . uh, husband. Yeah. They're uh, they're here for the festival."

Reiter reluctantly turned his attention back to Chard. "You don't have a sister. You have two brothers. Try again."

"He's trying to convince us to leave," Mirian said quietly, the words running together.

"He should have called every soldier in this square over here to help take you back into custody," Reiter said at the same volume, gaze still locked on Chard's face.

"It wouldn't have helped." She sounded entirely matter-of-fact.

Reiter remembered the circle of trees and almost smiled. "I suppose not."

Chard opened his mouth. Closed it again. Then to Reiter's surprise said, "It's not right."

"No, it isn't."

"And you can't make me . . . What?"

"Have you told Private Chard why you're here?" She was here to free the mages because she sure as shit wasn't here to give herself up to any prophecy. Chard opened his mouth, confused, but Reiter raised a hand, giving Mirian room to answer.

"No."

He almost smiled again at the way she made one word, two letters, sound like a challenge. "Chard, go away."

"But, Cap . . ."

"Private, this is not something you want to be involved in. This is not something you want to be interrogated about, and every moment you spend talking to us brings you a moment closer to shit you do not want to be in."

"Yeah, I get that, Cap, and I'm getting that you know what's going on more than me, and I'm fucking thrilled you showed up, and I'm good with walking away and letting you deal because . . ."

"Chard. Get to the point."

Chard, who was squinting toward the square, swallowed and nodded past Reiter's shoulder. "Lieutenant Geurin's coming this way."

"He's never seen me," Mirian began.

"He hasn't," Reiter agreed. "But he's one of the few people in Karis who might be able to see what Tomas is, and that's as bad."

Mirian's lips pulled back off her teeth. "Worse."

Reiter turned. Lieutenant Lord Geurin's uniform had been draped in enough braid that anyone who hadn't been forced to endure court dress might mistake it. The plume in his bicorn was as high as regulation allowed and absurdly poofy. He'd recently been shaved and his narrow mustache looked like a dark line on his upper lip. He was, at the moment, the most dangerous man in the square.

"I see you finally made it back to the capital, Captain, although I hear you failed in your mission. My uncle seems to think he's seen you around the court, but given the . . . *inexpensive* uniform you're wearing, he must be mistaken." His smile was as self-satisfied as it had ever been. His gaze flicked past Reiter, over Chard, and paused on Mirian . . .

At the last instant, Reiter managed to lay off enough that he didn't break the lieutenant's jaw. Or his own hand.

Geurin dropped like he'd had his strings cut. His mouth opened and closed but no sound emerged. His hat spun away, the plume bent.

"You punched him, Cap!"

"I did." The soldiers by the meat pie cart had already noticed. Another minute and they'd be on their way over. "And when they ask you why, tell them I said Major Meritin informed me of what the lieutenant wrote in his report."

"What did he write?"

"I have no idea, but I'm certain it was self-serving and puerile."

"He's going to be mad you hit him."

"I'm a captain, he's a lieutenant."

"He's a lord."

Reiter smiled tightly. "Tell him to take it up with the Duke of Burron. And now, I'm going to take *my* sister and her new husband to the inn where they'll be staying."

Chard shoved his hands in his pockets and squinted down at the lieutenant. "Yeah, I'd have hit him, too, if he'd said that to me in front of my sister. If I had one."

"Thank you, Chard."

He shrugged and grinned, but he met Reiter's gaze squarely, and something in his face said he knew exactly what he'd been thanked for. "It's okay. No one likes him."

Her hand still on Tomas' arm, Mirian remained silent until they were far enough from Chard and the group of soldiers gathering around the fallen lieutenant they wouldn't be overheard. "Why?"

Reiter, walking on Tomas' other side, a shield against the curious, drew in a deep breath and let it out slowly. Why did he interfere? Why was he helping them? Why was he committing treason . . . again? "One of the mages was killed," he said at last. "I was there."

"And you did nothing to stop it," Tomas growled.

He'd accused himself of that more than once, so he had an answer ready. "I couldn't have stopped it. At best, I'd have died with her, and that won't help the rest."

"Who?" Mirian asked and Reiter heard a similar self-accusation in her voice. *Why wasn't I here in time to stop it?*

"You couldn't have stopped it either," he said. "Her name was Kirstin. Small, dark-haired, blue flecks."

"Kirstin Yerick. Her husband was one of the Pack Leader's advisers. She has twin sons. Had." Tomas' response had a soldier's rhythm. Superiors didn't want emotion in reports. "And Danika?"

"Danika is . . . alive." He remembered the dagger drawing a gaping red line across pale flesh, her expression when she threw Kirstin's choice at the emperor. "Uninjured."

Tomas actually stumbled, his breathing suddenly ragged.

Danika was family. That explained why *Tomas* was here.

"Captain, how did Kirstin die? *Why* did she die?"

"She died because the emperor is . . . insane." Saying it out loud made it real. Explained why *he* was here. "I'm not going to tell you how."

He could feel Mirian leaning around the boy to stare at the side of his face. He expected a protest. He didn't get one.

They left the square and started down a narrow street between a wine shop and a tavern, the tavern's patio extending far enough to mask them from prying eyes, but offering no cover should anyone try to overhear their conversation. Reiter didn't expect to be followed—Chard was right, no one liked Geurin—but this wasn't the time to take chances. "I have a question for you now." He moved out into the street just far enough for him to be able to look Mirian in the face. "As stupidly suicidal as it is, it's obvious he's here for family. Why are you?"

She stared at him for a long moment. Made longer by the danger they were in. Finally she said, "Someone had to do something, and I was there."

"That's it?" Reiter knew that tone. He'd heard it from young soldiers who suddenly found themselves called heroes because they were the last man standing. And every one of them—the ones who didn't brag and bluster and accept the accolades as their due—was a soldier he wanted to have at his side. "You're a mage."

"You've known that since we . . ." Her lip curled. ". . . met."

Tomas growled low in his throat.

"Unless you're planning to get her killed," Reiter snapped, "stop it."

The boy's back straightened as he went silent. Definitely military. Good. If he could be convinced to follow orders, the odds he'd survive this madness went up.

"Powerful?" Reiter'd seen what she'd done in Abyek. Seen a man burn where he stood. He knew she was powerful, but he was curious about what she'd say.

She didn't.

"Yes," Tomas snapped. "She's powerful." He began to move between them, but again a touch to his arm held him in place. "We don't need your help."

"Yes, you do. Among other reasons, I can get my hands on the artifact that'll remove the tangles from your mages."

"The net? We don't need it. I took the other net off."

The ab . . . *Tomas* came from mage-craft and the tangles suppressed mage-craft. "Did you feel anything when you touched it?"

"Me?" He frowned. "No. Why?"

Either the Pack had moved far enough from their beginning or Mirian had fried it before Tomas arrived on the scene. Given the blackened gold, he suspected the latter. "You won't be able to take the rest of the nets off."

"Why not?"

"Because they're not on her." They turned together toward Mirian.

She sighed and said, "We need his help, Tomas."

"Then why are we standing here?" Tomas demanded, glancing back toward the square.

"Because you don't just walk into the Imperial palace." Mirian shrugged, the movement so deliberate she'd obviously thought about making it. It was too common a gesture for the girl she'd been. "It's the logical reason," she explained. "If people could just walk in and out of the palace, it would be a security nightmare."

Reiter grinned. "Which brings us to tomorrow. The Soothsayers have Seen a public festival . . ."

"The banners."

"The banners," he agreed. "During public festivals, people walk in and out of the palace. You'll be able to disappear into the crowds." He frowned. They were so *country* he could see the emperor heading right for them, beaming broadly, wanting to share the wonder. "But not dressed like that."

Reiter knew Mirian was young, but he hadn't realized how young until he saw her in one of the clothing stores up by the garrison. The tallest of the captive mages, the one who wore green, wasn't very old, but Mirian was younger still. Once convinced she could do nothing until the next day, she'd relaxed. The tension that had her nearly quivering in place out on the square was gone. Even though the reason behind that tension still remained.

"If we can't go into the palace in homespun . . ." She'd steered Tomas away from the square. ". . . then we logically have to buy new clothes."

Given the quality of the clothes she'd been wearing when she came out of the river, Reiter found her to be surprisingly sensible about buying secondhand.

In spite of the pittance they were paid, junior officers were expected to take part in the socializing that might lead to promotion. Single men who had only to come up with a dress uniform managed, but for those with families who already found their pockets to let every pay-day, it could be a disaster outfitting wives and sometimes older children. The Duchess of Novyk, whose husband had been a past Commander-in-chief of the Shields, had convinced her wealthy friends to donate gently used clothing and Lady Shops had sprung up in every garrison town. The rising numbers of women in the army who suddenly had to outfit husbands had put a rack or two of mens' clothing in most of them.

Mirian moved from rack to rack, touching fabric, pulling clothes out to hold against her. Reiter thought it was the first time he'd seen her smile although, given their history, that was hardly surprising. It was definitely the first time he'd seen her wrinkle her nose and roll her eyes at what he'd thought was a kind of pretty pink-flowered thing.

Both of them clearly came from money. Tomas pulled what he liked from the racks without looking at the tags. Mirian checked the tags, but weighed quality against price. Then she put Tomas' choice of jacket back and pulled another that even Reiter could see had been badly mended down the inside of one sleeve.

"You're not going to be wearing it long enough to pay the price of the other," she told him quietly. Sensibly.

Reiter found their relationship interesting. They weren't equals; she was definitely in charge. They didn't act the way he thought lovers should act, but while they weren't attached at the hip they stayed close and touched when they were close enough. Still, he'd noticed the mages did the same, so the touching could be cultural.

And it didn't matter. Whatever he felt about this young woman—and in all honesty he had no idea whether it was admiration, desire, guilt, or a mix of all three—he'd captured her twice, had her dragged through the woods, tied her in the back of a wagon, and drugged her. She might tolerate his presence for the sake of freeing her country-women, but she'd never trust him.

He recognized his purse when she pulled it out to pay and her brows lowered as she silently dared him to say something. "Spoils of war," he said. The shop girl frowned, Tomas scowled, but Mirian laughed, and losing his back pay seemed worth it. It wasn't like he'd need it after tomorrow.

Leaving the shop carrying a worn carpetbag, dressed in their new clothes, Tomas had the easy confidence of the aristocracy. Watching him move with a grace Reiter knew he'd never master, no one would suspect the younger man ran on four feet and ate raw rabbit.

Mirian twitched at her clothing and looked annoyed. "How can you run in a skirt like this?"

"Perhaps Imperial ladies don't run."

The skirt didn't look all that tight to Reiter. It fell straighter than what she'd been wearing, but with fabric enough gathered in the back for her to take a full stride. He'd watched her check the range of movement in the shop. On the other hand, he *did* have a sister even if he hadn't seen her for some years. "The color suits you." The dress was a deep burgundy with black trim. "You look nice."

"Thank you."

Any of the young men under his command would have jumped in with further compliments or a protest of how she shouldn't care what the enemy thought. Tomas remained silent, clearly very certain of his place.

"Where are you taking us now?"

Reiter tried not to resent the easy way she'd tucked her hand into the bend of Tomas' elbow. "To a guesthouse where relatives of officers stay when they're in Karis. The Soothsayers didn't give a lot of warning for this festival, so there should be room. My sister lives in Aboos, it's a northern port. That should be enough to explain your accents." The narrow streets off the square were still essentially empty and, as he had no way of knowing who else might be at the guesthouse, it was safer to talk while walking. "Get into the palace as early as you can tomorrow then make your way to the first assembly room. It's powder blue with winged babies on the ceiling. I'll find you there. He has them—the women—on a shifted sleep schedule, and if we can get to them early, it'll still be night in their rooms."

"Cells," Mirian corrected.

He let it stand because she was right.

"Won't having to wake them slow us?"

"Fewer guards on at night," Tomas told her.

Reiter nodded. "There's a limited number of guards. I'll bet most of them sleep when the women do."

"If there's a garrison right on the square, how can there be a limited number of guards?"

"The guards in the north wing are his private guards. They're not army, not soldiers, they're . . ." He took a deep breath and locked down the memories of them watching as Adeline slashed open Danika's chest, as they dragged the wolf from the observation room. ". . . they're prison guards who've bought into his insanity."

"If it's so bad, and you know how to get the nets off, why have you waited?" Tomas asked. "You know the palace. You know where they're kept."

"You think it's easy to commit treason? You could turn on your . . ." What was he called? ". . . on your Pack Leader?"

"I wouldn't get the chance. If a Pack Leader went crazy, the nearest Alphas would take them down."

"Seriously?"

Tomas frowned. "Of course. A crazy Pack Leader can't take care of the Pack."

"Politicians . . ."

"They'd likely be the nearest Alphas."

No using the insanity of their leader to consolidate their own hold on power. "I like your system."

"So do we."

"So, if it isn't easy to commit treason," Mirian said quietly, "when did you decide to make the effort?"

"When I saw you in the square." When he saw *her* in the square, but with luck he sounded like he meant both of them. "If you were stupid enough . . ."

"Hey!"

". . . to come into the heart of the empire," Reiter continued, ignoring Tomas' protest, "knowing what would happen to both of you if you were caught, then I can be stupid enough to help."

"It's not stupid."

"It's not smart. He has . . . Pack as well as the mages. It's going to take all three of us to get them out. This is it."

"This is what?"

"The guesthouse."

There was a room available, and his old purse held just enough for one night, so he took them to the tavern next door and bought them dinner, emptying his new. Leaving them on their own unsupervised was just asking for trouble. They had better table manners than he did.

He escorted them up to their room and stepped inside to murmur, "The palace gates will open at nine. Be careful. Don't attract attention and, most of all, don't . . ." He waved a hand. ". . . you know. He knows you're coming. It was Seen and he's had word from Tardford."

She flushed. "That was an accident."

"Don't have another." He nodded and backed away, allowing the door to close between them.

The first night after they'd escaped from the Imperials, Mirian had slept curled around him, clutching his fur, taking what comfort the presence of the Pack provided. They'd slept together in caves, old barns, on a filthy carpet in the midst of the homeless, under trees, in a nest of blankets on Jake and Gryham's floor. She'd defined both the distance and the closeness between them.

But this, this wasn't adventure. This wasn't war. This wasn't excusable. This was something he'd have to explain to his mother. Or worse, to *her* mother. He couldn't pace in fur; his toenails clicked against the wooden floor exposing him to the people in the rooms around them, so he paced in skin. And his trousers.

"Tomas."

Wiping his palms against the fabric covering his thighs, he turned and faced her.

"Take a deep breath."

A pillow hit him in the face as he inhaled.

"Through your nose!"

Familiar. Powerful.

"Tell me how I smell?"

He rolled his eyes but told her. "Amazing. You smell amazing."

His trousers ended up on the chair with the rest of his clothes. The mattress gave under him as he rolled onto his side, then gave again as Mirian fitted herself against his back, her hand over his heart. The same way they slept when he was in fur. The sheets smelled of soap.

Her breath lapped warm against the back of his neck when she sighed. "I can't believe after all we've been through and what we have to face tomorrow, you got upset by a bed."

When Danika closed her eyes, she dreamed of the white room. But not of Kirstin, of Ryder. Of his skin hanging from jutting bones, of his throat pierced by silver spikes, of his teeth . . . of blood on his teeth.

She lay in her nest on the floor by the door and she stared into an artificial darkness. She whispered strength to the others and listened for the fall of Stina's door.

Reiter stared at the ceiling and thought of treason.

Mirian woke with the Sunrise bell, snuggled her face into the pillow, and wished that she'd stayed in the carriage and continued on to Trouge with her parents. That she'd never been cold or wet or hungry or afraid. That she'd never had to discover how a man's flesh smelled as it burned. That she'd never had to wake in the morning and face anything more difficult than the new books *still* not having arrived at the lending library. That she'd tested too low to enter the university and she'd married the dark-haired young clerk at her father's bank who had sad eyes but had nearly smiled at her once or twice. That she wasn't about to get up and get dressed and walk into the Imperial palace and do whatever she had to do to steal both Pack and Mage-pack away from a crazy emperor.

After a moment, she sighed. Given the chance to do it again, she knew she wouldn't stay in the carriage, so there was no point pretending she could have faced a life of walks and shopping and a safe, affectionate marriage without screaming. She couldn't honestly say she'd been fundamentally changed by everything that had happened to her and around her since that morning. She was who she'd always been. Practical. Stubborn. More aware of what she could do. Less naive, perhaps. But not really any different.

She carefully pulled away from the warmth of Tomas' back, rolled over, and slid out of bed.

The bucket of hot water had already been left outside the door. She didn't see it at first, stubbed her toe on the side, then brought it in and emptied it into the large washbasin. At home, one of the maids would have brought in a pitcher of hot water, opened the curtains, and lit a fire depending on the time of year. The guesthouse, with the chipped basin, the frayed wash flannel, and the mug half filled with soft soap, would have appalled her mother. Her mother had never spent a night under the bent boughs of an evergreen. Or in a cave. Or on a pile of straw that smelled strongly of goat.

Mirian liked the room. She liked the worn furniture, the too-soft mattress, the uneven floor. She liked that someone had made an attempt to dress it up with chintz curtains and bits of glass that hung in the window to catch the sun. Although, they worshiped the sun in the empire, so maybe the glass pieces were religious rather than decorative.

The window faced east, and she reached out a finger and touched patterns of light that danced across the faded wallpaper. Followed the places where sunlight poured through clear pieces of glass and broke into rainbows. When she was young, Mirian used to sneak down early to the dining room and open the curtains to watch the crystal drops on the chandelier paint the walls with rainbows, courting a lecture on how sunlight faded expensive, imported silk carpets.

Light that broke into colors . . .

White light. The Soothsayer by the well in Herdon had touched her and said *white light.*

Leaning over the washstand, Mirian stared into the small oval mirror, forcing her eyes open as wide as possible. She'd tested high but had no mage marks. She smelled of power but had no mage marks.

Her eyes were paler than she remembered. The edges of her pupils no longer smoothly curved. As she turned her head, she could see patches of silver slide across the black, the blurring of her vision following the movement.

The more powerful the mage, the more mage marks they carried.

The Air-master at the university had marks enough that, at first sight, her brown eyes looked almost blue.

Gryham told her that mages had become unwilling to pay the

price the old way of power demanded and had bound mage-craft in rules.

She could work in all six crafts. Blue, green, gold, brown, red, indigo . . .

Her mage marks were white.

The more power she used, the more there were.

Eventually . . . No. She touched the mirror. *Soon*, if she kept pouring power through the crafts, there'd be marks enough to fill her eyes and blind her. Logically, inevitably, given what they were about to do . . . She clutched the mirror's frame to keep her fingers from shaking. *Now* she wanted to go home more than she'd ever wanted anything in her life.

Her vision blurred.

Cleared.

"Lorela?"

Her sister turned, dress half on, and staggered toward her side of the mirror. "Miri! You're alive! Lord and Lady, you're alive! Where are you?"

Leaning so close her breath fogged the glass, Mirian swallowed and said, "I'm in Karis."

"What? What are you doing . . . ? Mama said you died! That you were killed trying to rescue the Mage-pack, but there was no body. The elder Lady Hagen actually visited her. Mama was in her glory. But you're not dead. Cedryc said you weren't. He said he Saw you, but I couldn't tell . . ." Lorela swiped her palm across her cheek and took a deep breath. "Were you captured with the Mage-pack? Have you escaped? Are you coming home?"

"No, I wasn't captured. Well, I was, but I escaped." She almost giggled as Lorela frowned, clearly about to accuse her of not taking things seriously. "I'm here, with Tomas Hagen, to rescue the Mage-pack."

"Tomas Hagen is alive and you're with him?"

"Yes." Mirian braced herself. Her mother was, after all, Lorela's mother.

Lorela ran both hands up through her hair. "Lady Hagen needs to be told her younger son is alive."

"Yes." She blinked away tears and remembered she had information to give her sister in return. "Lor, if you touch Cedryc when he starts to See, it might bring him back. Touch him as much as you can, skin to skin."

"You're not supposed to touch a . . ." She couldn't say it.

"Because then what they See will be lost. Maybe they go so deep and fall so far because as soon as they start to See, people stop touching them. Maybe that's why they find what focus they have when they get to touch people. It's a stupid, selfish rule."

"Cedryc . . ." Lorela stopped, took another deep breath, and wiped her eyes. "All right. Thank you, Miri. Now then . . ." She squared her shoulders and frowned again. ". . . what do you mean you're in Karis to rescue the Mage-pack? And who set up this link? This isn't even a crafted mirror!"

"Just what I said. I did. Love you." She lifted her hands from the mirror, closed her eyes, and when she opened them again, she saw only the blurry image of her own reflection.

"Who were you talking to?"

Mirian turned to see Tomas sitting up in bed. "My sister."

"Through a mirror-link?" He sounded impressed, but she couldn't make out his expression. "Danika has one set up with her mother—Ryder kept hanging his jackets over it, said the last thing he need was the abiding presence of his mother-in-law. I didn't know you could link with an uncrafted mirror, though."

"Neither did I." Teeth clenched, she lifted the first layer of the stupidly restrictive Imperial undergarments off the hook and pulled it over her head. By the time she tugged it down into place and brushed her hair back off her face, Tomas stood less than an arm's length away.

"Are you all right?" He sounded worried.

She shrugged. "Busy day."

"Is it the captain?"

"Is what the captain?"

"I know you're willing to work with him because he let you—let us—go on the road, but what if this is a trick? A trap? I mean, he's already told us we're expected. If we get grabbed, he's still in the clear and he can play the sympathy angle with you."

"Why would he do that?"

Tomas shrugged in turn. "I don't know. He likes you."

"Funny way of showing it. Pass me the thing with the laces." She wrapped it around her waist and began hooking the busk in the front. "If he plans to stop us, why didn't he do it yesterday in the square."

"He didn't have a net and he knows what you can do."

After the sound left her mouth, Mirian thought it might have been better had she not tried to laugh. "*I* don't know what I can do."

"Anything."

"What?"

Hands on her shoulders, he moved close enough she could finally see his face. Close enough one leg bumped against hers and she could smell the warm, musky, morning scent of him. "You can do anything," he said.

And he believed it.

"Thank you." Mirian let her head fall forward and rest on his shoulder for a moment. Then, as a cart rolled by outside on the street, she straightened and took a deep breath. "We have to trust him."

"But you don't want to."

"What I want doesn't matter, at least not until after we rescue the Mage-pack. And the others."

"Okay, then."

"Okay, then?"

He grinned as she leaned back to look up at him. "Whatever you decide, you know I'm right beside you."

Beside. Not behind. "You'd better get dressed, then. They're not going to let you into the palace in fur."

There was no way he could do this and hide his involvement. This time, having Mirian knock him out as the emperor's captives fled the palace would only make it easier for him to be caught. He could get the necessary artifact only because he'd been sent to get it before. Because he was known to the Lord Warder. "*The emperor requests that I be given . . .*"

"It's a festival day. I could tell from the bunting." The Lord Warder sighed as he unlocked the cabinet. "The palace will be swarming with people." The old man snorted, carefully opened the cabinet's front, then slid a smaller key into the lock of one of the exposed drawers.

"People. They'll touch things with their dirty fingers. They always do. I plan on hiding down here until it's over."

He always did, according to the pages Reiter'd overheard complaining. He went to the Archive early and stayed late, sometimes sleeping on a cot in the corner if he felt the palace wasn't yet empty enough. The pages hated traveling all the way down to the Archive. The service halls didn't extend that far and they had to run to get the food there still warm.

Jiggling the key, the Lord Warder finally got the drawer open. He pulled out the fork and stared down at it for a moment before handing it to Reiter. "His Imperial Majesty will have no time for hobbies today."

Reiter slipped the small artifact into the inside pocket of his tunic. "I don't know about that, Lord Warder," he said, closing the frogging and trying to get the ridiculous amount of braid to lay flat. "I'm just following orders."

The old man snorted again. "Aren't we all, Captain? Aren't we all?"

Back in his room, Reiter changed out of his court dress and into his regular dress uniform. With half the garrison pulled in on extra duty and the other half wandering through the halls gawking, it granted him even more invisibility than usual. He had no reason to sign his sidearm out of the armory and being mistaken for an officer on duty could cause problems without it, but he missed its weight by his side. Not as much as he missed the weight of his musket over his shoulder, but that was a whole other level of not going to happen.

Ten past nine.

Reiter snapped his watch closed and slid it into his pocket. Walking over to the window, he buttoned his tunic and stared at the golden arc of the emperor's balloon, a hobby the emperor'd had no time for for a while. At least the aeronauts wouldn't be bored today.

Just before nine, they joined the crowd already gathered in the square, staying well back from those who clearly intended to be first in. Mirian didn't know if there were prizes or merely bragging rights, but the people nearest the gate were weirdly intent. She didn't need to be able to see their expressions; the need to be first in rose off them like smoke.

The food carts set up around the edges of the square were doing a brisk business among the more casual attendees. Although she hadn't eaten the dumpling the guesthouse had provided, and she should be hungry, the smell of the food made her stomach churn.

When she stepped back against Tomas, he jerked away.

"What have you got under your skirt!"

"The telescope. I left everything else in the room, but . . ." It wasn't that she thought she'd forget the soldier she'd killed, it was just that it was the only memorial he had. She couldn't carry it, so she'd tied it to her petticoat and figured it would remain unseen with all the extra useless folds of fabric. "What did you think it was?"

Before Tomas could answer, trumpets blared, loud enough the echo chased itself four or five times around the square.

A few people shrieked, a few more laughed at them, but the crowd quickly quieted.

"His Imperial Majesty Leopald, by the light of the Sun and the strength of his people, Exalted ruler of the Kresentian Empire, Commander in Truth of the Imperial army, Supreme Protector of the Holy Church of the One True Sun welcomes you, his people, to this public festival."

"Where's it coming from?"

"There's brass . . . I don't know, horns? Bells? Up on top of the gate."

Mirian could see the gate. She took Tomas' word for the bells.

"When the gate opens," the voice continued, "the palace will be laid out for your enjoyment. Your emperor trusts you'll behave in his home as he would behave in yours."

"Kidnapping, murder . . ."

"Shhh."

"Do not open doors that have not been opened for you. Do not speak to the soldiers. May the Sun grant warmth and life to His Imperial Majesty!"

A cheer went up, the gates opened, and the first few ranks surged forward.

Mirian's palms were damp as they followed, her mouth dry. She tightened her grip on Tomas' arm, frowning at a familiar noise. "You're growling."

"Sorry."

As they finally crossed the inner courtyard, heading toward the stairs leading up the open double doors, Tomas leaned in and murmured, "There's guards on the roof with muskets watching the gate." He didn't sound surprised.

"Just the gate?"

"It's a lot of roof."

It was a lot of palace. Mirian wondered how they'd find the first assembly room and Captain Reiter. Then she saw there were signs designed to look like theatrical scene cards by each open door and a soldier by each sign. The edges of the signs were soft and worn and they looked like they'd been used a number of times before. Most of the soldiers looked bored already. They'd be thrilled for the chance to chase escaped prisoners. More thrilled, no doubt to be able to shoot them in the back.

"You put half of Tardford to sleep," Tomas murmured against her ear.

There was that. But how did he . . .

"And you're cutting off the circulation in my lower arm."

Oh.

She tried to look overwhelmed by the magnificence, but suspected she looked like she wanted to throw up. Although, logically, that could be interpreted as overwhelmed, it would definitely attract more attention than they wanted.

The hall eventually dumped them into the small assembly room they were looking for. Most of the people around them kept walking out the open doors on the other side, one loudly declaring that only first timers stopped so close to the gate.

Mirian followed Tomas' gaze up to the ceiling and the naked, winged babies that cavorted across the painted sky. She couldn't see details, but they were large enough and gold enough, she couldn't mistake what they were. "My father says expensive ugly is still ugly."

"Your father's right."

"My mother never agreed."

"The emperor's mother had it restored just before she died."

She hadn't noticed Reiter arrive. Tomas hadn't started, so he must have picked up the captain's scent.

"If you're interested in her restoration work, she saved some ornate plasterwork as well." He looked as bored as the guards on duty, but then he would, showing his sister and her husband around the palace.

"I'd love to see the plasterwork." Mirian smiled broadly, then toned it down a little as his eyes narrowed.

They fell into step beside him as he led the way out of the assembly room and along a broad hall. Outside the narrow windows that provided light, was a small interior courtyard dominated by a tall post covered in trumpet vine.

"It's what's left of the old gibbet," Reiter told her, catching her staring. "That was the palace's execution yard before they built this wing."

"Foreshadowing," Tomas muttered. "Ow."

"Why would they keep the gibbet?" Mirian asked as Tomas rubbed his side where she'd pinched him.

Reiter shrugged. "Sentiment."

The prison on the southern edge of Bercarit had an execution yard and hangings were open to the public, but Mirian's mother had declared only the low and the vulgar attended. Mirian didn't care who went; she only knew she'd never see death as entertainment.

The vine burst into flower.

"Mirian."

"I didn't mean . . ."

"What did I say about accidents?"

"If I could control it, it wouldn't be an accident. It would be a deliberate!"

"Fair enough." Reiter's voice had gotten deeper. "Now keep walking. Look at the pretty flowers if you want to. Aren't they nice? Don't make a big deal of it."

It was a voice intended to calm soldiers. Mirian had heard it in the woods when she'd been his captive. She could almost see him walking along a line of men in uniform, speaking quietly, calmly, steadying them to get the job done.

"I'm not one of your soldiers." She didn't know why she said it.

"No." He almost smiled. "At this point, I expect I'm one of yours."

Her elbow stopped Tomas' growling almost before he got started. "Where is everyone?"

The hall was nearly empty.

"I was told the emperor often shows himself in the antechamber of his private wing in the first hour on a festival day. The crowds are crazy, though. I was warned away. There'll be other chances."

About to make it clear she had no interest in seeing the emperor, Mirian realized Reiter was once again talking to them like they were visiting family, assuming he'd be overheard. At the end of the hall, most of the crowd had turned right, but they stopped and stared at the plasterwork on the ceiling while Reiter opened a door and slipped into the room, pulling the door closed but not latching it behind him.

After a moment, of pretending interest in a white blur, Mirian heard. "Follow me when it's clear."

When the halls were clear? When no one was looking their way? "Tomas . . . I can't see that far."

His hand was warm on the small of her back. "I've got it. Look at the plaster . . . at the plaster . . . Move, now!"

She let his shove carry her forward, her weight opening the door. Tomas latched it behind them. The room wasn't large and held only a long narrow table at one end with a single, high-backed chair behind it. There was a smaller door on the back wall.

"This is the first room I was ever in, in the palace." Reiter stood by the second door. "Come on.

As Mirian stepped closer to the rear wall, she managed to identify the repeating blue pattern of the wallpaper as a shepherdess playing the flute. Her mother would have loved it. The door opened into an empty hall. Painted a soft gray, with gaslights along the left, it had little in common with the high ceilings and ornate paint effects in the hall they'd just left.

"Service hall?"

"Imperial shortcut. There's service halls that connect to it, but this will take us to the mages."

A sigh as the wood crumbled.

A crack as the bolt hit the floor.

A bare foot on slate.

A slow creak as the door at the end of the hall began to open . . .

. . . opened faster.

The hollow melon slam of a head against a wall.

A grunt. A groan.

A body hitting the floor.

Being dragged . . .

Danika scrambled to her feet as the bolts of her door were eased open. Although the light from the guard's lantern abandoned at the far end of the corridor didn't spill as far as Danika's cell, it was enough to turn the black to deepest gray, enough for her to see Stina's unmistakable silhouette on her threshold. She pressed two fingers against the other woman's mouth before Stina could speak, then leaned in close.

"The speaking tubes can be used for listening as well. We need to tie him and gag him if we're going to leave him here."

She felt Stina nod.

They had no time for sentiment, but she took a moment to hug the older mage and breathe, *"Well done. You're amazing."*

The guard was still conscious, but only just. There wasn't light enough to tell which guard it was even as they stripped him and tied him with his own clothing, afraid the sound of tearing sheets would warn any listener something was up. Danika checked that he could breathe while Stina checked his weapons.

Then they shoved him under the bed and locked him in.

Out in the hall, Danika ran to Jesine's door while Stina freed Annalyse.

"We can't go through concrete blocks," Danika whispered as they huddled together, needing the contact. Annalyse was shaking so hard Danika could feel the tremors through Jesine. "So we can't get out the way we came in. The lower level goes by the dark cells, it goes to . . . well, it goes somewhere we don't want to and there's a greater risk of running into guards that way. But they move food and furniture in and out of the big room, so there has to be another door."

"Probably a hidden part of the wall," Stina pointed out. "Like the emperor's rathole."

"We find it and we get out through the palace. No one will be up at this hour."

Jesine's hand closed around her arm. "And the captive Pack?"

"They're past reason. We have to get the nets off before we can release them." Danika laced Jesine's fingers with hers. "We will do everything we can to come back for them, but if we have to sacrifice them to save our children, we will."

"I hate the thought of leaving them."

"I know." She'd promised she wouldn't leave without them. It was a promise she couldn't keep, and breaking it cut more painfully than Adeline's dagger. "Come on."

In the big room, the guard's shielded lantern provided a pale circle of light, not strong enough to push the darkness back beyond its border.

"Find the door with your fingertips, with your nails," Danika told them. "Find the seams. I don't care how good the empire is with gears and motors, if you push two solids up against each other, there will be a crack!"

"Before we get going . . ." Stina handed Annalyse the guard's baton. "I'll keep the pistol, I expect I'm the best shot of the four of us, but you've got the longest reach and a good strong arm. Best this is with you if we need it to be used."

"You took his stick?"

Stina's teeth flashed white. "I would have, sweetheart, but Lady Hagen thought it would make too much noise."

One hand clutching the baton, Annalyse covered her mouth with the other to stop the spill of giggles.

"How did you deal with him?" Jesine asked.

"While he was still thinking we were harmless, I flicked his hat off him and slammed his head into the wall. Once he hit the floor, I kicked him in the chest, and knocked the air out of his lungs. Wouldn't have worked, though, if he hadn't hesitated."

"The door," Danika said, pushing her gently toward the wall. "We can hear your tales of battle when we're out."

They'd find the door, they'd slip through a quiet castle, and they'd disappear into Karis before the capital woke. Aydori had withdrawn their ambassador when the Imperial army crossed the border into the Duchy of Traiton, but the embassy was still there. Empty as far as Danika knew. It would, of course, be the first place Leopald would look, but they'd have time to . . .

She froze, fingertips splayed against the plaster.

She could hear voices coming from above. From Leopald's rat-hole.

"He watches the mages from here. It's the only way I know to get to them." With the emperor held by the duties of a public festival, the lamp in his little room hadn't been attended to. Reiter lifted the glass chimney off and set it on the chair. Then he pulled a fire-starter from his pocket, rolled up the lamp's wick, and lit it.

He turned and saw Mirian blinking in the spill of light. She rubbed her eyes, looked down, and jerked backward.

Tomas barely grabbed her in time to keep her from falling down the stairs. "What is it?" he demanded as he hauled her upright.

When she pointed, Tomas' lips drew back off his teeth and he began to growl. This time, Mirian didn't stop him. She kept swallowing as though she were about to be sick.

Reiter had no idea . . .

The rug!

Burn it, it wasn't even anyone they knew! He dove for the chair as Tomas clawed at his clothing, impressed, in spite of the danger, by how fast the boy could undress. The glass chimney toppled, fall cushioned by the thick fur underfoot. His hand closed around the lever in the side of the chair and he yanked it back, turning to see if . . .

It was one thing to know they changed. It was another to see it happen. Or almost see it happen. There was a glimpse of limbs stretching, changing, pale skin suddenly covered in black fur, a flash of silver on one shoulder, teeth . . .

Which was when he realized that the wall was taking longer to open than Tomas was taking to change and he was stuck in a small room with an enraged wolf. "Mirian."

Hand on Tomas' shoulder, she shook her head. "You don't understand. How would you feel if you saw Private Chard's head on the wall?"

He tried a laugh. "Chard may not be the best example."

"Captain!"

"We can't save *him*." Heart pounding, he waved a hand at the pelt and moved up and out and to the right of the chair as the wolf moved forward along the left. "And we don't have the time to waste on . . ."

Tomas leaped forward, out through the still opening door in the wall.

It looked like a shadow leaping out of the spill of light. It cleared them easily, landed, spun around, took a step forward, head up . . .

"Tomas?" Danika knew that silhouette and if her heart said *Ryder* first, no one had to know. He turned toward her, made a sound half whine, half word and she threw herself at him, her arms around his neck, her face buried in his fur repeating his name over and over. Then Jesine and Stina and Annalyse were there, touching him, stroking his ears, his shoulder . . .

When he began to change, they backed away and only Danika held the young man whose strong, callused hands lifted her head off his shoulder so he could look into her face. "Are you hurt! You're not hurt? You don't smell hurt . . . Is the baby all right?"

"The baby is fine." She dropped one hand to the curve of her belly, kept the other on his shoulder. "Tomas, what are you doing here?"

"We're here to rescue you."

"Ryder . . ." Twisting in his hold, she stared up at Leopald's rat-hole. No, not Ryder. Captain Reiter and a girl she didn't know. "No, of course not. The Pack Leader can't leave Aydori." When she turned back to Tomas, his cheeks were wet. "He sent you, though."

"No, he . . . There wasn't . . ." Tomas' grip on her arms tightened to the edge of pain. "Ryder's dead, Dani."

She wanted to scream, to weep, to wail, to lie on the floor and kick her feet and refuse to believe him. Except she could hear the pain in Tomas' voice. Her belief was irrelevant. And they didn't have time for her to fall apart.

Tomas stood as she did.

"Mirian and I came to rescue you."

Unexpectedly, Annalyse spoke next. "You were at the opera. I saw you on the promenade."

"My mother's idea."

Danika looked up to meet the gaze of a girl probably no more than Tomas' age. Eighteen. Nineteen maybe. Younger by three or four years than Annalyse, who Danika had been thinking of as so very young. "You're the sixth mage."

She nodded. "Mirian Maylin. I've been following you since you were taken."

"You should have gone to Lord Hagen . . ."

"That was the plan, but first I ran into Captain Reiter and then Tomas."

"I rescued her."

Mirian smiled pointedly at Tomas. "We rescued each other."

"So just the two of you?" Jesine moved to stand by Danika's side. "There must have been someone else."

"Everyone else is fighting a war. Or dead."

"If you were captured . . . How did you get the net off?"

"I heard your warning, Lady Hagen, and I twisted resin and sticks into my hair. It hasn't been cut in Pack fashion, so there's more of it."

Hasn't been? Hadn't been. Danika listened to Tomas breathing beside her and thought, *It could be now.*

"We could have defeated the net with a hat?" Stina snorted.

"So it seems." The girl, Mirian, reached back to pull Captain Reiter to the edge. If the skin was still up there, it had been rolled back. "The captain has the artifact to remove the nets."

"The fork," Jesine said in Imperial.

"That is what it looks like," the captain agreed, reaching into an inside pocket and pulling out the small wooden fork they'd used to remove Jesine's net before cutting into Danika's chest.

The scar throbbed. She only just managed to stop herself from touching it. He'd been there when it happened. He'd been there when Kirstin died. "Why are you helping us? "

"There's a difference between serving the needs of your country and supporting a madman." Because he looked so miserable about realizing it, Danika decided to believe him.

"You didn't know he was mad when you let Tomas and me go." Mirian spoke to the captain almost the same way she spoke to Tomas.

He stared at the girl for a long moment then said, "I knew he was wrong." But the look on his face told Danika he hadn't been think-ing of Leopald at the time.

"You have no mage marks." Danika squinted up toward the rat-hole. Even from here she should be able to see the color in Mirian Maylin's eyes. "You can't be the sixth mage without mage marks."

"My mage marks are white, Lady Hagen."

Beside her, Tomas made a questioning noise—it seemed as though this was news to him as well—and Danika shook her head. "There's no such thing."

"Yes, there is." Stina spoke in Aydori, but it was clear she'd under-stood at least the gist what had been said in Imperial. "My mother was from Orin. Most Earth-mages have closer ties to the old coun-try, but that's neither here nor there. When I was young, she told me stories of mages with white mage marks, mages who could work in all six of the crafts."

"All six?" Annalyse shook her head. "My professors always said that to divide your power between disciplines would keep you from realizing your full potential."

Stina snorted and, watching her stare up at Mirian through nar-rowed eyes, Danika wondered what she knew the rest of them didn't. "All our professors said that. I suspect it depends on how much power you have and how much you're willing to let it shape you instead of you shaping it."

Smiling tightly, Mirian said only, "If you could throw the artifact to Tomas, Captain. It would be best to leave this discussion for an-other time."

"Sensible," Tomas murmured as he caught the fork. He grinned up at the girl, she smiled down at him and Danika could hear history in the word. They'd have a lot to talk about, her and Tomas. Her and Mirian Maylin. Later.

He didn't give her a chance to tell him to free Jesine first. He shoved the prongs through her hair and forced the net up off her head. There was a flare of pain and then the headache she'd had since that morning on the Trouge Road lifted with it. It felt like a cool drink of water running down a dry throat. Like the first straw-berry in the spring. Like stepping out of too-tight shoes. Like a lover's touch . . .

"You could have warned me it would feel this good," she said quietly to Jesine as Tomas freed first the Healer-mage then Stina and Annalyse.

"I was too distracted the last time to notice," Jesine reminded her.

"Tomas, boost them up and let's go. This is the only way I know to get you out," the captain added as Danika turned her attention to him.

"They can't go through the palace dressed like that," Mirian protested. If Mirian wore current Imperial fashion, then she was right. Her wine-colored dress with the bulk of the skirt fabric gathered at the back below a fitted waist and hips looked nothing like the loose, high-waisted dresses they were wearing.

"Does it matter?" Annalyse asked. "It's night."

"Not out there," Tomas told them. "Out there it's midmorning, and there's a crowd of people in the palace for a public festival."

"But . . ."

Captain Reiter cut her off. "The emperor time shifted you, possibly to make it more convenient for him to observe you eating. Probably because he's insane. Let's move, people."

"Their clothes will give them away." Mirian grabbed his arm. "Even in the back halls, if a servant sees them . . ."

"We don't have any other clothes," Danika snapped. "Unless you want us to dress up in bedsheets."

"There you go." The captain pulled free of her grip and dropped to one knee at the edge of the wall. "Tomas! Boost them up."

"Wait!"

Tomas froze, responding to Mirian's voice. Danika added his reaction to the list of things they had to talk about later. He was far too young to make any kind of a commitment, no matter what he thought the girl smelled like.

"You have bedsheets?" Mirian asked. "Tomas, the Sisters of Starlight!"

Tomas grinned. "What was it you said, like they wore sheets over nightgowns?"

"Who are the Sisters of Starlight?" Danika demanded.

"A charitable religious order," he told her.

"An Imperial charitable religious order." Mirian grabbed the captain's sleeve and released him almost immediately. "Would they be noticed in the palace?"

The captain glanced down at his arm, then up at the girl. "Not today."

"Get the sheets . . ."

"We also have nightgowns." Danika bent and picked up the lantern. "Jesine you're with me. Stina, Annalyse, jam the door leading to the dark cells. I believe that's the way the guards arrive, and it has to be nearly morning. We need to delay them."

"You need to *hurry*," the captain snapped.

Both Tomas and Mirian made a small sound at the emphasis.

"Run," Danika said, and led the way.

Chapter Sixteen

WHILE SHEETS OVER NIGHTGOWNS wouldn't attract any less attention than what the mages had been wearing, Danika assumed it would attract a different kind of attention and with her head through a hole in half a sheet and it hanging down both front and back like an extra long historic tabard, she could only hope people would fill in the blanks in the illusion on their own.

"Kirstin would be better at this," Danika muttered as she jerked Captain Reiter's knife through a piece of leftover sheet. Kirstin took the fashion chances. Kirstin never cared what people thought. Kirstin was dead. Kirstin had to die to convince the captain to free them from the nets. Kirstin died to free them from the nets. She swiped her palm over her cheeks. "There's no way this will ever look like a shoe."

"The Sisters wear white slippers," Mirian told her dropping to one knee and wrapping a square of fabric around Danika's right foot. Her nose inches from Danika's leg, she tied the fake slipper in place with a long strip of sheet—around the ankle, down under the arch, back around the ankle. "And no one," she added, moving to the left foot and cutting off whatever protest the captain had been about to make, "would go barefoot in the palace. Perception is important."

"Getting out before we're overrun by armed guards is more important," Reiter grunted, lifting Jesine out of Tomas' hold and up into the small room. It was crowded already, particularly since none of them would touch the . . . body . . . folded up over the chair. Fortunately, Jesine was small. Mirian held up a hand for another square and shuffled over to wrap Jesine's feet.

"Forget it, Captain."

Danika turned to see Reiter on one knee, holding out his hand to Stina, who, fortunately, looked amused as she added, "Get out of my way, I can manage on my own."

When Danika translated, Reiter stood, hands spread, and backed to one side. She considered it a point in his favor that he stayed close enough to lend a hand if necessary.

It was definitely crowded with Stina in the small room. Danika moved closer to the edge, but maintained a hold on the billowing panels of purple fabric. Sheets weren't known for traction. Glancing down as Tomas bent to boost Annalyse to the ledge, she saw a fan of light spill into the room below. Before she could speak, Annalyse threw herself forward and out of sight, Tomas right behind her.

There was a meaty thud and a groan, then Tomas reappeared dragging Adeline.

The triangle of light disappeared and Annalyse stared up at her, eyes wide, green flecks gleaming. "I hit her with the baton!"

"Good girl," Stina called.

There was light enough to see Annalyse flush.

"Is she out?" Reiter demanded. He couldn't look right at Tomas, Danika noticed. Imperials had such strange ideas about skin.

Tomas showed teeth. "Close enough."

Annalyse needed even less help than Stina had, but then she was taller and almost fifteen years younger. Mirian, still on her knees, moved to her feet with the last two squares of sheet while behind her, Stina peered down at her own fake slippers and shook her head.

"Right, then." The captain nodded at Tomas. "Let's go."

Tomas changed and trotted to the far end of the room. As he started to run, Danika wondered why it looked so familiar . . .

"The Pack! Tomas, stop!"

His nails raked the floor as he slid.

"Catch me, I'm coming down! Lord and Lady . . ." Danika spun around, to find the others staring at her. ". . . how could I have forgotten. The nets are off!" She turned back to the edge. "We have to get the Pack out!"

"Stop her!"

Danika's foot was in the air when Captain Reiter threw an arm around her waist and dragged her back against his body. She called the wind, more than willing to knock them both down into the room where Tomas waited, but he held her with one arm and grabbed at the wall hangings with the other.

"Lady Hagen! Stop it!" Mirian grabbed her arm, and Danika got a close look at her eyes. None of the original color remained—only white and pupil—and the edges of her pupils were frayed. It was wrong and frightening. If this was what came of allowing the power to choose, the masters were right and she wanted no part of it.

When she flinched away, the wind stopped although she wasn't positive she'd been the one to stop it.

"Captain Reiter will take you to safety. Tomas and I will free the Pack."

"Tomas and you?" Fear sharpened her voice. "You're children!"

Mirian released her arm and stepped back, bumping into Jesine. "And you have your child to think about plus another four. Sorry . . ." She glanced at Stina. ". . . five. You're having twins."

Stina rolled her eyes. "Oh, joy."

"You could tell from touching her?" The gold flecks in Jesine's eyes glittered.

"I didn't mean to," Mirian muttered. "It's like first level metals by way of healing. Identify infant."

"That's not possible."

"And yet . . ." She shrugged and turned her attention back to Danika, lip curled. Danika suddenly realized this girl would challenge her if it became necessary.

"They've been tortured and starved," she growled. "What makes you think you can control them?"

"She has a better chance than you do." Tomas said.

Reiter let his grip ease enough that Danika could look down at her brother-in-law. "Tomas, so help me, if you say she smells amazing . . ."

"She does. But she also has metal craft, and you don't. They're using silver to control them, right? I mean, logically, they have to be."

Mirian's mouth twitched at that although Danika saw nothing to smile about.

"You'd have to figure out the mechanics, if there's even a way to get the silver off. Mirian wouldn't. She can get rid of any silver, fast. And she's . . ." He spread his hands although Danika wasn't sure if words had failed him or he considered it blindingly obvious that Mirian was his Alpha. And probably Captain Reiter's as well, although Danika doubted any of them had acknowledged it.

While age certainly had its place in Pack dynamics, in the end, position came down to power. Not only raw power, but also how that power was used. Ryder was . . . had been both strong and smart. Danika was the strongest Air-mage in Aydori. Mirian Maylin had made her way from Aydori to save the Mage-pack, even knowing she was the sixth mage Leopald searched for.

Danika stopped fighting the captain's hold, and he allowed her to pull free. Meeting the girl's eyes, forcing herself to focus on the white-on-white in spite of how uneasy it made her feel, she said, "I promised them."

"Let me keep your promise for you."

After a long moment, Danika tipped her head to one side. Behind her, Annalyse gasped, but the others were silent. Kirstin, who'd challenged and challenged and challenged, would have had something to say. Danika suddenly missed her so much she had to press both fists to her chest to hold in the pain.

Mirian looked past her to the captain and said, "I'm trusting you."

"I'll get them out."

And Danika heard *if it's the last thing I do* in Captain Reiter's voice even if Mirian didn't. Even if she was too young to realize that by helping them, by doing the right thing, he'd destroyed his own . . .

Mirian stepped off the edge.

Danika choked back a scream.

"What?" Mirian frowned up her as she floated gently to the lower level. "If I can float a leaf, I can logically float myself."

"The Air-master said it was impossible."

The frown became pique as she touched down. "Not to me."

Stina snorted. "They'll be fine."

Mirian was close enough to Tomas when she landed that her skirt wrapped around his legs, the deep burgundy making his skin look even paler than usual. "Your clothes?"

"I'll be more use in fur."

"Told you you wouldn't be in a jacket long enough to buy the expensive . . ." A sudden noise pulled her attention to the far end of the room. The guards weren't banging on the door, not yet, but they'd definitely realized they couldn't get it open. Reaching out, she touched Tomas' shoulder, ran her hand down his arm, and finally laced their fingers together before she glanced up at the emperor's nasty little room. "Where is he keeping the Pack?"

"Down the stairs," Lady Hagen answered. "Turn left and go through a metal door to a row of cells."

"Down the stairs behind the door that's jammed shut and has increasingly frustrated armed guards lined up behind it?"

"Only two at this hour. They start the day by escorting us one by one to the water room."

"Only two." Although she couldn't see faces, it wasn't hard to find Captain Reiter. He was the only one up there not dressed head-to-toe in white. "Next time we do this, we're coming up with a better plan."

"Next time." She could hear the smile in his voice. "Mirian, the . . . the Pack . . ." The smile was gone. ". . . you have to know, one of them, he ate the other mage."

"It was Kirstin's choice!" Lady Hagen protested.

Mirian didn't want to know what the alternative had been.

"And she convinced him to do it," Lady Hagen continued. "He was starving, but she convinced him to take her strength."

"So he could what?" Mirian asked.

"Survive. Kirstin couldn't live as a captive, and it's not like she knew what the arrival of the sixth mage meant."

Jake had told them to hurry. They hadn't moved fast enough.

"And now," Lady Hagen added, "he's lived long enough for you to save him."

"The emperor could have had him shot after we left." Reiter spread his hands as Lady Hagen turned on him. "We don't know."

Kirstin's decision sounded crazy to Mirian, but then she hadn't been locked up by a madman. "It doesn't matter if he's been shot. Well, to him, obviously, but he wasn't alone, was he? He wasn't the only Pack held captive."

"No."

"Then thank you for the warning, Captain, but it changes nothing." At the other end of the room, the guards' attempt to open the door grew more vigorous. At her feet, the woman taken down by the baton groaned. Mirian bent and touched her. "Sleep." She looked up again and couldn't believe they were all still watching. She'd thought Lady Hagen, at least, had more sense. "Get them out, Captain!" Slipping her hand in Tomas', she dropped her voice into his ear alone. "Leave the lantern and take me to the door."

"You can't . . ." He grunted when she shifted her grip and pinched the back of his hand. Pulling her close, he turned her toward the other end of the room and under the sound of the Mage-pack *finally* leaving said, "We have to talk about this."

"You could leave with them."

He snarled, but kept them moving. "*We* could leave with them."

"No." She thought about closing her eyes and seeing if it made any difference, then remembered they were crossing a dark room. Maybe her vision wasn't as bad as she thought. Although it was bad. "I can't see well enough to adjust to other people reacting up in the palace. If I go with them, I'd endanger their escape. I'd be responsible for the Mage-pack being recaptured. If *we* go with them, you'll defend me instead of them. Of course, if you go with them on your own, you'll be able to help protect them."

"You can't . . . How much *can* you see?"

That would be what he got his teeth into. "When we were standing by the lantern, I could see where you were, but not beyond you."

"It's dark. Really dark," he added as though that made the difference.

"I'm afraid . . ." She took a deep breath and let it out. "I'm afraid that at the rate I'm losing vision, I'll be blind before I finish what needs to be done." She was impressed by how calm she sounded. Saying *blind* like it didn't mean what it did.

"So floating down from that upper level wasn't the *sensible* thing to do."

"I guess not."

"You were showing off for Danika." He sounded amused.

"Shut up."

He stopped, tugged her to a stop beside him. When Mirian stretched out her hand, she felt the wood of the door and the vibrations of the guards banging on the other side. It was either thick enough she couldn't hear them shouting or they were trying to get through in complete silence. The latter was a little creepy.

Before she could decide what to do, Tomas wrapped a callused hand around her jaw and turned her face to his. "You don't need to see beyond me."

It took a moment to figure out what he meant. "Because you'll always be there to be my eyes." She didn't mean for it to sound as much like a question as it did. This was absolutely not the time to be questioning . . . things.

But Tomas only laughed as though he had complete confidence in her ability to make the right decision. As though he didn't know she was making it up as she went along. "Both metaphorically and actually."

She rubbed her cheek against his hand. "Big words. I'm going to open the door and sleep these guards now."

"You sure you can do it on purpose?"

Skin changed to fur under her hands as she poked him in the side where he was ticklish in both forms, well aware they were whistling in the dark.

The door had been saturated with water and the wood swollen to the point where the top of the doorjamb had buckled. Mirian moved the water out, then pushed the puddle far enough along the floor it would be out of their way.

Parting water. Moving water. Logically, it was still nothing more than second level water.

The door cracked and light from the guard's lantern traced patterns around and across it. A boot pounded once. Twice . . .

Mirian jumped back as the door slammed open and shattered against the wall.

The guard at the top of the stairs managed to clear his weapon from the holster. It fired as he fell, the lead ball flattening against the stone. His weight bowled over the guard behind him. One of the two lanterns went flying, the other landed upright, not only unbroken, but still lit.

When Mirian could hear again, she heard boots against stone. Running. Running away from the bottom of the stairs. Lady Hagen had been wrong. There were three guards.

Tomas dove past her.

Mirian picked up the unbroken lantern and followed, feeling for each step, extinguishing the flames devouring spilled lamp oil as she went.

"Gunfire!" Danika jerked around, the others turning with her as though they were connected by strings.

Reiter had to move quickly to stop them from racing back. "Keep moving."

They weren't soldiers. They didn't follow orders. They looked to Danika, not him.

"If it rouses the palace . . ."

"No one hears the sounds that come out of the north wing," Reiter told her grimly. They locked eyes for a moment—he had to fight to look at her, not the blue flecks—then she nodded. Kirstin may not have screamed, but someone surely had.

As they reached the end of the short hall, he raised a hand and checked that the way was clear before beckoning the mages forward. Emerging into the larger Imperial shortcut, he was amazed by how much better they looked than they had up in the emperor's rathole—where they'd looked like women wearing sheets over nightgowns. He started to think they might be able to pull this off.

"Da . . . Lady Hagen is weaving a glamour," the redhead told him quietly, falling into step beside him. Reiter glanced past her. Danika's lips moved as she walked and the edges of the robes . . . *sheets*, the edges of the sheets moved as though in a constant breeze. "She's telling anyone who looks our way, that they're seeing Sisters of Starlight. It's very high level. She's probably the only Air-mage alive who can . . ."

Her voice trailed off and Reiter knew she was thinking of Mirian. Who'd flown, or floated, when that wasn't apparently possible. He thought of Mirian facing the wolf . . . thought of turning, of needing to be by her side, thought of the wolf already by her side . . .

"Get them out, Captain."

He had his orders. He forced his thoughts back to the problem at hand. "If she can make a glamour, why waste time on a physical disguise?"

"She can only convince people to see what they want to see. When they look at us, they already think first of the Sisters of Starlight. Lady Hagen is smoothing out the edges."

Given that he knew what they looked like and the glamour still affected him, Reiter was impressed. And uneasy. Out of the nets, the mages of Aydori could change a man's thoughts.

"Get them out, Captain."

She'd changed his.

Helped change his.

Had she used mage-craft?

Did it matter? He couldn't leave the mages where they were, so he was either under the control of a mage barely out of her teens or he was a decent man. He knew what he wanted to believe. Needed to believe.

"Captain?"

Careful not to brush against the illusion, Reiter moved through the women, preferring to lead rather than herd. "Keep your eyes down. This glamour thing, it's not hiding the mage marks."

It was no darker at the bottom of the stairs than it had been at the top—an absence of light was an absence of light—but as Mirian stepped off the stairs onto the uneven slabs of stone, the darkness took on an almost physical presence. The circle of lantern light seemed both dimmer and smaller than it had a moment before.

Which was ridiculous.

It might have lessened the oppressive weight if she could have seen into the darkness, seen what it was hiding—in her admittedly limited experience, imagination added weight to the unknown—but she could see nothing past the line between dark and light. On the other hand, it felt damp and smelled terrible, and maybe she didn't need to know.

She could hear Tomas, so she turned, lantern in her right hand, fingertips of her left running along the wall as she moved toward him.

"Mirian, he's bolted it behind him."

A steel door. Her fingers slid over the oil on the upper hinges. Down the crack between the steel and the stone.

A steel bolt as well.

"Get behind me." She patted Tomas' chest, a large pale blur in front of her. "I'll try not to take the whole door down."

"It'd be better if we could close it behind us," he agreed, rubbing his shoulder against hers as he passed.

What did she know about steel? Iron tamed, made flexible. It didn't burn, fire had helped make it. It didn't break, violence had given it strength. She concentrated on the bolt. This steel had never been laid over a single anvil, pounded into shape. It had come from a foundry, a molten river poured into molds. Most relevantly, it was between her and where she needed to be.

She felt it sag, heard it drip. Pushed the door open.

For a moment, the howling was as solid a barrier as the door had been.

Then it stopped.

"Tomas, find out where he went." When he growled, she added, "We need to know there's not a division or two of the Imperial army on the way."

He changed and went reluctantly, but he went. He'd been a Scout in the Hunt Pack. He knew better than she did the value of an advance warning.

Mirian pushed the door closed and softened one edge. Hopefully, as it hardened, it would seal to the stone. She felt along the wall and hung the lantern on a steel bracket, carefully trimming the wick to lessen the light. At this point, it made little or no difference to her, but the Pack she could hear waiting . . . breathing . . . whining. . . . had been kept in the dark and she didn't want to blind them.

Too.

She didn't want to blind them, too.

Reaching out both arms, she touched damp stone. A narrow hall.

"There's a flight of stairs and another steel door." Tomas' hand brushed against hers. "It's bolted, too."

Mirian laid metal-craft on the air and sent it to fuse the bolt. She knew steel now. "What do you see?"

"Nine cell doors. Ask me what I smell."

"Tomas."

"There's nine alive, one to a cell. There used to be more. There's at least three bodies down here."

She stumbled past him, felt her skirt brush fur as he changed. Both her palms slapped against rough metal. Iron. The cells might not be older than steel, but they were older than foundries. Iron was simpler. Changed less after being pulled from the ground before being put back into the ground . . .

The door sagged. Collapsed.

Mirian gagged at the smell. Heard scrambling. Heard Tomas growl. Felt something push against her leg, damp and foul even through the layers of fabric. She reached down, slowly slid her fingers over matted fur and open oozing wounds, felt the silver before she touched it. It wanted to slide away as she removed it, so she let it go, let it run down a stinking drain. As long as the palace stood, no one would ever use it again.

She had to swallow before she could speak and even then she didn't dare unclench her teeth. "Convince him to change, Tomas. He needs to heal."

As she moved to the next cell, the howling started again.

They'd had to move out of the straight lines of the shortcuts twice. Once to cross a wide, three-story hall where sunlight fell from the upper windows to gild the mosaic floor. Once to skirt the back wall of a small room that held two enormous ceramic vases and nothing else. They'd passed servants—looking harried—and courtiers—looking supercilious—and neither seemed surprised to see an Imperial army officer leading four women dressed in torn sheets through the hidden halls of the palace. Hands clasped in front of her, Danika murmured the words of the glamour over and over.

She heard Stina say something quietly in Aydori.

Jesine brushed past her to walk by Captain Reiter's side. "You're leading us deeper into the palace, Captain."

Earth-mages of Stina's power didn't get lost.

"Yes, I am."

"How do we get out by going farther in?"

"You'll just have to trust me."

Mirian Maylin trusted him. Danika wasn't certain she did. Had it been as early as she'd believed it to be, she might have risked walking away from him, having Stina lead them through a nearly empty palace and out into the predawn streets of Karis. But the palace was full. The streets would be full. And the captain *had* brought them the artifact to remove the nets.

And Mirian Maylin trusted him. This was not the time to second-guess her submission to the younger mage.

The captain paused at the end of the hall and beckoned them in close. "From here on, we'll be out in public. We go straight to the Sun Gallery and then left, out into a courtyard. There's a balloon there. You're going to steal it."

"A balloon? With basket large to carry all?" To Danika's surprise, Annalyse seemed to know what she was talking about even if her Imperial wasn't entirely fluent.

"It's the emperor's personal balloon. It's not so much a basket as a boat."

"And the aeronauts? We steal them, too?"

"No." He nodded at Danika. "You have an Air-mage."

Annalyse frowned. "Should work, but . . ."

"No buts. It has to work. I'll go out and . . ."

The elderly man who slipped into the hidden hall saw them first, and his annoyed expression turned to one of bland welcome.

Politician, Danika thought as she murmured. *"See Sisters of Starlight."*

He stepped to the far side of the hall, inclined his head, said, "Enjoy your visit, Sisters." And then he froze. "Captain Reiter?"

"Lord Coving."

Danika risked a glance at the captain's face. He wasn't happy. Two of the other courtiers they'd passed had called him by name, and it hadn't seemed to matter. What was different about Lord Coving?

"What are you doing, Captain?"

"Helping Major Meritin, sir."

"But why take the Sisters through the . . ." Danika could feel the weight of his gaze. Feel the glamour slipping. She didn't know what reason Lord Coving had to suspect they weren't as they seemed, but she couldn't hold him. "These aren't . . . Are these?" He drew in a deep breath and she felt the glamour break. "Are you out of your mind, Captain?"

The captain's lip curled. "Funny you should ask that, sir."

"This is treason! In fact, this is more than treason, this is stupidity! His Majesty knows the sixth mage is in the palace!"

"How . . . ?"

"The flowering vine. According to your report, she did that same trick back in Bercarit! His Majesty was just informed of it and is on his way to the north wing where he is expecting to find her captive after trying to free the mages. When he finds the mages are already gone, he'll turn his guards loose. He'll send them out into the rest of the palace regardless of what he has agreed! These are not men I want among the citizens of the empire! These are . . ." He paused, glaring at Danika and then the others. "Where is she?"

"We were not the only captives, Your Grace!" Danika snapped.

The honorific startled him. Which was why she'd used it. "The abominations? She's freeing the abominations?"

"You know this is wrong," Captain Reiter growled. "You sent your son away to protect him *because* you know it's wrong. This is your chance to do the right thing. You don't have to help . . ."

"Help?"

". . . just look the other way. You're good at that."

"And die beside you? I don't think so. You're a dead man, Captain. A dead man."

As he opened his mouth—Danika assumed he intended to give the alarm—the captain charged toward him. Jesine was faster. Lord Coving hadn't been told she was harmless, but she was small and beautiful, even in torn sheets. More importantly, the empire had very few mages left and none of power. He didn't try to stop her.

When she touched his forehead, he frowned.

"Sleep."

The frown smoothed out, and he crumpled to the ground.

Danika thought the captain might try and catch him, but he didn't look very upset when the older man's head cracked against the floor.

"There's nowhere to hide him. If he's found, how easy will it be to wake him?"

Jesine knelt and checked Lord Coving's pulse, ever a Healer-mage even to their enemies. "He won't wake for some hours, no matter what they do."

"With luck, they'll think his heart gave out. Good work." He nodded to Jesine who flashed dimples up at him—Danika suspected she wasn't even aware she'd done it. "Although I *was* looking forward to punching the hypocritical old shitbag. We're just lucky he was alone; he isn't usually."

"We need to warn Mirian."

"About the emperor?" Reiter looked back down the hall and worked out how fast he could get to the north wing. "We need to get you out of here first."

Mirian rested her forehead against the iron door of the last cell, feeling the rough layer of rust against her skin. She'd lost the glow of the lantern three doors in. She'd thrown up twice, and the last time she'd been this tired and still awake, she'd just run the skin off her heels. Behind her, lying on the damp stone were eight scarred and starving wolves. She couldn't see them, but she'd touched the ripple of ribs and spines, hollow cheeks, corded throats in the moment they spent in skin before fur covered them again.

They'd changed to heal, but they wouldn't or couldn't stay in skin.

They whined. They twitched. They snarled. They snapped at nothing. They scrabbled at the stone unable to stop themselves.

Seven men—ages hidden by dirt and dried blood. One boy. Maybe six. Maybe younger. He'd been in a cell with his father's rotting, three-legged corpse—although all four legs were in the cell. When she dissolved his collar, he'd changed and thrown himself into her arms, blood seeping from wounds on his neck and between his legs. It wasn't until Tomas peeled the boy off her, both of them murmuring meaningless words of comfort, and he'd checked the wounds that they realized he'd been surgically castrated.

That was the second time she'd thrown up.

Tomas changed with him, and changed back with him, and that was enough to stop the bleeding, open wounds becoming twisting ridges of scar tissue. He'd whimpered once or twice, but had said nothing. He wouldn't tell Tomas his name.

There were no women.

Mirian suspected there were no women among the Pack for the same reason there were no men among the Mage-pack. Suspected. She didn't know. She didn't want to *know*.

Now, Mirian could hear banging against the door of the last cell. She didn't need Tomas to tell her this was the captives' Alpha. She didn't need anyone to tell her that this was the wolf Reiter had warned her about. The wolf who'd eaten Kirstin Yervick.

Eaten.

They didn't fetishize the dead in Aydori like they did in some cultures. She'd remembered reading that in Cafren they built small ornate houses for bodies, shared by the corpses of whole families. In Aydori, bodies were returned to earth in the land around the Lady's Groves. Historically, the Pack had eaten the hearts of their enemies, but in this modern world, even Alpha battles no longer ended in death.

There were overwrought novels written of extreme circumstances where the dying had said, *Let my body keep you alive.*

Apparently, Kirstin Yervick had read them, too.

Would he be more or less likely to eat her? He'd already done it once, so any social barriers against it had already been broken. But he wouldn't be as hungry . . .

"Mirian?"

"I know."

They didn't have time for her to settle it all in her head.

At this point, moving air from place to place made no difference in the smell, so she sucked as little as possible in past her teeth and rested her fingertips against the cell door.

Somehow, once the door was open, she didn't think the wolf behind it would sit quietly with his head in her lap while she dealt with his collar. But then she hadn't touched the silver in Tomas' wound when she'd drawn it to her, so, logically, she had no need to actually *touch* the silver in the collars. It took only a moment to find the metal and a moment more to deal with it. To have it slough off his neck—out of his neck—and down the drain.

Mirian took a deep breath, gagged, and got rid of the door.

Expecting his charge, she managed to keep from cracking her head against the floor as he knocked her down and scrambled over her. Still in fur, he ran up the stairs. Snarling, he threw himself at the bolted door.

She dragged herself up onto her elbows as Tomas raced past, up onto her knees as he reached the top of the stairs, and onto her feet just barely in time to move out of the way as the two came back down in an interlocked mess of growling and snapping teeth. From the sound of the impact, Tomas had landed on the bottom, limiting the damage to the starved wolf's prominent bones.

He fought like a crazed animal. Tomas had not only strength and speed, but reason on his side.

The fight quickly became toenails scrabbling against stone and Tomas growling with a mouth full of fur. Mirian inched forward until her boots touched something solid then she dropped carefully to her knees, bent forward, and moved enough air to wrap her scent around the tangled muzzles. "You're going to change when he lets you go," she said. "You're going to change because you need to heal. Now, Tomas."

The matted fur under her hand turned to greasy skin.

"Give me . . ." His voice was so rough she could barely make out the words. "Give me . . . a reason . . . to live." Skin turned back to fur, rising and falling under Mirian's hand as he panted.

She heard Tomas grunt as a small body dove back into his arms.

They could go back the way they'd come in. Get the men up into the palace. Sleep a few tourists. Get them clothes. Put them in the guards' clothes if it came to it. Get out the north gate and find a place to hide until dark. Feed them. If she had to sleep half of Karis to get them out, she would. That was the plan and there was nothing in it she couldn't do. Hadn't done—sleeping, stealing, feeding, sleeping again.

At the top of the stairs, the guards worked to free the bolt. Guards who'd locked a child in a cell with his dead father.

They had guns. Silver shot.

They thought they knew what they'd be facing.

Revenge seemed like the best reason she could give him right now.

They were almost across the Sun Gallery before they ran into a problem. Thanks to Danika's constant murmur as well as the Sisters' reputation for aggressive solicitation, the crowds peering at the wall of glass, at the golden tiles, at the golden Sun, parted before the five of them and closed up behind them, willingly blind.

Unfortunately, there were always priests in this part of the palace.

Reiter saw a smiling face perched above that ridiculous court collar closing the distance between them, clearly intending to intercept them before they reached the open doors to the courtyard. He sped up as much as he dared, but a soldier leading four Sisters of Starlight out of the palace at a dead run wouldn't help them remain unseen. With luck, this particular priest had never had contact with the charitable . . .

The priest's smile turned to a puzzled frown. Puzzled turned angry.

Seemed their luck had run out.

Although not entirely, as the priest chose to grab the redhead's arm before he yelled, "Impos . . ."

She tapped his forehead. "Sleep."

If they hadn't just been so thoroughly screwed, Reiter would have found his expression amusing. "Can you lot run in your condition?" he asked as the priest slowly crumpled to the tiles.

"Our condition?" When he gestured at her stomach, the redhead narrowed her eyes. "We walked out of Aydori in our condition. We were thrown into dungeon cells in our condition. Danika was tortured in our condition. We can run."

"Good. About that," he added when her eyes narrowed even further. Far too close already, a trio of priests hurried toward their fallen comrade. "Run!"

A pair of soldiers flanked the courtyard door. Reiter shoved the redhead left. As the soldier on the right moved to intercept, Reiter drove a fist into his stomach and, as he folded forward gasping, gave him a hard shove out the door and down the four broad stairs. A mass of vines came up through the cracks between the pavers and held him in place. Although Reiter knew they couldn't afford the time, he turned to stare at the brown-eyed mage.

She shrugged as she ran by him. "Like weeds, those. Leopald's gardeners is idiots."

Two small fountains erupted with force enough to blow a stone lion to pieces. People screamed and scattered. Roses grew to hedges. They had a clear run all the way to the balloon.

There were Shields stationed on the palace roof, but it was a big roof and they were in an interior courtyard. Reiter grabbed the downed soldier's weapons and ran to catch up, an itch between his shoulder blades.

"Ready!"

As the guard on the other side of the door sheared the bolt, Mirian dissolved the hinges then reached out and called every piece of silver she could feel. She let the metal splash against the other side of the door, then reached deep for her last reserves, blowing door and silver out to slam into the mass of men. As Tomas and the eight adults charged past her, she lifted the boy onto her hip—skin and bones and light enough that, as exhausted as she was, his weight meant nothing.

It seemed reasonable to assume that the light making her eyes water had been intended to blind the freed Pack as they attacked out of darkness. Bad planning. The Pack depended on their noses more than their eyes. Mirian could smell nothing over the stink of the boy in her arms.

But she could hear.

Wet tearing. Crunch of bone. A yelp. Even disarmed, the guards weren't helpless and only Tomas was at anything near full strength.

When the screaming stopped, the sounds grew wetter. She was about to set the boy down,

Then stopped.

Someone howled—it didn't sound like Tomas.

It bounced off walls and ceilings and floors, then faded and turned to the sound of nails against tile as the pack raced away.

"Tomas?"

Of course, he'd gone with them. Or after them.

Mirian set the boy on his feet, pried his hands off her skirt, took his left in her right, felt his right grip her thumb. She could see shadows on the floor that might have been guards' bodies, but, given the medieval dungeons already in use, they could have been pit traps. "I can't see." She could tell herself it was because she'd come out of darkness into bright light, but she knew it had more to do with the mage-craft she'd used freeing the Pack. "You need to direct me around obstacles. Can you do that?"

He whined and hung on.

She'd been speaking Aydori. When she repeated herself in Imperial, he sniffed and began pulling her carefully away from the door.

When her foot caught under what felt like an arm, she kicked it out of her way.

The boy understood Imperial. The ninth freed Pack had asked for a reason to live in Imperial. Mirian hadn't noticed because she'd been speaking it for days. The emperor had not only encouraged Imperial citizens to kill and skin Imperial citizens, but he personally had them imprisoned and tortured.

He was making war not only on Aydori, but on his own people.

As the boy tugged her toward the sound of snarling, she ignored the way her boots slid on the wet floor.

"Mirian!" Tomas grabbed her arm and pulled her into a room so bright she thought for a moment she could see.

The aeronauts watched wide-eyed as four women ran past them, torn sheets flapping. Reiter grabbed the arms of the young areonaut he'd spoken to earlier and yanked her out of Danika's way.

"They're not allowed on the balloon! No one is!" She twisted in his grip. "His Imperial Majesty's orders!"

Danika and the redhead were already on board, ignoring the aeronauts demanding they come down. The brown-eyed mage was nearly at the top of the half dozen stairs, an aeronaut hanging off the lower edge of her sheet. While waiting her turn, the youngest seemed to be causing more havoc with the fountains, spraying them toward the doors, keeping people inside. Smart.

"Look at me!" Reiter tightened his grip, pulling the young woman's attention from the balloon. "You don't want to get blamed for what's about to happen, and I don't want to hurt you. Go!"

"But they're . . ."

"You can't stop them from taking it."

Her eyes widened. She seemed more indignant than angry. "It's not that easy!"

"You told me the balloon is always kept ready, in case the emperor decides to go up."

"Yeah, but . . ."

"It's a big bag of air." He glanced at Danika now staring up into the balloon. "Trust me, it's that easy for them."

Four ropes hit the ground, the balloon surged up against the four remaining. The brown-eyed mage grinned, chips flying from the mahogany railing as she wielded the ax.

Maybe it was the grinning. Maybe it was the ax. The aeronaut jerked free of Reiter's grip, put two fingers in her mouth, whistled a complex pattern, and ran. The others ran with her. One held a length of sheet.

The youngest, the Water-mage, was on board now.

Two ropes remaining.

He heard the shot the same time he saw the musket ball kick up dirt. The first man to the edge of the roof hadn't taken the time to aim. Probably wasn't entirely certain what he was supposed to aim at.

"Captain!"

He turned to find Danika staring down at him.

"Are you coming?"

He hadn't . . .

He'd assumed . . .

He didn't even know their names. He knew her name and Kirstin's name, the name of the dead mage, but then they were redheaded, brown-eyed, and youngest.

"If you'd rather die, Captain Reiter, I won't stop you."

Another two shots. Not from the roof. There were Shields fighting their way out through the spraying water. He couldn't get back to Mirian. But he had . . . *they had* pulled Shields from all over the palace and created one flaming fuck of a diversion for her. She'd be able to slip the Pack out in the chaos. Hide them in clothing as she'd hidden Tomas.

Reiter had been a soldier most of his life. He'd always expected to die fighting for something he believed in. From the moment he saw Mirian in the square, he'd known he was a dead man. He hadn't actually thought there was another option.

As the balloon broke the final two tethers and surged up into the air, he ran up the stairs and launched himself at the break in the railings. Slamming down on his elbows, he bit his tongue, swallowed blood, and managed to get onto his feet in time to see the roof of the palace fly by.

In time to see two men with raised weapons. In time to dismiss one and identify the other as Corporal Hare.

Hare had been one of the first handed a musket with the new rifled barrel. Greater accuracy over a greater distance, and Hare had already been one of the best shots Reiter'd ever known.

The balloon was basically a big bag of air. Put a hole in it and it was a big bag.

Reiter raised his stolen musket to his shoulder. He might be able to distract . . .

The sandbag hanging by the redhead's hip exploded, spraying sand. She stared down at the mess, then up at the balloon. "He missed!"

"No." Reiter lowered his musket without taking a shot. On the roof, Hare took his time reloading. The wind whistled by, and Danika carried them out of range. "He hit exactly what he aimed at."

When Mirian blew the door open, one of the guards had tried to run. Tomas, less distracted than the others by the rich meaty scent of fresh blood on his muzzle, had slammed him to the floor, closed his jaws around the back of his neck and crushed his spine. By the time he spun back to the mass of bodies by the door, growling low in his chest, the screaming had stopped and the feeding frenzy had begun.

Not unexpected.

The guards didn't smell like Pack, or power.

He'd been warned, entering the Hunt Pack, that this happened in war. He was the younger Lord Hagen, and he'd sworn to himself he'd never . . .

They smelled like meat.

The guards had taken strength away. They could give it back.

Then Nine—he wouldn't change again and tell Tomas his name, if he even remembered it, so Nine—Nine had lifted his head. Lowered it. Scrubbed his muzzle on the shoulder he straddled. Lifted it again, and howled.

By the time the howl had faded, the whole Pack was running.

A man.

Over the scents of metal, and death, and piss, and lamp oil, Tomas had been able to catch the very faint scent of a man. Not one of the lingering scents of the many men and women who'd been through these halls. Fresh. A man standing somewhere close. Waiting.

Whoever he was, he was more than merely a man to the freed Pack.

He'd been enough to pull them from food.

Not far down the hall, Nine had turned, dove through what looked like an open cage with gears and pulleys up above and chains running down through holes in the floor, and into a white-tiled room.

"So you got past the guards." The man standing alone on the upper level had peered down through the bars into the room. He looked short, but that might have been the angle. When Tomas, caught up in the attack on this final enemy, had nearly sunk his teeth into the toe of a glossy boot, he'd danced back, but he'd seemed pleased rather than frightened or angry.

Then Mirian's scent had brought Tomas up onto two feet. Attention split between the enemy and the Pack, he'd gone to the hall to get her.

He lifted the boy up into his arms as she walked carefully into the room, adding bootprints to the smeared red pattern on the floor. The boy nuzzled up against his throat, soft tongue licking along the line of his jaw.

"Stop it." Tomas reached across with his free hand and pushed the boy's head away.

The boy whined and snapped at Tomas' fingers, trying to push his face back to . . .

To the blood.

"Fine. But no biting."

The Pack, exhausted, sat panting. And twitching. Except for Nine. Nine paced. Back and forth. Through the resting wolves. He brushed against Mirian's skirt hard enough to leave a dark, wet stain behind but not so hard she stumbled, so Tomas let it go. He understood the need to move. The frustration at not being able to take this final enemy.

He sucked blood off his teeth, shifted the boy to his other hip, and leaned closer to Mirian's ear. "Twelve o'clock. Up about fifteen feet." Her chin lifted. "Alone. No visible weapons, but he smells like power."

"Mage?" she asked quietly.

"No. But sort of similar. Not a guard. Expensive clothes. *Very* expensive boots."

The man looked at Mirian like she was his. Tomas growled. The boy in his arms echoed it. Nine picked it up and then, one by one, the other seven. It grew, filled the room, until Mirian said, "Enough."

"Fascinating." He smiled like a schoolteacher Tomas had particularly disliked. "So you're my sixth mage, are you?"

His sixth mage? Tomas tensed. The boy whined.

Mirian's lips pulled back off her teeth. "Ignore it. Reiter *said* the emperor was insane."

"Are you encouraging her to use mage-craft against me, abomination?" The emperor rocked back on his heels. Tomas wanted to snap the approving smile right off his smarmy face. "Well, that's definitely a good idea, credit where credit is due and all that, but she's already making the attempt. I can feel all six of my protective artifacts heat up. Actually . . ." Reaching into his trouser pocket, he pulled out a ceramic disk and slipped it into his jacket. "That was getting a little uncomfortable. Now . . ." Even at this distance, his eyes were so brilliant a blue Tomas thought for a moment he had mage marks. And mage marks on this man would be wrong for so many reasons. "According to the report from Abyek, you can use—and I think it's fairly and unfortunately obvious why I say *use* and not control, isn't it?—fire, air, water, metal, and earth. And then Tardford gave us healing." His smile stretched into broad approval. "Six in one. As happens far too often I'm afraid, it seems the Soothsayers were misinterpreted. You're the mage I was looking for all along. And let me tell you, understanding *that* makes it a lot easier to accept that the others have escaped. There is, of course, still the unborn child beginning it all to deal with, of course, but if that's not a factor currently, I'm sure we can arrange things. Although, this time . . ." He wagged a finger at Nine who snarled and took another leap at the ledge. ". . . we'll do it scientifically."

"Is he lying?" Tomas asked, not bothering to hide the question from the emperor.

"About mage-craft having no effect on him?" Mirian tucked a strand of hair back behind her ear. "No."

Nine set up for another run. Tomas growled, and he settled, reluctantly, by Mirian's other side.

"First, why would I lie? Second," the emperor continued as To-mas soothed the boy, "thank you for keeping my property from dam-aging itself, and third . . ."

He opened his hand. Nine jumped for the flash of gold. Missed.

Mirian felt the net snug up against her scalp, thought about hats, and bit back a giggle. It didn't hurt this time, but that was possibly be-cause she couldn't feel anything but tired.

"You didn't think I only had the original six, did you?" The em-peror smiled broadly. "This is the artifact we used for primary testing back when we first discovered the cabinet in the Archive, so I know this one, unlike the one you wore before, is entirely functional."

It didn't feel functional, it felt old.

Mage-craft had been wound through and around the gold links—a twisted combination of healing and metals.

Gold. Soft. Malleable. Never tarnished. She'd seen coins of red gold once from Talatia in the Southern Alliance at her father's bank.

"Mirian, there'll be more guards soon."

"I know."

The guards would have silver, and she couldn't . . .

She knew the gold. Not as well as she'd come to know silver, but well enough. Except . . . she had nothing left. She was only still standing because she was too stubborn to fall over.

The emperor said the Mage-pack had escaped. That was good.

But now he had Tomas. That was bad.

"What is wrong with your eyes? They're white, aren't they? At first I thought it was just the room because, in all honesty it can be just a little overwhelming—the tile, the lights—but no, they're white. No color to them at all. Wait, I've read about that. Hang on." He lifted a hand as if he actually thought the gesture would hold them in place. "I'm sure I'll remember in a moment. I know it was an old scroll. Very old . . ."

"Used to be, everyone had to do a bit of everything to survive, but civi-lization means specialists because suddenly everything's so bleeding compli-cated with foundries and gaslights and brass buttons, it takes all a person has to learn how to do just one thing and if everything's that complicated, then mage-craft can't be simple . . ."

"You need to be a river, not a bucket. Way I heard it, the power is every-where, but the mage has to open themselves and say fuck these bullshit rules."

She had essentially blinded herself with the limited power in her bucket. In this room, in this light, she could see shapes, although she had to trust those shapes were her Pack. She felt as though she were looking through a series of overlapping veils. If she turned her head quickly, the veils shifted and she almost thought she saw Tomas watching her.

What would unlimited power do? How many more veils would it add? What else would she lose? Sight. Hearing. Touch . . .

Life?

"Mirian?"

Running off to rescue the Mage-pack from the empire might have been a bit crazy, sure, but she didn't want to die.

Or lose Tomas and the boy and the eight others in their broken Pack.

Her life weighed against ten lives.

If completely opening herself to power did kill her, at least she wouldn't have to live with having failed them.

So, that decided, how did she find the power Gryham had heard about?

She knew how it felt lying dormant—*trapped, heavy, not fitting in the skin that should be yours.* She'd known that for years.

She knew how it felt being used—*like a breeze, a cool drink of water, warm earth underfoot, knowing the parameters of your body, silver run-ning silken.* Although that was more recent.

Oh.

Reaching out, she found Tomas' hand and squeezed it. There was no time to explain, but if the worst happened, she hoped he'd re-member and understand. "Fuck these bullshit rules."

"Mirian!"

Gold ran down her cheek and caught against the collar of her dress.

When she screamed, the Pack howled.

When she turned toward him, her eyes gleamed white from rim to rim.

Her body felt like it dissolved.

It hurt.

Then re-formed.

That hurt more.

"Mirian!"

She turned toward his voice. She could see the way the air moved over and around him. Defining him. She could see his shape in the air, see him. He was mostly water. She hadn't known that. She could see all of them for the first time. Faces. Expressions. Scars. For all the detail, there were no colors; it was all shades of gray. All but the silver fur that marked where the Pack had been collared—that blazed.

Mirian pulled her hand from Tomas' grip and stroked the backs of two fingers over his cheek. The movement shot pain down her arm as her new body figured out what she wanted it to do. The contact burned, then faded to a dull throb. "Don't look so worried. I'm . . ." In all honesty, she wasn't sure what she was.

What *else* she was.

She was Mirian Maylin.

"You can see me?"

"I can." She rubbed her face against his shoulder, savoring the burn as each new bit of skin settled. Turning toward the other end of the room, she rose on the air until she was level with the emperor. His gray body gleamed with points of blue and green and red and brown and gold and indigo. No silver. No one had tortured him. She pulled the iron rings from the walls, formed it into spears, and sent them through the bars.

They flattened against a flare of indigo and dropped to the floor.

"Amazing! But that's metal-craft and I told you, I'm protected. You can't blow me over, you can't move all the water out of my body, you can't wrap vines around me, or bury me, you can't light me on fire, you can't put me to sleep." He hauled out the artifacts as he spoke. Mirian saw them as their power rather than actual physical things. She could see how that power protected them.

"You can't hurt me."

She tried anyway.

She couldn't set him on fire, so she cracked the walls—the tiles were originally clay and threw the metal from the pipes . . .

. . . the water in the pipes.

Air spun around him.

He didn't fall. He didn't sleep.

He was right.

Exactly right.

She let everything fall and said, "That artifact that protects you from Healing is limited. It only stops me from putting you to sleep."

The emperor smiled disarmingly from within a knee-high circle of debris and rubbed the gold light between his thumb and forefinger. "Well, yes, but healing is hardly aggressive now, is it? You can't exactly heal me to death."

Mirian remembered the rabbit and smiled back at him.

This time, no one was close enough to break his neck. He died thrashing, fingernails digging into his face, heels drumming against the floor.

It didn't take long. She hoped he was terrified. She hoped it hurt.

Her Pack stood and watched silently as she rode the air back to the floor.

Tomas watched as she made her way through them—stroking shoulders, heads, ears, calming them, if only for the moment, with her touch. He was as silent as the rest.

"Tomas?"

"You smell . . . There isn't . . . words. There aren't words." He reached out and stroked her cheek with two fingers. A mirror of what she'd done. Only her fingers hadn't been trembling.

"We need to leave."

"How?"

"This way." Mirian meant to use the whirlwind to punch a clean hole through to the outside. She could feel the place where the weight of the palace no longer rested on the earth. When the dust settled, the north wing ended at the toes of her boots.

People screamed in the distance. Behind her, her Pack twitched and snarled and snapped at nothing. If anyone had been in the north wing when it fell, she wouldn't mourn them.

"You didn't mean to do that, did you?" Tomas sounded slightly amused. Or almost hysterical. Mirian wasn't sure which.

"Not exactly, no. Still . . ." Her body didn't seem sure of how to take a deep breath. ". . . no point in wasting it. Let's go."

"Where?" Still holding the boy, Tomas grabbed her arm and pulled her back from the edge. "We can't take them to Aydori. They're . . ." He was about to say *broken*, she could see it in his eyes, but he shook his head and said, "The boy's the only one who can stay in skin for more than a moment or two."

The gray light that defined the boy had become muted. His head lolled on Tomas' shoulder, his eyes barely open. And she still didn't know how to heal. "Times are changing," she said slowly, touching the boy's fur, watching dirt and dried blood flake away from her fingertips. "Science and reason are taking over. Soon everyone will have a chance to abuse power, not just those given it by an accident of birth."

"You won't abuse your power."

"Maybe not, but a sensible person would learn to control it. I need to find someone who can help. Help me. Help them." Everyone needed help except . . .

"Don't say it. Where you go, I go." His teeth were bared. "Tell me to stay behind and I'll follow."

Mirian found it more comforting than she could say that Tomas had known what she was thinking. *She* barely recognized the inside of her head. Still . . . "You could go home, Tomas. To your family. I'm as much a throwback to an earlier time as the emperor was, but you *can* go home."

He shook his head as another slab of masonry fell from the part of the palace still standing and crashed into the ruin of the north wing. "We're Pack. Where you go, I go. And Reiter said the emperor was insane, so you're nothing like him."

Mirian glanced up at the body. Had he always been insane? How had it started? Said, "All right, then. We're going to Orin."

Reiter put the newspaper down and stood as Lady Hagen came into the room. It had taken a while, but he'd learned to think of her using her title. They weren't friends.

"Sorry to keep you waiting, Captain." She lowered herself into the wing chair on the other side of the small table and nodded at the newspaper as he took his seat. "Are you back in the news?"

"Not this week."

For the first few months, the Imperial papers brought into Aydori had featured him prominently. Reading the stack sequentially, Lord Coving had declared him traitor, accused him of releasing the abominations and the mages, of turning both sets of captives loose to destroy the palace and the Imperial government. It was only due to Lord Coving's leadership that things hadn't gotten worse than they were. He called for Reiter to be dragged back to the empire to pay for his crimes. He even suggested that the ancient traitor's death be reinstated in this one case, and Reiter, when captured, be staked out in the sun. In the next issue, which looked to have been a rushed second printing later that same day, he accused Reiter of killing the emperor. In the next, it turned out that one of the scientists who researched in the north wing had found the body and took her findings straight to the newspapers. She had photographs. Reiter almost admired the adherence to scientific principles that led to her setting up a camera after finding the emperor's body at the edge of the wreckage before raising an alarm. She not only had photographs of the emperor's body, but files documenting everything that had been happening in the north wing. In later issues, the newspapers printed engravings based on the photographs—both of the emperor's body and of the experiments he'd had performed. Lord Coving accused her of being bought. Then one of the men who'd been guarding the Mage-pack came forward and supported her story.

"Bruised-thumb!" Reiter had no idea how Lady Hagen had recognized that feature in the engraving, but she'd been pleased by the guard's sudden discovery of a conscience.

After that, accusations flew thick and fast. The newspapers had to resort to broadsheets to keep up.

What had the politicians known? And when? Why had they done nothing about it? Adeline Curtain was found and interviewed and became a bit of a celebrity. The emperor's doctor came forward and even the Prelate took his moment in the sun, covering his ass with meticulously reported bullshit, rescinding the declaration of abomination. The church and the court expressed sympathy for all Imperial citizens murdered during this horrible loss of grace, but refused to prosecute their murderers because they had been, after all, doing nothing illegal at the time, the emperor's word being law.

In the end, Lord Coving sat in one of the five seats that made up the Board of Regents for the young prince—who would not be declared emperor in fact until his fifteenth birthday—and Captain Sean Reiter was still a traitor under sentence of death by more conventional means should he ever set foot in the Kresentian Empire again.

Which seemed like as good a reason as any for him to work to keep the Aydori border secure. Through the influence of Lady Hagen and the others, Reiter found himself in charge of building a garrison for Aydori in the meadow by the bridge where he'd spoken to General Denieu. His official title was consultant. He wasn't actually in the Aydori army—he doubted they'd ever trust him enough for that, nor was he sure he wanted to put on the uniform—but because Lady Hagen and the others still called him captain, so did everyone else.

During border negotiations, Major . . . no, Colonel Halyss had demanded he be turned over. The new Pack Leader and her council had refused, and the colonel hadn't mentioned it again.

The empire had withdrawn to the new Imperial Province of Pyrahn and were busy reinforcing the new Imperial border. Reiter doubted it would move during the life of this emperor.

Of late, he'd been in the Aydori papers more than the Imperial.

The Imperial papers had other stories to cover.

Reiter rubbed his finger over an engraving of a young woman flying above a pair of wolves. He still lost the track of conversations if the people around him spoke too fast or spoke over each other, but he was fluent enough in Aydori to speak one on one. "There is a story about the Ghost Pack visiting Verdune."

"Lord and Lady." Lady Hagen sighed, both hands laced over the curve of her belly. She was due soon. In the empire a woman of her rank would have left public life, but that wasn't how it was done in Aydori. "What have they done now?"

"They attacked a money lender in the night. Gave his money to the poor."

"No." She shook her head. "Verdune is too far into the empire. They wouldn't have left Orin for something so foolish. They're being blamed for things they couldn't possibly have done."

There were a number of things they *had* done crossing the empire.

In the early days, the stories of a flying woman and a pack of wolves with silver markings had fought with treason for the front pages of newspapers. They'd stopped a runaway coach, saving five. The wolves had herded the townspeople to safety while the woman put out a spreading fire. They'd rescued a flock of sheep from a spring flood. They'd found a little boy down a well and, according to his mother's interview in the paper, he'd cried for three days wanting the silver doggies to come back. They released two donkeys from the millstone they'd been tied to their entire lives and flattened the mill. Reports varied on what had then happened to the donkeys. In more than one, they'd been eaten.

The Ghost Pack probably hadn't flogged a foundry owner, known to take advantage of those young and attractive and dependent on him for a living, then chased him into a manure pit. It had happened close enough to the line from Karis to Orin it couldn't be ruled out, but it was the first of the stories not entirely tied to geography.

"It's not blame," Reiter said, pulling his hand back from the engraving. "It's myth."

Lady Hagen rolled her eyes, blue mage marks glittering. "Well, I just got another letter from Stina's cousin in Orin, and myth sheared off half a mountain, blocked the river, and flooded the village. There's a good chance he wasn't exaggerating this time since after the last council meeting the ambassador from Cafren asked me if I had any information on the stories she'd heard about earthquakes from her side of the border. The Pack Leader is thinking of sending someone north to see what's going on."

Reiter didn't pretend to misunderstand. "I can't . . ."

"Yes, you can." The baby kicked hard enough, it visibly adjusted the drape of her dress. It was a soft butter yellow, perfect for early fall. Her husband had died in the attack on the border, but the Aydori didn't wear mourning. Reiter tugged at a black cuff. He did. "The garrison is nearly finished . . ." She raised a hand as he opened his mouth. "Fine. The part we need you for is nearly finished. We lost too many to send Pack or Mage-pack up into the mountains. You're the obvious choice."

"I'm expendable."

"Yes."

He'd helped free them, but he'd also been responsible for helping to capture them. And only four of the six had come home.

"You're hiding here, Captain Reiter." She didn't sound unkind, but neither did she sound as though she'd allow him to stay in Aydori. To stay hiding in Aydori. "There's only one way to find out if you have a place in her Pack."

"And if I don't know if I want a place?" There were songs about the Ghost Pack—in two languages—and rumors around Bercarit of a new opera.

"In the Pack or the myth?"

"Both. Either."

Lady Hagen smiled. Reiter had been in Aydori long enough to recognize the difference between a smile and a show of teeth. This straddled the line. "There's only one way to discover that as well."

Snow had already fallen on the upper slopes of the mountain, but in Harar, the largest settlement in Orin, the reds and golds of fall still lingered. Dusty happily dove through drifts of fallen leaves, chasing a sparrow he had no hope of catching. Mirian was guessing about the reds and golds—her world remained grays and silver—but anyone with eyes could see Dusty's mood. His tail and his ears were up and his tongue lolled from his half-open mouth and every now and then he barked as though he couldn't help himself—in spite of lessons in the need for silence on the hunt from every single older member of the Pack.

The boy's recovery had been remarkable. His fears were the fears of the Pack as a whole—none of them could face darkness—but his strengths were his own. The starved and wounded silent child Mirian had taken from the Imperial cell had become a curious, joyful, much loved heart of the Pack. He spent almost as much time in skin as he did in fur and in a few short months he'd become almost fluent in Ori. Not only had his nightmares stopped as long as he slept touching another of the Pack, but those touching him never woke screaming. Mirian had drawn up a complicated sleeping rotation that Tomas and Nine enforced. Fortunately, no one in the Pack had a problem with putting Dusty's needs first.

Currently on guard, Bryan and Dillyn watched him from the porch. Dillyn had his head down on his front paws, but his eyes were open and all his attention was on the boy. Matt and Jace had gone hunting. They hadn't gone far enough from the settlement to actually catch anything, which was why Mirian could sense matching pissy moods as they returned. They hadn't yet determined how far apart she could be from her Pack and still maintain the connection—no one wanted to be the first to suddenly find themselves cut off from their Alpha. And, in fairness, she didn't want to find herself cut off from them.

When the Pack Leader in Harar had curled his lip and informed her that kind of contact wasn't normal for Alphas, only Tomas' elbow had kept her from laughing. Laughter would be considered a challenge, and the last thing Mirian wanted was to end up responsible for the entire settlement. The Pack she had was responsibility enough.

She could hear Jared and Karl behind the house, arguing as they chopped wood. Seventeen and eighteen, they could manage skin as long as they had something that needed hands. Stephen would be watching them from the wellhead, the silvered stub of his tail tucked under his haunches. Stephen seldom wore skin. The emperor had taken something from his insides as well—his belly fur split by a diagonal silver streak—and he'd almost died before they'd reached a Healer-mage in the mountains. Nine had changed and carried him the last two days, snapping and snarling at anyone who tried to share the burden.

Tomas and Nine . . .

Mirian frowned. Nine felt angry. That wasn't unusual. Unless he was with Dusty or her, anger was a constant with Nine. He'd refused to tell them his name . . .

"That man is dead. Nine will do."

. . . and he fought at the slightest provocation. The settlement's Alphas had learned to steer clear of him. No, Nine angry wasn't unusual, but Tomas felt unsettled and that couldn't be good.

Both Bryan and Dillyn rose to their feet as Mirian stepped off the porch. A gesture held them in place. The dead grass whispering under her boots, she crossed toward the path that led through the trees to the rest of the settlement. They'd been given land on the outskirts, half cleared, house half built and abandoned. Working together to make it habitable had smoothed out most of the Pack's remaining twitches. Most. Not all.

She'd acquired a few twitches of her own.

"Just as you do not define the mage-craft, do not let it define you. If you fly everywhere, what use are your legs? You want to be the person you were as well as the person you are, walk. Sweat. Wait for strawberries to ripen the same as everyone else." Hayla blinked eyes as much white from cataracts as from her scattering of mage marks and grinned toothlessly. *"Don't let young Master Hagen define your body, as enjoyable as that is. Define it yourself lest you lose it. You and the mage-craft are one, but you must be Alpha. Where are you taking those strawberries?"*

"You said . . ."

"I said you should wait. I'm old and have a pitiful fraction of your power. Hand them over. Now, go pick up that mountain you dropped."

Before Mirian reached the path, Nine trotted out into their clearing and crossed to where Dusty was stalking a beetle. Hackles up, he turned to face the trees, saying as clearly as if he'd spoken, that whoever was coming would only get near Dusty through him.

Tomas was in fur although the man with him wasn't. He wore an Aydori greatcoat pulled tight under the straps of the pack rising behind his head.

"Captain Reiter." Not a question. And Tomas felt unsettled, not surprised.

Nor did he look surprised after he changed and moved to stand by her side.

"Miss Maylin. Lord Hagen." Reiter had gotten better at ignoring skin and looking Pack in the eye although a fresh scar on his jaw suggested it had taken him a while to learn. "The Pack Leader sent me to check on you."

It was strange to see him in gray and white. The gold of his hair, the red of his whiskers, the blue of his eyes were gone. Mirian found herself missing color in a way she hadn't for months. "To check on me?"

"On all of you." Reiter looked calm as he swept his gaze over the visible members of the Pack. Nine stopped Dusty's advance with a growl, then growled again in Reiter's direction.

To Mirian's surprise, the captain tipped his head to the side before saying, "Did you know they call you the Ghost Pack in the empire? You've become part of the stories people tell."

"Really." Tomas snorted. "What do they call you in the empire?"

"Traitor."

Harsh but true.

"The Pack Leader," Reiter began, but Mirian cut him off.

"Isn't Alpha here. I am." Mirian laid her words on the breeze. "She knows you've arrived, and that's all she needs to know for now." When Reiter drew in a deep breath and let it out slowly, Mirian saw he breathed in through his nose, like Pack. "What do *we* call you?" she murmured.

"I guess that's for you to say."

"Do you have a first name, or is it captain?"

He stared at her for a long moment. "Sean."

"Sean." His eyes had been a pale enough blue that seen through mage-craft they were almost silver. "I guess if you want to know what we call you here . . . She could feel his life at the edges of her senses. ". . . you'll have to stay for a while until we figure it out."